Dedalus Europe 2015
General Editor: Timothy La

Light-Headed

Olga Slavnikova

Light-Headed

Translated by Andrew Bromfield

Dedalus

Supported using public funding by
**ARTS COUNCIL
ENGLAND**

Published in the UK by Dedalus Limited
24-26, St Judith's Lane, Sawtry, Cambs, PE28 5XE
email: info@dedalusbooks.com
www.dedalusbooks.com

ISBN printed book 978 1 910213 34 6
ISBN ebook 978 1 910213 35 3

Dedalus is distributed in the USA & Canada by SCB Distributors
15608 South New Century Drive, Gardena, CA 90248
email: info@scbdistributors.com   web: www.scbdistributors.com

Dedalus is distributed in Australia by Peribo Pty Ltd
58, Beaumont Road, Mount Kuring-gai, N.S.W. 2080
email: info@peribo.com.au

First published by Dedalus in 2015
Light-Headed copyright © Olga Slavnikova 2011
Translation copyright © Andrew Bromfield 2015

The right of Olga Slavnikova to be identified as the author and Andrew
Bromfield as the translator of this work has been asserted by them in accor-
dance with the Copyright, Designs and Patents Act, 1988.

Printed in Finland by Bookwell
Typeset by Marie Lane

A C.I.P. listing for this book is available on request.

The Author

Olga Slavnikova was born in 1957 in the Urals. She now lives in Moscow where she works as a journalist and as the director of the Debut Prize which champions the work of new authors.

In 2006 she won The Russian Booker Prize for *2017*.

Light-Headed was shortlisted for the 2011 Big Book and 2012 Russian Booker awards and won the Book of the Year Award 2011 at the Moscow International Book Fair.

The Translator

One of the founders of the Russian magazine *Glas,* Andrew Bromfield is one of the most important translators of Russian Literature in the English-speaking world. His many translations include *Light-Headed* by Olga Slavnikova.

Maxim T. Yermakov, the happy owner of a three-year-old Toyota and brand manager for several appalling varieties of milk chocolate, drove up to his chocolate office with his customary feeling of having no head on his shoulders. Meanwhile, the head was smoking and it could see the wet car park, with the inflatable snowman standing in a black January puddle. But even so – it wasn't there.

When he was a child Maxim T. Yermakov used to ask his parents a stupid question: How do people know that they think with their heads? His father, whose head was flanked by a pair of ears large enough to suggest it had the secret ability to fly, tried to explain about the two hemispheres of the brain: his mum anxiously touched her child's warm forehead, seeking for an illness in that space where thoughts drifted about like cosmonauts in zero-gravity. The concentration of the human sense of identity in the head, above the arms, legs and everything else, was the greatest human mystery of all to the young Maxim T. Yermakov. He disliked games that required agility and active movement because he was afraid of the strange void through which the wind blew freely between the neck of his tee-shirt and his denim cap; afraid that a branch might accidentally poke into that void, or a bronze beetle might fly into it.

The nurse at his kindergarten, who survived in his memory only as a pair of icy hands and a tiny mother-of-pearl mouth, used to put the group on the weighing scales every month and then inform his parents that their boy, although he appeared to be well developed, was lagging about four kilos behind the normal weight for his age. His mum, who didn't understand what was going on, stuffed little Maxim T. Yermakov with cloudy oils from the pharmacy and high-calorie casseroles. As a result, the sluggish, force-fed Maxim T. Yermakov grew into a chubby youth with large pink cheeks and a second chin with the delicate texture of cream: anyone who looked at him realised instantly that only the very finest produce had gone into the construction of that body. After the young man's weight reached a hundred kilograms, the missing four were not so obvious. But even so, the heavy bearer of a light head remained constantly aware of the lack of weight on his shoulders.

Despite his lightheadedness, which at first he did not realise was a strictly personal trait, peculiar to him alone, Mikhail T. Yermakov's grades in school and college were all As and Bs. But even so, he still didn't understand what his teachers meant when they told him to "get something into his head". The information that he was given – on everything from Pushkin's poetry to product rebranding techniques – immediately escaped from his virtual cranium to become a free element of the world around him – which, properly speaking, was what it already was in any case. The world presented itself to him as a flexible information environment, and the knowledge, released into freedom, returned to him fully structured, bearing, like an industrious bee, nutritious nectar that it had gathered in parts unknown. It sometimes seemed to Mikhail T. Yermakov that he could acquire information without any books or the internet, quite literally out of the air.

These personal peculiarities, however, were not enough to make Maxim T. Yermakov into either a genius or a master of life. While still a student, he found himself a job, just like everyone else did, and ended up in a commercial structure that promoted a range of transnational food products. For a brief initial spell he handled an instant coffee that supposedly possessed a ravishing aroma, which wafted through the air in the form of bluish-grey silk ribbons, but since that time the life of Maxim T. Yermakov had been focused entirely on chocolate. Chocolate bricks, chocolate bars, cream-filled chocolate, half a dozen different kinds of chocolate sweets, white chocolate, honeycomb chocolate – all of it positively demanding enjoyment from the consumer in the same way as war demands feats of heroism. For in real space, the product consisted of a sweet, bitty clay with the addition of soap, a mixture that was produced in a factory somewhere near Ryazan.

The jokes linking Maxim T. Yermakov's figure with the object of his creative endeavours were groundless: Maxim T. Yermakov did not eat his own chocolate. However, his entire appearance as a flourishing fat man made him an entirely apposite representative of the product, with the ruddy bloom of his cheeks extending right up to his eyes and the sugary bristles on his head producing free-flowing rainbow effects in response to the movements of his thoughts and skin. As already stated above, the delectation presumptively deriving from this chocolate was entirely incorporeal in nature. Maxim T. Yermakov knew a lot about the incorporeal. By combining images in the correct proportions, he created the visual representation of a flavour that did not actually exist in reality. Sales increased. Even the executive director, V.V. Krapinov, commonly known as Crap, a superannuated monster overgrown right up to his eyes with grey stubble that the efforts of stylists had transformed into something akin to a coil of barbed wire, was reluctantly obliged to admit that *whatchamacallim*, the young chocolate guy, had a good head on his shoulders.

Youth is ambitious. It took time for Maxim T. Yermakov to accept his common fate. He was a member of the international army of millions of corporate clerks, a single droplet who fused with the masses in the hours of struggle to negotiate the traffic jams of Moscow, which resembled an agglomeration of flies on strips of sticky paper. Meanwhile, in his light head, with its apparent lack of all physical boundaries, a clear truth gradually took shape – things were not looking black, on the contrary, they were looking up. Because, in these modern times, the human rights defended by serious international organisations had been superseded by the Rights of the Common Individual. Maxim T. Yermakov condensed down the essential meaning of numerous messages, apparently originating from a wide range of different sources, to the concept that the Russian dilemma posed by Dostoyevsky, "Shall I let the world go to hell or skip my tea?" had nowadays been resolved in favour of the tea. To choose tea was to choose freedom, which is what our hero did, focusing his efforts on acquiring several square metres of floor space within Moscow's Garden Ring Road. Twice he was almost suckered out of serious money, but that only lent a final polish to his character. Maxim T. Yermakov was now entirely prepared for his freedom, which distinguished him favourably from millions of his compatriots who, according to numerous media channels, were entirely unprepared for freedom and were, in fact, totally unfit for anything.

However, he found himself completely unprepared for the sequence of strange and surprising events that began at the moment when the alarm system of his Toyota switched on with a liquid glug and his mobile phone simultaneously swelled up to twice its size and started squirming about in his pocket.

"Max! Why are you so late?" said a mini-micro voice in the phone. The voice belonged to Little Lucy, his immediate boss's secretary. "Vadim Vadimich wants to see you urgently! We've been searching for you everywhere!"

"Okay, I'm on my way, I'll just drop my coat off in the office," Maxim T. Yermakov muttered, increasing the speed of his stride through the listless winter rain that was mottling his fine cashmere.

"No, no, no! Straight to the seventh floor!" little Lucy squeaked and Maxim T. Yermakov immediately switched her off when he heard a second signal forcing its way through the first one and literally erupting out of his phone.

"Maxim Terentievich? Vadim Vadimovich wants you to come to his office immediately." This time it was Big Lida, Crap's own secretary, speaking in a distinctly husky voice, as if her temperature was rising by leaps and bounds.

Maxim T. Yermakov started feeling alarmed. But the sense of alarm was actually pleasant: he had the brief, brazen thought that the outcome of all this ballyhoo would probably be an opportunity to earn money, since everybody needed him so urgently. As he trotted across the soundless synthetic carpeting of the seventh floor, he had visions of those elegant little toy building bricks of life – ten-thousand-dollar wads in bank wrappers. In the outer office Big Lida sprang up, rising to her full towering height as he came in and gaped at him as if she had never seen him before. Pale-faced, with new silicone lips that resembled two pieces of mild-cured Atlantic salmon, she dragged Yermakov's damp coat off his shoulders and shoved him into the office before he had time to catch his breath.

There were two visitors sitting opposite the boss of the entire enterprise, who seemed poised rather uncertainly on his imposing chair. They were reflected in the glass desk top like dark islands, with the absolutely pristine, empty ashtray gleaming between them like a thick circle on water.

"Ah, well, at last! Twenty minutes late!" Crap exclaimed in the voice of a jovial school headmaster, which was quite unlike him. "Here you are. Our young colleague," he said, turning to his visitors and baring a clutch of bluish crowns in a grin.

"Good morning," Maxim T. Yermakov said to them, and thought to himself: "Fifty grand, at least."

"May I go now?" Crap enquired, half-rising to his feet.

"Yes, dismissed," said one of the two visitors, but Maxim T. Yermakov couldn't tell which.

Crap, who had obviously been waiting with desperate anxiety for the moment when he could bolt from his own office, acted entirely out of character, scurrying over to the doors and giving Maxim T. Yermakov a farewell flash from his dull, metallic old-man's eyes. Only then did the visitors turn towards the person they had come to see. Their faces were entirely bloodless, with prominent foreheads. The individual sitting on the left had totally blurred features, with a tuft of dry hair on the very top of his head; the second or – to judge from the invisible currents running between the two of them – the first and more important individual, resembled a human foetus that had not been born, but developed and matured in some other, more obscure fashion. The thin skin of the inordinately large, bald head seemed semi-transparent, but it was impossible to make out anything

11

inside it, and hideous flames blazed in the wreaths of purple wrinkles below the hairless arches of the brows.

"What an ugly pair of freaks," thought Maxim T. Yermakov, making himself comfortable in a chair.

"Good morning, Maxim Terentievich," said Foetus, with his gaze fixed on a spot somewhere above Maxim T. Yermakov's shoulder. "As you have probably already realised, we are here as representatives of the state."

In synchronised motion the two opened their ID cards – not the usual format, but large and square, similar in shape to the chocolate slabs of his closest competitor. Glowing in bright gold inside them was the predatory emblem of the state, with solid gold letters stamped into the paper: "Russian Federation. Special State Committee for Social Forecasting". Despite the strange appearance of the documents presented to him, Maxim T. Yermakov realised immediately that the IDs were genuine and these were very, very serious guys. Far more serious than all the VIPs he had ever seen before, all lumped together. The joyful anticipation of money suddenly switched temperature from warm to icy cold. "A million. A million dollars," Maxim T. Yermakov thought quite distinctly, twining his fingers together more tightly on his stomach.

"The actual title of our department is rather different," Foetus remarked casually, lowering his ID into some crevice in his blank, featureless clothing, which seemed not to have a single button on it. "And now, permit me to enquire, Maxim Terentievich: is your head in good order?"

Something like a small tornado took shape in Maxim T. Yermakov's absent head, drawing the ceiling lamp down into itself. Maxim T. Yermakov thought: "I have a pain between the ears, as the Red Indians – I think it was – used to say". Out loud he said:

"Well, actually, it's *my* head. And whatever might happen to it is my own personal business."

The state committee freaks exchanged glances. "Like something straight out of 1937," thought Maxim T. Yermakov, amused at the thought that in this old game he knew everything in advance, and he knew in advance that he was right.

"All right, then we'll tell you," Foetus said imperturbably, crossing his legs to display a lacquered shoe as simple as a plain galosh. "Your head happens to cause a certain slight, just a tiny, little disturbance in the gravitational field. That is the feature by which we located you."

"Do smoke if you like," Blur put in, nudging the virginal ashtray in Maxim T. Yermakov's direction. "We know you smoke Parliament. It's not really allowed in here, but you can smoke with us."

Feeling annoyed, Maxim T. Yermakov took out a pack of Parliament, which had instantly come to seem trashy and tasteless. He really was feeling a quite savage desire to smoke. As usual, the cigarette smoke filled up his head, rounding it out and materialising it, streaming about inside it with a pleasant sensation.

"And why are you interested in me?" Maxim T. Yermakov asked cautiously, trying to figure out the smartest way to haggle with these two, who had opened the bidding with their artless state security gambits.

"I shall not attempt to conceal the fact that we are extremely interested in you," Foetus declared, puckering up his face. "In a nutshell, our department deals with relationships of cause and effect. I won't go into the theory and the know-how involved, especially since I have no right to do so. I can only inform you that these relationships are entirely material structures, one could even call them living organisms. And our research indicates, for instance, that the human sacrifices in pagan cults were not mere superstitions, but rational actions. Every so often, cause and effect relationships enter a vegetative phrase. And then the individuals whom we call 'Alpha Objects' appear. And, strange as it may seem, the future course of many, very many events depends on them. You, Maxim Terentievich, are precisely such an Object, if you will pardon us for saying so."

While Foetus spouted this raving gibberish, Maxim T. Yermakov gaped, as if he were hypnotised, at Foetus's loosely assembled fingers, tapping out some kind of faltering scales on the desk: they looked as if they were made of ice, and the gold wedding band on the crooked ring finger glinted in the sombre light of day as if it was iron. Naturally, Maxim T. Yermakov did not believe what he had heard but, above and beyond the words, he could feel the character of the space around him changing. "I wonder which presidential candidate is going to be my chocolate now?" he thought, and his heart started bobbing up and down, like a small object set in motion by the impetus of heavy footsteps.

"So you want to offer me a job?" he said out loud, assuming an air of indifference.

The state committee representatives exchanged another quick glance from under their domed foreheads, as if they had instantly dealt each other cards.

"In a manner of speaking, yes," Foetus said in a dreary voice. "You have to commit suicide by shooting yourself in the head."

Maxim T. Yermakov smiled politely. A shudder ran down through him and back up again, as if someone was using him like a tinwhistle to play a shrill melody. He screwed his cigarette into the ashtray so hard that it squeaked, emitting a stream of unused smoke straight into the face of Blur, who narrowed his slim nostrils squeamishly.

"And if I refuse, you will eliminate me yourselves?" said Maxim T. Yermakov, not even hearing himself speak.

"No. Unfortunately not," Blur answered this time, speaking in the same tone as Foetus, but in a different voice. "It must be your will and your hand. If we perform the deed ourselves, we will not merely fail to achieve the required result, but will also deprive ourselves of a quite indispensable opportunity."

Phew. The thick snow that had started falling outside the window suddenly seemed to Maxim T. Yermakov more blindingly white and festive than any snow he had ever seen in his entire life. It was falling at an angle, sometimes accelerating to a dense, stippled blur, sometimes hanging in the air and swaying back and forth, together with the pale office towers, which looked like wet, shaggy towels. Still feeling stunned, and soaked in joy as if he had been doused with a tub of cold water, Maxim T. Yermakov asked:

"And what reasons do you think I have for shooting myself?"

"You have very important reasons, Maxim Terentievich," Foetus replied with a disdainful smile. "If you are not sacrificed – pardon me for calling a spade a spade – the relationships of cause and effect will develop in a highly undesirable direction. You can already see the beginning: tsunamis, climate change. It would be hard to list all the consequences. But in the very near future, they will affect very many people directly. Out of the full range of possibilities, only the most negative will be realised. Take Ludmila Viktorovna Chebotaryova, your boss's secretary. Her little son is ill, a congenital heart defect. He will die. In Moscow and St. Petersburg, shopping centres and amusement halls will collapse and the dead will be counted in thousands. There will be a major accident on an oil pipeline. A new war will break out in the Caucasus. We can expect a major terrorist attack in some large regional centre in Siberia. Then a global economic crisis will develop…"

"Hang on, hang on!" cried Maxim T. Yermakov, interrupting the state security man's tedious recitation of disasters. "Terrorist attacks, accidents – these are all part of your job, aren't they? You've given me an interesting overview of why you need my, shall we say, sacrifice. Now explain to me what I need it for. Only in a way that makes sense to me."

"Name your own terms," Foetus said icily, wrapping himself tighter in the loose, shaggy item that covered him all the way down to his galoshes.

At this point Maxim T. Yermakov suddenly felt like laughing again. Once again he had the distinct feeling that he had wandered into some film about the year 1937, only with a big initial signing-on bonus, unlike all those ardent revolutionaries who cried out at the end: "I am innocent before the People and the Party!" "Well, if they want me, it's going to cost them," he thought, his earlier certainty confirmed, then he clicked his lighter in front of the cigarette wobbling about in his mouth and declared:

"Ten million dollars, gentlemen."

"We accept," Blur said quickly in a humdrum voice. "Ten million.

Will you be writing a will?"

"What will? What for?" Maxim T. Yermakov asked in surprise. "I can give you my bank details, but cash is better."

"Unfortunately, Maxim Terentievich, that's not the way it works," Blur said with a smile: if you looked closer, what he resembled most of all at that moment was a collective-farm accountant. "You see, we cannot deceive you. The connections that we deal with are in a very delicate state at the moment, we must not damage them. Every cause must have its effect and so, as soon as you shoot yourself, your heirs will receive the money. But you can scam us. Take your millions, and then refuse to shoot yourself. Or ask for an advance, blow it all, smash up a couple of Mercs and decide you want more. You'd have the entire state working for you. We can't allow that to happen, so it's better not to start. I tell you in all seriousness: you personally will not receive a kopeck. So give instructions for your nearest and dearest to get the money."

And so saying, he pushed a blank piece of paper towards Maxim T. Yermakov, with a cheap ballpoint pen lying across it that had been chewed like toffee. Maxim T. Yermakov stared blankly at the white surface. He tried to imagine his parents if they suddenly became rich. When was the last time they called him? On New Year's Eve? His father did nothing but act cheerful and boast, breed rabbits with fat backsides at the dacha and go to Communist Party meetings with a half-bottle of vodka in his pocket. His mother gave music lessons and in the evening she played "for herself" on the old piano, as if she was doing the laundry, heaving her shoulders and shoulder blades like a washerwoman, hammering out tangled gibberish on the keys as if they were a washboard. They'd get a life and move to Moscow. But if not his parents, then who? Well, not Marinka, that was for sure. What kind of nearest or dearest was she? All she had were her long, long legs and her extravagant ambitions. Maxim T. Yermakov's future wasn't bright enough for her. The other women? Absurd. All they left behind in the morning was a stuffy little hollow in his pillow and a little mousehole gnawed in his budget. A sudden feeling of revulsion for all the people who made up his presumptively humane and comfortable world set Maxim T. Yermakov shuddering inwardly. They weren't people, just empty holes. And now the stroke of luck that this morning had unexpectedly dangled in front of him was down the tubes too. They just wanted to screw him for free, in the name of the state and the people. When the devil bought your soul, at least he let you live for a while – but not these guys.

"No. No deal," he snapped, pushing back the pen and paper which, it turned out, he had already covered with bold lacy squiggles. "Please, catch the terrorists and build the hypermarkets properly, so they don't fall down. But I'm leaving, I've got a lot of work to do."

"But what about the higher considerations?" asked Blur, suddenly raising his voice. "It's not entirely unpaid and anonymous. We have good script writers. They'll work up a legend for you, you'll become a national hero. Would you like us to put up monuments to you in Moscow and your home town?"

"No, that I don't want! Who do you think I am, Alexander Matrosov?" Maxim T. Yermakov shouted furiously, exulting in the knowledge that in the front office they could hear him yelling at these state security bogeymen, who had frightened everyone half to death. "Higher considerations! You can stuff that totalitarian eyewash up your backside! You're not using me as raw material for your propaganda! Like some kind of Gastello! If they'd paid the soldiers in that war properly, they wouldn't have let the Germans get right up to Moscow!"

"An interesting idea," Foetus laughed, and the semi-transparent bubble of his head turned slightly pink. "Well then, Maxim Terentievich, this isn't the last talk we'll have, you realise that. Here, take my card. It has my numbers, call me if anything comes up."

He held out the rectangle of cardboard to Maxim T. Yermakov in his finger and thumb, like a pair of pincers. It had the same double-headed eagle glowing on it as the rowanberry-red page of his ID. "Sergei Yevgenievich Kravtsov, Senior Expert" was stamped above two seven-digit telephone numbers, in which the first three digits were 111. While Maxim T. Yermakov sceptically twirled the little card in his fingers, Foetus squinted sideways at Blur's formless outer garment. Blur understood, nodded, stuck his hand into a deep, crumpled fold and pulled out a heavy item, which proved to be a large revolver with a fluted grip. Maxim T. Yermakov shuddered. Grinning with half of his wrinkled mouth, which had sagged open like a pocket, Blur launched the pistol across the desktop towards the Alpha Object, who gazed, mesmerised, at the weapon's slow revolutions, like the final turns of a roulette wheel.

"That's a Makarov PMM. A twelve cartridge clip. Loaded, reliable, easy to use," said Foetus, introducing the baleful apparition that had left Maxim T. Yermakov covered in fine beads of sweat. "Take it and keep it with you. It will come in handy, believe me."

The pistol was clearly not new: bare metal showed through on the fluting of the handle, like on an old black rasp, and the trigger in the lop-sided guard looked greasy from the squeezing of countless fingers. "Why, the lousy cheapskates, they even cut corners on this," Maxim T. Yermakov thought in amazement as he picked the weighty souvenir up off the desk. "But okay, at least it's a little clump of wool from the sheep's clothing these big, bad wolves are wearing. It's quite a toy, interesting."

"I don't promise to call. All the best, gentlemen," he told them out loud.

And with his jacket pocket weighed down by the heavy PMM stuffed into it, he set off towards the door at a waddling jog. Maxim T. Yermakov felt the souvenir smacking hard against his thigh and his soul seething with bitter fury.

"Maxim Terentievich! One moment!" called Foetus, stopping him right at the door.

"Well?" he asked, half-turning.

"You have not asked the question that all Initiated Objects ask," Foetus said imperturbably, swaying his foot.

"What question?"

"Was the man known as Jesus of Nazareth an Alpha Object?"

"Well?" Maxim T. Yermakov repeated irritably, trying to work out what would happen if he simply shot these two state security men who had taken up residence in Crap's office as if it was their own home.

"He was not. He was an instance of a phenomenon that lies beyond the comprehension of our present-day science," Foetus declared dispassionately, darkening to total impenetrability against the background of streaming snow, leaving behind only the intense purple shimmer of his intently gazing eyes, like the lenses of powerful binoculars.

The day passed somehow or other. Maxim T. Yermakov frittered away the time, sometimes calming down, and then lapsing into bitter fury against the morning's visitors. He had no ideas for the new "valentines" – brittle little chocolate hearts in violent pink wrappers. And in general, Maxim T. Yermakov suddenly had the feeling that his chocolate, which always congratulated the population of the country on every possible kind of public holiday, was somehow fusty and putrid, like a General Secretary of the Central Committee of the CPSU. Whatever office he visited, he was followed by furtive glances from beneath lowering brows and all the hands extended to be shaken seemed to have turned from men's into women's. He found himself casting sideways glances at Little Lucy, whom he had hardly even noticed before, always picturing her as a vague blob with something glittery on her mealy, ashen-grey little neck. He didn't notice anything special now, either – slivered hair, miserably thin eyebrows, spectacles. For some reason, he'd always thought of Little Lucy as not much over twenty years old but, to look at, she was actually thirty-something.

"Maxie, why are you so down in the dumps? They say you had a visit from the militia today?" Little Lucy asked in a quiet voice when Maxim T. Yermakov wandered into his boss's front office yet again for some unknown reason. "Maybe I should make you some strong coffee?"

"Maybe I should give her some money?" Maxim T. Yermakov thought drearily. But money was tight.

The estate agent Gosha-Cherdak called at half-past three. His voice sounded thick, as if it had been smothered with sauce.

"Max, it's like this, we have a problem," he said with gravitas. "The seller's upping the price by thirty grand. Remember, first I knocked them down by five, but now a new buyer's turned up, some sort of Armenian with big bucks. They've just gone to take a look at the apartment, and I'm going after them. You'd better get stuck in too. Think how much you can raise. Between you and me, the apartment's worth it."

"But we put down a deposit!" Maxim T. Yermakov protested, aghast. "No fucking way! What are they fucking about at? We already agreed!"

"Life is hard, Max, do you understand me?" Gosha-Cherdak admonished him solemnly. "Putting down a deposit is one thing, buying an apartment is something different altogether. Real estate is like a big fish, it can slip off the hook a dozen times. So get your wheels on down to Gogol Boulevard and along the way call everyone you can, beg and borrow. Okay, get on it!" – and he disappeared, like a coin into a slot.

Maxim T. Yermakov went hurtling down the stairs, muttering incandescent obscenities as he repeatedly failed to slip his hand into the sleeve of the coat trailing behind him like a crippled wing. People shied away from him, clutching their paper cups of coffee and files close to their bodies. In the car park the inflatable plastic snowman was tumbling about in the wind like a soft-boiled egg. Snowflakes swirled furiously, windscreen wipers swept aside streams of murky water, and brown puddles quivered under wheels, fed copiously by the wet mass of snow.

The apartment on Gogol Boulevard, which was tiny, although it was on two levels, was being sold as if it was solid gold. Maxim T. Yermakov had already wrung himself totally dry and he had been counting on the new annual chocolate budget, out of which he intended to filch a fair-sized chunk. He had no idea who to call, and he ferreted aimlessly through the memory of his mobile phone as he drove slowly through the snowy glop. The domes of the Cathedral of Christ the Saviour drifted past on the left, as pale as electric light bulbs burning during the day. As he turned into the courtyard where he had intended henceforth to park his Toyota in exalted proximity with other, more expensive, high-pedigree motors, Maxim T. Yermakov almost believed that the Armenian buyer with the big bucks would actually turn out to be a phantom.

His hopes were shattered ten minutes later. Hovering in the centre of the apartment which Maxim T. Yermakov had already divided up into such neat style zones in his dreams, was the owner of the property, a bulky old woman with carats of gold glinting dully in her stretched ear lobes and a face that looked like a flabby peach covered with grey fuzz. The old woman's estate agent, a red-haired businesswoman in a tight-fitting crimson suit, was working the new client with a vengeance, detailing the merits of the living space and emphasising the limited number of similar opportunities on the Moscow market. The client was nodding patiently; his big head, like an irregular boulder, didn't even turn in Maxim T. Yermakov's direction as Maxim stumbled into the studio. Gosha-Cherdak was nowhere to be seen. "The bastard's late, he's dumped me with this lot," Maxim T. Yermakov thought spitefully and immediately, in the half-light by the stairs that led up to the bedroom, he spotted the individual for whom the apartment was evidently being acquired – this apartment of which, in his dreams, he had already made every square centimetre his own. About eighteen years old. More likely the Armenian daddy's daughter than his girlfriend: little white collar, boring black skirt, like the slip cover of a man's umbrella. Sumptuous curls with no gloss to them – fuzzy, pinned back with a crude piece of glass; huge great moist eyes, exactly like a sheep's. It took at least a minute for Maxim T. Yermakov to realise just how lovely the Armenian girl was. The thought that the apartment would belong to her, and she would never belong to this unsuccessful competitor, whom her rich father was about to grind into the dust, made him want to smash something. "So okay, she'll soon get fat and grow a moustache," Maxim T. Yermakov thought vengefully, feeling a little tornado dancing on his shoulders in the place where a head ought to be.

"Right, the gang's all here!" Having finally reached the place,

Gosha-Cherdak shook himself in the doorway, with water streaming off his leather jacket as if he had just got out of the shower. "Sorry, bro, the traffic and on top of that, the snow," he said, holding out a cold, wet hand to Maxim T. Yermakov – the thumb alone was the size of a chicken leg.

"How the fuck could you creep here so slowly that it took three hours? The traffic, he says. And here I am hanging about like a spare prick at a wedding," hissed Maxim T. Yermakov. "Come on, talk to them, or I don't know what's going to happen."

"All right, all right, relax," Cherdak said soothingly, directing a watery smile at the opposition's estate agent.

"Ah, and here are the other buyers!" she announced in a tourist-guide voice, as if Yermakov and Cherdak were part of the flat's furniture and fittings. "Gosha, are you still in the bidding, or is it already out of your range? I phoned you about the new price. Careful now, everything will go up again in a month."

The Armenian didn't say anything, merely turning his entire short torso to glance at the competition; his eyes, set in heavy folds of brownish skin, looked like old mushrooms.

"Ninochka, sweetie, of course we're still up for it, of course we are!" Cherdak warbled, oozing syrup. "I'll just have a quick word with my client! Five minutes!"

So saying, he grabbed Maxim T. Yermakov by his thick forearm and dragged him towards the window, stepping on his shoes in the process

"Right then, how much dough have you come up with?" he asked vehemently, looming over Maxim T. Yermakov with streaky rainbows on his poorly cleaned glasses. "I checked out all the databases before I came: prices are absolutely unreal everywhere. So it makes sense to step up, and sharpish. Come on, the train's leaving, and we're trying to jump on the last carriage!"

"I haven't come up with anything! That's it, end of the line, we're screwed," wheezed Maxim T. Yermakov, squinting at the redheaded estate agent's surprisingly fat back, which looked as if it was quilted. "You pressure them on our agreements. Ask if they think they can treat us like total patsies."

"What are talking about, bro? Are you the great Chocolate Kid or some pansy just out of nursery school? What agreements? Can you see anybody here who owes you anything? Well, that's down the tubes, then. Moscow's just chockablock with money, but he's too bloody squeamish. Come on, get that mobile out! Start calling people! Well!"

Wrinkling up his mealy forehead so that it looked like heavily peppered semolina pudding, he drove Maxim T. Yermakov back against the wall with small prods and pokes, then carried on pummelling him quietly until he forced a mobile phone out of the whisked heap.

"Okay, then step back a bit," said Maxim T. Yermakov, puffing and panting.

Cherdak growled, released his grip and moved away a couple of steps. Maxim T. Yermakov suddenly felt a new, almost unbearably intense sensation licking at his heart, like a flame. This old woman, the owner of the studio apartment, who had just lowered herself heavily onto the only stool in the place, spattered with paint from the renovation work – what did she want with so much money? It was obvious she'd never had any: that string of amber beads on her wrinkled neck, those dull earrings, those murky, rust-coloured little eyes, with the fine streaks of albumen – her life was practically over already. But for some reason he, Maxim T. Yermakov, had to fire someone else's pistol into his own insubstantial head, like firing a dense little bullet into a sumptuous, trembling New Year tree, jingling with decorations. Fuck it, where was that business card... Maxim T. Yermakov carried on squirming, amazed at how deep his own pockets were, until eventually he pulled out the rectangle of cardboard with the eagle on it. Sergei Yevgenievich Kravtsov... right then... His fingers seemed to stick to the keys of the phone, as if they were made of iron and there was a bitter frost; fine rivulets of sweat trickled down his back.

The number that began with three ones answered immediately, mysteriously not ringing even once, and Foetus's voice sounded as close as if the state security man was actually located inside the handset.

"Maxim Terentievich, good day today. Well, you see, you've called already."

"Ah… E-er… Sergei Yevgenievich, good day to you too," Maxim T. Yermakov declared vivaciously, glancing at the card. "Something's come up… I urgently need thirty…" – he squinted at Cherdak, who was shaking outstretched fingers at him – at least six or seven of them – "…no, sorry, sixty thousand. Dollars, naturally."

"We know, Maxim Terentievich," Foetus responded in a benevolent tone of voice.

"Well then?"

"Well, Maxim Terentievich, we already discussed that with you, didn't we?" the state security man said paternalistically, and Maxim T. Yermakov thought he heard a note of derision insinuating itself into his ear together with the words. "Our position hasn't changed in the meantime."

At this point Maxim T. Yermakov could physically feel the blood tinting his nebulous brain, like dirty water flowing through it. He hunched over, concealing the conversation with his cupped hand, and hissed furiously;

"So that proposal you made my day with this morning, is all free and for gratis? Save mankind, you said. But what's in it for me? Absolutely nothing! Oh no, gentlemen, screw you! Give me the money, and I'll give your proposal some thought. If you don't, you can go to hell and further."

"We won't give you it," Foetus informed him sadly. "And you're wrong to say it's all for gratis. It's just that the only thing on your mind is loot. Think it over properly, communicate with your inner self; what would you like to leave behind you? There really is a lot that we can do and we're prepared to go to great expense, very great expense. Believe me, it's not often that anyone gets this kind of chance to change something in the world. It's just that you need to have wishes that extend beyond the bounds of your own body and your own physical life. Do you really not have even one?"

"Ah, go jump in a lake!" Maxim T. Yermakov roared, and immediately felt everyone's eyes on him. The redheaded business-woman turned away rapidly, the glinting edge of her smile scraping across Maxim T. Yermakov's heart like a match across the rough side of a matchbox. At the back of the room, by the stairs, a tender oval glowed gently, and that glow made the white collar seem as crude as plaster of Paris.

To recover his breath after this humiliation, Maxim T. Yermakov turned away towards the window. The falling snow was like a net being dragged through the air. The evening light was thickening and the yard was spread with white twilight, like a sheet. A spotty dog the size of a cow was wandering across the hoary grass. Someone in a short, dark coat with snowy shoulder straps was striding up and down the length of the narrow pavement, performing an about turn to the left at the point where the trampled trail of his footmarks ended. There, now he had stopped and raised a mobile phone to his ear, lighting up his hollow cheek with a blue glow. Immediately a second man with his hair trimmed short like plush got out of a parked minibus and the two of them spoke briefly, tilting their foreheads as they took a step backwards to look up at Maxim T. Yermakov. He recoiled. The two inclined faces reminded him of white buttons on a keyboard with unfamiliar signs on them. Maxim T. Yermakov immediately guessed the number from which the call had been made to the mobile that had lit up the stranger's face, and which government department owned the old minibus coated in mud that seemed to have grown on it like moss. The writing on the side of the minibus said: "Green Garden. Moscow's finest garden furniture," – but those two individuals with the epaulette-square shoulders were definitely not furniture delivery men.

That was the first time that Maxim T. Yermakov saw the men whose presence he sensed constantly from then on. For the most part they drove around in minibuses ("The Village Milkman. Good Health and Good Humour!" "Kitchen World. The Market Leaders." "The World of Leather. Style for all the family.") Sometimes they drove ageing imported cars, or even old first-model Zhigulis with a thick coat of rust showing through a crude paint job – but they all darted along the road with a fine turn of speed. These vehicles were all as filthy as pots and pans with baked-on dirt. The moment his Toyota left the car park, they appeared in his rear-view mirror – he could always pick them out in the general flow of traffic by the intense way they shuddered – even standing in traffic jams they looked as if they were about to come to the boil.

The agents of the Department of Social Forecasting always worked in pairs and they were all about the same age, all dressed in grey, Soviet-style coats or airy padded anoraks, buttoned shut all the way up to their formidable chins, as solid as sledgehammers. From a distance their faces were all like buttons from the same keyboard, some of which seemed to display letters and others numbers. In the stairwell of Maxim T. Yermakov's building, an empty pickled-tomato can appeared on a windowsill from which the door of his flat could be surveyed and gradually filled up with fragrant cigarette butts. Maxim T. Yermakov could literally sense the surveillance on his skin: prickly sand trickled down his back between his shoulder blades, and he himself felt like an edifice of sand, damp on the inside, crumbly on the outside, gradually being eroded by a chilly breeze. In order to escape, at least briefly, from the relentless minibuses, he started going down into the metro for the first time in many years. But it was pointless: the moment he stepped onto the escalator, a burly figure sprang up behind him, setting a massive ham of a hand in a black, wrinkled glove on the moving handrail and, just two or three people ahead of him, he spotted the back of the other partner's head, looking like a fat hedgehog.

The flat on Gogol Boulevard was sold in a flash. Gosha-Cherdak was bitter, but he carried on hustling, taking Maxim T. Yermakov to view other possibilities every evening. There was no point in even trying to grab anything in the centre: prices had shot up across the board, and sellers were running ahead of the market, trying to sell their property at the March price in January. Just at the moment nothing was happening; the market had stopped dead and the very air seemed to have followed suit – after the short-lived snowfall it had returned to that bleary, turbid state typical of confused dreams. There was no season outside: if snow tried to fall, it dissolved into the dampness like washing powder, the ground sucked in the foam and, deceived by a temperature above freezing, put out feeble, pale-green blades of grass. The low, even pall of cloud didn't let through any sun; the naked trees were obscure black shadows; the winter was like a burnt-out electric bulb.

Gosha-Cherdak, rapidly running out of enthusiasm, dragged Maxim T. Yermakov off to an area near the Kozhukhovskaya metro station, to concrete-panel apartment blocks with windows overlooking the rat's maze of a derelict market; to grey-brick five-storey buildings somewhere out beyond Voikovskaya metro station, where a rotten two-room apartment was being sold for a king's ransom, complete with blistered floors and warm water that felt greasy to the touch flowing out of rheumatic pipes. Prestige was no longer an issue, the money available simply had to be invested in square metres of floor space – but everything slipped away, moving out of reach in literally just a few days. As the unreal rise in the city's price continued, the city itself became spectral; the rise, taking in even residential areas where nothing at all was being sold, was reflected in the unconvincingly rarefied substance of the buildings, in the strange, shimmering glint of their windows. The bright scrolling-text advertisement of the bank where Maxim T. Yermakov's money was withering away met his eyes on almost every high rooftop, reminding him of a school chemistry experiment in which the combination of a crimson liquid and a green one always resulted in a pop and a puff of smoke.

Ten million. Ten million dollars, fuck it! And with a bit of haggling, even more. And it seemed as if all he had to do was reach out his hand. Maxim T. Yermakov had not the slightest doubt that he was worth all that money. He could sense that he was only separated off from the opportunity to buy any flat, in fact any property at all in Moscow or Europe, by a strange, taut, semi-transparent membrane. He had never given any thought to the nature of this barrier before

– except perhaps in his childhood, at the age of about six, when he suddenly realised that he would inevitably die and his parents would die too. The object lesson on the subject had been grumpy old Grandad Valera, whose way of walking with a stick used to make all of his heavy bones obvious – he had laid down in a long box lined with cloth and suddenly stopped smelling of tobacco. Maxim T. Yermakov was haunted by the vision all summer, and after the event certain phenomena – the clamorous chirruping in seaside thickets at night, green rain in the countryside, the squeaking of children's swings, the rigid flight of a lean, dry dragonfly – aroused a quiet melancholy in Maxim T. Yermakov. But afterwards, in September, it had all come to a sudden end, as if the school bell had cut it short.

Now, however, it had come back again and the nights had turned hostile. Unable to sleep, wallowing like a seal in sheets that were damp with sweat, Maxim T. Yermakov struggled to come up with ways to get his money and stay alive. Unrestrained by any brainpan, his thought performed elaborate acrobatic somersaults, inventing a docile double, willing to do anything he wanted, or imagining a phony shot fired on some not-too-high bridge, with a body tumbling down into the oil-slicked water, down into the safe, murky refuge where a trusty aqualung, concealed in advance, lay waiting.

It was all too unreal, it all required preparation, including physical training – but Maxim T. Yermakov had never been a sportsman and he was especially afraid of diving, knowing that under water his virtual head was transformed into a cold dome of air, as fickle as mercury, constantly trying to divide into several parts. He needed helpers, loyal people, as an absolute minimum he needed good-quality false documents in someone else's name. To feel secure, he ought to toughen up his pampered body that bounced about when he ran and discharged pink steam into his head when he bent down to his shoes. But he couldn't buy an exercise machine or other equipment in secret. Vigilant social forecasters always dogged Maxim T. Yermakov's footsteps to the supermarket, jostling at their charge's rump with the trolley into which they tossed all the same items as Maxim T. Yermakov had amassed for his own entirely innocent needs; if there was only one specimen of any particular item left, after a brief struggle for the box or the bottle, the victor was always the imperturbable social forecaster with the cast-iron body under his coat. After trundling their trolley out into the car park, the special committee agents tipped their duplicates of Maxim T. Yermakov's shopping list into a black plastic rubbish bag, tied it in a knot and dumped the bulging bag into the boot of their car – evidently for further analysis, to determine whether meat ravioli and shampoo could be used to produce plastic explosive. Every move that Maxim T. Yermakov made was scrutinised. Suspecting that any spot on the wallpaper or any bead in the skimpy Chinese chandelier might be a concealed camera, he examined his rented flat more thoroughly than he had in all the previous four years: to the observers he must have looked like a spider creeping around the corners, secreting its sticky thread.

Maxim T. Yermakov had only one advantage over the social forecasters: he had time, and they did not. The Europa megamarket came crashing down. Two hundred and twenty-six people killed – so there you go. Maxim T. Yermakov ostentatiously drove over to take a look. The glass corpse of the megamarket looked like a theorem that had committed suicide for lack of any proof: triangular elements of the carcass still jutted up here and there through the chaotic jumble, supporting expanses of glass that reflected crooked, slanting slabs of grey cloud cover, as if the sky itself had been cloven asunder above the disaster area; the decks of the structure were suspended precariously above the gaping black pits of the shopping levels. Men in orange vests with frowning faces were walking around everywhere; beside the barrier of metal mesh wet with tears, withered carnations lay on the asphalt like fresh spots of paint.

After standing there for a decent interval, marvelling at the dummies in business suits that had survived, looming up out of the chaos of concrete and glass, Maxim T. Yermakov climbed back into his car. On the way home he was swamped by a mixed wave of merriment and horror. The world was becoming as pliable as plasticine. Maxim T. Yermakov could not have articulated clearly the nature of his newly acquired power. But the feeling of power was so unmistakable that the Toyota literally tore through the traffic, escorted by a modest little van that wagged like a dog. They'd pay up, they had no option. They had already done Maxim T. Yermakov a great favour by allowing the Alpha Object to probe the thin barrier between this world and the next and stop feeling afraid. Despite the rather feeble materiality of his own head, Maxim T. Yermakov did not believe in the realms of heaven or hell, which were no more than vaporous emanations of human thought. He acknowledged only things that were concrete and real. For him "the next world" was now to be found in the prestigious flats in Moscow's old, neatly restored mansions of the nobility – that was where he would go as soon as he could get his hands on his money, those appetising little bricks of dollars that he could see so clearly through the cold membrane that had now moved up so very close. To be on the safe side, now that the negative forecasts had started coming true, Maxim T. Yermakov decided for the meantime not to visit any large shops, but buy his groceries close to home in a cosy little basement, where he was always greeted by the good-natured security guard with the fat backside and the elderly check-out lady with the yellow fringe and the abundant rivulet of gold trickling down into the narrow defile between her mottled breasts. "But there's not going to be a shot, gentlemen, oh no!" Maxim T. Yermakov crooned to some jolly little tune as he pressed the magnetic tab against the lock of his building's iron door with its blisters of water and paint.

There was a surprise in store for him in his flat. Sitting there in the only armchair, in the only room, wearing a tracksuit with worn, shaggy stripes, was Sergei Yevgenievich Kravtsov in person; his thin-skinned head seemed to be swollen like some animal's stomach, tightly stuffed with food. Standing behind the boss, with their hands clasped over their reproductive sectors, were several geometrical figures, four in number. Standing in front of Foetus on the small, crooked coffee table that leaned so badly that one of its legs seemed to be a crutch, was a glass of golden French cognac, taken from the bar without permission.

"Well, did you admire the sight?" the Senior Expert asked his charge instead of greeting him.

"How are your relations of cause and effect coming along, boss?" Maxim T. Yermakov replied acidly, taking off his coat. "Are they all multiplying autonomously? How are they feeling? Not ailing, I hope?"

"They are ailing," Foetus confirmed, giving Maxim T. Yermakov a glance like a swivelling of decrepit ball joints under his naked brow arches. "You've seen everything for yourself, you're only just back from the site. An unnecessary question. I haven't seen such an impudent villain as you in a long time."

Maxim T. Yermakov bowed politely. There was nowhere for him to sit in his own room, apart from on the open bed, where Marinka's panties lay like a crushed blue butterfly among the chaos of the bedclothes. Maxim T. Yermakov sighed and plonked himself down.

"And how about illegal entry into a private residence?" he enquired, sliding a mocking glance over the faces of the bodyguards, on which the harsh wrinkles were like tribal war paint. "Or I'm sorry, do you have a warrant? Perhaps I have broken some law? Killed someone? Or have you already tipped snow into my washing powder and now you're waiting for the witnesses?"

"Drop it, Maxim Terentievich," Foetus said, wincing. "Your door wasn't locked and we just walked in, as old acquaintances. We're sitting here, guarding your property. And we only came in order to ask you a single question: Which number is larger – two hundred and twenty-six, or one?"

"One, of course, if that one happens to be me. What did you expect?" Maxim T. Yermakov responded skittishly. "Can you give me another life? Can you give one to the people who were killed in the Europa? Instead of putting tails on me, ferreting through the groceries I buy and smoking in my stairwell, you'd do better to try tracking down the terrorists! Yes, I went and I saw it. I'm not to blame, you are! And I don't need your exercises in arithmetic. You're not doing your job properly, gentlemen!"

31

"Well, you really are an impudent villain," Foetus repeated thoughtfully, warming his host's cognac in his bloodless knuckles, which were coated on the back with translucent hairs, like hoarfrost. "Yes, the state's tasks are mostly arithmetical in nature. We have a simple sequence of natural numbers: a hundred and forty million inhabitants in the country. And from this arithmetical point of view, one is precisely two hundred and twenty-six times less than two hundred and twenty-six. What surprises me is something else. You, Maxim Terentievich, act as if you're not afraid of us at all. But you should be. Everyone has a sensitive spot where they can be grabbed. And if we set our minds to it…"

"You can't touch me!" Maxim T. Yermakov informed them happily. "I'm as round and smooth as a billiard ball, all inside myself, there's not even anywhere to pinch me. Shall I be honest with you? I don't need anybody but myself. That is, I used to love mum and dad once upon a time, but now – well, I'd feel sad for a week or so, if anything happened. Maybe I'd get drunk. Even if feelings do come up, I'm not afraid. There are some nice women, of course, but not nice enough to shoot myself for. I would be afraid of you, of course, if you could use force to pressure me, but you can't act arbitrarily, outside the law, thanks to those relations of cause and effect! So we have an ideal situation here; if a citizen doesn't break any laws, there are no questions he can be asked. By the way, if I take that pistol of yours and start firing at people in the street, what will happen?"

"Well, then we'll arrest you, acting entirely within the law," Foetus said with relish, and from the buttery softening of his stony stare, it was clear that such a turn of events would be most welcome to the committee that he represented. "Yes, then we'll arrest you and initiate a perfectly legal process of investigation and trial. But we'll arrange it in forms that will soon have you asking us to let you have the pistol in the cell for a moment."

When he heard his uninvited guest say that, Maxim T. Yermakov suddenly felt himself go limp. He wanted to get into his bed immediately, just as he was, in the business suit of wool cloth that prickled the tender folds behind his knees, and call in sick. Pull the impervious blanket up over his insubstantial head and pretend that bogeymen didn't exist.

"Why, you're a coward, Maxim Terentievich," said Foetus, pressing his advantage, and he immediately seemed to be hovering over his victim, although he hadn't moved a millimetre from his chair. "Your very flesh is cowardly, every cell trembles and weeps if you are merely shown a knife. Remember that time when you lost badly at cards as a student? Those tough guys, Skewbald and Cossack, put pressure on you. To pay back the debt, you stole two and a half thousand dollars from a student in your year, Vladimir Kolesnikov. But he turned out to be a vicious thug too, and although he might not have had a knife, he had huge fists. Remember how you used to hide from him in the women's rooms in the hostel? The way you sat it out in the wardrobes among the skirts and the sandals?"

"They certainly get great training, all right. Appearing right there in front of you, moving through space without even stirring a finger. That's some trick. I wonder how they do it," Maxim T. Yermakov thought feverishly, trying to use his thoughts to exorcise the shudders running from his heels all the way up to his blurred head. But it was too late. Vladimir came back to life, as if he had escaped from the cell block of memory – Vovan, Big Vovan, with the stubbly, unshaven face that looked like a dirty sponge, with the wild woolly growth on his chest that jutted out like straw, forcing apart all the blue and pink shirts he had bought at the village general store. Vovan had ended up in jail later, after getting involved in a bad fight outside a dingy beer parlour beside a metro station – that was what had saved Maxim T. Yermakov from physical mutilation and a nervous breakdown. Vovan, by the way, had also been a player in that exceptionally slippery game of poker, but with peasant cunning he had thrown in his hand and escaped with only a miniscule loss. What Maxim T. Yermakov should have done, instead of getting carried away with taking more cards, was pay attention to the strange way the dealer caressed the pack, and the way cards literally grew between Skewbald's fingers, like the webs on a frog's feet. What the hell, was he supposed to take a knife for two and a half grand? There really was a knife, by the way – a vicious flick knife with a composite handle made in a prison camp. Those two, Skewbald and Cossack, had stroked Maxim T. Yermakov all over with it, spreading steely mirror-bright terror over him like butter over a sandwich. Maxim T. Yermakov had acted rationally: he scanned the surrounding space and discovered the only accessible sum of money large enough to pay off his debt in Vovan's rustic peasant jacket, sewn into the inside pocket with dirty white thread. Big Vovan shouldn't have boasted before the game about how he had earned money on a building site and now he was going to screw the lot of them; it was a simple matter to feel out the rich crunch of money in his trashy, eau de cologne-soaked wardrobe.

Yes, Maxim T. Yermakov had saved himself by choosing the lesser evil over the greater. Yes, he had sat it out on sandals in wardrobes, like a chicken sitting on its eggs, while big Vovan tried to explain himself to the girls in a wild roar and flung chairs about. Anyone with any nous at all would have pulled the same stunt. How terrifying the thick, acrid, almost surgical smell of Vovan's cologne was when he hoisted Maxim T. Yermakov up by the collar and his cornflower-blue eyes turned blank and lifeless, like a doll's. That fragrance of the common people, "triple eau de cologne", was already a discontinued product line by that time in the late nineties (Vovan's kulak family must have maintained reserves, less for the sake of social propriety than as a cheap hangover cure) and by now the stocks had run out in all the warehouses – but it continued to exist in Maxim T. Yermakov's mind. His virtual sense of smell, which drew fragrances directly into the brain, occasionally captured a few stray coarse molecules drifting about from some source or other, and that was enough to trigger panic, setting his solar plexus – that spot into which Vovan's tattooed fist used to sink, instantly cutting life short – thrumming like a rubber band.

"What are you thinking about, Maxim Terentievich?" The uninvited guest's voice seemed to come from behind Maxim T. Yermakov's back, although Foetus was still sitting there in the same brown armchair, like a picture in a frame.

"Oh nothing, just reminiscing about my young days," Maxim T. Yermakov replied with a smile, wiping his wet palms inconspicuously on the sheet. "You got the names right: there was a Skewbald, and a Cossack, and a Mr. Kolesnikov. My God, even a tiny sum was enough to trigger a conflict then... Small change, phooh! How stupid people are at the age of twenty. It might seem that only the young need money – what good is it to people who are getting on a bit? But I'm only just beginning to understand that the older a man gets, the more money he needs to live a decent life. Don't you agree, Sergei Yevgenievich?"

"Are you counting on living to see your ten million?" Foetus enquired ironically. "I can guarantee that will never happen."

"But you will manage to make me a national hero posthumously?" Maxim T. Yermakov answered in the same tone of voice. "You won't get anywhere with that either: that's not for me. That's for some collective-farm worker who's read Ostrovsky's *How the Steel was Tempered* in his village hut. Mr. Kolesnikov could have done that, if he had ever opened a book at all. Laying down your life for your friends – that doesn't cut it nowadays. Not even because there are no morals, but the aesthetics have changed. The art gestures are all different now. My videos about chocolates mean more today than that entire stupid heritage of multiple-volume editions with morals and heroes. Is that news to you? I understand. No doubt I'm not your first Alpha Object. And in their foolishness the Objects before me went charging off to save mankind, and even thanked you for the honour. You used to be able to scoop that foolishness out of people by the spoonful, without the slightest problem. They built the Baikal-Amur Railway and cultivated the Virgin Lands. But that's all over now. No more freebies, gentlemen. Now, I'm wasting time on you, when I was planning to have supper and take in a movie."

At that Foetus chuckled darkly, leaning back in the chair to display an Adam's apple like a chicken's egg swallowed by a snake. The four geometrical individuals, who so far had not made a single sound, apart from the squeaking of their square-toed shoes, chuckled back to their boss in chorus, like swamp frogs.

"Well, just wait a while, Maxim Terentievich," the Senior Expert said when he was all chuckled out. "I still don't understand your intimations that we ought to pay for your time. After all, we're not discussing morality or modern art with you, these are purely practical matters. Responsible as I am in certain respects for the arithmetic of the state, I have to effect the exchange of the one for the many. You wish to haggle. But let me tell you again: it's useless. And let me explain that in fact you *are* afraid of us. We shall have to make a hero out of you anyway, but there are various different ways we can go about it."

"But I am a hero already, haven't you noticed? You're pressuring me, but I'm not giving in! Why is that, you may ask?" Maxim T. Yermakov reclined slightly, supporting himself on a pillow with one elbow although, through his suit and his sweat, the expensive fine-cotton bedding felt repulsively woolly. "I am defending in my own person the rights of the human individual against the state machine. And from the position of those rights it makes no difference whether that individual is a hero, a genius or a common man in the street. You may be a triple Hero of the Russian Federation, but that's all hogwash to me. The freedom of the individual consists in the fact that he himself is the supreme value. Simply by virtue of his own existence. If someone wants something from him, they conclude a contract with him. But you don't want a contract, so you have nothing to interest me. You're trying to intimidate me. What I'm wondering is if I ought to get together the heavy journalists I know. Arrange a press conference, tell them how the rights of Russians are violated by all sorts of murky state committees."

"Now that's a serious subject. Well, you're a genuine human rights advocate, Maxim Terentievich. Maybe you'd like to ride the impetus of this wave into politics?" Foetus enquired mockingly.

"No, I don't want to go into politics. You have to put your face around the place and lie. I can't be bothered. I'm better suited to being an image-maker. A politician or chocolate – the technologies are all the same," said Maxim T. Yermakov, but to himself he thought: "I could fancy a candidate for president. Not the primary one and not his full-frontal opponent: those slices of the pie are too big for me, I'd choke on them. But give me some Siberian peasant, rough-hewed with an axe. Someone who could roar and bellow for the common people and pick up one and a half percent in the election. Financed by non-ferrous metals. And an exclusive contract for me!"

"Your chocolate, by the way, is appalling rubbish," Foetus observed. "It should never be given to children. Only to blondes of a Balzacian age, to get them out of the way as soon as possible."

"As if our politicians were all St. Georges," Maxim T. Yermakov parried. "Just take a look at them apart from their images. Focus your eyes properly! Either some office-supply manager, a real slab of meat, or a good-looking lad wearing his father's tie, or a general, wearing his three cerebral convolutions on his forehead. There are far better characters in any TV soap. Politicians seem to be chosen specially to make the creative task of the political technologists more difficult. But I'm not afraid of difficulties like that! In fact I enjoy them. Have you seen my latest creative idea with the cute little model bathing in this stream of thick chocolate, like she's in a swimming pool? Makes you want to lick it off straight away. But if the chocolate itself was any good, the job would be boring."

At this point, there was a loud, jangling sound in the depths of one of the geometrical individuals, somewhere in the region of his stomach, as if he were a tinny old Soviet alarm clock. Opening the flap of his jacket to reveal numerous technical devices, including a strange-looking weapon resembling a hairdryer, the geometrical man unhooked a small flat oval plaque and held it out to his boss with a crisp, precise gesture. Foetus clicked a thin, wriggling string out of the plaque and Maxim T. Yermakov's ears were suddenly blocked, making it darker in his head than it was in the room. Foetus said something into his special state-security mobile, rustling his cellophane mouth: invisible volumes of space seemed to distend and froth up around Maxim T. Yermakov, surging against his awareness, the light bulbs in the chandelier swelled up, the uninvited guests moved with a repulsive viscous susurration, like beetles in a matchbox. And then sounds suddenly came back, but all with a strange, coarse lining.

"The unpleasant sensations will soon pass off," Foetus informed him, no doubt speaking at the top of his voice, but sounding as if he was whispering. "Actually, it's time we were leaving. But I'd like to say a few words about freedom before we go. A man appears to have many freedoms – go ahead, develop in as many directions as you like! But there is only one genuine freedom: to act correctly. All men, unfortunately, are blind. They have an opinion about everything, because they feel the need to have one. But there are very few matters concerning which a man can make a decision on the basis of his own personal experience. All the important things, the things that are most important for his life, are communicated to him by the television. A blind man can only move about if he knows the arrangement of the items in his home and has an approximate idea of how everything is arranged outside. The world may be nothing at all like what it seems to be to a blind man. But if the blind man acts correctly, he won't bump into anything. And he will never even be aware of our presence."

So saying, Foetus got up out of the armchair in his idiotic tracksuit with bulges that betrayed the presence of concealed equipment or monstrously protruding bones. One geometrical man hurried into the hallway and spoke to someone on the landing. To judge from the sound of voices, the entire stairwell was full of social forecasters, from the entrance door right up to the top floor.

"You have surprised me, Maxim Terentievich," said Foetus, looking down at Maxim T. Yermakov, who was still stunned and deafened and didn't have the strength to separate himself from the pillow, which seemed to be stuffed with the same substance as his dark head. "I thought you would come back from the Europa in shock, I brought you a psychotherapist…" he pointed to a member of his retinue, who looked exactly like all the others. "Very well. So you still don't fully appreciate the situation. I leave you, Maxim Terentievich, with a heavy heart. As you quite correctly understand, we cannot violate the provisions of the law. But civilians who have no connection with our committee can. Bear that in mind."

One by one the uninvited guests disappeared from Maxim T. Yermakov's field of view, as if they had dissolved into the stale air of the flat. The final sound was the demonstrative grating of a key turning three times in the lock. Maxim T. Yermakov reached out an unsteady hand for the TV remote control. The screen unfolded into a frightening picture: a conflagration undulating like a medusa against a dimly lit sky, little helicopters glinting pink, a taut pillar of blackness, braided together out of greasy smoke, rising up into the clouds.

"...According to sources in the administration of the State Fire Fighting Service of Krasnoyarsk, the blaze covers an area of more than four thousand square metres..." a fruity, anxious woman's voice informed him, speaking rapidly. Maxim T. Yermakov turned over onto his back and roared with laughter.

So they had keys. Maxim T. Yermakov's first impulse was to change the locks as soon as possible. The door of the flat, covered with black imitation-leather cloth, the kind used to cover dilapidated books in district libraries, contained three locks – one functional and two dead, fossilised like trilobites into the door's battle-scarred slab of iron. Maxim T. Yermakov was slightly upset when he estimated how much it would cost to replace the fossils with something reliable, like DORI or RIFF, but he managed to find an acceptable offer on the internet and booked a visit from the locksmiths, who promised to fill his order within a week. He realised perfectly well that the social forecasters would get in anyway, if they wanted to, but as a matter of principle he didn't want to leave an invitingly defenceless door between himself and them. Let those two who sat on the windowsill in the stairwell, chewing on their plump sandwiches, see that the Object was doing everything he could to create difficulties for them to overcome.

That left the problem of the flat's owner – Maxim T. Yermakov didn't want to give her any keys. His landlady was called Natalya Vladimirovna – "Just Natasha", as she had asked him to call her, although she was approaching fifty. Large and garrulous, always dressed in a pink jacket, with dyed blonde ringlets, which looked soapy because of the grey that had grown through them, Just Natasha plied her trade in various feeble media outlets as a correspondent or advertising agent. Several times she had tried to suggest that Maxim T. Yermakov should direct part of his advertising budget into the evening newspapers, literary newssheets and youth websites that she represented – and she had proposed such modest commissions for herself that her actions seemed to be quite disinterested, if not self-sacrificing. Naturally, with the kind of product range that Maxim T. Yermakov had, only a madman could have gone for vehicles like that. The refusal reduced his landlady to a state of angry despondency, she could go on for hours about how she never got paid anywhere. When she met someone new, the first thing Just Natasha did was enquire – with lively curiosity in her voice and a convex glitter in her large, watery, bulging eyes – how much the other person earned. Before she rented out the flat, Just Natasha had given it a cheap lick-of-whitewash renovation: she had pasted up silver-ribbed wallpaper, laid basic and incredibly slippery tiles, and hung up acetate curtains through which the sun shone in the morning as if they were glass. Four years later, in Just Natasha's mind all of this was still brand new, and when she came to collect the rent, she searched anxiously for flecks of dirt, rubbing them off with a forefinger that grated over all the surfaces. When she heard that Maxim T. Yermakov was going to buy his own place, she artlessly named a price for her one-room flat that was twice the going market rate, assuming that if someone had already moved in, there was no point in him moving out again.

"If Just Natasha sees the new locks and doesn't get any keys, she'll think her toilet bowl's been smashed," Maxim T. Yermakov thought as he rode up in the lift to his flat on the seventh floor, still feeling annoyed by a tedious meeting with Crap and the crooked faces of his colleagues, all looking as if they had just had their mouths forcibly wiped, and the mother-of-pearl nails of his immediate boss, Irina Konstantinovna – or Ika in the people's vernacular – which she had drummed on the desktop for the best part of two hours. When he saw the door of his flat, Maxim T. Yermakov recoiled. "DIE,

ASSHOLE!" was daubed across the black imitation leather cloth in white industrial paint. The fresh paint, which gave off a stupefying stink, was creeping down the door in thin dribbles, as if it was putting out little roots. Catching a soft drop on his finger and smearing it across the door, Maxim T. Yermakov flew into a wild fury.

As usual, there were two men perched idly on the windowsill, with professionally conventional faces that had been made as smooth as gravel by the crowds in the streets. They were just about to start their supper: one was pouring strong tea out of a thermos flask covered in cloudy condensation, the other already had his mouth open wide for a roll that looked like a bread mitten grasping a sausage.

"Who did this? Who?" Maxim T. Yermakov roared, running down the steps towards them, with the paint on his finger staring like a blank wall-eye. "You sit here, so why don't you use your fucking eyes"

The social forecasters glanced at each other and gave identical shrugs. Then they stared at Maxim T. Yermakov with two pairs of eyes that were as clear as glass beads and expressed nothing but amazement.

"They've buggered up my door, were you too bloody idle to see them off?" Maxim T. Yermakov carried on yelling, his fury escalating even further at the sight of a substantial still life, with slices of large tomatoes and pieces of boiled chicken as pink as little cupids flaunting themselves on a paper plate.

"Mr. Yermakov, we're not employed as your watchmen and security guards," the one with the bun replied coolly.

"And we don't present our reports to you either," the second one added.

"Why, you lousy scumbags! *Bon appétit*!" Maxim T. Yermakov shouted, and the social forecasters nodded calmly in reply.

Maxim T. Yermakov slipped through warily into the hallway, grasping the desecrated door by the handle with his finger and thumb, as if he was holding a huge fly by the wing. Despite all his care, he found white marks on his Hugo Boss coat, as if someone had licked the expensive cashmere against the nap. Glancing at his watch, Maxim T. Yermakov realised that the locksmith was due to turn up at any moment with the new locks. There was no way he could receive any kind of visitors with that fresh, sticky slogan on the door. It filled Maxim T. Yermakov with a childish kind of shame. He quickly called the firm and swore with every second word as he replied to the insolent, drawling voice of the young hussy of an operator, who set about teaching him business etiquette. The only thing he wanted to do was wash off the sweat of this day and then set about cleaning his coat. He had only just filled the landlady's resonance-chamber bath, in which the taut jet of water awoke distant echoes of the railway, when the bell in the hallway started screeching in frantic fury. Maxim T. Yermakov swore and shuffled off to open up, wearing his tight-fitting plush dressing gown over his wet body. While he was trying to hurry, fiddling with the belt of his dressing gown and losing his slippers, the bell whipped up the contents of his head into a murky lather. Savouring the thought of what he would do to the locksmith, who had turned up anyway to earn his one and a half kopecks from other people's problems, Maxim T. Yermakov swung the door open without glancing into the peephole.

Just Natasha was standing on the doorstep. Her watery eyes were gaping wildly, her eyebrows had shot up so high onto her forehead that they had almost jabbed into her hairstyle, like needles into a ball of wool. She reached out to Maxim T. Yermakov with a white index finger bearing a sample of the outrage, visual proof of which had not been enough. The slogan on the black imitation leather cloth was smeared in several places and the bell push, also spattered with white, looked like a large flattened moth.

"What is this? What's going on?" Just Natasha demanded in a trembling voice. "What's this surprise you've arranged for me? Who's an asshole, is that me, an asshole?"

"Ah, what makes you think that? Do you think this is my rotten daub?" Maxim T. Yermakov retorted resentfully. "Some local hoodlums or other plastered it on!"

"Why are you dressed like that?" Maxim T. Yermakov's landlady hissed, advancing with the crumpled corner of her bloated dirty-pink handbag aimed at him.

Oh, mama! Maxim T. Yermakov saw himself from the outside. The old dressing gown barely even closed across his overgrown belly, which bore a tortured scarlet stripe from the tightly-drawn belt – and God only knew what else the rancorous bitch could glimpse as she stood there in her coarse leather coat that looked like cardboard trimmed with cat's fur.

"Why, was I expecting you today? Just a moment, I'll get dressed," Maxim T. Yermakov muttered, stretching the edges of the dressing gown together and mincing off to the bathroom like a woman.

"You weren't expecting me? Well, that's nice! Today's the second!" her voice called after him. "So you don't need to pay for the flat, then? Never mind me, I can survive on bread and water. But who's going to support my sick mother? You live in my mum's flat, by the way!"

That was right. The second of February. Just Natasha appeared with the implacable inexorability of Don Juan's Stone Guest. The fact that Maxim T. Yermakov occupied her mum's living space, thereby excluding from her place in life the Honoured Teacher who had left behind in the flat the woeful writing desk with prehistoric ink stains and drawers that smelled of the graveyard, somehow imposed additional moral responsibilities on Maxim T. Yermakov. Just Natasha had attempted to convert these obligations into additional rent. Muttering obscenities, Maxim T. Yermakov pulled on his sweat-soaked office shirt with a collar that felt like cold rubber, buttoned up his crumpled trousers somehow and counted out the thirty thousand roubles that was due. Shuffling into the kitchen, he heard the water leaving the bath in stentorian gulps, as if an entire cave was disgorging its contents.

"You have to empty the water, so it won't leak, and you have to clean the cooker with a special ceramic cleaner, not leave filthy marks on it," Just Natasha informed him nervously, examining the mirror-bright surface of the Indesit cooker from various different angles – it bore a faint mark from a saucepan, like a lunar eclipse on

43

a black sky.

Just Natasha counted the rent three times: her damp, freshly washed fingers, with the blinding tears of massive, wet gemstones glinting on them, left the money limp and swollen. Just Natasha held her unscrubbed index finger out to the side – like Maxim T. Yermakov's, it was covered with a kind of whitish mildew.

"All right, and for the door?" she asked in a brazen voice when she finished counting.

"It wasn't me who loused up your bloody door. Ask whoever did it to pay!"

"Do you think I'm going to conduct a criminal investigation? You live here, you pay. That's another fifteen thousand you owe me, if you don't want serious trouble."

"A new door doesn't cost that much!" Maxim T. Yermakov exclaimed, startled.

"How would you know how much it costs, you didn't pay for the repairs!" Just Natasha retorted, immediately raising her voice. "I spent my last roubles on that laminated flooring and covering the door and buying the tiles! I went into debt, I've never had so many debts in my life. With the amount of money I earn, the cost of those repairs was like a million for anyone else."

"Tell me Natasha, do you think that you rent out the flat, someone lives in it, and the renovations just get newer and newer?" Maxim T. Yermakov asked as calmly as he could manage, taking out a cigarette.

"Don't smoke in the flat!" Just Natasha squealed and slapped Maxim T. Yermakov on the hand. "All the men smoke out there on the stairs!"

Maxim T. Yermakov shuddered when he realised which men she meant.

"Okay, I won't give you fifteen, I'll give you seven," he muttered rancorously and set off to the bedroom with long, rolling strides.

"Nine!" Just Natasha shouted after him.

Raiding his rouble stash once again, Maxim T. Yermakov held the diminished wad of money up in front of him, feeling like a maple tree in autumn, with its leaves fluttering off in the wind. He separated off nine one-thousand notes, stood there with them for while and put one back, as if he had made a small, cautious move in a card game. "All right, screw you," he thought, stuffing his stash back under the cover of his old appointment book. "Some sodding dame rooks me for dough like there's no tomorrow. And I can't rook those freaks. Why is that?"

Just Natasha pursed her lips into a tight knot before she even finished counting the thousand-rouble notes, but didn't say anything, just put the money away in her handbag with a sigh of resignation. She had already made herself a half-litre mug of instant coffee from Maxim T. Yermakov's supplies: the spoon clattered in it with a wooden sound and brown streaks floated on the surface like paint; now he had to wait for her to finish drinking it.

Just Natasha was in no hurry. Her discontent filled the tiny kitchen, setting the weak bulb in the doughy-coloured ceiling light blinking: as if the landlady was sucking out the energy she needed to continue the row and wasn't going to leave things at that.

"You wash that door down properly. I'm not having any assholes written on my door. With petrol!" she declared. "If you've got a car, you can scrub it off with petrol."

"I've paid for the damage, now you have to wash it," Maxim T. Yermakov retorted, and immediately regretted his lack of restraint.

"Me? You ought to be ashamed of yourself!" said Just Natasha, coming out in blotches of the poisonous-pink colour that was intrinsic to her by nature and was repeated as often as possible in her clothes. "Suggesting something like that to a woman who's older than you! So I have to feed my bedridden mother with a spoon, wash her dirty things and then scrub your door for you? I'm telling you seriously, I've warned you: if you don't want serious trouble, behave like a decent human being. We've got an official contract, with official information in it, and I know where you work. I can write a complaint to your firm. Then we'll see how your bosses like that."

Maxim T. Yermakov knew they wouldn't like it at all. Sending a screed "to the firm" was pretty much the same as complaining to the Party Committee in former times. They might dispatch the trashy scrap of paper to the rubbish bin, or they might study it and discover that their employee's domestic mores amounted to a contravention of corporate values and damaged the company's image. Admittedly, Maxim T. Yermakov was in a rather special position these days. He strode round the offices like a ghost in its ancestral castle, and his colleagues avoided meeting his eyes, as if they could all see the clotted blood in the bullet hole in his forehead. Somehow they seemed to have guessed that the aggregate state of Maxim T. Yermakov's head was not the same as that of normal individuals' heads. And that made Maxim T. Yermakov feel like a small bottle without its top screwed on: jolt it and everything will spill out. His tacky creative idea for the national holiday of St. Valentine's Day – a chocolate heart, pierced by an arrow that looked like a fish skeleton – had been accepted without a murmur at today's meeting, and no one had come up with any disagreeably intelligent comments, everyone had pretended that Maxim T. Yermakov wasn't there.

"Write a stinking letter, I don't mind," Maxim T. Yermakov declared nonchalantly. Just Natasha stared hard at him and rested her heavy elbow on the table. "If you want to simply waste your time."

"Why, you shameless lout!" Just Natasha exclaimed indignantly. "All right, let's get to the bottom of this. I have a right to know what's going on!"

"Why?"

"What do you mean why, what do you mean why?" jabbered Just Natasha, looking very much like a large chicken with ruffled feathers. "The militia have been keeping watch on the stairs for more than a week now! My mum and I were always poor, but we were respectable! And now the neighbours, who've known me since I was a little girl, call me up about you: Natochka, they say, your tenant's been put under surveillance by the militia. We've got an ambush here, they could start firing at any moment. Who knows what might happen to the flat now, you'd better come over and sort it all out!"

"What business is it of theirs? And what makes them think it's the militia? And why have they decided it's me they're watching?" Maxim T. Yermakov asked irritably. "Maybe they've decided to keep an eye on the winos on the fifth floor? What do I do? They're the ones who are always partying non-stop day and night. The landlord Vasya never even dries out, he lives off letting in whores and their clients. It's a real dive, and you go on about respectable people and a respectable stairwell! Sometimes I see a face in the lift and I dream about it all night afterwards. And Vasya's the most handsome of the lot, with his burnt beard and his cap from the garbage tip. I suppose they all watched him grow up too. Maybe you shared a desk with him at school and you danced together at the graduation ball?"

"Don't you dare talk like that about Vasya Shutov!" Just Natasha retorted indignantly. "He was a good man, he used to buy my mother expensive medicines. He's only been drinking for three years. First he started believing in God and then he took to drink. You've never done a single thing for my mum, so don't you say anything about him to me."

Maxim T. Yermakov cleared his throat sceptically. It was extremely hard to believe that Vasya the alcoholic had only been drinking for three years. If that was so, Vasya was cruising through life at an incredible pace and, if his fate had turned in a different direction, in the same period he could have built, for instance, an entire factory. Instead of which Vasya had destroyed himself, and now he was a bandy-legged little hobgoblin with a face like minced meat and a mindless eagerness in his vodka-soaked eyes – eagerness for villainy or heroism, whichever way the spinning bottle landed. At night the muffled sounds of drunken merriment emanated from his lair, and the entirely unsavoury flat jiggled about like a cardboard box full of broken glass. The local militiaman, red-nosed and as fair-haired as a goose, regularly dropped in to the lair, in fact he spent quite a lot of time there. But even so, the alcoholic Vasya was a Muscovite, he had grown up here, in this leaden-grey dormitory suburb with a fierce wind blowing from round every corner – and therefore he was regarded as more reliable than some outsider, quietly renting a tiny flat for serious money.

"But all the same, what reason have you all got for deciding that this surveillance is down to me?" Maxim T. Yermakov asked irritably.

"A very good one!" Just Natasha exclaimed triumphantly. "They've arranged with Maria Alexandrovna in 406 to use her toilet. Civilised people, they are, don't pee on the stairs. They showed her their ID too, and, as it happens, they pay her money, almost as much as you pay in rent. Maria Alexandrovna keeps a special towel and soap just for them. She invited them to eat lunch in her kitchen, so they wouldn't have to chew their sandwiches on the windowsill, even offered them fresh tea. But they told her: No Mrs. Kalyazina, we can't do that, we have to keep an eye on flat 410. That made her nervous, after all, she's getting on, and she asked them: Why, what's happened? They told her: We're very interested in the tenant in there. So, how do you explain that? And there are these odd characters hanging about in the yard all the time! Only yesterday Maria Alexandrovna went out to take her dog for a walk and they were standing there: about twelve of them with placards, and they had 'Die, asshole!' written on them. It was your door they wrote that on, nobody else's! But that door happens to belong to me!"

While she was speaking, working her little painted mouth intensely, Maxim T. Yermakov felt a strange thirst building up in the entire substance of his being, as if some of the essential elements of Mendeleev's periodic table that constitute the organic matter of life had been sucked out of him. He mechanically tugged a cigarette out of the pack; when Just Natasha raised her narrow grey-blue eyebrows to form a right angle, he gave her a look over the vertical flame of his cigarette lighter that set her coughing into her mug. The first drags filled his body with a pleasant, languorous sensation and eddied around in his head, and in those eddies, which assumed the spectral forms of a brain, a certain attractive idea started taking shape.

"So you want money, do you?" asked Maxim T. Yermakov, handing Just Natasha a paper napkin because she had a trickle of coffee running down her large flannelette chin.

"Do the shops sell me everything for nothing?" she snarled back.

"All right, then, I'll give you the kind of story that makes a journalist's name forever. Worldwide fame! And money will follow as a consequence. Okay, the subject: the rights of man and a new twist in the KGB's flouting of the law. Because it's not the militia who are camped in our stairwell! It's the special services. The state fucking committee for driving citizens to commit suicide!"

Just Natasha's handbag with the money in it gradually slid off her limp knees. She listened, breathing through her open mouth, as if she had grabbed a mouthful of food that was too hot and simply couldn't swallow it. Maxim T. Yermakov tried to describe the special committee men, hung all over with weird equipment, their crazy ideas about cause and effect relationships and their violations of civil rights. Of course, Just Natasha wasn't the best possible choice as a media agent, and he felt rather sorry to waste the story on her. But, with his hand on his heart, Maxim T. Yermakov would have had to admit that the big-time journalists, with whom he had tried to frighten the state committee freaks, existed more in his imagination than in reality. Of course, he was acquainted with a certain number of individuals from the promotional departments of influential media structures. For the most part they were successful women, still sort of youngish, but already of indefinite age, with skin and clothes that were too taut, as if the loose folds were clutched in someone's fist behind them. These individuals were indifferent to any human story: for them every phenomenon in the world was an opportunity for self-publicity and it was their job to ensure that none of the promotional assets found their way into the parallel media-reality for free. They were the metaphysical heirs to the Soviet censors, and their weeding of the field of reality reduced it to a series of bald patches that gave even Maxim T. Yermakov the creeps.

Maxim T. Yermakov had acquired other acquaintances in the realm of the media at presentations of his milky-clay product and at outings arranged by the firm for members of the press. There was a certain Dima Rozhdestvensky, always half-drunk, always in a dark shirt and a light silk tie that looked like a freshly-filleted fish, and with something fishy in the tint of his freshly-shaved cheeks; there was another Dima, whose surname he thought was Kavkov, always three-quarters drunk, who wore coarse denim trousers that looked as if they were made of elephant hide and a waistcoat of the same material with multiple pockets, all of which was half-concealed behind his ginger beard. And there were the girls – fat-faced, skinny, various – their names were confused forever in Maxim T. Yermakov's consciousness because, for the life of him, he couldn't remember which one of them it was he screwed at the Shchukino Holiday Camp, far from the corporate shish-kebabs, by the wan, flickering light of a thunderstorm that seemed to clothe their damp bodies in electric fur.

These were all semi-unemployed journalistic small fry, regular freeloaders at buffet lunches, not a single political wolf capable of spinning the story and really giving the social forecasters what they deserved. True, there was one man, the intelligent scoundrel Vanya Golikov, who used to present the trenchantly sardonic TV programme "Murmurs in the Ranks", on the NNT-TV channel about three years earlier, when the entire country knew his bony features, decorated with two bushy eyebrows and one pre-eminent nose reminiscent of a primeval stone axe. But then some kind of friction in the works had generated oily smoke and political sparks, and the channel had given Vanya the push, since when he had been a plaything of the winds that blew him round Europe, from where he would return carrying a bit more flesh and looking more and more like a placid rat. Maxim T. Yermakov's path and his had crossed in random fashion, in middle-of-the-road clubs, with sofas hot from backsides and toilet mirrors gummy with traces of "snow". Despite the innate meanness that prevented Maxim T. Yermakov from becoming a fully-fledged Moscow city clubber, he and the party animal Golikov had struck up a relationship involving an easygoing mutual-credit arrangement for minor sums that were instantly forgotten, so that it soon became impossible to tell who owed how much to whom. This unlikely financial affinity generated a spiritual one: the conversations that they held, ignoring the chilled-out babes snuggling up from the right and the left, concerned the entire world order and, in particular, the techniques of success. In fact Golikov had asked Maxim T. Yermakov to toss him a "subject, a topic, some little screw-up" to which he could add a detonator and a fuse to create a bomb. But Maxim T.

Yermakov had no idea where to find the intermittent Golikov now. The latest reports had him working for some radio station in Prague – or maybe not in radio and maybe not even in Prague. Golikov's e-mail responded with automated messages and his mobile number announced its own non-existence in funereal tones.

For Just Natasha, Maxim T. Yermakov's story was an excellent chance, one which, all things considered, she didn't actually deserve. But somehow the proffered gift failed to fill her with delight. As the story unfolded, the hot pink coals on her sagging face turned to ashes.

"You want me to defend you in the newspapers?" she asked, outraged, when Maxim T. Yermakov paused for a minute or so in order to raise a rather shaky section of the double glazing and secure it in place with a rasping crunch of the handle. The open pane tensed like a sail under the crackling assault of rain that splashed inside, and while Maxim T. Yermakov was struggling with the recalcitrant frame, he thought he glimpsed a movement down below – several black umbrellas springing into the air at the same time where low, grey banks of snow had settled round the edge of the flickering asphalt like soap scum.

"Sorry, what?" he asked, looking round.

"I said you want to exploit me for your own indecent purposes," Just Natasha declared, bristling on her stool. "I always make an effort to help people, and I made an effort for you, I went to the senior editor and pushed for your advertising campaign. You didn't take the opportunity then. I have a career and a reputation too. I'm not going to go putting myself out for your business again. Especially since your position is so dubious. If you can make certain that terrorist attacks are prevented, but you don't want to, how will the relatives of the victims feel about the article? I personally have no sympathy for you at all. What if tomorrow I get into the metro and they've planted explosives in it? Do you think I'd like that?"

"Have you gone totally gaga? Completely lost your marbles?" asked Maxim T. Yermakov, twirling a finger beside his temple and generating a small whirlwind in his head. "How can someone sitting quietly at home possibly be responsible for bombs going off anywhere?"

"All sorts of things happen," Just Natasha declared haughtily. "It was the Soviet regime that indoctrinated us with the idea that there was nothing but the leading role of the Party. But now just look how many healers and people with magical abilities have appeared. They used to hide them from the people before! But there were psychics working in the Kremlin, they kept Brezhnev on his feet when he was already a corpse. So don't you try to tell me! The only reason I'm still alive is that I work on my subconscious, I don't have enough income to spend anything on doctors."

"Income's exactly what I'm talking about!" exclaimed Maxim T. Yermakov, trying to step harder on that sure-fire pedal. I repeat: my theme is political. A real hot potato! Just listen closely to the key words: human rights, freedom, KGB. Can you imagine the kind of financial recompense we're talking here?"

Just Natasha started blinking her eyes and rapped her rings on the table. A little grey cloud of fine dust rose into the air from the ashtray that Maxim T. Yermakov had filled right up to the brim and then settled back down onto the plastic surface.

"Stop trying to involve me in this filthy business of yours! I don't want to hear any more! I write about the theatre, about culture, if that word has any meaning for you! People's Artists know me, they kiss my hand. I've worked all my life for that, and now you're trying to arrange things so that everyone gives me the cold shoulder, right, is that it?" Just Natasha trembled in indignation as she fumbled around hastily for the flabby carcass of her pink bag lying at her feet. "This is what I have to say to you, young man. I was only going to raise your rent for the inconvenience and risk. But now I realise that I can't let you stay here. I want you out of mum's flat in a week, is that clear?"

So saying, Just Natasha stormed out into the hallway and started pulling on her terrible cardboard-leather coat, pinning down her criss-crossed scarf with her multiple chins.

"Have you forgotten we have a contract? Have you read it

carefully? You have no right to throw me out, I haven't violated a single condition!" Maxim T. Yermakov shouted after her.

"I don't give a shit for the contract! Just you try staying even one day longer! I'll throw your faggoty suits out of the window!" Just Natasha retorted, wrapping her arms round her bag and shooting out into the stairwell.

"Fuck it, what a whore! The old scrubber's got problems with her private places!" Maxim T. Yermakov thought as he padded after her, intending to close the desecrated door. But instead he opened the door as wide as it would go and yelled loud enough to set the entire damp, dingy stairwell ringing:

"I won't move out! Stick a chimney stack up your ass and another down your throat!"

He saw Just Natasha threatening him from the lift with a white fist, adorned with an ink-black gemstone on it, before the lift, shuddering like a rickety cart, lugged its load off to the ground floor. Two dark male figures with sharp noses were silhouetted against the silver-foil background of the rainy window, and Maxim T. Yermakov launched a slipper in their direction. It vanished without making a sound.

Where had that pistol been all this time?

The hand-me-down Makarov PMM was still where Maxim T. Yermakov had stuck it immediately after his first encounter with the social forecasters. It was lying in the middle drawer of his office desk, surrounded by all sorts of petty trash, like faulty computer disks, empty cigarette lighters and dried-out felt-tip pens; it skidded about in there, smashing the fragile plastic with its heavy ordnance weight. At first Maxim T. Yermakov had hoped the PMM would simply disappear; he thought that if he left something that was usually hidden in an easily accessible spot, it was bound to get stolen. But no such luck. Even the cleaning lady seemed to have given Maxim T. Yermakov's workstation a wide berth: the desk had grown a thick coating of dust and a slick of coffee that had been spilt one day was developing into a furry birthmark. Maxim T. Yermakov's habitat in the office was like some obscure island, where the inhabitant could be found, like a bear, by following his fresh tracks.

Eventually one day Maxim T. Yermakov picked up the weighty Makarov PMM and started pondering. Since the weapon was only intended to perform a single, one-off operation – a brief mechanical convulsion between his finger and his temple, like the exaggerated gesture people use to show that someone has a screw loose – the social forecasters had not bothered to provide the Alpha Object with any contrivances for carrying the pistol around: a holster, straps or whatever else they had to do the job. When the PMM was placed in his jacket (and Maxim T. Yermakov liked jackets of fine wool with silk linings), the way it weighed down the pocket looked god-awful; and apart from that, his liver reacted to its dead iron weight, hardening instantly into sclerosis, even seeming to borrow the right-angled corner of the PMM that was jabbing him in the rib. The best idea he could come up with was to put the PMM in his briefcase so that, at the right moment, he could detach the flap from its delicate lock, shake the briefcase off the weapon and shoot.

He could sense the cool, minty breath of danger with every inch of his sensitive skin. He'd had a bad feeling since the morning, as if the social forecasters who were in the flat hadn't left, but actually dissolved into the air. They communicated their presence through acrid technological smells and strange darknesses, and he only had to click the light switch in the early-morning winter twilight for the lamps to burn out and burst with a gentle clinking sound. At night Maxim T. Yermakov's head flailed away like a washing machine, swirling round gigabytes of soggy information, sucking out and draining away the scummy swill that he dreamed of as a sea that had to be laundered, together with everything in it. He got out of bed feeling shattered, thwacked Marinka, who was staying overnight more and more often, across a cold buttock that resounded as crisply as a football, and shaved frenziedly, snarling into the mirror at the approach of the bleak day preparing its malign surprises for Maxim T. Yermakov.

It could be that the relationships of cause and effect for which the person of Maxim T. Yermakov represented a node of morbid sensitivity were setting traps for him by exploiting the general conditions, as it were. The icy steps at the main door, which slipped out from under the sole of his shoe, making him sit down suddenly on what felt like a vertical bolt of lightning, could be explained by the previous day's atmospheric precipitation and the touch of overnight frost that had transformed the road surface into a washboard. Everyone crept cautiously over these treacherous humps, with Maxim T. Yermakov the most cautious of them all. Even so, just two traffic lights before the office Maxim T. Yermakov slipped into a sideways drift down an inclined slope, feeling the solid ground shifting away with every nerve of his battered and bruised backside, and gave a six-sided streetlamp a neat smacker of a kiss.

All of this was lousy shit, but it didn't exceed the bounds of the general order of things. The next day, however, as Maxim T. Yermakov, having left the crumpled Toyota at a friendly repair shop, was simply walking along the street, the object that whistled down through the air and shattered at the spot where his foot would have been in one second on completing the step for which it was already raised, was not an icicle, but a thick champagne bottle. Maxim T. Yermakov froze, with a trembling in his stomach, contemplating the black star that had exploded at his feet. He took no notice of his custodians, also on foot, who came running up, fingered the back of his head, as yielding as a tussock of grass in a swamp, and craned their necks to gaze upwards at the launch point of the glassy death that had missed its mark by mere centimetres. Casting off the long arms of the KGB and moving like some animal with a neck that nature never intended to be cocked backwards, Maxim T. Yermakov twisted and strained and squinted up at the small, dark faces hanging over the side of the Stalinesque edifice's balcony, which resembled a box in a theatre.

Well, let's assume that some unspecified group of merrymakers could have got carried away celebrating something or other and dropped the bottle from the balcony to fall on whoever God put in the way. But how could he explain what was going on with the door of the flat? Maxim T. Yermakov had conscientiously washed off "DIE, ASSHOLE!" But the very next evening he had emerged from the lift to see a fresh text daubed in sweeping strokes: "SHOOT YOURSELF, DICKHEAD!" And furthermore, the wall all around the door and lower, down the angle of the stairs, had been defiled with cans of spray-paint; the obscene words swirled and eddied like blue and red fog and at one prominent spot there was a drawing in soot, a tight bunch of three balloons that made up a 50-centimetre prick with balls. The two faithful retainers were perched all present and correct on the windowsill, but there was no food spread out between them this time, instead there was a painstakingly arranged game of chess, over which they hovered, fingering the pieces. Maxim T. Yermakov stood there and thought for a moment, then stepped back into the lift, in which an empty beer bottle clattered about uninhibitedly, and went back down to the ground floor. In the yard he said a polite hello to Maria Alexandrovna, a cultured old crone in a decayed beret, dragging her fat bolster of a dachshund along on its lead. Out of the corner of his eyes he spotted a group of people smoking, but ignored them. At the sight of Maxim T. Yermakov, they spread out hastily, unfurling a long banner that snapped in the wind. "Yeah, yeah, demonstrators like that come for a dime a dozen, the same ones take money from the same place to hassle dissenters, or guys trying to save Russia, or the talk show 'Voice of the People'," Maxim T. Yermakov thought spitefully as he walked down into the basement minimarket. After greeting the yellow-haired woman at the checkout, who replied with an affectionate gold-toothed smile, he made a modest purchase. Ten minutes later he was back standing on his own floor of the building, holding a three-kilogramme bag of wheat flour in each hand, like fat little infants sitting on his palms.

"Just why is everybody so afraid of you after all, Messrs State Security Agents?" he said to himself as he walked down towards the pair, who looked up indifferently at him from the chessboard, on which the black and white pieces were locked together stubbornly with a terrible, meaningless strength, like the knuckles of two fists. Since the bags had been opened in advance, the flour flowed out freely onto the threadbare tops of the social forecasters' heads. They

56

both accepted three kilos of the crumbly, clinging substance without stirring a muscle, only blinking their identical white eyelashes as they were transformed into two humungous honey agaric mushrooms.

"And now off you go to Mrs. Kalyazina's place for a wash," Maxim T. Yermakov said in a didactic tone when the bags had breathed out their final white sigh and their contents were exhausted. "Ah, but I believe Maria Alexandrovna is still walking her dog. You'll have to be patient for a while. Perhaps while you're waiting you might recall who's been playing the hooligan here in the stairwell? Or is that your own eager handiwork? If, so please wash the door, I washed it yesterday, I can't be bothered to do it again."

Suddenly a hand as white as the fingers of a skeleton grabbed hold of Maxim T. Yermakov just above his watch, and the pain was so bad that the paper bag slipped out of his immobilised fingers like a blurred cloud. The window shuddered and the bright electric spots outside it suddenly looked exactly like freshly decanted, bloody egg yolks. A pair of red eyes glared at him from close up, and the expression in them suggested that the social forecaster was the one in pain, not Maxim T. Yermakov.

"Listen, you, have you got any conscience at all?" the state committee freak wheezed exactly like some ordinary man in the street with a cold.

"Bugger off!" Maxim T. Yermakov responded with aggressive bravado, although the pain from that grip was rising in taut, throbbing rings and blossoming in his head.

"Do you have any honour or dignity? Do you have a heart? Do you know what people suffer under a collapsed building? And what about the hostages? Have you no compassion for anyone but yourself?" asked the state-committee freak, continuing his tedious sermon.

"Go screw yourself!" Maxim T Yermakov replied with the same cheerful conviction, even though he could no longer feel anything below his shoulder.

At that, the social forecaster screwed up his face and shoved Maxim T. Yermakov away with a jolt that shed a light sprinkling of flour onto the windowsill and the chess pieces. Chortling and hissing by turns, Maxim T. Yermakov walked up the flight of steps and started fiddling one-handedly with his keys, which stubbornly tried to slip out of his grasp: his left arm dangled limply and only got in his way, like an inflatable limb. About an hour later, after he had hung up his clothes somehow, despite them repeatedly slipping off the hangers, and tied the belt of his spacious new dressing gown with the help of his teeth, Maxim T. Yermakov indulged himself by looking out to see how the KGB sentries were baking in their dough. But the social forecasters were not on the landing: old Mrs Kalyazina was sweeping up streaks of flour off the tiled floor with a gingerish broom that was shedding its stalks of straw. "Lord, Lord, the things that happen, everyone's lost their minds, Lord, how are we supposed to live," she muttered, with her earrings and her chins jiggling; the tuft of grey hair on the top of her head was like a solid pellet of dust. At the sight of the old woman, Maxim T. Yermakov experienced a clear physical sensation – a solid barrier in his chest, immediately behind the ribs, against which this pitiful, tear-jerking little scene smashed to smithereens. "Want my heart, do you? Fuck you, you scumbags," he thought spitefully, slamming the door hard against the jamb.

Apparently the old crone who provided aid and comfort to the KGB had managed to get through to Just Natasha on the phone after all. Maxim T. Yermakov awaited the day appointed by his landlady for the defenestration of his suits with a certain degree of apprehension. However, nothing happened, and Maxim T. Yermakov calmed down, smiling to himself mockingly as he recalled that plump fist threatening him from the lift. But it was a mistake for him to relax, and he shouldn't have trusted the good mood he felt when he finally got his Toyota back from the workshop, all straightened out and repainted, but still with a surprised look on its face, as if it couldn't forget that six-sided pillar with its husk of ice-glazed-paper notices. As he rolled up to the entrance, aiming to slip adroitly into the gap between an amiable Honda and the rusty carcass of a Moskvich that looked like a horse's skull, he saw the disaster. The naked, blue-grey tree that had been a scrawny maple during the summer, now resembled some kind of umbrella-shaped growth from the African savanna. The flat patchwork crown had a strangely anthropomorphic appearance, and Maxim T. Yermakov immediately guessed what was hanging there. The feeling with which he recognised his things was the same as when he recognised himself unexpectedly in a street mirror. He had bought that mustard-coloured tweed jacket in a sale at Harrods and that charcoal-grey suit with the supremely fine light stripe was from the Galleries Lafayette in Paris. Now it was all dangling there, absorbing the dirty drizzle, a blurred mass of formless blotches.

A group of thoroughly damp gawkers were standing in a circle, like children round a New Year tree. Maxim T. Yermakov walked closer, keeping his hands in his pockets. One quite respectable-looking character, plump with glowing health right up to his leather cap, was cautiously shaking the recalcitrant, comatose trunk; another, with a skewed woolly hat set on dirty clumps of grey hair, was pawing a pair of soiled and totally defenceless light-coloured trousers with his swollen mitts. Loitering there among the others, hoiking his burnt beard up in the air, was the alcoholic Shutov from the fifth floor, accompanied by two of his girls of extremely easy virtue: one lanky-legged and long-nosed, looking like a sick ostrich in her short jacket of waterlogged silver fox, the other small and insignificant, gazing in fright at Maxim Y. Yermakov with smeared, blotchy eyes and clutching across her chest a pair of small hands with fingers like white sticks of school chalk. Here and there on the sleety lawn, on the grainy layer of disappearing snow, small coins shaken out of the pockets of suits glinted palely, and a crushed cigarette packet was a lone white spot.

Even if he had all his things cleaned, there was no way he could ever wear them again. Muttering under his breath, Maxim T. Yermakov shuffled off towards the lift. Upstairs, the air in the flat was as fresh as outside: it probably wasn't long since Just Natasha had perpetrated her frenzied feat of heroism. The doors of the empty wardrobe were standing open, exposing its plywood back and the empty hangers, clumped together crookedly. With the chandelier switched on, the inside of the wardrobe was so bright that it hurt his eyes. Still hanging there, untouched, on a small rack specially installed by the tenant on one of the doors, was a restrained, silky rainbow of ties – carefully selected to match the things that had already been ruined. Lying in open view on mum's dreadful desk was his old appointment book, crudely forced open with its spine cracked apart; the money extracted from inside the cover had been laid beside it, with ostentatious hypocrisy, and weighted down with a marble inkstand that looked like a lump of greyish soap. There was also a page ripped crookedly out of the appointment book, besmirched with straggly little wormlets of words that Maxim T. Yermakov could barely make out, even when he screwed his eyes up. The note said: "I warned you, and you thought it was all just talk. All the neighbours are dead set (illegible) against you. Good people live here, war veterans and labour veterans, no one wants to live with you around. Clear out! I've taken seven thousand roubles from your (crossed out) money to pay for the door."

So Maxim T. Yermakov was left with nothing but what he was standing up in, the clothes he had come home in. Not that he'd been so very attached to those duds… Ah, but yes, the fucking bastards, he *had* been attached to them, he'd loved them and pampered them, he liked the way he felt in all that comfortable, slightly conservative stuff, he adored the super-light, intense, enveloping warmth of cashmere, the raw roughness of linen, he relished unhackneyed tones, precision-perfect manufacturing and what was called "line" – the kind of real quality for real men that was obvious from a casual glance. Maxim T. Yermakov felt as if he himself, and not just his clothes, had been tossed out into the cold and filth from the seventh floor. He was infuriated by the thought that the social forecasters' cheap flock-pelleted coats that had been ruined by the flour were not worth as much as the lining of his handsome tweed jacket, the original price of which in Harrods had been six hundred and fifty pounds.

In the morning the branches of the naked maple that had accepted the humanitarian aid for the local street bums were empty and broken, half of them dangling on frozen ribbons of bark, making the remains of the tree look untidy, and at the same time it all resembled a tattered spider's web, complete with long-legged insects that had got caught up in it. In his only remaining suit (the Gianfranco Ferre that was his favourite, even though it was from the year before last), Maxim T. Yermakov felt as if he had slept without getting undressed. He put off a meeting with the brainless whiners from a production studio and instead of lunch went on an intensive shopping expedition. For the first time ever he was irritated by the military bearing of the empty jackets hanging in close formation and the wanton glances of the gauche hussies who only came over into the men's department to barge into fitting rooms at the most inappropriate moment with a random armful of tatty threads. Squirming about in the brutish confinement of those solitary cells, with their crooked curtains of unreliable rags, Maxim T. Yermakov was swamped by terror at the thought that in the next cubicle, right there on the other side of the mirror that reflected the various stages of his undress, at that very moment someone was setting up a bomb. The suit that was eventually purchased, which in the hot shop-floor lighting had looked very much like one to which he had taken a fancy on the Boulevard Haussman, turned out at home to be a piggy-pink colour, with large padded shoulders and bug-eyed buttons.

All this time Maxim T. Yermakov was thinking, thinking, thinking. He had wanted his personal war with the social forecasters to be beautiful, a struggle that would put to shame the wretched Bolsheviks who, instead of bumping off that half-pint Stalin, had flooded into the camps in droves. But it had turned into a communal-apartment squabble, with the opposing sides crapping outside the single rusty toilet bowl and spitting in each other's soup. Maxim T. Yermakov was beginning to understand all the pitilessness and hopelessness of communal wars, fraught with material losses and ultimately, absurd as it might seem, dangerous to life. He simply couldn't find in himself that intense, essentially womanish, domestic fury, which, when dissolved in the slush of the humdrum daily round, provides the drive and energy to do the dirt on the enemy relentlessly. His fury was of a different, metaphysical kind. The rights of the Common Individual, who wished to drink his tea and eat his bun with no hang-ups and no hindrances, were being violated with impunity and without compensation – and Maxim T. Yermakov intended to stand up for his own commonness. In the face of the overwhelming force of the special state committee, he felt like one of those little black stones coated with dust that find their way into grain, get boiled up in the mush and break one of the diner's teeth.

However, war at the level of the common people seemed to play straight into the social forecasters' hands. They intended to run this contrary Alpha Object into the ground using the energy of the civilian population, with its industrial-scale reserves of communal spite and innate inclination to cosy up to the secret services. Maxim T. Yermakov was almost certain that the picketers with the gloomy faces who suddenly came to life like large rag dolls when he appeared, had been rented out to the KGB men by some piddling little political party – there was nothing personal in their shouting, or the way they flung the squishy, rotten vegetables. But there was something deadly dangerous in his neighbours' festive excitement, in their sudden mutual cordiality, in the stout bearing of three or four vodka-soaked old men, who seemed to have recovered their health out of the blue.

At first glance, the most rational thing to do was to move out of Just Natasha's one-room flat and leave all these lamebrains behind. But on sober reflection, it became apparent that moving out was the last thing he should do. It wasn't likely that an Object under siege from all sides would be able to rent another flat – they would hardly allow him to do that. He could even end up as a vagrant – transformed from a proud Common Individual into a mindless bundle of organic matter with cyanotic blood, absorbing the deathly chill of Moscow's asphalt and stone through his stinking rags. Or he could cut loose from the capital and head for his officially registered place of residence, the regional town of Krasnogorie, which boasted a glorious metallurgical plant and gigantic Lombardy poplars, like tangled masses of thick cables. That region, enveloped in sun-bright toxic industrial haze and managed hands-on by a Mr-Nice-Guy governor, would be the easiest place in the world to grind anyone down. So he had to hold on to this little flat, and Moscow, and his chocolate, for which they still hadn't got around to allocating the biannual promotional budget.

In point of fact, the social forecasters had no real levers they could use to prise Maxim T. Yermakov out of his accustomed perch. Or was he being too naive? He had to watch his step very carefully, fastidiously observe all the traffic regulations when he was driving, not stick his nose into any more large shopping malls, not wander nonchalantly under balconies or any kind of awnings or canopies where crooked icicles grew, as murky and cock-eyed as jars of homebrewed hooch, but still capable, in the warped coordinates of the relations of cause and effect, of plummeting downwards and smiting with the precision of an arrow. What else? Alcohol and drugs – cut them out completely. Actually, in that area Maxim T. Yermakov had long had the reputation of an eccentric. Always dressed, as Sasha-Cherdak put it, "like a government minister", drinking and snorting as if he was doing the entire party crowd an immense favour, he was regarded by the glammed-up, low-order party animals as either a vulgar attention-seeker or a great careerist in embryo. In reality Maxim T. Yermakov simply didn't get a hit from strong drink, or pills or snow. The entire effect amounted to no more than his anti-gravity brain responding to the blow by transmitting innumerable copies of itself into space for a few minutes – and then a piercing clarity descended, as painful as the screech of a knife scraping across glass. Maxim T. Yermakov wasted money on these anti-pleasures purely out of a sense of propriety – something he would have to forget about completely now: even a brief loss of self-control gave the cause-and-effect relationships an increased opportunity. It was even more important not to go sticking his nose into dark archways and alleys, with those special acoustics that transformed someone out walking at a late hour into raucously tramping bait. And he absolutely must not trim time off the short walk from the minimarket by cutting through the next yard, where the lamps glowed so feebly and the derelict foundation pit lurked in the rain that transformed its clay into thick pea soup.

In a world spread thickly with danger, like butter, in a slippery world with no brakes, a prudent man probably looks like the same kind of madman as someone stoned out of his mind and driving with his speedometer needle off the scale in a stable, normal world. Perhaps it was indeed a kind of madness that had come over Maxim T. Yermakov. Perhaps he had started suffering from delusions. Whatever, but when, in a state of utter despondency, he did set off back home with his purchases across the next yard, Maxim T. Yermakov thought he heard someone behind him cough into their fist, and then someone suddenly tugged very hard on his ear. The cough was immediately repeated, a piece of metal that had been hit fell to the ground with a clang and several more bullets buried themselves juicily in the clay. Maybe this twitchy, nervous response of the darkness was the manifestation of Maxim T. Yermakov's own personal neurasthenia, but he tossed away the light-coloured bag with his upended supper in it and made a dash for the garages.

All this was extremely improbable. All this was not what anyone wanted, especially the social forecasters themselves. Nonetheless Maxim T. Yermakov, with a Band Aid on his ear where a small piece appeared to have been nicked off by an eyelet punch, took the government-issue PMM out of his drawer at the office and transferred it to his briefcase.

"Ah, drop it, Maxie, don't let it get to you. You're the lucky type, you are," Marinka remonstrated with him, squinting lovingly at the tenderly swollen little brush tracing a scarlet stripe along her fingernail.

"Oh yeah, sure. Lucky as a drowned man, I am," muttered Maxim T. Yermakov, who had just emerged from the shower, a study in pale droplets and steamed moles. "Every step I take, luck just kicks my ass."

"Look at things objectively," Marinka exclaimed reasonably, carrying on painting her large, sturdy nails, each almost the size of a hen's egg. "You could have snuffed yourself against that lamppost, but all you did was dent your bumper. That bottle from the balcony was headed straight for your noodle, but it missed. Maybe someone did even take a shot at you – but they didn't kill you, did they? – and look, your ear's almost healed up now. Someone's warding off disaster for you. My granny would have said you've got an angel standing behind your shoulder. Even those morons in the yard, throwing the tomatoes, they missed too…"

"The tomatoes got me," Maxim T. Yermakov informed her morosely, flopping into bed.

"Why, the cackhanded jerks!" Marinka exclaimed. "How bad is it?"

"I tried the Italian cleaners for the coat, but they wouldn't take it," Maxim T. Yermakov replied reluctantly. "Said it was no good, it's ruined, the stains won't come out. And there's no point in getting a new one. So from now on I'll be walking around Moscow dressed like a collective-farm worker. I'll dig out the old leather job, the one I bought back home in Krasnogorie, at the market, and wear that."

"Oh, great. We could walk around dressed like collective farmers at home. What was the point of coming to Moscow just to wear old rags from the Krasnogorie Market?" asked Marinka, pulling a wry face and twisting up her long, thin mouth – she tried so hard to make its contours seem plumper, constantly running the lip-liner over her light-coloured fuzz, that it often looked as if she was bleeding from the nose.

She picked an invisible little fibre off her scarlet nail and leaned back, admiring its beauty. She had recently got into the habit of laying out her full manicure kit at Maxim T. Yermakov's place, including the small bent and broken tubes, swabs of coloured cotton-wool and fat little bottles that looked like decorations for the New Year tree – all with a fierce reek of acetone, as if there was major renovation work in progress. The processes involved were fiddly and finicky, Marinka spent at least an hour drying her nails, manipulating her fingers as if they were delicate little pincers. Previously she never used to spend any more time at Maxim T. Yermakov's place than was necessary for a quick spot of love-making and a slightly less hurried spot of making-up to restore her smeared face to its original untouched state. But these days she seemed to be assimilating Maxim T. Yermakov and everything to do with him all over again. She scattered lipstick cartridges and lacy lingerie around the place and then, having marked out her territory in this way, took charge in the kitchen, concocting the only thing she knew how to make: super-heavy borsch with a marrow bone that looked like an oak tree boiled whole. She fleshed out the simple lovemaking with a whole set of freakish tricks, the cinematic origin of which was clearly revealed by the scintillating glance that she cast through her tangled hair in the direction of an imaginary spectator. She rotated her derrière with the gingerbread suntan and toyed with the thin strip of her panties like a young hooligan fiddling with his catapult. She scratched Maxim T. Yermakov like a favourite pig with her bright-coloured fingernails. Her tongue stung and melted, like a never-ending sip of brandy. In this new sex, she was the aggressor and Maxim T. Yermakov was a goody-goody prude with his nerves ablaze. But then, when he reached bursting point, she turned out to be unresponsive inside, like a shoe stuffed with sand. Maxim T. Yermakov didn't understand how that could happen.

"Ma-axie! Ooh Ma-axie, don't look at me like that!" Marinka said, turning away to screw the top onto a wobbly little bottle. "I didn't ruin your coat, did I?"

"Why are mia-a-a-owing like that, like some Moscow pussy ca-a-at?" Maxim T. Yermakov responded irritably. "Do you think I can't hear how hard you're trying? They may all be kittens and pussy cats here, but we're doggies. Grrr! Grrr!"

"Growl like that and you'll end up selling bananas at the market," Marinka snapped, then she blew on her extended fingers and slumped sideways against Maxim T. Yermakov. "Maybe I'm your guardian angel?" she said skittishly, butting him on the shoulder.

"That's not very likely," muttered Maxim T. Yermakov, putting his arm round Marinka just below her breasts. "My angels are out there on the stairs, sitting on the windowsill."

"Sod them," Marinka whispered fervently, grinding herself more intensely against Maxim T. Yermakov. "Sod them and screw them! Moscow's a mean old place, it doesn't want us. But we're even meaner! Someone picked you out and they're putting the pressure on, to teach our kind not to come here any more. But you turned out to be a hard case. Much harder than all those loudmouthed kids who shit themselves if you just wag a finger at them! So there!"

Marinka's whisper was as palpable as thick, hot fur. Maxim T. Yermakov grinned broadly despite himself.

"Maxie, you're a tough nut, like Bruce Willis in *Die Hard*!" said Marinka, piling on the heat and wiggling her hips even harder. "Maybe all the bad guys are against you, but I'm with you! Mmmm... Wow! Maxie! Maxie, remember when I came to your school graduation ball... With that pimply Lyoshik... And you brought me an ice cream, remember... And you trod on my shoes and crushed my feet... I wasn't angry with you at all then, I wasn't... That's right, pull that zip open. Maxie, I didn't want to tell you before, but I came to Moscow for you..." Marinka wriggled, staining the sheets with her nails, her face blazing behind a tangled web of hair. "Maxie, would you like me to marry you?"

Holy shit!

Provincials who have come to Moscow are not fond of others from back home. As they turn over the first leaf of a new life in the capital, they prefer to feel that they are not the children of their crummy fathers and mothers who have been used up by life, but the offspring of trains that have toiled all the way to Moscow in a state of pregnancy and deposited their iron brood on the platforms of the station. Nobody wants witnesses who remember the present-day super-cool party animal from his back-of-beyond, home-town disco, taking an elbow to the nose from the wildly flailing chick he was walking across to, to ask for a dance or, five years before that, in a hideous little wool-mixture suit, reciting verse about the wide expanses of his native parts at the school poetry-reading competition. Those endless expanses – the infinite lines of smooth-combed fields sweeping away in all directions, the mirages of combine harvesters, the turbid, sluggish little river that looks as if you could write on it with your finger, the old bell tower, as ordinary as an empty bottle, and over it all the bright, sunny air that possesses a strange and terrible strength, as if a process of electrolysis taking place in it is coating the clouds with blinding metal – these proverbial expanses really did harbour within them profound latent meanings, but in Moscow they became superfluous and their price was marked down to zero. Here the victories of pre-Moscow days proved to be more shameful and damaging than the defeats of the past. According to this logic Marinka, who had arrived to conquer the capital fresh from victory at a municipal beauty contest, held under the aegis of the ebullient mayor, should have given Maxim T. Yermakov a wide berth, never coming within a kilometre of him.

Marinka was a genuine, extremely fine example of female perfection, the kind that could only be bred by that lazy, undulating land that sat so low beneath the sky because of the dead weight of iron ore in its belly. The elements of this beauty, encountered so frequently on the streets of the regional centre that they seemed to have been handed out to the entire female population with an even-handedness that did not, alas, connote happiness, had been combined in Marinka with excessive abundance, the result being that her large, slightly puffy eyes and smooth black hair, reaching down to the pockets of her tight denim skirt at the back, seemed to be not her own, but stolen from someone else. Marinka was like Gogol's little Polish witch. It must have been from the age of thirteen, or even earlier, that she started attracting swarms of individuals of the stronger sex, from her hormonally harassed classmates to hairy bikers and members of the municipal committee for youth affairs, with their premature stoutness that seemed to assign them all to a single, fundamental male type. It was said that Marinka's father, a hundred-kilogramme drunkard with a round red face that looked as if it had just been baked in a deep skillet, used to thrash Marinka with an army uniform belt. Among the inflamed rivals buzzing around her there were plenty who would have liked to confirm that in practice. All this was water off a duck's back to Marinka. She participated in action groups on youth development and danced in the Green Fields Sunrise ensemble, her heavily outlined eyes glinting from the stage as if they were filled with tears, kicking up her ivory-skinned leg against the background of the regional crest, which combined a swan with a stylised excavator on the march.

This insolent young creature had not turned up at Maxim T. Yermakov's school graduation party simply for the fun of it, she had come as the leader of a youth leisure creative workshop: broad-shouldered Lyoshik, who wasn't pimply at all – on the contrary, his face was as fresh and florid as a poppy – was her secretary. She looked straight through Maxim T. Yermakov. She hadn't come to have a good time, but to supervise: she gazed through narrowed eyes at the tense graduating couples shuffling on the spot to a slow number like rickety four-legged stools, and chatted to the director of the school, who coughed into his fist in embarrassment, clearly very aware of the precise line of her minimalist skirt, as if it marked the level of water rising towards his groin. Maxim T. Yermakov had brought Marinka that melted ice cream – the final glass of the turgid substance – with malice aforethought and crushed her shoes quite deliberately: those long-nosed fancy doodads covered in beads and artificial gemstones roused a quiet fury in Maxim T. Yermakov and the desire to trample and shatter them was absolutely irresistible.

There was a scene; Maxim T. Yermakov had supposedly got as drunk as a skunk and brought shame on the school, and they didn't want to give him his school graduation certificate. He could never have expected that subsequently Marinka's patchy girlish memory would construct out of this incident an entire romance that never existed. But then, anything at all that happened to her at that time was raw material for love-story plots; all male individuals expressed exactly the same feelings in different ways, and to Marinka those feelings probably seemed even more identical than they were in reality. Although he was directly aware in his own head of only non-material processes, Maxim T. Yermakov had perceived Marinka as super-dense material, a solid ingot of materiality. Naturally, she hadn't caught a whiff of anything out of the ordinary in the fat school graduate who, to be quite honest, didn't smell of drink at all, but merely gave off a strange, insipid kind of draught. And at that time Maxim T. Yermakov himself was not aware that he had been born with an anomaly in his upper storey – an Alpha Object, fuck it!

Of all people, Marinka, the leading beauty and prime bitch in the junior category in her native parts, was the very last who should have made the move to Moscow. She was a born Leda for the heraldic regional Swan, spreading its triangular wings over that square excavator. If she had stayed at home, she would probably have become some kind of top-level boss and the campaign bride of the governor – a moustachioed old gent of generous proportions with a generous spirit to match, who was very fond of encouraging talented young people. Everything had been spoiled by the beauty contest, when Marinka, parading in her tight swimsuit, knocked the stern jury dead with the line of her thigh, which propagated shock waves at every stride. Marinka's victory and her coronation with a diadem of Swarovski paste crystals had marked her price up substantially. And she wanted to realise that price.

Maxim T. Yermakov thought she had moved from the local commercial college to one in the capital, or something of the kind. She had shown up at his office in order to tap him for some dough and there and then – with typical Krasnogorie diligence – repaid her debt on the office desk, setting it shedding papers in all directions and slamming its drawers furiously. Ever since then Maxim T. Yermakov had become a kind of spare wallet for her, also doubling as a friend with whom she discussed the insidious wiles of Moscow.

"You can't even imagine how many whores there are here," she complained after escaping from yet another adventure with tear-stained eyes and a heavily powdered face. "Thanks to them the rich guys aren't even human any more. Why would a guy like that bother with a relationship with a girl? He only has to crook his finger to get any kind of sex he wants. And all for a few kopecks, by his standards. He can't even find a place to drink a cup of coffee that doesn't have three or four loose bitches sitting around in their whores' thigh boots. Whores are like a virus. They wreck a man's normal programming. People say: look at all these whores who have come piling in from Ukraine and Moldova! But if you'd like to know the truth, the Moscow girls are worse than the outsiders. The way they get themselves up! And the lies they tell! They think they need more and they're entitled to it, it's theirs by right. Then why do they hire themselves out for two hundred bucks a time? For pocket money? Don't mummy and daddy give them enough? The lousy sluts should stay at home in their flats…"

Maxim T. Yermakov just shrugged at that. A price of two hundred bucks suited him fine. But at the same time, he sympathised with Marinka, in his own detached fashion. Marinka had tried really hard. As far as she could, she had eliminated that southern Russian sound halfway between "h" and "g" from the turbulent rhythms of her speech and assiduously imitated the catlike vowels of Moscow, especially that broad "a" – although, to be honest, what she came up with was actually more like quacking than miaowing. She had upgraded her wardrobe at the sales, swapped her idiotic gold for stylish fashion jewellery and no longer looked out of place at the mega-glam corporate events and private parties she managed to worm her way into by hook or by crook. Sometimes she even seemed to get lucky. She had been spotted arm-in-arm with the big-time restaurant owner Mamedov, a large, moist figure of a man, whose contours showed through his fine linen shirt the way the form of a salted herring shows through its newsprint wrapping. She had also been seen in the company of General Yartsev, covered all over in scars and robust as a firmly inflated football, who, since he suspected all his helpers of distorting the meaning of words, was toiling away in person on his book of memoirs, constantly astounded by the cockroach-like evasiveness of basic Russian vocabulary. Marinka, who had always been the first to hand in her school essays – and always with half the commas between clauses missing – had supposedly been engaged to help with this book. From General Yartsev she had moved on to the publisher Polyansky, who took her round the international book fairs for a while and even bought her a mink coat in a Turkish shop round at the back of the Bahnhof in Frankfurt – a spot that was less like a fur emporium than a dark chicken coop with a lucky dip selection of fluff and feathers.

The coat, as it happens, suited Marinka remarkably well. She would have been equally well suited by a small single lady's apartment with a huge silky bed and a bright-coloured compact automobile like a very expensive children's toy. But somehow things never got as far as the apartment and the automobile: her mentors suddenly took off on unexpected business trips, after first handing Marinka a skinny envelope "just for a start". But that damned start never came to an end. Marinka was stuck in a time warp, in which all the thick, salty oysters and insipid winter strawberries were absolutely tasteless, and the beauty spots of European capitals, parading past her like a series of postcards, were tedious and boring. Marinka suffered really badly, howling and cursing in her cooling bath, shedding floods of tears into the honeycomb foam as it subsided into ashes – but there was no authority to which she could apply to redress this suffering. The men she wanted to possess were not so much movers and shakers as moved and shaken by their own business affairs: these serious matters choked their brains and even their blood vessels so completely that they physically could not take Marinka seriously too.

"All right, never mind, we're no age at all yet," Marinka reassured herself, grinning into an open powder compact. "You know what I want, Maxie? I want to marry an old man. Some People's Artist of the USSR. With a great huge mouldy old dacha and an apartment on Kutuzovsky Prospect stuffed with old junk. Five years on active service with him – and there I am, a rich Moscow widow!"

"Why marry an old man?" Maxim T. Yermakov asked in surprise. "Don't the young men have any money? No old man can screw you the way you need, I can tell you that for certain."

"Maxie, don't be so dumb," Marinka replied, switching to a brisk businesslike tone. "A Moscow widow's in a different price range. It will be like I never came to the capital from the back of beyond, but I'd always lived here. I'll take his name, some name that the in-crowd respects. You see, Maxie, getting widowed the right way is like being born again. In a good Moscow family, not with my lame-brain old folks who didn't even have the wits to gouge a flat out of the factory. Don't frown like that, you get the idea: we've been born and we're living our lives, but no one's set a place at the table for us. It wouldn't be a sin to help myself along a bit. I want to do it honestly, after all. As long as my People's Artist can still creak a joint or two, I'll love him like my own dear father. And after my shitty old man that won't be too hard, you know that…"

Maxim T. Yermakov didn't want to upset Marinka, but he found it hard to believe in the feasibility of her matrimonial plans. Marinka had made good headway in Moscow and almost stripped off her provincial crust, together with her moulting Krasnogorie Market glad rags – but in the meantime the capital had managed to grind her down. As he studied Marinka's long body, bulging slightly around the joints, Maxim T. Yermakov no longer perceived her as a solid slab of materiality, the gold ingot that back home had seemed to represent a special value and a special fate. Moscow, this immense mass of stone, concrete and metal, flooded with crowds of millions and millions, had robbed Marinka of her material autonomy, reduced her to an almost nonexistent particle of itself. Moscow had proved difficult terrain for Gogol's little Polish witch; she wasn't flying through the air with her long mane fluttering freely in the wind any longer, but scraping dourly at the asphalt with her skewed stilettos. Every time Maxim T. Yermakov walked arm-in-arm with Marinka, he was left with a crumpled sleeve. In Moscow, Marinka's big greenish eyes with light flecks had become specimens under a microscope, with the melancholy, meaningless quivering of cells in an aqueous medium. And the tears poured out by these round springs seemed to be teeming with viruses – although they were perfectly ordinary drops of salty water.

"Maxie, tell me, what's wrong with me?" Marinka sobbed, going to pieces after the wild abandonment of sex.

"Stop bawling, you fool," Maxim T. Yermakov replied rudely. "It's just that there's such a shitload of whores in Moscow."

Probably the only thing that could help Marinka was some truly exceptional concatenation of circumstances. After Maxim T.

Yermakov, totally blown away by her proposal, had allowed himself to be mauled passionately, with the bed hammering wildly against the wall, he suspected that such a concatenation might already exist.

The plans of the social forecasters, whose own bloated heads were obviously not in good order, made Maxim T. Yermakov the ideal old man. Bearing in mind that he should already have shot himself by now, the Alpha Object's matrimonial age must be about ninety. And ten million dollars was no mean inheritance! But how had Marinka found out? Had they really had a quiet KGB word with her in a dark little conspiratorial flat and at the same time checked out her qualifications on the small brown Soviet sofa bed? Unlikely. Stupid. It didn't give the Alpha Object any additional motivation to put a bullet through his bonce. Marinka's behaviour only made sense as her own personal gamble, an attempt to grab a large piece of the pie. Naive people, thought Maxim T. Yermakov. Making plans as if he, the main player in the game, didn't have any interests of his own. As if the only thing he was dreaming of was how not to screw things up for them. But then where *had* Marinka got hold of the information? Were they putting ads in the newspapers? Such and such – first name, surname, address – represents an intolerable discrepancy in the relations of cause and effect. Because of him, dear citizens, all your sandwiches fall with the buttered side down, but if he voluntarily eliminates himself, his nearest and dearest will receive fifty million greenbacks.

Absurd. But even so, not all the manifestations of popular protest against Maxim T. Yermakov's existence could be explained by the protesters having been recruited and briefed. One fine morning, as he tramped through the icy slush from the car park to the steps of the office building, Maxim T. Yermakov saw a picket line. "EUROPA CASUALTIES" said a home-made poster written on thick Whatman paper that rattled in the wind like sheet metal. Maxim T. Yermakov's heart skipped a beat and sank into his stomach. There were about fifty people standing in a ragged line in front of the steps and, although they were dressed in decent civilian clothes, somehow they seemed like a military detachment that had lost two thirds of its men. Maxim

T. Yermakov had the clear impression that there should have been far more of them standing there. The missing were symbolically present in the white void behind the picketers' backs – and they were obviously also the people in those photographs with their corners tagged by black ribbons of mourning. Every picketer was holding one of these framed photos, on which the snowflakes melted in a wet glimmer of farewell. Just to be on the safe side, Maxim T. Yermakov pulled his stiff leather collar erect as he peered at the casualties. "Actors?" – he wondered. "No, not actors."

That fresh grief, already dusted with the indifference of life, couldn't possibly be acted out or faked. An elderly couple with tearstained eyes were holding up a portrait of a young man with thick eyebrows, wearing a paratrooper's beret – he had probably been working as a security guard at the Europa; every now and then they straightened up, as if someone had prodded their stooping backs, and took a meaningless little step. An old woman with short-cropped hair, wearing a round astrakhan cap, was holding someone's photographic smile out in front of her, as elusive as a fleeting spot of sunlight; the old woman had an extinguished *papyrosa* dangling from her lower lip. Maxim T. Yermakov wasn't convinced by the old people, he knew that hiring them was a piece of piss – they were political small change, and their infirmity was sold cheap. For the same reason he wasn't convinced by the students and other young lummoxes, who earned a bit more for beer and crisps as extras in political crowd scenes. But most of the demonstrators were of an age when they had other things to do with their lives apart from standing in picket lines. Maxim T. Yermakov noticed a tall, imperious-looking woman standing slightly in front of the others, clearly by force of habit. Although she had the stamp of arrogance and there was something tigerish in the folds of her heavy face, the woman was trembling in her thin, plucked-mink coat, and her eyes were as empty as dried-up inkwells. She spotted Maxim T. Yermakov first and waved a red-gloved hand. A movement ran through the line, as if they were passengers in a jolting suburban train.

"Coward! There, there, look at him run!" the woman shouted in a damp, broken voice, disinterring something from her deep pocket.

"Stop! Stay there! You snake! You traitor! We want you dead!" – the cry ran along the picket line like an echo and the demonstrators held up their mourning photos awkwardly as they all started taking out guns.

Maxim T. Yermakov didn't realise immediately that the shooters aimed at him were toys. There was a moment when he froze, shrinking precipitately towards a point at some bottomless depth within himself, while he gazed obtusely at those empty black holes pointing his way. And then all that hollow plastic weaponry crackled and chattered, and there was an acrid smell of scorching pistons as dull plumes spurted from the poisonous green water pistols. The short-cropped old woman waved a mummified gismo that looked like an absolutely genuine Mauser from the old revolutionary days. The hand in a red glove clenched convulsively on the precious item of burnished-metal, as if it was a stone out of which she was trying to squeeze water. Maxim T. Yermakov, soaking wet under his solid covering of leather, stamped his feet furiously and ducked in through the door of the office.

The picket had not disappeared by that evening, or the following morning, although its composition changed somewhat. Life had summoned the more responsible participants to deal with their affairs (Maxim T. Yermakov never saw the imperious woman in the plucked mink again); but others had dug in and were still standing there with impassive smiles on their faces, as if they were waiting in the arrivals lounge for some flight from the next world with their dear ones on board. The Europa casualties were joined by victims of the fire in Krasnoyarsk, a terrorist attack in Krasnodar and an explosion on a gas pipeline at an unpronounceable village near Ufa. The consolidated groups of activists represented two major air disasters and five or six passenger train crashes; the crashes had come one after another without any apparent cause, as if the railway line had got jammed like a zip fastener on various stretches between Vladivostok and St. Petersburg.

On the patch of land between the office towers tents sprang up, flapping wildly in a strong wind and emitting a kind of damp cough in the severe gusts. Wet, multicoloured garbage flew everywhere, light beer cans pranced and clattered across the black asphalt: the wind snapped the spokes of umbrellas hoisted into the air as if it was breaking flies' legs. The most conspicuous of the picketers were the Siberians, accustomed to respecting their bitterly cold winters; here, in their pine marten and fox furs, under the soapy Moscow sleet, they looked like newborn chicks with wet feathers. The casualties in wheelchairs took up a separate position, under a snapping tarpaulin. Some of them, shackled by plaster into ludicrous and pathetic poses, resembled fallen statues. The wheelchair casualties included only one young woman (in any human gathering, and especially since Marinka's proposal, the first people Maxim T. Yermakov noticed were the pretty young women); this young woman smoked and spoke constantly on her mobile, but appeared detached from everything because of the pallor of her sharp-featured face, which looked small against the huge, billowing swell of her light-brown felted hair with its sprinkling of tiny coloured beads. Maxim T. Yermakov could have felt sorry for her – the only one out of the whole lot. Just recently he'd been feeling a strange agitation and inclination to search for something, despite all the social forecasters' exhausting filthy tricks. The gentle, understated charm of the Armenian girl now peacefully installed in the flat on Gogol Boulevard had left a strange, deep cavity in his soul, like a break in the clouds that is a continuous cause of annoyance, because it never fills up with sunshine, and that useless splotch of blue amid the gloom is simply going to waste. Poor Marinka had nothing at all to do with these feelings. While she snored, with her firm round knee thrust out towards Maxim T. Yermakov, he could sense her brain working away on the pillow next to him, illuminated by bright running lights that spelled out ten million dollars. His irritation held him suspended right on the verge of tenuous sleep. And in the morning he had to go to the office, still drowsy, accompanied by fresh escorts who had only just come on duty and steered their pseudo-commercial vans dashingly through the murky atmospheric precipitation.

The picketers greeted Maxim T. Yermakov's appearance with a universal chorus of obscenities and a crackling storm of toy gunfire. Not having come up with anything better yet, they carried on flinging rotten vegetables and other unappetising foodstuffs at the enemy of the people; Maxim T. Yermakov had learned to repel these items deftly with a spring-loaded umbrella, throwing the canopy open to counter the semi-liquid bombardment. Nonetheless, many of the missiles found their target, and any colleagues of the treacherous snake who had the misfortune to arrive late and try to slip past got the same treatment. The result was that at the start of the working day the toilets were transformed into a washing and laundering station, with a morose queue for the washbasins and a black quagmire on the flooded floor. People shunned Maxim T. Yermakov, only casting hostile sideways glances in his direction, so he found himself rubbing down his leather coat and rinsing off his umbrella in his own personal gunk-spattered basin, humming some jolly little tune to himself as he did it.

Maxim T. Yermakov was not disciplined for arriving late; everyone would only have been delighted if he didn't show up at all. His immediate superior, Ika, a former Komsomol leader who had missed out on a big career, was like a wild beast, caged in her cheaply furnished twenty-square-metres office. About once every three days she suggested that Maxim T. Yermakov write a letter of resignation.

"Max, surely you understand," she said, feeling cautiously at her coiffure, in which every single hair seemed to have been gilded and arranged individually. "Everything that's going on around you is incompatible with the firm's image. It's like a railway station now in front of the office, I swear it is. You'll find a great job with no problem afterwards! But in the meantime corporate loyalty requires you…"

"No it doesn't," said Maxim T. Yermakov, interrupting his boss as he sprawled back in the pitifully squeaking chair with thin legs, on which he had not been invited to sit. "I'm not writing any resignation letter. No, and that's it."

"You have the nerve to tell me 'no'!" Ika exclaimed in surprise every time, turning pale under her powder to reveal two faces that didn't completely match up, one drawn on and the other genuine.

"Yes, you, you, Irina Konstantinovna," Maxim T. Yermakov confirmed imperturbably. "For the fourth or fifth time, by the way. If you want to, you can fire me yourself, by the book. Nobody's repealed the Labour Code yet. Give the order, a reprimand to Yermakov for violations of work discipline, for instance. Do I violate it? Yes, I do. What are you waiting for?"

"You not only come late, you've also completely stopped working." These words were accompanied by a subtle rattling sound, emanating either from her broken Komsomol heart or the small glass with sharp-pointed pencils in it.

"Work? Without a budget?" Maxim T. Yermakov asked sarcastically, stung on a sore spot by the question of money. "Am I supposed to pay for the billboards out of my own salary? And the stickers in the metro? Now wouldn't that be convenient: pay an employee six thousand bucks and let him handle everything else himself. He can lay out his own mazooma if he needs to. Maybe I should ask the Ministry of Culture for a grant for our advertising?"

"Yermakov! You never used to talk like this!"

"We never used to have a dozen state-security men hanging about on every floor," Maxim T. Yermakov reminded her soulfully. "Go on, try it, sack me!"

At this point his boss leaned back in her chair and started trying to hypnotise Maxim T. Yermakov with her cold, light-coloured, spider-webbed eyes. In better times this must have sent a light frost creeping across the skin of her subordinates. But the effect was nowhere near that good any more. No doubt Ika seemed to herself like a cobra with its hood extended in menace, but Maxim T. Yermakov saw an angry failure with a painted mouth like a withered autumn leaf, who was no good for anything any more apart from siphoning off agency commissions to pay hairstylists and beauticians. "What are you, compared with my state-committee tadpole-heads?" he thought with a certain degree of satisfaction – and then in the reception area he would actually run into a modest example of a social forecaster, either placidly reading something or fiddling with the wheezing coffee machine. Little Lucy, incidentally, was absent from her work position more and more often. And even if she was sitting at her neat little secretary's desk, she seemed to be absent anyway. Maxim T. Yermakov guessed that she was dashing over to the hospital to see her son, or taking him round the specialists for consultations, or something else of the kind. Little Lucy looked so bad that Maxim T. Yermakov couldn't even imagine the pain someone close to her would feel at the sight of her swollen little face in the blurred spectacles and her bluish nails, as transparent as fish scales. Maxim T. Yermakov was even prepared to help her sick little son, only not in the most radical fashion possible. After all, he had parents of his own too. Old parents who smelled of medicine and cooking, who had failed so completely to understand anything about the changes of the past two decades that Maxim T. Yermakov couldn't even imagine how he could have a heart-to-heart talk with them.

In the intervals between Maxim T. Yermakov's appearances, the camp followed its own daily round. Twice a day a state-security van with an advertisement for garden furniture on its side brought hot food. The back door was swung down and mature ladies clad in overall coats of dubious whiteness moved out aluminium containers, waddling them to the edge of the platform as if they were heavy infants just learning to walk. Metal vessels as shapeless as potholes in a road were held up from below and greyish lips grabbed at hot potatoes – there was something of the front line, something forlornly heroic, in all this, and the office clerks consuming their free corporate lunches in the staff cafeterias felt an inexplicable discomfort at the sight. Order was maintained in the camp by a pair of bored militiamen, who sometimes communicated with each other on crackling walkie-talkies; they observed the malicious hooliganism – which is what the hurling of vegetables undoubtedly was – with their keen eyes sparkling, like trained marksmen, as if they were betting against each other on whether anyone would hit the fat man in the long coat or not. Not far from the two cops a large first-aid tent flapped its red cross in the wind. The brisk medical personnel included a dark-skinned female doctor with a broad leonine nose and grey hair like the froth on a cup of cappuccino; Maxim T. Yermakov was hoping it was some kind of international mission, until a cyclist rode into this venerable matriarch and she harangued him in robustly obscene Russian.

But the strange thing was that in two – no, it must have been three, or even three and a half weeks – not a single TV camera showed up at the camp. There wasn't a single lousy journalist, not a single story in the news.

After work Maxim T. Yermakov now experienced a desire to get drunk – which in his special case was much the same as wanting to fall asleep during an attack of severe insomnia. Tossing the stinking leather coat, which now resembled a freshly flayed sealskin, into the boot of his car, he set off to make the rounds of familiar drinking establishments – fortunately his body produced no results to any of the traffic cops' tests, even if he poured an entire bucketful of booze into it. In the evening Maxim T. Yermakov sought islets of normal life, from "pre-war life" in the language of his Grandad Valera, who called the scarce Meteorite sweets "downright pre-war", to the Consul eau de cologne he got for his birthday after it had only just appeared in the commercial kiosks of perestroika.

Maxim T. Yermakov discovered Dima Rozhdestvensky in an establishment called "The Good-for-Nothing", which, in all fairness, was exactly where he belonged. The yellow journalists' journalist was sitting at the bar, sniffing intently at the yellow contents of his glass. His glazed eyes glimmered with the same convex gleam as the paunchy glass that the barman was polishing; Rozhdestvensky had a dark streak that looked like an exclamation mark on his light-coloured silk tie.

"Here, have one to be sociable," he said, moving the glass towards Maxim T. Yermakov, who had sat down beside him. And then, unable to find another glass to clink with the first, he nudged Maxim T. Yermakov on the shoulder.

The word was that Dima Rozhdestvensky had been promoted and was now in charge of the "Society" section in his moribund tabloid newspaper, which was like a neglected vegetable plot, with a senior editor who locked himself into his office for days at a time and emerged as red-faced as a Martian, having almost forgotten the Russian language. There was practically no one left to work on the paper, which probably explained Rozhdestvensky's promotion. The yellow journalist didn't have much idea about social matters, but he knew how to tack a mocking commentary onto any fact in order to create the impression that the author knew much better than society what society needed when it woke in the morning, clutching its aching head. The same mocking manner had also infected Dima Rozhdestvensky's way of speaking. He adored frightening young female journalists and PR agents by hinting at the dark secrets of the professional world. He hypnotised his victim with the heavy gaze that he raised from the table with some effort and the friendly gesture with which he took hold of his colleague's breast, in the same way that some people put their hand on the shoulder of the person they're talking to.

Obliged to conceal the fact that he knew life less well than others – when could he possibly have got to know it: Here, have a drink! – Rozhdestvensky had imagined, literally breathed out of himself, an impenetrably dense cloud, which contained, as he thought, the dark reasons for society's disorders and his own personal ones. He could sense this dark cloud above his head as he hammered out his latest material on his grubby keyboard. He was secretly convinced that it was impossible for a human being to make a judgement about anything at all, and he issued his own judgements with the facile ease of a lottery drum, at a rate of three or four hundred lines in every issue. Ignorance – as a self-sufficient substance and dense bulk filler for the head – had developed in Dima a certain intuition that passed for journalistic nous in publications where no great intellect was required from the writers or the readers. This intuition not only compensated for Dima's lack of information and experience, it also saved him from all sorts of unpleasantness. It indemnified him, you could say. He never ran into the editor in chief as he was tumbling along the corridor, smashing his bony fist against the wall. On those bad days when the editorial team felt like a family whose father was in the middle of a heavy drinking bout, running around the house with an axe, Rozhdestvensky was present in the office, but remained as invisible as a ninja. In precisely the same way, as he drove his unwashed Mazda along the street in a state close to passing-out, he never ran into the traffic cops, as if he could somehow avert their eyes. Dima quite literally sensed danger with his highly sensitive nose, which had a velvety birthmark that looked like flower pollen; danger had a rank smell, it stank, and Dima, surrounded by these metaphysical odours, confidently asserted that life itself was a heap of garbage and shit. This was the reason for his excessive use of fragrances. Sitting there with half his backside on the tall bar stool, the journalist was as aromatic as a tropical shrub in blossom.

"What's that you reek of?" he asked Maxim T. Yermakov, lifting his nose out of his glass.

"Vegetable Warehouse," Maxim T. Yermakov replied laconically, trying to attract the attention of the barman, who was artistically twisting a striped cocktail together out of two bottles.

"I think it's Dead Meat," Rozhdestvensky said definitively. "I'm shocked. Haven't just climbed out of the grave have you? That shirt you have on looks as if it's rotted a bit."

"Shut those big jaws, shark of the pen," Maxim T. Yermakov advised him amicably.

"Okay, it's a fine piece of gear. Very stylish, a spot of rot, I like it a lot," Rozhdestvensky declared, grinning broadly and exposing his uneven teeth, which looked as if they had been parted by a bottle-opener, like a metal cap. "You do reek of Vegetable Warehouse as well. Well, why are you just sitting there? Are you going to booze or not?"

The bald barman, whose bow tie was a perfect match for the shape of his pampered moustache, finally responded to the call and Maxim T. Yermakov ordered vodka, three hundred grams all at once. He immediately regretted the choice, because vodka made him sweat copiously: all the liquid he had swallowed immediately started trickling down his back, and he got the feeling that his body had been wrung out, like a rag. But it was too late to retreat: the barman set three little glasses of Finlandia out in a row in front of Maxim T. Yermakov, together with a reheated ham sandwich. Maxim T. Yermakov winced and downed the first hundred grams, there was a gentle thud inside his head and the drunkenness immediately dispersed like a puff of smoke from a canon. Maxim T. Yermakov set about the sandwich, which was at human body temperature, with a feeling of revulsion.

"Me and alcohol don't get along too well," he explained, either to Rozhdestvensky or himself.

"Ah, but alcohol and me get along just fine, couldn't be better. Alcohol is my friend," Dima commented. "But drink anyway, while you're still alive. Since the people haven't shot you yet."

"How come you're in the know, I don't get it," Maxim T. Yermakov replied, suddenly feeling annoyed. He wanted to knock this laid-back hack down on the floor and watch him get up onto all fours.

"Of course I'm in the know," Rozhdestvensky said pompously. "The day before yesterday I went to a press briefing at a charitable foundation, their office is opposite yours, and I watched for a while! You're a dab hand with that umbrella. The tomatoes come flying and the umbrella springs out to meet them – hup! The glop goes flying back – splat! Know who you look like in a long black leather coat? An executioner. All wet with blood, soaking in it. Very fucking romantic!"

"So why don't you dash off a fucking column, then?" Maxim T. Yermakov enquired, pulling a wry face. "It's your area, isn't it? There's society for you, as large as life."

Dima Rozhdestvensky sighed and ruffled up his thick thatch, so wild that it seemed to feed directly on the tissues of his brain, as if they were soil.

"My friend, it grieves me to tell you this, but the fact is that you're not news. I mean you as such. You're not a newsmaker. Do you understand that or not? Just as soon as you become a newsmaker, I'll be the first to come running, with a dictaphone and a photographer. But in the meantime, sorry…"

"I don't understand. The owners of manky old housing scheduled for demolition only have to set up a picket and you're all there like a shot. A heap of cameras, all the channels, an interview with the local mayor… But here you have a demonstration right in the middle of Moscow that's been going on for weeks. And it's not just some old pensioners in their berets. People have come from all over the country. You've got the survivors from that plane in Siberia, and all the top bastards from the train crash near Peter. You mean you haven't got anything to say about all that?"

"Well we wrote about the crash near Peter. Gave it a whole double-page spread. And we wrote about the plane, I actually flew out there with the guys from the Ministry of Emergencies. Heavy stuff, eh, how about that! They landed on a main highway, the traffic underneath them was going crazy. Then they missed the bend and ploughed up a field. That Tupolev was reduced to tatters. There's something you really should take a look at!"

"No great hurry," said Maxim T. Yermakov. "I'm apathetic, got no curiosity. But you tell me, as a super pro: Why does one event become news and another doesn't?"

"Well get you, a man with no curiosity! Drink. Don't you even try to slack off with a veteran of the campaign to exterminate alcohol like me."

And so saying, the journalist parked a lightly bitten cigarette in the ashtray, picked up one of the two remaining shots of vodka and handed the other to Maxim T. Yermakov, who had to swallow more of the harsh liquid that stung his lips as if they were cracked. Maxim T. Yermakov realised that with the indefatigable Rozhdestvensky's active participation, and especially if a pally crowd flooded into the bar, he would down enough of the futile poison to turn his stomach into a sack of hot coals the next morning. Having survived the scorching of his stomach and the thud in his head, he lit up a cigarette too, and the smoke beatifically softened his hazy state, dispatching the ponderous files to a different location.

"Well?" he asked, moving closer to Rozhdestvensky, who at a certain stage of inebriation started looking soulful and benign. "I've had a drink, now you spit it out. Or I'll smash your face in."

"No, did you hear that, la-dies and gent-le-men?" Rozhdestvensky appealed tearfully to the barman and two hussies sitting a short distance away, with their plunging oval necklines resting on the bar. "Him! Smash my face? How will you do that?"

"Physically, that's how," Maxim T. Yermakov explained coolly. "And not just smash it, smash it *in*. Feel the difference."

"Listen, my friend, you're so fat, and so aggressive," Rozhdestvensky said reproachfully. "Well, all right then. So, let's think it through together. Collectively!"

For some reason Rozhdestvensky found that last word funny and he barely managed to stay on his stool. Maxim T. Yermakov had to give the journalist a resounding thump on the back, forcing him to pour out his giggles rapidly, the way a slot machine pours out coins when it takes a hard blow.

"Hey, Max, get your hands off," Rozhdestvensky protested hoarsely, goggle-eyed and runny-nosed, but apparently slightly more sober. "Do you want to clobber me for real? What for?"

"No, all right, I don't really want to," Maxim T. Yermakov replied wearily. He was starting to feel depressed by the bar lamps' dim glow, with a murky kind of residue on the bottom, and the clicking of billiard balls that he could hear through the half-light. "Give me the lowdown on the news, or I'll stop wanting to listen to you soon."

"You think I'm just dying to give voice to all that claptrap?" asked Rozhdestvensky, slowly rotating his empty glass in front of his unseeing eyes. "A quick question: Who produces the news – the mass media or life?"

"The media, it stands to reason," Maxim T. Yermakov replied angrily. "But life plays a part too. As the raw material, let's say."

"Right, but wrong too. Imagine what would happen if just any bum could come out in the street with a placard and become news. If the opportunity was there for the broad masses of the population.

What would happen, eh?"

Rozhdestvensky looked up at Maxim T. Yermakov with a sad glance, in which an intelligent light seemed to glow feebly through the alcoholic pall.

"But the opportunity isn't there, believe me! It's too expensive, like a detached house on the Rublyovskoe Chaussee. News is pricey. O-ho, very pricey. News requires serious investment. The finest example of the present age: Al-Qaeda's fucking planes slamming into the twin towers. Let's add it up. They planned the attack for a certain number of years. They trained those fanatics, and fed them. Then there's the cost of the two Boeings, and the two skyscrapers, with everything that was in them, plus the huge fucking number of people who were wiped out. Plus the consequences. On September 11, Bush ordered all planes in the air over the States to land and stay hunkered down. They landed and they hunkered down. That cost money too! Think of the round number for everything that mega-news story sucked in. Now your example about the owners of those lousy old apartments. Would anyone be interested in those pickets if land in Moscow wasn't worth its weight in gold? Raw material, you say. Right, Max. But raw material has to be rich and thick, like crude oil. No one's going to make candy out of shit for you. Amateur efforts from below are not encouraged. That is, of course, an average klutz can pop up in the news too – provided he pays for it big time. If he douses himself with fucking petrol and burns himself to a crisp to spite President Medvedev. If you shoot yourself, Max, like they want you to do, we'll put in an info note about you. But just one paragraph, mind you, for the whole of your fucking life! And next day your little mark in the sand will be washed away by the next wave. And that's all. So, my friend, don't try to get yourself in the news. For you the price of a place in the papers is a place in the graveyard. And now go away, shove off…"

Exhausted by this long stretch of continuous speech, the journalist lowered his head, dangling his hair, and slid his elbow along the bar, clearly intending to take a rest. Maxim T. Yermakov squeezed Rozhdestvensky's flimsy shoulder, sensing his hazy, limited awareness, like a sleepy jelly-fish trembling in the ether.

"How do you know about me shooting myself?" he asked, shaking the journalist a bit harder. "Does the name Kravtsov mean anything to you? Sergei Yevgenievich Kravtsov, bald, with a terrifying pair of peepers?"

"I don't know any Kravtsov!" The journalist suddenly jerked upright indignantly, almost swiping Maxim T. Yermakov across the lips with his fingers. "You're in a real bad way, Max. Don't you look around as you run? Take a little peep out from behind the umbrella. Those people flinging stuff at you are waving texts. Like: 'Shoot yourself, Yermakov'. Neat, eh? Rea-lly neat... And they shoot at you with their toys – brrr... But you watch out, they're not all toys, I saw one with a Sai-ga car-bine... If he goes crazy and starts blasting, that umbrella won't protect you. D'you re-al-ise what I'm saying? That's it, scoot, you've worn me out..."

"Well, screw you then."

Maxim T. Yermakov let go of the hack journalist and, feeling his heart constrict painfully behind his wallet, pulled out a credit card. The barman, having received a hundred roubles tip in cash, bared his teeth in a genial grin. Above the billiard table, in the low cone of light iridescent with cigarette smoke, someone with long arms and dangling braces was aiming a cue at a blindingly bright ball with the gloss of dead ivory.

"The people are freaks and stupid geeks," Rozhdestvensky suddenly said drowsily, speaking in rhyme and gazing straight through Maxim T. Yermakov with blank, glazed eyes.

This idiotic rhyme combined with the crisp explosion of the billiard ball to shift something in Maxim T. Yermakov's awareness. The words started swaying, as if they were on a wave, receding and advancing again. "I can't recall how long is it since I realised life is shit," Maxim T. Yermakov said to himself, highly astonished. That phrase was still fading away when another came dashing up to take its place; "Never mind that life is shit, you'll soon see the end of it". There was something else drifting up too, he could almost hear the rhymes ending in 'it' or 'at' – but the oscillations receded, leaving nothing but a heavy rippling in the region of his stomach. "Have I started writing poetry, then?" Maxim T. Yermakov thought, now in his normal manner, as he walked towards the door. Suddenly he realised the meaning of his composition. You'll soon see the end of it. He stopped, staring obtusely at the billiard table, where four balls were trundling gently to a halt and two were standing motionless.

Well, sod them – soon! Not for a long time yet. Home to Marinka, give her a screw, go to sleep and tomorrow we'll see how things stand. Maxim T. Yermakov felt a fleeting regret that he hadn't made a move on the girls who had been flirting invitingly with their clarified-butter eyes while he was arguing with the journalist like some lamebrain. On the way out he saw one of the glittering hussies, with a bright piercing in her navel and a rhinestone button set much lower than her navel on her denim trousers, sit down by Rozhdestvensky and take a tick-like grip on his neck.

Before he even opened his eyes properly next morning, Maxim T. Yermakov thought he must have forgotten to switch the light off for the night. The room was filled with half-forgotten sunlight, like fine dust; the built-in mirror of the crooked Soviet wardrobe had a metallic gleam. What day was it today?

The seventh of March, fuck it. Tomorrow was the eighth, Women's Day.

One massive pain in the ass.

Marinka was taking a shower, spraying the plastic curtain generously with water. Right then, calm down. There's a whole cartload of time before tomorrow. Maxim T. Yermakov rinsed off the cobwebs of sleep still clinging to his face and went into the kitchen to brew coffee in a battered Turkish coffee pot. After she'd finished splashing about, Marinka appeared, heated and aromatic, half-blind, eyebrowless and without her make-up; Maxim T. Yermakov had always thought her wet hair looked like the black twigs of a broom and made her look a bit of a gawk.

"It's our office party today!" Marinka announced, straining out some green tea for herself. "When's yours?"

"Today as well," said Maxim T. Yermakov, suddenly remembering.

Strange, the firm's male community, whose motto on the Eighth of March was: "Do the right thing, give," hadn't sent anyone to him for money, he had been passed over. Maybe he should buy his boss an independent bouquet? Or maybe a bouquet wasn't the right thing?"

Marinka, having shuffled on something radically yellow, with a line of silky surf above her tightly squeezed knees, ran off to celebrate the holiday at her office – he thought it was some kind of investment fund, where Polyansky had considerately set her up with a job when he left her. Muttering angrily, Maxim T. Yermakov put on that suit, the piggy-pink one: too hot and well-padded for the warm period of the year, too light-coloured for the cold, chemical-laden Moscow slush. The pants, despite all Maxim T. Yermakov's efforts to clean them, had literally been burned through by the brown splashes, like cigarettes. Not a single decent necktie from his remaining stock would consent to match this outrage. And Maxim T. Yermakov's disgruntled face was no less reluctant to fit in with today's female festivities. Always regarded by its owner – because of the anomaly in his head – as a personal mirage that expressed nothing in particular, that face had now acquired a strangely expressive quality, of a kind that Maxim T. Yermakov had sometimes observed on the faces of other people who had been seriously unsettled by something or other. The sharp folds from the nose to the small, crooked mouth were new, and the nose itself, a frozen pink colour, looked as if it had been ripped off and sewn back on again by a surgeon. It was high time he had a haircut: his sugary bristles had sprouted, covering his virtual cranium with pale chicken feathers.

Well, fine. Maxim T. Yermakov ignored the frozen-solid demonstrators in the yard, clambered into his Toyota and trundled off through the sunny streets. The sunshine and the bright blueness extending across almost the entire sky had brought frost, not warmth; glassy puddles burst with a pop under tyres, here and there the ragged asphalt had been patched with needly ice and women's heels clattered on it crisply, as if it was hollow inside. Standing beside every metro station was a line of street traders with buckets full of small, chilly roses and carrot-coloured tulips, their feeble little blooms tied round with rubber bands so that they wouldn't fall apart. There were heaps of buyers. Practically every pedestrian in the street was carrying a bouquet wrapped in brittle cellophane that looked as if it had just come out of the freezer: and every bouquet was destined to be passed from hand to hand throughout the day.

Maxim T. Yermakov parked near a lively little flower market. As soon as he entered the stream of people, he immediately felt them looking at him. Whereas previously, like all Muscovites, he had known how to avoid meeting anybody's glance, even in the very thickest of crowds, now he kept running into strangers' eyes trying to glance straight through his brain to the back of his head. The strangers' eyes were cautious, malicious, curious; the more malice there was, the more salty the glare. Some of the curious ones moved as far away as possible, others tried to rub up against him, to touch him; Maxim T. Yermakov couldn't get rid of the feeling that he was being worked by several pickpockets at once.

"Look, is that him? It is, it's him!"

Baggy teenagers gaped avidly at Maxim T. Yermakov; the young predators hastily pulled mobile phones out of their broad pants with pockets down to the knees, clearly intending to snap the Object without any permission from the federal special services. Maxim T. Yermakov blocked off their view with his own back and trotted into a flower kiosk, where the goods were a bit brighter and more luxuriant than in the rows on public view in the street. Standing behind the counter was a beefy, breezy wench in a huge, freckly sweater with green leaves dangling on it, as if it was a camouflage net. At the sight of Maxim T. Yermakov, she opened her pale eyes wide and squeezed her mouth tight shut, as if she had just managed, at the very last moment, to catch an expression that was about to slip out, something like "Clear off!". Instead of saying that, the powerfully-built flower lady shifted from one massive foot to the other and spoke in a high-pitched squeak:

"How can I help you, sir?"

Maxim T. Yermakov made her work for fifteen minutes as he examined one after another of the expensive bouquets, in which everything was bright and succulent and seemed to have been crimped with curlers; while he did so, the flower woman's glittering eyes darted about rapidly in her head and her red, scratched hands kept dropping things. "Fuck it!" thought Maxim T. Yermakov. "What a pain in the ass!"

His annoyance was soothed by a clump of incredibly fresh white roses, with a greenish flush on their plump sides, which somehow looked as if they weren't quite mature yet – and that really made him want to give them to someone.

"Seven," commanded Maxim T. Yermakov.

As he cleared off with his bouquet, which felt wet and prickly through its mirror-surface wrapping, he spotted his social forecasters beside a van with "Bread" written on it. The men were jigging about to keep warm in their short, cheap coats. One of them was holding out in front of him a few cellophane packages of mimosa, looking like something dried to go with beer; the other was breathing on his crooked fingers as he counted the money.

"Compliments of the season, dear comrades!" Maxim T. Yermakov shouted to them as they raised their bluish-grey faces.

However, presenting the bouquet to his boss proved to be not that simple. As always on holidays, the lady was somewhat out of sorts. She eventually deigned to show up for work at a quarter to ten and, after flinging aside her clumpy second-hand chinchilla in the reception area, locked herself in her office. Everything was finally ready for congratulating the women, who were all freezing at their computers in their bare-armed little dresses in slightly absurd flesh tones, as if each of them was dreaming of being different from what she was in reality under the dress, and this dream showed through the thin material. Crap himself, wearing a superlative tie of raw silk, had already delivered his holiday speech to the collective and done a runner. In the cafeteria, the plates standing on the white cloths covering the tables that had been moved together gleamed a medicinal white and at the bar the ranks of vodka bottles were gradually thinning out. But they couldn't start the office party without congratulating Ika.

Maxim T. Yermakov loitered in the reception area with the congratulating team, led by Big Lida, who always liked to be in charge of something. Big Lida was angry now and she kept tugging hard on her white, crunching fingers. The congratulating team had brought a basket of chrysanthemums, as plump as curd-cheese pies, and a bunch of balloons – the men had blown them up and the women had drawn coloured smilies on them. After waiting for more than two hours, the smilies had turned a bit sulky and the balloons themselves, which had been inflated with live human breath, if not actually gusts of spontaneous goodwill, had become turbid, as if they had started to ferment. The office was filled with a tense silence; it felt as if more and more silence was being pumped in and it would burst at any moment.

Of course, all complaints were addressed to Little Lucy. Every now and then she called the inner office on the intercom and then smiled slow-wittedly as she dropped the receiver onto its cradle and announced.

"Irina Konstantinovna said later, she's still working."

"Aha, she's working, sure," muttered Big Lida, striding round the tiny reception area and stepping on the feet of her team, which was seated untidily on the uncomfortable chairs around the walls. "She's taunting us, just taunting us."

Little Lucy was completely out of it today. She seemed to have dressed and put on her make-up without a mirror. Maxim had seen that sheep-grey knitted suit on her all the time just recently. Little Lucy's luminous eyes glowed with meaningless brightness and a vein twitched steadily on her hollow temple, as if blood was oozing into her body drip by drip. "Could the kid really have died?" Maxim T. Yermakov thought, hiding the heavy bouquet behind his back as he felt a chill enfold his heart.

He didn't think he'd blurted anything out loud, but Little Lucy turned towards him,

"Not yet, but they say any time now," she said, wincing as if she'd bit a lemon.

"Any time now! How much longer?" Big Lida asked, clattering her long beads against the secretary's desk as she pounced. "We've been waiting more than two hours, she could at least have the grace to see people!"

Immediately the door behind her back opened with ostentatious theatricality. Everyone jumped up, donning their smiles like gas masks at the sound of a chemical weapons alarm.

"Two hours of working time in my reception area, how sweet," said Ika, standing in the doorway as if it was the frame of an official portrait. "And what a lot of people there are here! Well, it is Women's Day, so I can understand why they're here, but why are the men taking it easy? Have they taken the Eighth of March off as unpaid leave?"

"Vadim Vadimich has already gone, he told us all to enjoy ourselves" Big Lida said ingratiatingly, wagging her hands to the team behind her back to get them to start on the congratulations.

"But I'm here," the lady boss retorted coolly, gazing at Big Lida's chin, clenched into a powdered clump. "Or doesn't that count? I'm just an empty space for you, am I? Why are you jiggling your backside like that, like some stupid wagtail?"

Big Lida despairingly pulled her hand out from behind her back and grabbed at her beads, which immediately tumbled to the floor with a clatter and went clacking across the bare parquet.

"Good God! What have I done to you?" Big Lida exclaimed in a tearful voice, backing away from the cascading facets .

"You? To me?" asked Ika, narrowing her cold eyes ironically.

"Just what the hell did I come here for?" thought Maxim T. Yermakov. "I've got better ways to waste my time than watching this performance. First train crashes and plane crashes on all sides, now this lot with their plotting and intriguing. And the holiday spirit to top everything off!"

To mark the holiday, Ika was rigged out in all her finery, a thoroughly planned ensemble in painfully consistent green and beige tones, every detail of which seemed to vouch for several others; her unhealthy grey face, with dark patches covered by downward-smeared make-up, looked as if it had been sent by fax. Ika obviously had no intention of allowing the party of congratulators into her sunny office, with the pristine, humdrum order of its desk, on which a single caramel sweet lay like a threadbare bow of ribbon. The thoughts and feelings that Ika had been elaborating for two and a half hours while she shut herself away from the women's holiday still seemed to be floating in the air in there; entry into her petty, narrow soul was forbidden to outsiders. "Fuck it, what the hell do I want with trying to understand this lot?" thought Maxim T. Yermakov, backing away into the corner of the reception area, where rolls of draft design print-outs were standing: the rolls slid along the wall in an arc and plonked down heavily onto the floor.

"Max, you're here too!" Ika exclaimed with dark delight, and the congratulators hastily moved aside, leaving Maxim T. Yermakov and the heap of paper junk that he had knocked over at the lady boss's mercy.

"Aha, hel-lo!" Maxim T. Yermakov responded in a repulsively childish voice.

"Aha, and I was just about to send for you," said Ika, mimicking his tone. "Good news: the budget has been confirmed. Haven't you heard yet? A big, handsome budget. And it has been decided to release you for creative work. That's your most important activity, isn't it? I'll handle the placement of all the clips and billboards. All you'll have to do is put forward creative ideas and hold presentations on them. The financial side of the projects is no longer your concern. Isn't that just great?"

Maxim T. Yermakov had the impression that all the lights, including the sun, blinked off for a second.

"I wouldn't exactly say so," he said cautiously, presenting Ika with his very broadest positive smile, the one that made him hear a squeaking sound behind his ears. "I work hard, I know people in all our partners' companies. It takes more than a month or two to pick that up. And in general I have experience…"

"I know, I know," the lady boss interrupted coquettishly, "thanks for being so concerned. But I'll manage somehow, Max, you must understand that."

"Why you rotten cow," thought Maxim T. Yermakov, still smiling frenziedly, as if he was pulling along a truck with his clenched teeth. "You've just gone and lifted thirty thousand greenbacks out of my pocket, at the minimum. And I'm a lot more economical than you, you scum. I live on almost nothing but the discounts that I earn for myself. Who's going to give an old scrubber like you any discounts? No, you'll grab everything the crude way, with kick-backs. I can just imagine the kind of budget you've worked up for yourself..."

"You've turned pale, Max," Ika said sympathetically. "You know what? I think we'll probably hand over part of the creative work to some big advertising agency. We need to refresh the image of our product. Liven it up a bit, you understand me?"

And with those final words, to show how the brand needed to be livened up, the lady boss squared her shoulders and sliced an aggressive fist covered in froggy skin down through the air. Many members of the congratulatory team immediately straightened up, demonstrating the requisite vigour, and here and there eyes glinted.

"You can hand it over, of course," sighed Maxim T. Yermakov, seating himself sideways on Little Lucy's loudly complaining desk. "Only what will it cost? The agency will draw up an estimate for you, and what will it put in there? Its own accountants, its own rent, its own car park. The firm pays plenty for our car park, doesn't it? Well now it will shell out for someone else's."

"That's none of your business!" Ika snapped spitefully, and Maxim T. Yermakov realised he had hit the bull's eye. "Well, you all came here, I didn't send for you. What did you want?"

"Actually, I didn't come to see you, Irina Konstantinovna," Maxim T. Yermakov said with a broad, complacent smile. "I came to see Lucy here. It's a holiday today. I wanted to congratulate her and all the rest of it..."

This absolutely unprecedented insolence made the team gasp. Someone tugged on the balloons, which had been dozing peacefully on a cupboard, someone else dashed forward with the basket of chrysanthemums. Big Lida surfaced from all this kerfuffle for a second: her ponderous cheeks were as red as bricks and her sweet perfume gave off a poisonous heat, as if it had been splashed onto a red-hot stove.

"Why, you lousy snake," she hissed straight into Maxim T. Yermakov's face. "The people are right to hate you. You're both snakes," she said separately to Little Lucy, who somehow seemed absolutely transparent in her estrangement, letting everything pass through her without perceiving anything.

"Lusienka, may I wish a happy holiday to you on this day at the beginning of spring," Maxim T. Yermakov declared in a loud, solemn voice, and set the bouquet down in front of Lucy.

Those flowers seemed to be the first ones that Lucy had really seen that day. And they were worth seeing. Inside the cellophane wrapper beaded with moisture the white roses had opened very slightly, as if they had just taken a breath in; the tender green hue of the petals was like the plant's natural blush, the thorns were enveloped in pure drops of water, like tears. The miraculous charm of something as banal as seven roses suddenly lent Maxim T. Yermakov's vulgar congratulations a significance so reverent and exalted that he felt embarrassed.

"Oh, how..." Little Lucy whispered, picking up the bouquet as if it was an abandoned child.

The congratulators didn't give Ika a chance to admire this strange scene. Discordantly declaiming sycophantic verses, the human tangle tumbled out into the corridor. Big Lida grabbed the insulted lady boss's clumpy chinchilla out of the wardrobe, shook the coat as if she intended to cover her entire exuberant mob with it, and fell in at the rear.

"Yermakov! Get off my secretary's desk!" the lady boss's cracked voice called from out of the tangle. "You can both climb up there when I'm gone! But don't you dare do it on my desk, understand? I'll know straight away if you do."

"What a bitch," Maxim T. Yermakov muttered quietly. "Take no notice, sweetheart." He gave Little Lucy a paternal kiss on the dry top of her head, which had an aftertaste of iodine.

"Thank you, Maxie," Little Lucy said in a quiet voice. "They're very beautiful flowers."

Silence fell, with just the plump echo of receding congratulations ringing somewhere in its depths, then the central lift jingled melodically as it swallowed Ika and the silence relaxed, flooding freely across the entire floor. A small-format social forecaster glanced cautiously into the reception area and, once he was sure that the space was free, trotted across to the sofa where his colleagues always kept vigil, plucking at the houseplant that looked like a cockerel. Maxim T. Yermakov had noticed a long time ago that big men with thick, strong necks were used for street surveillance, but the men assigned to surveillance duty inside buildings were small and skinny – probably so that an officer could still perform his duty even when he was cramped into the most awkward little corner. This day-before-the-holiday model looked absolutely useless: his dappled, buckwheat-coloured jacket reached down almost to his knees and he had a crimson boil the size of a woman's nipple blushing shamefacedly on his cheek. "Well, now I'm right up shit creek. Just my salary to live on. I can't believe it," Maxim T. Yermakov thought miserably, perfunctorily observing the state security man, who reached into his pocket and took out a battered paperback with a glossy pistol on its half-ripped-off cover, and dived headlong into this low-density reading matter. A void had formed at the spot where Ika had extracted money from Maxim T. Yermakov's plans for life together with his very soul. Maxim T. Yermakov could feel this void when he breathed air in and out. "All right, the day's not over yet," he told himself, staring at the social forecaster and replacing his helpless gaze with a masterful one. "So your firm is my sponsor, it's decided. You freaks owe me ten million greenbacks for real, and I'll get that dough from you fuckheads, even if I have to turn you inside out, you assholes."

The small-format state-security man, sensing the Object's attention on him, looked up from the ragged page and his brown eyebrows climbed up his forehead interrogatively, like stale crusts of bread. Maxim T. Yermakov strode up to him resolutely and the state-security man got to his feet as if he was facing a superior officer, with his forefinger marking his place in the book.

"Well done! You're a hero!" said Maxim T. Yermakov, slapping the state-security man on the empty shoulder of his jacket and feeling something like a small, smooth stone under the stage-prop padding. The state-security man's face didn't flinch, a lead shutter simply seemed to come down in the unblinking eyes. "Right, I'm off," Maxim T. Yermakov flung out and headed for the door.

"Maxie, wait," Little Lucy called to him in a trembling voice. "I really need to talk to you about something."

"Let's go for a smoke," suggested Little Lucy, nervously tugging out the drawers of the desk as she searched for cigarettes.

The smoking area was a long way away, on a whitish side stairwell, and it was arranged with every inconvenience appropriate to a corporate campaign against an unhealthy habit and the consumption of someone else's product. They had to walk right across the entire level, go up, walk along beside an interminable glass wall that oozed icy cold, then go down four cramped, steep flights of steps in order finally to reach the bin with a thick, moss-like coating of ash that mechanically lowered cigarettes butts into black water. Today, since it was a holiday, everyone was smoking and clamouring without restraint in the offices (to be on the safe side, several condoms had been stretched over all the smoke detectors), but Little Lucy and Maxim T. Yermakov had no corner all to themselves. As he resignedly followed Little Lucy down into the shaft that reeked of stale-tobacco fumes, Maxim T. Yermakov stared in pained embarrassment at the narrow back of her inclined head and the limp little collar that had come away from her neck.

At the bottom of the flight of stairs a dense crowd was buzzing and smoking away, gesticulating with its cigarettes; a tight crush, like folks packed together on the devil's frying pan. Down there, against the wall, Maxim T. Yermakov spotted the distinctive, firm and prickly tops of two heads – or perhaps he was just imagining state-security men everywhere by this time?

"This way," he said, pushing Lucy, who had lost her bearings, in through an opaque glass door.

They found themselves in a quiet corridor on someone else's floor. A short distance away they could see a red designer sofa like a plump woman's mouth, and a plant in a tub, looking as if it had been glued together from stiff embossed paper. Fresh cigarette butts protruded from the plant's mouldy little patch of soil, and Maxim T. Yermakov had no qualms about taking out his Parliament.

"This seems like a quiet spot," he said, speaking soothingly in an effort to calm Lucy, whose cigarette was dancing about in her fingers, refusing to accept a light.

"Max," Little Lucy said in a hoarse, damp voice, "you know I have a son, Artyomka… Well, you know about everything… He had an operation at the cardiac centre. A successful operation, I took the surgeon flowers and a bottle of cognac. Then suddenly all his organs started failing… As if someone was switching him off, one system after another… He's in intensive care, hasn't come round for twelve days now. The doctors say he never will. Perhaps he can hear me…"

At this point Little Lucy's eyes suddenly expanded to twice their size and started glimmering with an alarming, flickering light; two tracks of hot moisture crept down her nose and dripped off her chin. Maxim T. Yermakov was disturbed by this. He had never seen tears flow down a motionless face in a continuous stream like that, like water over a rock.

"I'm so sorry," he replied in the positive words of a character out of a Hollywood movie. It sounded stupid, and in his annoyance Maxim T. Yermakov tugged on a palm leaf, which set the plant rattling over their heads.

"He might only have a few days left." Little Lucy was biting her cigarette rather than smoking it. "Perhaps a week, or two. Artyomka's fighting, he doesn't want to go. His skin's completely cold, only his forehead's hot, and his hair's gone dry, it's like some synthetic material. He's completely dependent on artificial life support, I sit beside him at night and this corrugated thing hoots like an owl.

That's Tyomka breathing. He's still so little, he doesn't understand what death is at all, and how can he die? He's thinking something, after all, and I sit beside him, trying to imagine what it is. It's easy to plant the idea in a little child's head that he's to blame: he broke the toys, drew on mummy's handbag with the felt-tip pens. I'm afraid he thinks this is all his punishment for the handbag. A child believes he'll be forgiven if he promises not to do it again. That mummy will forgive him... sometimes it seems to me that I'm already alone, completely alone with all this, do you understand, Max?"

"But why doesn't Ika give you leave?" asked Maxim T. Yermakov, switching to a whisper for some reason.

"I don't tell anyone," Little Lucy answered, also in a whisper, turning her wet, completely Martian face towards Maxim T. Yermakov. "They only know the general situation. I'm afraid somehow. It seems like if they all realise just what Artyomka and I are going through, it will be even worse. They'll smell blood and they'll go for our throats. Can you believe it, Maxie, I walk along the street and go down into the metro and dream of being invisible?"

"Then why are you telling me?"

Little Lucy answered by smiling the half-witted smile that her well-gnawed face had been wearing all the time just recently and grabbed hold of Maxim T. Yermakov's fat wrist.

"Maxie, they're going to get you anyway," she whispered fervently, fluttering her clumped eyelashes.

"Who are they?"

"They..." said Little Lucy, squinting in the direction of the glass door. "They won't back off, Max. I'm saying such terrible things now... But afterwards you'll do it anyway... Fire the pistol into your head... But it'll be too late for Artyomka and me... If you could just make up your mind! It's appalling, asking you like this, but I'll do anything now, anything!"

"Wait. Wait, will you, stop blubbering!" Maxim T. Yermakov squatted down in front of Lucy and folded her completely in his arms, like a frightened little goat that was kicking out with its feet. "Concentrate, look at me. You're an intelligent, grown-up person.

Do you really believe that if I shoot myself, Artyomka will live? Come on, apply a bit of logic. Do you really think that?"

Little Lucy slowly raised her empty, wet eyes to look at Maxim T. Yermakov and slowly shook her head.

"There now, you see!" Maxim T. Yermakov said delightedly. "You know yourself that it's not possible. Where's the connection? How can one man who lives his life without bothering anyone be the cause of accidents, catastrophes and deaths? Do you think I go around at night derailing trains?"

"Then why?" Little Lucy asked, glancing round again at the opaque door of ribbed glass, behind which dark, dense patches rippled, numerous feet tramped up and down the stairs, someone cackled loudly and an angry woman's voice was raised above the complacent male murmur.

Of course, Maxim T. Yermakov understood what she meant. If he disregarded his quite distinct gut feeling that everything was exactly the way the state tadpole-heads had explained it to him at that first memorable meeting, this business could have numerous different explanations: some special kind of training, for example, or some tortuous, complicated gambit being played out by the fuckheaded special services, who had mistaken Maxim T. Yermakov for an international terrorist. And what was a "gut feeling" anyway? You couldn't touch it or break a piece off it.

"I don't know," Maxim T. Yermakov told Little Lucy almost honestly, looking almost effortlessly straight into her face, which still slashed at his almost open gaze, like the light of a low-power electric bulb. This uncomfortable smarting sensation suddenly brought large tears, a teaspoonful each, welling up in Maxim T. Yermakov's eyes.

"Maxie, you're so good," said Little Lucy, touched; and wiped her flabby cheek with the back of her hand. "If only I could help you…"

"You can, as it happens," said Maxim T. Yermakov, suddenly thinking of something. "You can see they're putting me under pressure, and I don't understand a thing. Those psychos out in front of the office – who are they, where did they come from? I've got another crowd of the same kind of retards in front of my door at home. Okay, so I was given a special talking-to and fed a load of bullshit. But how do they know about my head, about the pistol? You, for instance, where did you get your information from?"

"You mean you don't know anything about it?" Little Lucy's surprise jolted her briefly out of grief and into reality. "How long is it since you entered your own name in a search engine, in Yandex, for example?"

"Why would I search for my own name?" asked Maxim T. Yermakov, surprised now himself. "I'm not a celebrity or a star. There's nothing about me on TV. Yesterday a certain gutter journalist explained very clearly to me that the cameras won't come because the PR isn't paid up. I understand all that anyway, I wasn't born yesterday."

"No, you don't understand," Little Lucy interrupted briskly, looking as ugly as a little old monkey. "The Maxim Yermakov on the internet is not you. It is you, of course, but it's like this character in a computer game. The game's called 'Light Head', it's top of the online ratings. And then the bloggers are always writing about you. That is, about the Yermakov who's a character, but really... I tell you what, let's go back, it's better if I show you. Oh, Max, it's so incredible!"

"Right, let's take a look," Maxim T. Yermakov muttered to himself as he hurried after Little Lucy along the icy corridors and smoky stairways. They could hear the sound of heated voices and pounding music on all sides, as if the Eighth of March had given the cold office leviathan a heart attack. Every now and then a gaggle of unhinged office workers swept along the corridor, boisterously waving little corporate flags – and then it was suddenly empty again, and the frosty sunlit panorama outside the windows seemed to be made entirely out of textured glass. Lucy, suddenly unnaturally cheerful, wobbled ahead of Maxim T. Yermakov on her crooked heels, and the glance that she cast over her shoulder seemed inappropriately playful, reminding him of a prostitute who has picked up a client.

But, of course, this was a distorted image, in her present unfocused state Lucy could have appeared like absolutely anyone, that was beyond her control. Coughing into his fist, Maxim T. Yermakov suddenly remembered Marinka and her ballistic-yellow dress. The memory was uncomfortable, and somehow that was connected with Little Lucy, but Maxim T. Yermakov didn't understand how exactly.

All that remained of the social forecaster in the reception area was the open book, lying flattened out face-down, and the husks of waxed paper wrappers from cheap sweets. People are only human, this was everyone's holiday. Maxim T. Yermakov took the keys from Little Lucy and locked the door thoroughly with three turns of the lock. Meanwhile Lucy had clambered into her slouching office chair and awoken the computer with a tap of her nail on the keyboard.

"I'm downloading it, Maxie," she told him, squirming in agitation.

Maxim T. Yermakov squeezed though into the secretary's cubbyhole, setting the furniture groaning, and stared at the monitor.

Right, then.

He didn't know anything about computer games and he'd never played them in his life, but even to him it was obvious straight away what a monstrous amount of loot had been thrown into making 'Light Head'. The graphics were incredible; the building in which Maxim T. Yermakov lived was recognisable not only from its stocky, twin-column-desk silhouette, but even from the mournful expression of the balconies, which looked like packing crates piled one on top of another with all sorts of trash in them. Maxim T. Yermakov's seventh-floor window flashed red, like a panic button.

"Maxie, look." Lucy moved the mouse, and the building started getting bigger, dissolving into a blurred lattice and then acquiring definition again. A blue plaque appeared on the corner: "16 Usov Lane, that's your address," Lucy declared, but Maxim T. Yermakov had already figured that out for himself.

"Click on the window," he told her with a loud sniff.

He suddenly had the feeling that half of Moscow had broken into his flat. The pictures were so realistic, it was astounding. There was the room, there was the crumpled bed, with a rug carelessly thrown over it, there was the Honoured Schoolteacher's reddish-brown desk with the cubistic inkstand, there was the armchair, and the silk ties tossed onto it this morning, squirming like a brightly patterned tangle of snakes when the mouse was moved. With her eyebrows angled together, Lucy unscrolled the scene, leading to the left to bring the hallway looming up, and Maxim T. Yermakov suddenly recognised his own ruined cashmere coat, hanging on the coat stand with its back to the viewer.

"So what is it, a cross between a game and a reality show?" he asked himself, quickly trying to recall what was scattered about in the bathroom.

"I don't know Maxie, there's all kind of strange bits and pieces in here," Little Lucy replied guiltily. "And you know, this is only the skin! You can go out onto the stairs, ride down in the lift, get into your car…"

"And where am I?" Maxim T. Yermakov interrupted rudely.

"Just a moment, look."

Yes, it was a good likeness all right. A white face filling the entire screen. Cheeks like pockets stuffed with something, a bulging grin like a reflection in a samovar. And then the face drifts away a bit and up rises a fat-fingered white hand with a black sleeve and a black pistol. Bang! The head turns transparent, rather like an X-ray, the bullet slowly rips the air apart, trailing a beautiful rainbow-coloured plume behind it. Splat! The bullet enters the head and starts frolicking about inside it, like a goldfish in a round bowl. Then the grin again, as if nothing has happened, the monster scratches his thin-skinned head with the barrel of the pistol in comical deliberation, and a window opens on the screen: "CLICK HERE!"

"I see," muttered Maxim T. Yermakov, trying to conceal his discomfiture. "Lucy, you send me the link, I'll get it on my e-mail at home and play with it, see what's in there."

"Of course, Maxie. Only, Maxie, don't get really upset," Lucy said anxiously, clattering the keyboard with her bony little fingers. "Okay, I've sent it. Maxie, wait, I'll show you something else."

"What?" Maxim T. Yermakov asked sharply, looking round just as he was all set to clamber out of the secretary's cubbyhole and dreaming of smashing up all the furniture in the reception area.

"I found a few things on the internet. It's important, honestly. You see, people confuse the game with reality. That's what they're encouraged to do!" Little Lucy put on the meaningless face that she had been wearing so often recently. "Look, someone loses their nearest and dearest in a plane crash. Imagine the state they're in. If your husband's not there any more, or your child, it's a different world, strange and alien. And if you can believe that your husband and child have been killed, you can believe in all sorts of other incredible things. Even devils, even flying saucers. Those victims who throw vegetables at you are taking the game as a prompt. They think someone in the know is giving them a hint. Especially since they find out immediately that the address is real and the character really exists…"

"I already figured that out," Maxim T. Yermakov interrupted. "Are you telling me that grief turns people into idiots?"

"Not everybody," Lucy said quietly, offended. "Max, why not just watch? I really do want to help you."

An amateur video started up on the screen with a hiss and an indistinct rumble of voices. It was a shot of an airfield in winter, flat and frozen, with an ink-black strip of forest on the horizon. Here and there planes took off from the concrete, looking like solemn, fat-arsed ganders with their wings extended. The picture was unsteady. It jumped about, and every now and then a blurred round tower moved into shot. Suddenly the camera caught a grey silhouette hovering above the tower, like a fly. The silhouette started growing rapidly, trailing a fat black thread behind it. Suddenly the stricken plane was the size of a whale and it tried to dive down into the depths of the earth, splashing like a whale with its broken-off tail. Curly flames flared up and started spreading, the rumble of human voices became unbearably loud and then it was suddenly cut short. In the halted picture the flames froze like some gigantic ginger lady's hairstyle.

"That's the Kazan crash, genuine footage," Little Lucy explained, minimising the video.

"Aha," Maxim T. Yermakov muttered, immediately recalling the group of men from Kazan outside the office, all tightly packed into their black leather jackets, wearing identical round mink caps on almost identical round heads. Their leader, a man with absolutely no neck and an old, womanish Asiatic face that was propped on his chest, nonetheless had long arms and he threw accurately. His projectiles, launched with real force, flew in an almost straight line and struck the umbrella with a sound that reverberated in Maxim T. Yermakov's stomach. This Tatar was one of the most dangerous of the demonstrators laying siege to the office and Maxim T. Yermakov tried to run past him as fast as possible. Had he actually seen the events in the amateur video-clip? Had he realised straightaway that it was *that* plane, *his* plane? Who had he gone to with what he was feeling then – and was there anyone left alive for him to go to?

"Now look at this, there, the fourth level of the game," Little Lucy told him as she downloaded it.

Everything exactly the same, but as if it was wrapped in cellophane. Everything reproduced precisely: the rows of parked planes, the blunt silhouette of the tower, even a small caterpillar-track truck driving past, carrying miniature suitcases that looked like coffee beans. The difference was that there were small human figures, as black as letters, lying on the airfield, with a bloody red patch spreading out from under each one of them, eating away very naturalistically at the snow. Maxim T. Yermakov suddenly had the thought that the genuine bodies wouldn't look like letters, but like little piles of tattered clothes. The game seemed to be showing in playback mode: there was a gun fight taking place on the airfield without Lucy being involved at all. A cartoon-film character with shoulders as broad as a milkmaid's yoke and an agile fat man in checks were blasting round shells at each other, stringing them on threads of flame, like beads. The fat man hit the target. The broad-shouldered guy lay down on the concrete in disciplined fashion – and immediately the grey, trembling silhouette appeared in the milky sky, the plane crashed, broke apart, burst into flames and a small red window flashed open with a buzz: "You have been eliminated."

"They processed the actual recording, I just can't tell in what program," muttered Maxim T. Yermakov. "I can imagine the amount of dosh they laid out for that footage. The guy was maybe just filming for himself, messing about with his new phone, and all of a sudden he's a millionaire…"

"All of a sudden a hundred and sixty people are dead," Little Lucy reminded him, flashing her little eyes and frowning.

"And what about it? What's it got to do with me?" Maxim T. Yermakov snarled rancorously. "Have you any idea of all the stuff they're laying on me? These people were killed, those people died, here, there – and it's all down to me! There's always something like that going on in the world, name me a year when airplanes didn't fall out of the sky! Who do you have to be to take all that on board and go through it all with everyone? A Titan, Jesus Christ?"

"Maxie, I'm sorry," said Lucy, instantly relenting. "Of course, no single person could bear all that. Oh! That's what they're counting on, isn't it!" she exclaimed in sudden realisation, snatching at her cheek with one hand. "To get you to shoot yourself!"

"Aha, so you finally figured that one out," said Maxim T. Yermakov, scowling with his head lowered and sticking his hands as deep as he could into the pockets of his shamefully splattered trousers. "But I'll stick it out. I can promise you that for certain. I'll screw things up for them real good. And by the way, about the game. What is it, just an ordinary dumb shooter? Didn't they come up with anything fancier than that?"

"Yes, of course they did. There are different ways you can play it: one player can put together a team of characters with various abilities and then play online with other players, even go through training and earn a qualification. There are lots of complicated missions. The main purpose of the game is to get you – that is, the main character – to shoot himself in the head with a pistol. To do that you have to score hits on the character, I don't remember how many, more than a thousand, and with various different weapons. But on the first three levels, if a player scores a hit on Yermakov, then Yermakov only gets stronger and quicker, and better armed. So not many people get through to the fourth level. Only with the help of a special key…"

"That's all very interesting, of course, only, in case you've forgotten, Yermakov happens to be me," Maxim T. Yermakov said acidly, feeling more like he had been robbed than shot. By moving into the game, his appearance had become public property. Reduced in this way to his own inner content, Maxim T. Yermakov was like a ten-year-old child, only a hundred and twenty centimetres tall and, shameful to say, that child wanted to cry. "And what are the missions all about? Are they connected with the real disasters?" asked Maxim T. Yermakov, shredding some sort of paper trash in his pockets.

"They're directly connected," Little Lucy answered. "In that part I showed you, you have to save the plane and the passengers. If one of the team had survived and found a briefcase with a code, the plane could have landed and the fire in the engine would have been extinguished."

Maxim T. Yermakov slowly pulled his hands out of his pockets. The pieces of paper that he had reduced to shreds with his recently sprouted fingernails were two rouble notes – a hundred and five hundred. Fuck it!

"You could stick them together," Lucy said with a guilty expression as she watched the cash fluttering through the air.

"Never mind, forget it," said Maxim T. Yermakov, brushing off the scraps that had stuck to his pants. "What interests me is this, maybe you know the answer: these disasters in the game, what period are they from? The last year? The last two? Did I become the root cause of all evil just recently, or have I been a saboteur since I was a little baby?"

"Definitely not just one year," said Little Lucy, frowning in concentration. "As for when you were a baby – there's no way you can find that out for certain, there wasn't any internet then, or any mobile phones for people to film anything they fancy. If there are any old pieces of film, they're not on the internet, they still have to be digitised. There, look, a sports plane that crashed near Geneva in ninety-nine. That's the oldest thing I've been able to find."

This time the action was filmed from the plane itself as it bobbled about over the abyss. The engines must have cut out: there wasn't a sound to be heard, apart from a shrill grating, like the squeak of a garden swing. When he heard that regular rasping, Maxim T. Yermakov was suddenly grabbed somewhere below the knees by a piercing sensation of height. The distant ground shifted between lying horizontally and standing up on end – and then it seemed as if the battlements of the mountains, moving in from the left like the steel tongues of a door lock, would rip through the taut wing of the little plane at any moment. Down below, suburbs as neat as packs of tablets glowed white and the rim of water in a lake shone as if it had been traced out in phosphorous. It all seemed impossibly far out of reach, the little plane was more likely to pick up speed and go soaring up into the heavens, where the circle of the sun, polished to painful brilliance, shone blindingly first on the left, then on the right. But suddenly the little plane flipped over, the mountains hung down like gigantic icicles, the ground lurched closer and everything started flickering and flapping, like a line of washing being dragged through bushes.

"Shall I show you how they do it in the game?" asked little Lucy, clearly pleased with her research. "Yermakov flies round the plane, like Superman, steering it with his fists, and you have to get him with a sub-machine gun at least three times!"

"Oh no, I've had enough. I'm feeling a bit tired," said Maxim T. Yermakov, rubbing his damp forehead with the back of his hand. There's only one other thing I'm curious about: why do you play this garbage? I mean, pardon me, in your circumstances?"

"It's not me, it's Tyomka!" Little Lucy exclaimed proudly. "There are thousands and thousands of people, all kinds, in this game, and Tyomka's in the fourth hundred by points, just imagine! None of the gamers know that he's a child. Everybody thinks he's already eighteen."

After she blurted that out, Little Lucy stopped short and the smile on her face froze in a crack. "Your son's never going to see eighteen," Maxim T. Yermakov thought detachedly, hoping she wouldn't start

110

bawling again and let him leave in peace.

"Well, I'll be off!" he announced cheerfully, twisting the key protruding from the lock of the door. "Congratulations again on the holiday, regardless of everything! And thanks, you really have helped me," he added in a normal human tone of voice, which made Little Lucy's blurred eyes flood with tears again and start glowing like crystals.

"Right, I didn't see that," Maxim T. Yermakov told himself sternly, skipping out into the corridor. "And I don't see this either," he added when he almost ran into the small social forecaster, pacing the synthetic floor covering in unpolished boots with toes as pointy as sunflower seeds.

The glow of the traffic jam extended for as far as the eye could see, like a large river shimmering with reflected lights. Crushed ice crunched under hundreds of ponderous wheels, backlit vapour rose into the air, the viscous puddles on the half-thawed roadway were like glue. The social forecasters' bread van was stuck like everyone else; carried ahead slightly at a tight fork in the road, it was trying to switch lanes, cutting across the traffic and provoking an outraged honking of horns; every now and then the headlights of Maxim T. Yermakov's Toyota picked out the side of the van, caked with icy mud, and the man at the wheel, with a round, shaved snowman's head and a crooked *papyrosa* jutting out of the face instead of the traditional carrot.

"Bugger it, more than two hours, like flying to Paris," Maxim T. Yermakov thought in annoyance as he finally turned into dingy Usov Lane, now familiar, apparently, to thousands upon thousands of lame-brains. His heart was aching at the thought of the money his shrewd boss would pocket now – and she would shoot down in flames all the business contacts that Maxim T. Yermakov had been nurturing, to mutual advantage and profit, for years. The car park turned out to be packed solid with rusty Soviet vehicles that belonged, no doubt, to the demonstrators in the yard. After squeezing into a space somehow, Maxim T. Yermakov, numb from his coccyx to the tips of the toes that were fused together in his shoes, clambered out of the Toyota – and only then remembered with a feeling of disgust that tomorrow was the Eighth of March. He still hadn't bought a present for Marinka, but at the very least he had to get champagne, sweets, some kind of cake. Never mind, never mind. Hang in there, Alpha Object, there's no one you can rely on but yourself.

The basement shop's electrical garland twinkled welcomingly, as if tomorrow was not just the Eighth of March, but the New Year all over again. "Maybe I'll get myself something too, a little bottle of something…" Maxim T. Yermakov thought as he walked down the steep steps that were all different heights. The cash desk in the shop was jangling away briskly, the saleswoman in the vegetable section was weighing a bunch of grapes the size of a chandelier, customers were jostling each other, clutching full baskets, with gold-wrapped and plain-glass bottle necks jutting out in all directions. A holiday! But the moment Maxim T. Yermakov attempted to step into the sales area, his way was blocked by the familiar security guard, who at close quarters gave off a strong smell of coarse woollen clothing.

"We don't serve you," he muttered gruffly with a scowl.

"What do you mean?" asked Maxim T. Yermakov. "I'm a regular customer of yours! Don't you recognise me, or what? I come here almost every day."

"I said: We don't serve you!" the security guard repeated more loudly, bearing down on Maxim T. Yermakov with a uniformed chest studded with metal buttons like the heads of firmly beaten in nails.

Maxim T. Yermakov gaped around helplessly. The yellow-haired woman at the check-out, always so affable, now showed him the undyed, muddy-brown, back of her head as she sorted through the baskets of trustworthy citizens with exaggerated concentration. Customers with tight-packed plastic bags pushed past Maxim T. Yermakov, casting sidelong glances at him, like timid little fish in murky water.

"Why, I'll sue you!" exclaimed Maxim T. Yermakov in a woman-ish voice that wasn't his. "Call the director!"

"The director's not here. He's gone home. Come on, stop

blocking the passage, outside with you, quick!"

And so saying, the security guard forced Maxim T. Yermakov out of the shop and then, wheezing and prodding him under the shoulder blade, made him climb the uneven steps to where a loathsome wind was sweeping handfuls of scanty grains of snow up off the asphalt and swirling them round in the air.

Daunted, Maxim T. Yermakov started patting his pockets, looking for cigarettes. The security guard hovered there for a moment and then took out a box of *papyrosas*. They both lit up, shielding the ragged flames of their lighters from the wind. Illuminated for a moment by the turbojet spurting from his fist, the security guard's face looked like a fat thumb eloquently stuck between two fingers. Casting cautious glances at each other, they took turns to shake their ash into the cast-iron litter bin that was full of crushed cardboard boxes and dry, broken stalks. "Maybe I should try talking nicely to him?" Maxim T. Yermakov thought drearily as his cigarette end almost clashed with his enemy's *papyrosa*, glittering in the wind.

But just then a gentle, almost silky tenor voice spoke behind him:

"Good evening, neighbour!"

Looking round sharply, Maxim T. Yermakov saw the alcoholic Vasya Shutov standing there. He had trimmed off the burnt part of his beard, leaving it as crooked as a straw broom worn down to a stump. The native-born Muscovite was wearing a putrid ear-flap cap that looked like a cat's corpse and a chipolata-pink woman's down jacket that belonged, no doubt, to one of his regular collaborators, who was busy at the moment with a client.

"What's this then, won't they sell you anything?" the native-born Muscovite asked considerately, blinking his warm little eyes, almost completely buried in bluish-grey bags of skin.

"Yeah, well..." Maxim T. Yermakov confirmed reluctantly.

"Listen, let me help you out, as a neighbour," Shutov suggested in a conspiratorial whisper. "You tell me what you want, and I'll have it all bought in a jiffy! And don't get any bad ideas, I've got an entire accounts office in my head. You just give me enough for a bottle of the white stuff, to mark the holiday.

As a commission, eh?" Shutov grinned obsequiously, showing his one protruding front tooth, as yellow as a chip of wood.

Maxim T. Yermakov hesitated. Doing business with the alcoholic Shutov had definitely not entered into his plans for the immediate future. But on the other hand – what else could he do? With a heavy sigh, Maxim T. Yermakov counted out three five-hundred-rouble notes into the alcoholic's trembling hands, then thought for a moment and added another one.

"Right then: a yoghurt cake, the best kind they sell, then a box of chocolates, champagne, cognac, a chicken fillet or a veal steak, see what they have…" Maxim T. Yermakov listed off, wincing fretfully at the joyful way the fired-up alcoholic nodded his head. "For your trouble, you take a half-litre, not the most expensive kind. They slashed my pay at work today, so from now on I've got to be very economical!"

"I gotcha! Gotcha!"

The alcoholic skipped friskily down the steps into the shop, holding the rainbow-bright five-hundred-rouble notes out in front of him. Maxim T. Yermakov was left outside in the wind that made the icy asphalt look too slippery to take even a single step. The bare branches of the trees reared up into the air, as if they were trying to catch the sparse, dull little snowflakes, flying past looking like moths – Maxim T. Yermakov fancied that if those black, groping fingers should catch any fluttering insect, they would clench into a bony fist. Time dragged. The cold turned the soles of his tight-fitting shoes to stone, he couldn't feel any feet in his shoes at all. "Now he'll go and pick up all sorts of garbage," Maxim T. Yermakov thought dismally, gazing down at the door of the shop.

His misgivings, however, proved unfounded. Vasya Shutov clambered back up to the surface, as happy as if he had already taken a swig from a bottle, lugging a plastic bag stuffed to overflowing with his purchases. He started transferring them one by one to another bag that he had prudently picked up at the checkout, at the same time checking them against a long receipt that was already grimy, and Maxim T. Yermakov was astonished to realise that Shutov had taken everything that he would have chosen himself. At the end two vodka bottles were left clinking against each other in the bag.

"Don't take it amiss, neighbour, I took two of them, because they have this discount, a special offer," said Shutov, crinkling up his face guiltily. "But if you're offended, take one for yourself!" He pulled out one to show it – an extremely dubious "Stolichnaya" bottle with a neck that looked like a crudely bandaged finger.

"Oh no, you can drink that stuff yourself," said Maxim T. Yermakov, recoiling.

"Well thank you, my kind man! My girls could do with a drop too. That's a tough job they do, hard on the health…" Shutov muttered contentedly, rummaging in the pocket of his down jacket. "The change! Right down to the last kopeck," he said, placing in Maxim T. Yermakov's hand a bundle of crumpled ten-rouble notes and a few coins that were as sticky as boiled sweets.

"That's okay, why don't you keep it," said Maxim T. Yermakov, embarrassed for some reason.

"Money – no way!" said Shutov, hoicking his beard up into the air spiritedly. "We only take money for services rendered. And we do an honest job! But as neighbours, we can always lend a helping hand. So you get in touch. You know the number of the flat. We'll buy the list, spot on, and deliver too!"

"Well, at least he didn't offer me his girls," Maxim T. Yermakov thought sourly as he took his leave of the scrupulous alcoholic. Shutov hurried on his way, holding the quivering bag with the bottles out to one side, like some lady he was leading in a dance. Maxim T. Yermakov trudged after him, falling behind, with the handles of his weighty bag vibrating and whistling in the wind. The demonstrators in front of the entrance had clumped together into a tight little circle and, to judge from the expressions on their faces, they were pouring vodka. So let them. A far less pleasant sight was the lanky figure of the local militiaman looming into view under the stooping streetlamp; the militiaman's tight little bracket of a mouth was squeezed shut angrily, his gait expressed the determination to carry out some action as yet unknown to anyone, including the militiaman himself. "Fuck it, what does he want with me?" Maxim T. Yermakov thought in annoyance, slowing down.

But it turned out that the militiaman hadn't come on his account. Spotting Vasya Shutov, the militiaman jerked his bony chin in his direction, and Vasya Shutov meekly plodded over, stuffing the vodka in the plastic bag inside the flap of the down jacket.

"So, we're wandering about the place, not sitting quietly at home," the militiaman said, displeased, raising his peaked cap and mopping his forehead with a handkerchief that was no longer fresh.

"I only just went to the shop and back..." said Shutov, starting to make excuses.

"Well, obviously you didn't just dash out to the library," the militiaman interrupted him mockingly. "Did I tell you about the raid? I did. So, it's set up for tomorrow, on the holiday. After two o'clock, you stay home, as if you were glued in there, we'll come to pick you up."

"Gotcha, Andrei Andreich!" Shutov exclaimed cheerfully, adjusting the rustling plastic bag that was protruding from under his jacket.

"Look here now," said the militiaman, piling on the pressure. "I need numbers tomorrow, statistics. You've got barley juice for brains, you go wandering off somewhere and I'll have to stick some decent citizen in the slammer instead."

"Only, Andrei Andreich... It would be better without, you know, eh?" said Shutov, cautiously fingering his spongy temple that looked as if it had been boiled soft. "Or at least not the full wallop, gently like? I'm coming in voluntarily, responsibly!"

"Now fancy that, he's coming in voluntarily!" the militiaman exclaimed, flashing a sharp glance from under his cap. "Your way of life, citizen Shutov, positively presumes regular pokes in the face. Do we keep a disorderly house? We do. And we drink like a fish. According to the law, you should have been put away for a five year stretch of minimum security a long time ago. You've got soft-hearted neighbours, they don't write complaints, only complain in person sometimes. And I've got soft-hearted too. A disaster like you on my beat, and I still talk to you nicely, like a human being, figuratively speaking."

"Andrei Andreich, I understand! I won't screw things up!" Shutov said obsequiously, mincing up and down on the spot in a way that made Maxim T. Yermakov want to spit. "I won't stick my nose outside tomorrow!"

"There you have it, our people," Maxim T. Yermakov thought spitefully. "Go, lay down your life for them!" At that moment the alcoholic Shutov seemed to him like a symbol of the irredeemably backward national masses in whose name the state tadpole-heads were pushing him to shoot himself. The wind twisted Shutov's trousers round his skinny, loose-kneed legs, tried to knock his cap off his head and frisked him, exposing his attempted concealment of the vodka. One of his hussies appeared out of the darkness and took her patron timidly by the arm – on her immensely high platform shoes she was even more unstable than Shutov, it looked as if she had heavy flat-irons tied to her brittle matchstick-legs. Without the slightest change in his expression, the militiaman twisted round and slapped the hussy on her backside, as flat as a pack of A4 paper. Wriggling her puny little body in professional style, the whore giggled and flirted with her mascara-lined eyes, sending the blood rushing to the militiaman's face and making him grunt.

"There you have it, the harmony of human relations," Maxim T. Yermakov thought as he darted in through the door of the building. "Those people are really colleagues, family in fact, you could say. Together they create, so to speak, the substance of life, weaving the broad canvas millimetre by millimetre. And I'm an awkward little knot that has to be trimmed off. Or is that the way that anybody who isn't simple-minded enough feels? Everywhere else in the world, solitude is a personal problem, but here it's an antisocial position. Or is the constitution of our national masses somehow special? It's hard even to imagine the number of threads that bind them all together: neighbours, relatives, godfathers, cronies, classmates.ru... More like a covering of moss than a nation of people. Well, no thank you. My dear compatriots, I shit on you from a great height. I just hope

Marinka's not going to put on one of her performances and start bawling, Lord, Lord, I'm so sick of everything."

But there was no Marinka in the flat. The toilet bowl was gurgling quietly in the darkness – Marinka always forgot to press its cold button to stop the water flowing. Maxim T. Yermakov switched on the light in the hallway and saw what he had observed three hours earlier on a computer screen: a coat stand, a coat with vegetable stains, his own cap looking like a vegetable. He had the strange feeling that all these objects were unreal. Maxim T. Yermakov had suspected before that the flat was under audio and visual surveillance, but now the walls of the hallway, covered with coarse wallpaper the colour of wooden planks, had become especially suspicious; the overhead light, in the form of a thick beaker of wavy glass, cast uncertain circles on the ceiling. Maxim T. Yermakov squeezed his eyes tight shut, shook his head; and when his surroundings re-emerged from the concentric green murk, they remained normal for a while.

Maxim T. Yermakov wondered where Marinka had got to. Her absence aroused in him almost the same odd blend of pleasure and irritation as her presence. Taking long strides that betrayed his fear of strangers watching his back, he walked through into the kitchen and swigged a litre of mineral water from a whooping, crackling plastic container. He put his purchases for a romantic evening in the unwashed refrigerator, with old waxy streaks of egg yolk running down its damp wall. Maxim T. Yermakov didn't feel like eating at all, but despite that he assembled a shaggy sandwich for himself out of a short baguette, lettuce and ham, shook some instant coffee into a blank cup and, after perfunctorily hanging up the suit that had grown so heavy over the day, plonked himself down in front of the computer with all this booty.

Little Lucy's message jumped out at him immediately, like a puppy dog that had been waiting, shivering outside the door. But Maxim T. Yermakov didn't click on the message, deciding that he'd seen enough for today. In actual fact, he was rather afraid of finding himself there, sitting at the computer, of finding himself in the kind of infinite suite of rooms that appears between two mirrors standing facing each other and seeing himself dwindling endlessly in symmetrical perspectives as overwhelming for the mind as the infinity of the universe. Instead of opening the people's favourite game, "Light Head", Maxim T. Yermakov went into Yandex and entered his name in the search line.

There was nothing about Maxim T. Yermakov in the news as such, that was dominated by a certain Maxim Yermak, general director of the charitable foundation "Happy Childhood", a man who looked like an ancient pink toddler and gave two interviews for every computer donated to his orphanage. Everything Little Lucy had talked about was in the blogs, where Maxim T. Yermakov's popularity shot right off the top of any imaginable scale. The discussions branched out in every direction, whichever way he looked the links extended like the surface of a bog; he felt that if he set foot on it, he'd be sucked in immediately, step by step, down into internet depths that had no meaning and no bottom. It seemed quite impossible to understand how all this was structured and what it all meant, at least to begin with.

"I'd never have believed they could handle projects like this here in Russia!" a certain *hell-demon* spluttered in delight: he presented himself as a user pic of an armour-plated monster that resembled a domestic pressure cooker. "So much for your Electronic Arts or SEGA, or Ubisoft! Revolutionary graphics, and the engine is simply mind-blowing! You can even make out Maxim T. Yermakov's buttons and the stubble on his face. Check out the latest gimmicks in game mechanics. Basically, I categorically recommend it to everyone! Gamers, I'm proud of my country!"

"We can do it when we want to," commented *milena*, represented by a thumbnail portrait of a little blonde beauty, which quite obviously had nothing in common with reality.

"Maxim T. Yermakov is a really classy baddy! Charming and attractive. And so appallingly dangerous for mankind. Hey, all you guys, and dolls! Everyone join in the fight against Maxim T. Yermakov," blue-eyed *paladin* exclaimed in support of *demon*.

"A fantastical fairytale game!" exclaimed the feisty *alex-leopard*, developing the theme further. "Two computer chairs fell under me like race horses. I'm only sleeping two hours a day. This is the life! My respects to the developers!"

"Will they translate it into English?" *milena* enquired ingenuously, popping up again with her sugary curls and glazed lips.

"Sure they will! What damn choice do they have?" replied *hell-demon*, bubbling over with patriotism. "Let's hear it for the Russian blockbuster!"

And so on in the same fashion. Maxim Y. Yermakov was well acquainted with these shady techniques for heating up the biosphere, he had paid for them himself on numerous occasions. Two or three users created the content, it was effective and inexpensive – only fifteen thousand roubles a month. Of course, it all depended on the users. According to the terms and conditions, they had to be real people with active blogs – but Maxim T. Yermakov had always suspected that specially prepared virtual ready-mades took part in the warm-ups. Just to be sure, he checked out *demon* by going into his actual blog. "This is me in front of the Eiffel Tower," said the caption under a photo showing a fat man in a check shirt hanging outside his pants, with ginger hair and a beard like a fox-fur fringe on his triple chin, while all that could actually be seen of the tower was one gigantic support strut, lit up in yellow, looking like amber. "This is me in Nice," – the same man in the opening of a narrow lane where every last window was covered with bars, making them look like washboards or birdcages. So the internet promotion of "Light Head" had been carried out properly, without any bullshit. Unpaid users got sucked into a whirlpool like that on a wide scale. Right then, let's take a look. Maxim T. Yermakov massaged his squishy eyes with his thumb and forefinger and carried on reading.

What came next was interesting.

Humanist: (a user pic of a cartoon cat with bright yellow-and-black bee stripes): "Yesterday I saw the real, live Maxim Yermakov. For real, friends! When they told me at first, I didn't believe it. Then I went to Usov Lane. The house is there all right. Then this guy dashes out of the entrance, flashes a glance right and left and hops into his ride. Some old-timers tried to belt him with their sticks – smack! But they missed! I would have got him!"

Verunchik: (another lovely, but not a blonde, a brunette with a smooth aerofoil of hair): "Well go and get him then".

Experiment: (a user pic of something abstract, with lots of legs, like a mosquito squashed on glass): "How many levels have you got through?"

Humanist: "Two. That is, one and a half."

Experiment: "Aha, and he would have got him. Instead of trying to be flash, why don't you try to hit him with a crossbow during the terrorist attack in Kazan, while his health indicator's almost down to zero?"

Anonymous: "Gentlemen, that's not a real guy, it's an actor."

Verunchik: "That's right! I remember him! He was in the soap 'Stay with Me', playing that oligarch Katya accidentally stabbed to death. What was his name? It's on the tip of my tongue."

Experiment: "It wasn't 'Stay with Me', it was 'Cruiser', and it wasn't an oligarch, it was the first mate."

Verunchik: "He was in both."

Fly-landed: (a user pic of a fly crawling along with its wings torn off): "It's a promo spin-off for the game. Pretty creative. They hired a lookalike actor and shelled out for him to run around looking like this dreamboat. Soon they'll start selling shirts and mugs with his portrait. I'll buy them!"

Anonymous: "I don't reckon this is commercial business. The game's free to play! They're flushing our cerebral convolutions, trying to flog us something. I just don't understand what."

Verunchik: "I'm slowly choking here. Where do these anonymous brainiacs come from? Have they taken a course on total brain relaxation? Of course someone makes money on the game. But how much is none of our business."

Humanist: "Something doesn't add up. Let's say they did hire an actor. Did they hire the building too? Or did they build it specially, so it would be old, post-Soviet-degenerate straight away? Maybe it's all the other way round. They drew the house from a real one and they drew the character from the actor."

Fly-landed: "Makesnodiff."

Experiment: "That actor, I can't remember his name either, he has this groove of his own. That's why he only plays black villainaceous types. Maybe someone rich has decided to give the people a present. What if, in the end, the actor really does shoot himself with a pistol? There'll be a huge party, to celebrate the triumph of justice. Millions of people's hearts will feel lighter."

Verunchik: "Aha, it'll be like everybody gets compensation."

Experiment: "Our people can be robbed and trampled down and their mouths can be stopped. But every now and then our people need a life to be sacrificed for them. So there's a proper balance and self-respect for everyone. Then they can carry on with their robbing and trampling."

Anonymous: "What sick freaks we all are."

Maxim T. Yermakov could no longer feel his backside or the chair under him as he read all this gobbledegook. It was the dead of night. In the silence he could hear the separate sounds of all the timepieces in the flat: the dull scrape of Just Natasha's old wall clock, the firm click of the metal alarm clock, the gentle cicada call of the Longines mechanical watch, taken off and abandoned somewhere in the bed. Maxim T. Yermakov went into the kitchen, made himself another sandwich and gobbled it down without tasting it, stuffing the watery leaves of lettuce into his mouth with his finger. Outside the window tiny little white midges swarmed in the heavy, hazy air, the columns outside the doorways of the opposite house glinted dully. There was something unnatural about Marinka's absence at this hour. No office blow-out rumbled on until this late at night. Maybe Marinka had found herself another adventure – a sugar-daddy with a thick wallet? Well, God grant her the chance. Otherwise it would be back to: "I'm going to marry you!"

Of course, he really ought to hit the hay. Maxim T. Yermakov's eyes were burning as if someone had sprinkled pepper into them, he had this murky water sluicing around in his head, drawing everything white into its vortex: the curtains, the bed sheets… But in Yandex there were megakilometres of posts containing the opinions of hundreds of strangers about Maxim T. Yermakov. They drew him irresistibly. Popularity was a kingdom of distorting mirrors, and Maxim T. Yermakov was careless enough to step into this region, into the icy waves of those silvered surfaces, in which he either swelled out sideways or stretched out into a thin needle, or divided into semi-liquid sections, like an amoeba under the microscope. It was surprising that the bloggers, who wanted their posts to be accessible to the internet community, had apparently not given any thought at all to the fact that Maxim T. Yermakov himself might read them. That lent his research the frisson of a semi-legal activity.

"I want to put everything out up front," wrote *Lady-Irena*, who chose to be seen in the form of a white rose that looked like a cup of thick sour cream mixed with sugar. "It might come out clumsy, but it just hurts too much. I want to get it out of myself and give it to the blog. Maxim Yermakov is a villain and a monster. How can he go on living when people are dying all around him? I almost died too. This winter is so grey, and my heart is as black as the depths of outer space. This winter I split up with Slavik. They may say there's happiness in solitude too. But that's just beautiful words. I only wish I could sacrifice myself for people! And Yermakov can, but he doesn't want too. I don't understand why.

"I've got lots of things even without Slavik. Here's my list.

"I'm intelligent. That's an indisputable fact.

"I'm beautiful and charming. There's no doubt about that either. Beauty and charm are the most important things for a woman. The glances that men give me are very eloquent.

"I have friends. I wouldn't swap them for anything. I get more than three texts a day from them.

"I have parents and a sister.

"But I'm ready to sacrifice myself without a second thought, especially if I could know that in a hundred years' time people will pass on my name by word of mouth. Everything inside me just turns topsy-turvy and I'm overwhelmed by this desire to do something useful for people, even at the cost of my life. But Maxim Yermakov runs away from his fate. I'll say it straight out, honestly. Maxim Yermakov is a shit."

"I've been stuck down in the dumps since the beginning of the year," announced a certain *Cyber22*, who for some reason visualised himself as a fat black man with a shaved head, looking like a cowpat. "Ever since I got smacked in the kisser on the night of January 2, I just can't pull myself together. Various dreggy people tell me I'm the one to blame for everything that happens to me. Even my friends too. Well, let's say maybe in that particular case that's right. But how can I be to blame for everything? Who needs that? I read various different posts here about the relations of cause and effect and Maxim Yermakov. They say he's the reason for all the bad stuff that happens. Friends, advise me please; maybe I should find Yermakov and grind him down a bit? What kind of dude is he?"

"I've read about Yermakov too," commented *Grampa-poke*, who represented himself with an image of an old man holding open a toothless mouth covered with a grey cobweb. "There seems to be some kind of scientific proof of his special role in history. I've thought about it for a long time. I think people sense scientific laws at the level of their physiology and everyday life. If I drop a stone out of my hand, I know it will fall downwards. Without any physics formulas. If I feel that someone is to blame for the way my life is, then that's the way it is. And lots of people feel that way. Most people in fact. What follows from that? All this about Yermakov isn't crap, it's the truth. Genuinely scientific discoveries. Someone will get a million dollars for the Nobel prize."

Cyber22: "But what do I do? Maybe I should smack Yermakov over the noodle with a crowbar?"

Grampa-poke: "You could do that. It's only a half-hour job."

The gallery of distorting mirrors retreated further into the boundless depths of the internet. After an indefinite period of time, Maxim T. Yermakov felt as if every letter in the text was weeping. The grey patch of the brightening window bled through the curtains, strata of cold tobacco smoke surged and heaved under the ceiling, a harsh scraping sound rose up from the depths of the yard as the Tajik yard keeper hewed at the icy asphalt with his spade, his blue and orange municipal anorak making him look like a tropical beetle living in sub-zero temperatures. Maxim T. Yermakov suddenly realised that someone must be to blame for what was happening in *his* life. The feeling licking at his soul with its slim, sticky little tongue was envy – envy for all his fellow-citizens who had found a culprit in the person of Maxim Yermakov. What a relief that was for them! Well of course, for almost twenty years the people in this country hadn't been given any real chance to figure out who was to blame for the changes that had swept over them, they had always been pawns in someone else's cunning schemes. Where the fuck are they, the enemies of the people? Stuff like this doesn't happen to the people without genuine, insidious enemies! Give them to us!

At this point Maxim T. Yermakov seemed to sink into a strange, fluid haze, a crepuscular murk. The millstone of his heart dragged him to the bottom. This was a new kind of condition that he had never experienced before. Every visual object became repulsive: his mug – because he had to drink out of it; his bed – because it was for lying in; his slippers – because he was supposed to put them on his feet and shuffle along in them. Despair, that's what this is, Maxim T. Yermakov guessed. He stood facing his computer, barefoot, in his dressing gown that had come untied, breathing heavily with his flabby, sweaty chest that had a crest of white fur at the centre. Stop, stop, stop, he ordered himself. This was all planned. This is what the social forecasters are counting on. They deliberately set all this up. He had to break out of this. He needed something to catch hold of, some kind of straw to clutch at. It was as if everything around him was painted, but just scratch the paint and inside everything was the same, all made out of the same grey stuff. And to top it all, that poisonous creep Ika had filched his budget.

Money – that was what would save him and warm his heart! Ten million dollars. The moment he woke up in the morning the thought of them greeted him – not yet fully formed, like the light from round a bend in a tunnel, grey and spectral at first, but opening up like an eye as it approached, gathering strength and life. Money – the vivifying substance that was the true habitat of the Common Individual: like water for a fish, like humus or the layers of heavy deposits on the sea bottom for certain species of micro-organisms. We're going to think about money. In our thoughts we'll open up a flat, heavy little attaché case like so – with a simultaneous click of both springy locks; we'll gaze in reverent awe at the neat, handsome brickwork of those wads of banknotes. We'll breathe in that smell: lots of brand-new dollars together smell like wormwood. Now we'll take out one brick, not exactly from the centre, and not quite from the edge. It's flat and compact, the money isn't bloated yet from the touch of human fingers, it's never given itself to anyone else before us, and the gratifying heft of the wad is like the mysterious, substantive weight of a volume of poetry that hasn't yet been read or even opened for the first time. Ten million dollars. With that money I'll become myself. Life will no longer be a cage. All the lousy freaks, from the state tadpole-heads to Ika, will be rendered powerless. All the hassles will evaporate. Everything that's been happening for the last few months will become insignificant. Tranquillity and freedom will triumph…

And with these thoughts drifting round the room, Maxim T. Yermakov fell into a sweet sleep.

He was woken by the coarse-grained rasping of a telephone. The call was on Just Natasha's landline, which Maxim T. Yermakov hardly ever used, since he had no limit on his mobile. The antediluvian device was located on a rheumatic locker in the very furthest corner and, despite Maxim T. Yermakov's efforts to dig himself deeper into the warmth of the bed, it carried on rumbling away. "What does she want on a public holiday, my best wishes and congratulations?" thought Maxim T. Yermakov, meaning the pestiferous Just Natasha, who never phoned his mobile in order to save money. Still groggy, staggering and slapping his bare feet hard against the floor, he plodded over to the locker, grabbed the slippery receiver, dropped it, caught it as it swayed on its grubby cord among the disturbed heaps of light dust and yelled hoarsely:

"Happy Women's Day!"

"And the same to you," replied an unfamiliar voice, small and whiny, but nonetheless male.

Swearing furiously, Maxim T. Yermakov slammed the receiver back down onto its cradle. He rubbed his palm round his face in a circle, making the stubble rustle, and saw his eyes in the mirror, scalded red by sleep, seeming to question him about something. The telephone immediately distended and started emitting its heavy-calibre trill again.

"What do you want?" Maxim T. Yermakov asked feebly, holding the receiver up with his shoulder as he lit one of yesterday's fag-ends, which tasted of dung.

"Don't hang up, I've got something interesting to tell you," the voice he had just heard said with a nasal twang. "We've got your fiancée, Marina Anatolievna Yegorova. Don't call the cops. Get three million dollars together in used bills…"

"Stop, stop!" Maxim T. Yermakov exclaimed, interrupting the stranger and finally waking up completely in the middle of the cold, smoky room. "Have you lost your fucking marbles, dude? Been watching too many movies? Where can I get three million? If you're short of ten bucks for a fix, then say so!"

"So maybe I should cut off a finger and send it to you?" the unknown caller responded resentfully. "Get this good, we're no softies. If you don't come up with the money, we'll send Marina Anatolievna back to you one piece at a time. First the fingers and toes, all twenty of them. Then the nose, and a foot, and something else that will still leave her alive. And at the end, the trimmed body, in a separate suitcase. Do you really want to receive packages like that?"

Maxim T. Yermakov shook his head, which made the objects in the room scatter and then come back together again, like in a kaleidoscope. Okay, how much did he have in his foreign currency account? If he took it out now and let the interest go hang? What a stupid fool Marinka was, stupid, stupid, stupid! They'd probably invited the great booby to a restaurant, but taken her to a basement where the floor was covered with dusty ice and empty, rusty radiators emitted plaintive cries. Better not think for now. Imagining scenes like that could scorch away all his money – and his nerves too. And worst of all, the dumb pinhead wouldn't even pay him back a cent afterwards!

"Maybe a hundred thousand greenbacks would be enough for you?" Maxim T. Yermakov asked the whining kidnapper in a hoarse voice. "That's all I've got. You ask Marinka, I'm no oligarch."

"You're no oligarch, you're just plain dumb!" the kidnapper exclaimed indignantly. "I told you: three million. It's your problem where you get it from. We couldn't give a toss, got that?"

Somewhere in the background behind the nasal whine, a female voice kept breaking into angry patter, making the kidnapper falter and mumble as he fended it off. There was some flimsy kind of music twiddling and skipping away too – Maxim T. Yermakov could hear the same music, probably being broadcast on TV, coming through the wall from his neighbours, creating the impression of a single open space in which he could reach out and touch the kidnapper.

"All right then, let me talk to her," Maxim T. Yermakov said in a placatory tone, also recalling the content of the relevant movies.

"To who?" the weepy bandit asked in sullen mistrust. "No, not you!" he said with the underside of his voice to the angry woman pressuring him in a fervent whisper that sounded like the hiss of a simmering kettle.

"Marina Anatolievna Yegorova," Maxim T. Yermakov chuckled.

"To her? E-er… Well, okay," the kidnapper agreed feebly.

The cretin dropped the receiver and it clattered on the coffee table, or whatever kind of furniture it was they had. The TV immediately became more clearly audible, now broadcasting (just like the one in the flat next door) a convoluted eastern melody that nagged like an aching tooth. Maxim T. Yermakov listened avidly. No, not a basement. Judging from the dense, bottled-in kind of noise that served as a background for all the other sounds, the accommodation was on a storey very high up, directly above a major thoroughfare, where there was a traffic jam just at the moment. Doors opened and closed in the accommodation, drowsy voices called to each other, plates clattered crudely as they were gathered up off a table, a spoon or fork circled round a plate and jangled on the floor. There were about six of them there, at least. "Come on, where is she?" he heard the weepy individual's voice say, half-sized in the distance. "In the little room, she's still sleeping," came the angry answer. "She's not there!" the weepy one wailed dolefully. At that, two women moving away from each other both started speaking unintelligibly at once, he heard the words "pissheads" and "where've you got to". "I'm in here!" Marinka shouted from somewhere, alive and well, and Maxim T. Yermakov felt an ominous chill in his heart. Another door opened, he heard the unmistakable sound of swirling water from a powerful, hot jet filling a bath. Whispers, exclamations, a plumpish patter of bare feet. Finally, Marinka's voice in the receiver.

"Maxie! They brought me here, they put a bag over my head. Save me, Maxie! They'll kill me! Please!" – every inflection false, the whole thing taken together reminded him of a badly performed refrain from some folk song.

"That's enough!" – that was the weepy one, snatching away the receiver. "Get the money together, you'll get a call!"

For a while Maxim T. Yermakov stared dull-wittedly at the old phone that looked like a skull, yellowed by age but still possessing the jangling remains of reason, as if it was the first time in his life he had ever seen anything like it. Then he went into the kitchen and pulled the festive cake decorated with semi-transparent jelly-like fruits out of the fridge with a crack as its plastic lid opened. He scooped up the slippery fruit with his fingers and devoured it, then wrecked the sweet confection's decor by carving off a fat, milky wedge and eating that too. He licked the messy kitchen knife, catching the sour taste of black metal through the sweetness as the blade tickled his tongue. Right then: what he'd heard on the phone sounded less like drunken bingeing by gangsters on guard duty than the hung-over awakening of a group of friends who'd been on a real bender last night. If someone's just been kidnapped, they don't shout "I'm in here" from the bathroom. And things didn't stack up anyway. Just suppose that Maxim T. Yermakov, impressed by the whiny individual's threats, did obtain the sum of money in the only way that he could, by rapidly scribbling out a will in Marinka's favour and then, like an idiot, zapping himself in the head. Even so, Marinka wouldn't come into her inheritance for at least six months. Were they going to keep her locked up for all that time? Let's say they were, the ransom was big enough to make it worthwhile. But then she would probably have to show up at the notary's office in person and go through the legal procedures. Or could that be done with a power of attorney? Even if it could, the whole game plan was too clumsy, there were too many "buts". It was all too dumb somehow. But then, weren't there plenty of cases when dumbness combined with greed had led to pretty terrible consequences, and the culprit merely fluttered his eyelids in dismay at an outcome that ran far beyond the short reach of his feeble thoughts?

Fuck it! Airplanes were falling out of the sky and buildings were collapsing, the victims were counted in hundreds. The struggle for the rights of the Common Individual required him to withstand all that pressure, and that was like holding up a heavy shield with the entire world pounding on it. Maxim T. Yermakov seemed to have managed it so far, although he was certainly no Titan. But now here was a blow that had sneaked through his defences, and from someone near and dear, you might say. Maybe he should give Sergei Yevgenievich Kravtsov a call? They hadn't talked on the phone for quite a long time already. After all, dealing with kidnappings was his job. Or was that actually the cops' job? Maxim T. Yermakov wondered what was happening right now in the online game "Light Head". No doubt rabid gangs of gamers were busy rescuing a kidnapped brunette, and the virtual visitors to Maxim T. Yermakov's flat were contemplating the ruins of the cake and the pistol-toting briefcase lying in the hallway in the pose of a stray dog.

Maybe he should go and check how his weapon was doing out there?

But just at that moment Just Natasha's phone started ringing again, choking on the grain it was milling.

"D'you think I'm playing games with you, butthead?" the same whiny kidnapper screeched hysterically into the receiver. "Decided to play dumb, have you? That won't work! Does a human life mean nothing to you? Does the life of your fiancée mean nothing? Is your own skin worth more? What sort of man does that make you?"

"Cool it, cool it," Maxim T. Yermakov said with a grin, now that everything had become more or less clear. "What's all the rush? The dames have put the screws on, have they? Including my so-called fiancée?"

"Why so-called?" the weepy individual asked in bewilderment, immediately softening his tone. "Tinochka, now he says…" he said, appealing to his unknown prompters somewhere in that echoing multi-room space. Immediately everything went garbled again, then there was an explosion of female indignation, like a cupboard full of crockery falling flat on its face. In among the general clatter and jangle, Maxim T. Yermakov clearly made out Marinka's cracked crystal.

"Tell you what, Mr. Doormat," he told the kidnapper briskly, "if the ladies wrote the script for this show, but they couldn't find anyone tougher than you to play the gangster, I feel really sorry for them. Especially on Women's Day. You could try cutting off Marina Anatolievna's little manicured finger, of course, only watch your eyes – she'll scratch them out. But don't call me again."

So saying, Maxim T. Yermakov slammed the receiver and its clump of curly cord back down on the cradle. Electrical pulses rippled across the surface of his soul. What if… after all? No, the way things broke down was pretty clear: Marinka feels impatient to get her hands on money she thinks of as hers; Marinka tries to do something about it and comes up with a plan that doesn't even deserve the name, something that could only work in some stupid soap, but no way in real life. The nasty people are so mean, they won't let kitty steal their cream: that was the way she lived, but just how long could that go on, when all was said and done? So she had tried to pull a fast one, thinking no one would actually be wicked enough to apply logic to her plan. But Maxim T. Yermakov had applied it, the ratfink.

Okay, but what if he was wrong after all? Then the promised package would arrive, followed by another call. Any other way simply wasn't worth their while. So what did that mean? It meant wait. And think, think, think about how he could rip his millions out of those social forecasters – those millions that somehow suddenly seemed vulgar to Maxim T. Yermakov – not money at all, but a stage prop in a cheap thriller that he'd somehow got mixed up in…

Yeah, what a great holiday! Maxim T. Yermakov surveyed his dingy residence with his hands propped on his hips. There was dust lying everywhere, it gathered on his finger in the form of coarse, grey fibrous wool. Just Natasha's flat manufactured this thick dust, using some special process that added cement to the fluff. The floor was littered with mandarin peels, desiccated to the tough consistency of dragon's scales, and dirty socks. The well-fingered mirror of the wardrobe was covered in rainbow bruises. Moving in slow motion, Maxim T. Yermakov changed into his baggy old jeans, poured some hot water into a red plastic bucket that turned it pink and set about cleaning the place up.

When all was said and done, it was the best possible occupation for such an indefinite and equivocal day. That pulse of electricity was still rippling through his soul. The bucket, the steamy rags and the effort he had to make to reach the neglected dark corners made him feel hot. The cubic inkwell of the marble writing set contained fossilised chewing gum; the glossy magazine stuck behind the bed in the pose of a pigeon winged by a huntsman absolutely refused to surrender. Here and there on the dirty cups containing black tar and greyish rainbow membranes, he could see the pockmarked traces of Marinka's lipstick: they were the hardest thing of all to wash off. When he ran an old rag over the light, dove-grey bloom left on the table following the destruction of Marinka's box of eye shadow (the eye shadow that gave her puffy, moisture-laden eyes their fake Egyptian slant), it suddenly produced a greasy streak of lilac. The draught that Maxim T. Yermakov had arranged to freshen up his sleep must have carried the ultrafine grains of the substance throughout the flat and now it manifested itself, like invisible ink, literally everywhere – on the floor, on the furniture, on the cold plastic windowsill, the rag brought to light dark hieroglyphs that even generous applications of detergent could barely defeat. The mirror squeaked shrilly as Maxim T. Yermakov, with his brows knitted, wiped it from side to side and bottom to top; he seemed to be sweeping aside a cobweb stretched over an opening and instantly recreating it, drawing it out of the tiny grains that contained an inexhaustible reservoir of pigment.

Fuck it, he'd never wash it off!

And then Just Natasha's telephone started clamouring for the third time. Maxim T. Yermakov shuddered violently, something jerked and snapped in his belly. Grabbing hold of the waggling receiver with a wet hand and lighting up a cigarette that was also wet, as if it was stuffed with mincemeat, he snarled:

"Well, now what?"

"Son, it's your mum," said an insufferably dear, insufferably cultured voice, like a weak solution of sugar in water.

Maxim T. Yermakov caught his breath. What time was it? Still only half past three. She'd got impatient again. She always phoned first on Women's Day and her own birthday.

"Mum, Happy Women's Day to you!" Maxim T. Yermakov exclaimed with a phony smile at the red bucket, in which the heavy water resembled borsht. "Good health, happiness and long life to you!"

"I was just worried you hadn't rung for so long, son. I thought something might have happened to you." His mother's voice was insufferably meek, insufferable in general in every respect, with an after-taste of that sickly sweet syrup the colour of his granny's cataract that he was supposed to take during the season of winter colds, one teaspoon three times a day. The things that came back to mind from his childhood. Maxim T. Yermakov could picture with exceptional vividness his parents' "telephone table", dried-out and fragile, trembling in response to human footsteps that set the venerable phone, even older than Just Natasha's device, jangling as if it was a heavy piggy-bank full of coins.

"So what's up, son? You're not ill, are you?" his mother insisted, ready to break into a shriek in her agitation.

"Mum, what on earth gives you that idea?" Maxim T. Yermakov exclaimed indignantly into the slippery receiver which this time led straight to his parents' home. "I was just busy, doing the cleaning, and I was just going to call you. Why do you go jumping the gun like that? Why are you always imagining things?"

"All right, all right, come on now! Don't talk to your mother like that!"

His mother always moved easily from a meek tone to the senseless banter that she used to drive the neighbours' piebald goat off their plot of land at the dacha – and she used that tone with people when she was caught out in some weakness that was inexcusable in a music teacher so well-known in the town. Indications of this state included fluttering her yellow fingers against the little frills up beside her throat and an abrupt attack of severe short-sightedness, with eyes narrowed in a trembling squint behind the lenses of her gold-framed spectacles.

"Sorry, mum," said Maxim T. Yermakov, retreating straightaway in the knowledge that objections would only lead to a long, drawn-out quarrel, with manoeuvres including insulted silences and phone calls after midnight that solved nothing. "So tell me, how are you getting on back there? How are you? How's father?"

Sighing sadly at first, as if she was reluctant, his mother started telling him. The doctor had prescribed his father a German gel, really expensive, for his joints. His father was really angry, he hollered that the doctors got a percentage for prescriptions like that. Next week, if the gel helped, he was going to go to the consumer protection association, but if it didn't help, he was going to stay at home. Some of his mother's pupils had already come to see her today. Did he remember Lidochka Malinina? She was a music assistant in a kindergarten now. And Tanya Noskova? She was working as a secretary for the director of the Krasnogorie Market. Tanya was really very talented, and look where she had ended up. And some others had come too, all grown-up and handsome, in leather coats. They had congratulated her on the holiday, given her a new coffee-grinder, brought tons of flowers. Last month his father had accidentally broken the big vase, the one with cornflowers on it. Now there was nowhere to put the bouquets, they were just lying on the piano. The trams in town had become very unreliable, but the buses were running well. Just before New Year they had opened a Chinese restaurant where the hardware shop used to be...

His mother's words poured out of the holes in the earpiece like water out of a shower-head, shifting between hot and cold. It seemed as if he could get the hang of the receiver and the cord, he could wash the whole room with that watery rustling. Maxim T. Yermakov couldn't reach his cigarettes because the cord was too short, and he really wanted to put an end to all this by shouting: "Yes, something has happened! Do you want to know what exactly?" But he knew that, paradoxically enough, his mother's perpetual fear that Maxim T. Yermakov had a temperature, had broken his leg or got picked up by the militia had nothing at all to do with reality. In that imaginary world Maxim T. Yermakov had not yet reached the age of eighteen, he was as virtual as a Tamagotchi. There were probably ways of somehow breaking down the wall of mirages so that the black wind of reality could blow into that powdered old face, forcing those screwed-up eyes the colour of a turbid sea wave finally to open properly. And what would be the result of that? No help for her son, no understanding, no moral support, nothing. More likely chaotic protest, an attempt to discover what her son was guilty of, the way he always was, in everything – and she would immediately end up in hospital with a combined attack of all her accumulated ailments at once. It would only be the worse for him. So he had to lie, say all the most natural things like: "Congratulations, mum..." in a lying voice.

"Now you tell me all about yourself," his mother told him strictly after she finished the recital concerning her native town, which from the distance of Moscow seemed to Maxim T. Yermakov like some kind of cardboard model.

"Oh, mum, there's nothing at all to tell," said Maxim T. Yermakov, still dissembling and trying to speak as cheerfully as possible. "I still work in the same place. I had the car repaired recently. Right now

I'm washing the floors… That's all, basically…"

"You're not being honest with me," said his mother, offended (No, I'm not, Maxim T. Yermakov thought to himself). "You're lying to me, of course…" (And how!) But do you remember how you used to tell me for hours about school, about the other boys and girls? You used to come running in, drop your briefcase in the corridor and the first thing you said was: 'Mummy, mummy!' (Now you're lying.) Well, have it your own way. Parents aren't very important to their grown-up children. Will you at least come for your holidays this time, or are you off to Cyprus again?"

"I'll try my very best, mum!" (What fucking holidays can I take now, and if I could, home's the last place I'd go!)

"That's good. You could go fishing with your father. The roof at the dacha needs repairing. Do come."

At long last she hung up. Worn to a frazzle and soaking wet, Maxim T. Yermakov made a dash for his cigarettes. His mother was a sickness. It just got worse and worse. Why were her calls, her meekness, her resentment so depressing? Why, after working on him for just five minutes on the phone, did she remain present for hours, far more distinctly than during the actual conversation? And she always dragged around with her the entire stage set of his childhood, boyhood and youth, incessantly humiliating Maxim T. Yermakov with them, after he had made such great efforts to break free of all that!

Suddenly he remembered, as if it had never disappeared, the long, three-storey, grey-brick building that seemed to be built out of blocks of dirty snow that didn't melt in the summer heat.

The closer it got to the sky, the more the building belonged to the town: the flat roof was overgrown with the dry iron stalks of aerials, on a few balconies there were even white satellite dishes, looking as if they were enamelled on the inside. The lower the building sank, the more distinctly it was mired in rural life. The front yard was enclosed by a sparse fence that looked like a comb with numerous teeth missing, not clogged with hair, but grass, nettles and even raspberry canes, on which bitter berries with three grains ripened in the summer. Inside the yard lazy chickens with axe-head tails strolled about in their grubby drawers. To bring a little culture into the daily round, the inhabitants of the building laid out flowerbeds that consisted of old car tyres with shaggy asters crowded into them. The only thing near the building that Maxim T. Yermakov liked was the old apricot tree: its branches had gone rusty, its twisted trunk was propped up by an iron crutch – but every spring the taut little white peas on it opened up, turning into a dove-grey cloud of blossom that could be seen all the way from the bus stop. The crippled support structure disappeared completely in the apricot's blossoming, only the cloud was left, with a colour and freshness that were entirely of one nature with the clouds of the heavens. The old tree's fruits were always rather wrinkled and seemed to be streaked with blood, the way chicken's eggs sometimes are. For as long as Maxim T. Yermakov could remember, his mother had been allergic to apricots.

The Yermakovs lived on the second floor. The distinctive, sweetish smell of the entrance hall, the distinctive clang with which the iron door cut a person off from the street. A four-room flat that his mother called "four-celled". Even in these times of high property prices it was worth no more than fifteen thousand dollars. There were always numerous flattened, threadbare slippers lying about in the corridor – and no one in the family had a pair of his own. Everyone's food was served in the same coarse pottery tableware, there was nothing personal, except that granny's tea was taken to her in a special, thin cup that looked like bone china, decorated with faded forget-me-nots. According to family tradition, his grandmother was the only one who had been able to play the piano properly, which was impossible to believe, looking at the gnarled yellow fingers knotted together on her stomach.

His grandmother was absolutely tiny, like a little grey monkey; her eyes, set in bitter folds of wrinkly skin, were the colour of chicken broth: the right one was clear, but the left one was clouded by something like the fine oval of fat on broth when it's taken out of the fridge. Granny occupied the very corner of a monumental metal bedstead – its barred headboard and footboard looked like sections of a cemetery fence. She had shared this bed with Grandad Valera until he died. The bed was fenced off from the front door by a narrow bookshelf, crowned with dark, carved battlements, like a tower. Somehow at least three times as many books as the little cupboard was supposed to hold had been crammed into it. It seemed as if one fine day the bookshelf, which weighed so much that no one ever moved it, would explode under its own internal pressure, like a wooden bomb. It was almost beyond the bounds of possibility to wiggle one of the solid, gilded volumes and drag it out, and there was probably no point anyway: all the words inside it must have been crushed. One day Maxim T. Yermakov did manage to get out one vastly thick book that wasn't standing quite in line by pulling it over onto its back, and it turned out to be true: some of the letters in the words were normal, but others had been squashed up and turned upside down. The book, with its spine like a hooped barrel and shabby scraps of tissue paper covering the illustrations with numerous human figures, could not be shoved back into the row, which had closed up tight as soon as it could catch its breath, and it had to be hidden under the divan.

Much later it turned out that the entire library that had fused into a black monolith standing like a dark cliff in the midst of the family's bustling and colourful life was in French. All these bookish riches belonged to granny, but Maxim T. Yermakov couldn't remember her referring to them even once, just as she never sat down at the musical instrument for which she felt a literally physical aversion. The Soviet "Elegy" piano, consisting of a modest shelf with worn keys and an equally worn body that didn't occupy too much space in the sixteen-square-metres "hall", provoked only a sarcastic grimace from granny. "Her standards are too high," Maxim T. Yermakov's mum used to say, in this way defining the absolute egotism in which the little old woman was wrapped, like cotton wool. In the daily confrontation that hovered in the air of those four gloomy rooms, he was on his granny's side. His mother was in the right: she cooked, washed, cleaned and ironed kilometres of bed sheets dried in the wind – but

Light-Headed

Maxim T. Yermakov hated the right and instinctively rejected a life in which all this had to be done. It was this rightness, accumulated over the years, that made his mother's rare calls to Moscow almost unbearable. And his mother's cooking had always been disgusting: cloudy soups with threads of meat and insipid little meatballs.

If only Maxim T. Yermakov's mother had known what he was doing now. He was watching Just Natasha's telephone. For half an hour or more he had been polishing Marinka's little perfume bottle, holding it in an old rag that was velvety with dust. The bottle was slippery and almost melted through, like a caramel, to the sweet yellow filling. Out in the yard some halfwits were setting off thunderous fireworks to celebrate the holiday; on their glowing threads the lights were like balls of different-coloured fluffy wool that had come unrolled. It was already half past seven, the water in the bucket had gone cold, the whole place was topsy-turvy, he ought at least to make some tea and maybe finish off that yoghurt cake.

It was strange how much garbage his memory held. At home for the holidays they always used to buy heavy, square cakes made locally, thickly impregnated with coloured margarine. The arrangement of the decorations on the cake followed the same principle as the checkered cloth on the table. His mother always cut the cake herself, avoiding any damage to a single greasy rose or flourish: she spent a long time measuring things with the knife and wrinkling up her face before she drew the line. For some reason it was very important to her to maintain the decor as if the cake hadn't been touched at all, maybe so that it could all be put back together again. Some of the confectioner's mouldings were entirely inedible colours; coniferous green, for instance, or that whitish blue colour that soap sometimes has.

Granny, to whom they always took the very richest piece, only prodded at it fastidiously with her own old, crooked dessert spoon, tumbled it over on its side and left it lying there on the fluted saucer with forget-me-nots. Maxim T. Yermakov only discovered the difference between a teaspoon and a dessert spoon in Moscow, at someone else's corporate event, with the kind assistance of a bony lady who looked

139

like a bandaged mummy in her designer dress consisting of strips of semi-decayed material. After that Maxim T. Yermakov had done everything possible to avoid meeting the mummy again, although he needed her for business and she had given him her embossed card. At home all the everyday knives, forks and spoons, once washed, had been dumped into the rattly kitchen drawer in a wet, clattering heap. Mum, mum, where were you when I was growing up such an idiot? Mum was at the bus stop by the central department store. She stood there in line with the other tradeswomen, in front of her wobbly packing crate covered with a sheet of newspaper. Standing in a white row on the newspaper, like unpainted matryoshka dolls, were different-sized jars of curd cheese and sour-cream. His mother found it somewhere for four thousand roubles a kilogram and sold it for six thousand. That was the time when the factory his father had been born to was at a total standstill, it had literally stopped breathing and no longer made its familiar hooting, hissing and muttering noises in the night; his father sat quietly in the kitchen with a scowling face and heavy hands that looked like roots torn up out of the ground, or spent his time at the dacha where, for some unknown reason, all his first batches of rabbits died. At that time it was only the women who got things done. Simple women, or women reduced to simplicity, like his mother, could somehow sense the shifting price differentials within the range of their familiar urban districts, the way fish sense the shifting pressure of water; they unerringly located the secluded basement wholesale outlets and set up their planking counters at lively spots. It was only the women then who were able to come up with a kopeck, literally making it out of the harsh, sunny air and the dusty wind that picked up and then immediately dropped its own treasures – glittering wrappers from the previously unknown Mars Bars and Snickers, from chewing gum and cigarettes. No one said thank you to them for that kopeck. His mother's curd cheese was dry and tasted like whitewash: weighing the product and dividing it up between the large numbers of sterilised jars gave the flat the appearance and smell of a children's hospital. Everything that hadn't been sold in two days and now smelled even more distinctly of nappies had to be eaten up, right down to the very last crumb. Even now Maxim T. Yermakov could feel that gauzy taste in his mouth, that insulting picture was still there in front of his eyes: his mother, windblown and erect as a guard of honour, standing over her packing crate counter with a strand of hair clenched in her teeth, squinting enviously at the woman next to her, from whom a particular gentleman with a fat backside is buying a pair of socks. Maxim T. Yermakov was teased about his mother's trade in milk products by all the kids on the block. Now he would have said just one word to those buck-toothed little jackals from the nearby flats – "business" – and they would have shut up instantly.

Until they reach the same height as their parents, children simply don't notice the life that is taking place above their heads. It's like the cloud layer, like the weather; although the virtual precipitation falling from those skies onto the white top of Maxim T. Yermakov's weightless head always generated a cold blizzard inside it, he had forgotten all about that now. One dark memory had been preserved of his mother crying silently, jerking her chin convulsively – from below it had looked as if her own teeth were bothering her. He could have said: My mother's tears scalded the back of my head. But the tears weren't hot, only warm, and they dissolved into the short-cropped hair very quickly somehow, as if Maxim T. Yermakov's hair and skin and very being were a desert, avidly soaking up raindrops. He had remembered this soaking-up for the rest of his life, which was why even now Maxim T. Yermakov didn't like to get caught out in the rain without a hat. There is no logic to the way memories are preserved or fade. The baggage of memory is like the baggage of a refugee, as if a man flees, emigrates, abandons all that he has amassed many times in the course of his life, grabbing in his haste only whatever happens to come to hand. Even while life might seem to be proceeding evenly and normally. What are these changes and breaks that do not rise up to the surface of awareness? Here, for instance, is another brightly-lit picture: his grandmother reaching out her wrinkled upper lip, like a dry laurel leaf, towards her inclined

141

cup in which the tea, visible through the thin wall, is as transparent as honey. Why that? What has it got to do with anything? It seems quite pointless, but if he tries to erase it, he can't.

Later everything more or less came together for his mother. Private lessons appeared and took the place of her lost job in the music school that had been closed forever (following the logic of a bad dream, its building, which was the colour of raw-smoked meat, with white semi-column ribs protruding from it, instantly went to a meat-trading firm). Some parents still believed that learning the piano was good for a child. For the most part it was the star pupils of the disbanded music school who came: a motley bunch, tiddlers and beanpoles, and one who was so large that untrimmed logs seemed to have been used in the construction of her six-feet-something frame. Having been given slippers in the hallway, they shuffled off to the open instrument as if they were on skis. Their soft, rubbery little fingers did not run, but walked over the black and white keys; something about these exercises was reminiscent of little girls' games of hopscotch. If he entered the "hall" during a lesson, Maxim T. Yermakov saw the backs of two lowered heads and four elbows working away – and somehow through the green wall he could also see his grandmother, huddled up under the blanket against the brutish sounds of the pupils' music. Somehow all musical sounds concerned his grandmother in a direct, personal way, they resonated inside her, seeming to affect her actual physical constitution. Sometimes on the radio they broadcast something that sounded like a jumbled, sugary mess to Maxim T. Yermakov, and the effect on his grandmother was like water on a fading rose. But that only happened rarely, all the music of daily life contained mostly poisons that instantly permeated the old woman's aged tissues and only failed to kill her because her blood carried them too slowly through the bluish veins that stood out in places, looking like dead worms. Unlike the rest of them, his granny couldn't listen and not hear; silence was her only refuge.

Not wishing to act as her torturer, and begrudging the time that was needed to torment his games console and hang about down by the garages, Maxim T. Yermakov resisted furiously when his mother tried to coerce him into this musical hammering too. His mother thought the reason for his resistance was that it was mostly girls who studied the piano. She brought up the example of a ginger-haired hulk by the name of Valuev, who had been deciphering the same stubborn little piece for a year, and another redhead, Lenchik Gernstein, with hair like the flames blasting from the nozzle of a rocket, who launched his entire skinny body into the air when he hit the loud, humpbacked chords with his spread fingers. Maxim T. Yermakov did not possess even the basic modicum of ability that these two apparently had. He supposed that his exercises, in the course of which his tangled fingers and thumbs sometimes knotted into obscene tangles, must be driving the old woman frantic.

That wasn't particularly important, of course, old women got all sorts of ideas into their heads. But Maxim T. Yermakov's granny was special, after all. She didn't feel the slightest kindred interest in her only grandchild, not even a shadow of sentimentality, absolutely nothing at all – but that was precisely why Maxim T. Yermakov respected his old gran. Useless and repulsive to look at, with strange deposits under her eyes and on her sunken cheeks, she was, nonetheless, genuinely cool. He couldn't possibly imagine wishing her a Happy Women's Day: the old woman didn't accept anyone's best wishes on any holidays. She was equally indifferent to all of them. Certainly, Maxim T. Yermakov did attract her attention on occasion, the result, as he realised later, of some profound affinity between the old woman's transparency to musically organised sound and the gravitational phenomenon resting on his own shoulders. Beckoning to Maxim T. Yermakov with an index finger that bent reluctantly, his granny would take his head between her hands in the way people hold a dish that they are about to take off a shelf. She felt at Maxim T. Yermakov's cranium with an expression of profound mistrust, setting the brain inside the cranium trembling in layers. The old woman glanced with the same curiosity into Maxim T. Yermakov's eyes and ears, like a cat looking into a mousehole. She must have seen or sensed something; at that time Maxim T. Yermakov had not yet realised that not everything about his head

143

was normal, and he thought a fly or a stick had got in there after all and his grandmother was looking for it, so she could take it out.

Now that was strange: when was it she died? Probably seven or eight years ago. Naturally, she had never called Maxim T. Yermakov in Moscow, and his mother had hardly ever mentioned her, and then the moment came when the not-mentioning lasted for so long that the old woman simply couldn't still be alive any more. Thanks to his mother, he had got the impression that behind her bookcase, the old woman gradually shrank in size and significance until she disappeared completely, without any doctors, official documents or funeral. She seemed to have dissolved into the stale air of their flat, like a lump of sugar crumbling away in a glass of water. Maxim T. Yermakov thought about her quite often – that is, he didn't exactly think, as much sense her presence in his own past, a far more distinct presence than that of his parents. Even so, he had missed her death completely or, rather, he hadn't taken the slightest interest in this distant fact.

His grandmother hadn't been concerned in the least about how he was getting on here in Moscow – unlike his mother, who had demanded detailed reports by phone at the beginning. Maxim T. Yermakov had taken a special kind of pleasure in lying about everything to her – the names of his friends, the names of his lecturers, the arrangement of the student residences, the titles of the new exhibitions and plays in the capital. This had built up in his mother's imagination an entirely fantastical fragment of Moscow, over which she kept mental tabs, clinging tightly in her own mind to the image of Maxim T. Yermakov studying for his exam in a green room on the third floor, whereas he was holding a tipsy female fellow student on his knees in a yellow room on the fifth floor. This telephonic mendacity gave Maxim T. Yermakov a delightful feeling of freedom. No doubt the big, genuine Moscow would simply not have noticed all these makeshift alterations, even if they had happened in reality. However, for his mother, who actually turned up one day to inspect everything, the consequences of this distortion of space were unpleasant. Failing to recognise the grey stuccoed building as the multi-columned and multi-gabled student residence described by Maxim T. Yermakov, she went back down into the metro and trundled from one station to another until late at night, like a ball shifting from hole to hole when a pinball table is tilted and shaken.

And she could quite easily turn up again, couldn't she? Right in the thick of events. He wondered what she would say if she suddenly discovered the whole truth. Her first response would certainly be horror and indignation at her son's failure to comply with the authorities. That little corner of every Russian mother's soul inhabited by self-sacrificing heroism, where the march *Slavianka, Farewell* was constantly playing, would definitely be activated. Her animal maternal instincts had been eroded by education – not only the one that she had received, but the one she had given to her child, based on the inviolable, unshakeable correctness of the surrounding world. "So, everyone marches in step, but you march out of step," she used to say when Maxim T. Yermakov, with his indeterminate head, skipped football – as dangerous as a battlefield with flying cannonballs – in PE, or refused to be dragged off with his class on some tedious and uncomfortable trek. His mother unconsciously used words associated with combat formations, marching, the army and discipline. Marching in step and the mindless unity of boots striking against the ground set Maxim T. Yermakov's head resonating and shuddering right down to his Adam's apple; he could unwittingly puke simply at the sight of a company of lop-eared young soldiers marching along the street in a movie.

He wondered if Marinka had phoned his mother in these last few days. She was quite capable of calling and passing on the news of a happy event: I'm marrying your Maxie. But then his mother would have subjected him to a full-scale interrogation on the phone. And anyway, why get close to your mother-in-law, if you were expecting a multi-million inheritance? Grab the money and make a dash for it, like a rat. Best of all to go somewhere in Europe. Or should he not think about Marinka that way right now? What if some smiling golden-toothed bandit rang the doorbell and handed him an envelope, and there in the envelope was a cold, pink shrimp: a severed finger.

And then you sometimes hear the opinion (Maxim T. Yermakov thought, continuing to chat to himself as he heated up the kettle for the umpteenth time after forgetting to pour the boiling water into the still-wet mug with the sulky tea bag that had soaked up the tap water)… there's this stupid opinion going around that Moscow isn't the real Russia and anything authentic, real life and so forth, only begins outside the orbital highway. In actual fact it was all the other way round. His mother's withdrawal from reality was explained precisely by the fact that she had lived all her life in a titchy, medieval, provincial town with short streets that hadn't given her the slightest mental or visual concept of life beyond its boundaries. The town itself was incapable of generating authentic reality and thereby providing its inhabitants with their own ground under their feet. With the exception of the minute historical centre (a group of squattish plaster-covered structures with geriatrical whimsies, such as a rusty weathercock or a little tower covered in tiles, looking like a pine cone), the town had been built up with structures of widely varying types: the four seven-storey "Stalin blocks" that adorned Factory Square; then the "Khrushchev blocks" only three storeys high here, because the town was so small; then the slovenly five-storey blocks of the nineteen-seventies, their concrete panels bonded together with crude black seams, which, in combination with the bars on the ground-floor windows, gave the impression of a prison; and finally, the buildings from the contemporary series, stylishly faced with ruddy brick, including even one genuinely large shopping centre, consisting entirely of panels of blue-tinted glass that seemed to add a false blueness to the pale sky. Whichever way you looked, you saw a copy, and felt that somewhere there were much better, much more real originals.

Formerly, during the quiet and gloomy Soviet years, the town had still possessed that tenebrous charm peculiar to mist, rain and endless drizzle on a holiday. Later, when perestroika happened and a certain, extremely small, group of citizens suddenly became gorged with money, the non-genuine reality of the place was revealed in all its obviousness. A gigantic green plastic cactus, looking like a bloated New Year tree, stood in front of a restaurant with Mexican cuisine, a fragment of curved, multi-storey roofing was installed above the Chinese restaurant, jutting straight out of the concrete-panelled building like a fish's gill. A new oddity was opened – a casino: in the darkness of night, jets of coloured electricity traced out the likeness of a domed building with two small semicircular wings, but by day it turned out that all this beauty was miraculously supported by a former cinema, so dowdy and dilapidated that it had barely survived the cosmetic repairs to its facade.

Now, after all these years, Maxim T. Yermakov believed that his mother had insisted on buying a dacha in order to give her "four-cell" flat the status of a genuine urban dwelling. The authenticity was derived from the contrast. The "dacha" was a plank-walled little trunk with a patched sheet-metal roof, on an inhospitable standard garden-collective plot, and its roof always leaked. Maxim T. Yermakov could never understand in the name of which ideals they had to go trailing out there every weekend in a filthy, asthmatic bus and then lug their heavy bags for another kilometre and a half, in the ambience, as it were, of their own native expanses, which consisted of prickly crops and stinking cows. Inside the planking box there was a room with two trestle beds and a kitchen with a heap of grey tableware behind a curtain, there was a flat little stove that blew acrid smoke out of its cracks as the coarse firewood caught light, squeaking from the damp. Life refused to take hold in this non-real little house; in only five days, a shirt left behind at the "dacha" developed a covering of delicate decay, the fine, sepulchral velvet that was typical of all the heavy "dacha" clothes; coarse-grained salt, tipped into the salt dish only the day before, set as hard as granite.

All this wouldn't have been too bad if, for instance, the dacha had served for children's games, like that fairytale hut that flaunted its bright painted walls on the playground in the courtyard in town and often contained vodka bottles that had rolled in under the bench. But his parents regarded their dacha with obtuse seriousness. His mother crippled herself on the vegetable rows, loudly singing the praises of the rich black earth that didn't exist anywhere else in the world, apart from her plot of land. The black earth was truly glorious: in a mild winter it coloured the melting snow like Chinese ink, and in summer it mostly nourished luxuriant weeds, for some reason begrudging the mighty power of its juices to the carrots and beetroot. Maxim T. Yermakov's father had beaten it into his own hard head that rabbits, since they reproduced so actively (he loved to repeat the words "in geometric progression") would solve all the family's problems with money and provisions. The little beasts were actually rather large, with donkey-sized ears and size forty rear feet. However, Maxim T. Yermakov could only ever remember the family eating rabbit meat once: it was tough and dark, it got stuck in his teeth, and his memory had preserved the picture of his father wiggling his scarlet ears and biting into a rabbit leg that was dripping grease, as if he were trying to comprehend some difficult truth.

Basically, his father's business plan was a resounding failure, the geometrical progression let him down somehow. But Maxim T. Yermakov didn't blame him for that. What he couldn't forgive his father for was never summoning up the will to buy a car, and therefore never teaching his son to drive. As the family, laden with its heavy baggage, trudged its way to the dacha along the rutted earth road and the neighbours' Zhiguli overtook them, crunching the shifting gravel, his father's face assumed an expression as if someone had loudly fouled the air. On the outskirts of the garden cooperative, close beside a bitter-green alder grove, there was an old Zaporozhets automobile that had once been blue and was now blind in both eyes, standing on bricks instead of wheels. Maxim T. Yermakov loved to climb inside it, onto the ripped driver's seat, and waggle the collapsing driving wheel about, imagining that he was driving a car, that he was already grown up. With the first money that he earned (by reselling two "400" computers), Maxim T. Yermakov bought himself a heavy IZhak motorbike, also very far from new, with a leaky accumulator and worn seats, built to a design that still preserved the memory of the glorious cavalry. He spent the entire summer reassembling the weary old warhorse. Of course, he wouldn't have dared to expose his fly-through head to a head-wind and all of its dangerous contents (he knew that the air always contained more objects than the average person thought: from insects and rotten wood dust to flowerpots falling from balconies), but that problem was solved by the helmet, which was actually one of the reasons for the purchase of the motorbike. In this cosy item his head became calmer and denser, it no longer sensed those ticklish draughts of information. But he couldn't just walk around in a helmet, like some kindergarten pupil dressed up as a cosmonaut for the New Year party, could he? Maxim T. Yermakov bought a new, expensive helmet. Red and sturdy, with double ventilation, the size of a vacuum cleaner, it gave him a sense of security with which absolutely nothing could compare. In effect, the purchase of the motorbike and accompanying outfit was the first real happiness in Maxim T. Yermakov's life. And that was when he really felt for the first time that he and his father were completely different people. Maxim T. Yermakov's father somehow receded abruptly and developed the habit of looking straight past him, and when he did address a few words to his son out of necessity, he seemed to be straining to see something behind his back – something important that his son was annoyingly blocking from view. The purchase of the motorbike had made Maxim T. Yermakov grown-up and unnecessary at the same time. Sometimes he was unable to hide his joy after a good spurt along the highway and plumped down at the supper table with a broad smile on his burning face. Then his father would quietly get up, hoisting up the table and its jangling dishes slightly as he rose, and shuffle off, stooped over, with his dull, sloping bald spot reflecting the light bulb, to his bed "cell".

Presenting his parents with bills for payment was an absolutely pointless exercise. The more points there were in those bills, the more it would cost him. Not only could he never mention any overdue bills, he had to try not to let anything at all slip out, not even hint in his intonation, in a single word. He had to smile crookedly and put up with family conversations in which there was nothing about the important things, in which each phrase was passed in the same way as salt or pepper is passed at the table (his mother broke plates occasionally, but not all of them). If he tried to wake up these grey-haired, sickly infants to reality, he'd end up with a catastrophe. With his mind (not his heart, alas), he realised that his mother and father had lived their lives inside a black-body radiator, that they were unfortunate people, that they could always come up with something in response to his grievances: two bouquets of chronic illnesses that had never been treated properly at the district health centre, two pairs of weary hands and hard, calloused feet, a green carpet trampled like a lawn, a cracked kitchen windowsill with the indelible impression of a newspaper that had once dried onto it, murky jars of some kind of food in a rattling fridge, ingrown toenails, broken spectacles, the perpetually leaking roof at the "dacha". They genuinely didn't realise what had happened to them. They didn't understand that the state had screwed them over real good, and so had the factory that was once their life, and that, as a matter of fact, no one had any plans for either of them to live long or prosper.

They should have opened their eyes to reality when they still had some strength left, some time before the age of thirty-five. It was too late now. Look, his father had gone running off to Factory Square again for his fix: red banners, revolutionary marches and a pompous orator on a grandstand, the two of them together looking very much like the bronze busts of war heroes and labour heroes that stood in a line in front of the factory's checkpoint. It actually seemed as if they had dragged one of those snub-nosed idols to the square and set it up before the people, and all the other blockheads had something to say as well. An absolute funny farm. Could his parents have changed anything, if they had lived with their eyes open? Hardly. It would still have been the same flat, the same factory and those shameful fermented milk products as a means of survival. But they would at least have been unhappy like human beings. They wouldn't have crawled from one state of abject misery to another, even worse, pretending that a trestle bed and a crooked privy in a vegetable patch were good things. There wouldn't have been any "dacha" for sure. And there wouldn't have been any holiday camps with tents for ten people and dancing-schmancing to a smartly lacquered accordion.

But the way they were now, he honestly didn't feel sorry for them.

Every child has a dark boundary line that cuts across his life, a line that he steps across, raising his knees high. Before that frontier, you're certain that mum and dad can do anything, that the only person better and stronger than them will be you, when you grow up. After it, you see your parents as they really are, and you have nothing to talk to them about. There are several such twilight zones in childhood, but their nature has not been well studied. The only one that is really well known and has been described adequately is when, at the age of five to seven, a child realises that he will die, and everyone will die, and mummy and daddy will die too. Maxim T. Yermakov made this discovery at the usual time – with some assistance from Grandad Valera, who was found already cold one morning, beside grandma, who had shared the lacy, dilapidated bed with the dying man to the end. The next period of twilight descended only six months later. Maxim T. Yermakov asked his father: "Dad, will you be the boss when you get old?" – "Maybe I will, maybe I won't," his father muttered, lowering his eyebrows over his rapidly blinking eyes. But back then Maxim T. Yermakov believed that all grown-ups or, at least, all proper grown-ups, became bosses when they got old, just as a pupil in the first class would graduate from school in eleven years' time, unless he was a hopeless dunce. Now, at the age of reason, Maxim T. Yermakov realised that the question he had asked his father was probably the most painful of all for him. But that realisation didn't change a thing. In his memory, his father remained helpless and angry, with a scrap of paper stuck over a cut on his shaved chin, pulling his belt out of his crooked twisted trousers – although he never could bring himself to use it for educational purposes. Well, and then there was the detestable "dacha", the tedium, the mosquitoes, the brownish canned-meat soup in enamelled bowls, the white Zhiguli on the next plot of land – the only one in the entire garden collective – the black little pond with its disgusting, silty bottom that felt alive, the rain, the damp fog, the coarse grass.

What are you thinking about, Maxim T. Yermakov. Not thinking about Marinka, are you? Not thinking properly at all. How often had he called her mobile before today? A couple of times a week, at most. But now he'd made maybe a hundred calls in a single evening. The pest had got what she wanted: Maxim T. Yermakov was dreaming harder than he had ever dreamed of hearing those mewling Moscow vowels of hers in the receiver. But then, so what? The thoughts of Marinka still left his head almost as soon as they entered it. An amusing memory: probably until about the eighth class Maxim T. Yermakov understood the expression: "It goes in one ear and straight out the other," quite literally, taking it as confirmation of the fact that everybody's heads were unbounded spaces. Otherwise, why would they say that? Now, there was an interesting thing: why did Sergei Yevgenievich Kravtsov have such an unusual, semi-transparent bubble on his shoulders? Maybe he was originally an Alpha Object, but had somehow been cured – with radiation treatment or injections directly into the head? There had to be a reason why he didn't have a single hair on his bubble and why that cephalic formation had such a strange shape, like an octopus. He could assume that like attracted like; probably all the top brass on their special committee had brain abnormalities. What if there was some kind of cure for this supposed Alpha problem? But they weren't telling Maxim T. Yermakov about it! Just shoot yourself, and that's it. Sure, coming right up. Why's the time dragging so slowly? The clock's barely even shuffling along. Here I am sitting like a wooden doll at a wooden kitchen table, left to my own devices for an entire eternity. It's hardly surprising that the colourful memories come creeping out of all the cracks. And my mother triggered the whole thing with her holiday phone call.

In childhood everything is authentic. "Our shop" – the one Maxim T. Yermakov used to call into with his mother on the way home from the kindergarten, was the most important shop in all the boundless neighbourhoods roundabout. There were diagrams as colourful as maps hanging up there, showing how to butcher a red-and-yellow cow's carcass; it was always dark there because there were so many people, and the people didn't pack into the shop just any old way, they always formed two thick queues, coiled into a single snail; there was a saleswoman in a gauze cap, who put the goods on the scales and froze the moment she took her hand away, enchanted by the mystery of equilibrium wrought by the pointer quivering to a halt.

Not far from the shop was the "Kremlin", a long wall of red brick with juicy burdock creeping out from under it with a special, insolently joyful kind of strength. Maxim T. Yermakov was certain that if he walked right round the whole wall, he would definitely see that tower with the golden chimes and the New Year tree star that they sometimes showed on television. And in general, everything around him possessed the vivifying power of authenticity. The old oak tree with the stone-coloured bark that grew behind the kindergarten and broke up the asphalt with its roots was the only one like that in the world: it looked as if it was much bigger under the ground than above it. There was mystery in the old communicating courtyards that mum used as shortcuts on the way home; the yellow, plastered buildings that surrounded them looked ordinary from the street, but in the yard they were covered with a pattern of cracks and blisters, they overlapped each other at strange angles, displayed dull, uninhabited windows and drainpipes like rusty dragons in surprising places. The foliage in those yards was always damp, like oil paint, in winter icicles, some as thick as a birch tree, froze onto the tinplate cornices here and there.

When spring came, the snowdrifts subsided, turning black and wavy so that they looked like mussel shells; streams murmured in low, guttural voices as they carved through the ice and soil, down to the whitish sand; in summer faint scars from the streams remained on the ground for a long time. The capricious little river that flowed through the town made a loop not far from their building, he could see a little bit of it from the window, glittering and glinting in delicate stars among the more material and coarse gleam of foliage. The river was delightfully small, but it smelled bad. They said its bed was tainted, rotten, so no one swam in it or went fishing there; his father brought his bloody, plump carp from "the lake", where Maxim T. Yermakov had never been. But he often used to run to the river without his parents' permission, together with the young neighbourhood jackals who were sometimes friendly, sometimes hostile. The lads used to scamper about on the concrete blocks that protruded from the water, overgrown with slippery, bright-green waterweed. There they used to catch nameless fish as black as leeches, scooping an old shirt into the water and hoisting it up, together with the mud and the catch, a heavy bubble of water foaming out through the material. There they splashed in the water, in the scorching heat, clambering out onto the bank with silt in their underpants and a taste of iron in their swollen throats, like the taste if you take a punch directly on the snout. There on the cluttered bank Maxim T. Yermakov, keeping slightly aside from the most boisterous hi-jinks, once found a woman's earring the size of a fishing hook. There he was once given a thrashing for no reason at all by some freaks he didn't know, with bulging foreheads and shaven skulls that looked like crudely peeled potatoes; it was strange that the blows to his head didn't hurt, but on the inside his head just got tighter and tighter, it felt as if any moment it would deliver a blast that would sweep aside the freaks and everything else with them.

In his childhood, then, a genuine world was built out of squalor and garbage, and that world was ready to extend its authentic reality beyond forests and mountains, to the entire country. Only it turned out that no one wanted him and his shit. Before entering into relations with Moscow, a young man like Maxim T. Yermakov becomes aware of himself and his place in life through his relations with the centre of his own town. There was a little capital there too – clean, neatly trimmed and washed and, by local standards, very expensive. As teenagers they went strolling along Lenin Street and sprawled on the chairs at the white metal tables outside the fashionable Bavarian Court beer hall, watching through narrowed eyes as a fat girl with a fat plait swept tenacious pieces of paper out of the lawn with a household broom and two other girls with expensive outfits and cheap little local faces slipped voluptuously into an elderly Volkswagen Golf. Lenin Street, Factory Square – that was the genuine little old town, everything else was submerged in dust and obscurity, it wasn't a town in the full meaning of the word. All the centre girls, carrying

154

their self-importance along on heels as high as fence posts, paid zero attention to the pimply-faced riff-raff who had rolled "into town" on their battered mongrel bikes for a swig of beer. The sophisticated in-crowd that eddied in the evenings around the little black Chekhov, reading his little black book written by God knows who, swept the rabble into the stiff, coarse bushes.

That was when Maxim T. Yermakov, who by that time had watched a whole heap of Hollywood movies on video tape, came up with the escapade that was the only good memory he had brought with him to cold Moscow from his native parts beyond the capital's Orbital Highway. Once upon a time, during his parent's youth, photographs indicated that the town had been populated by a large contingent of broad-shouldered statues that graphically illustrated the ideals of the time, patches of white in among every half-decent clump of bushes. They included copies of the infamous Soviet classic, "Girl with an Oar" and her close relatives: laid-back steelmakers with their visors raised; collective farm women with massive sheaves of wheat, like the capitals of thick columns; scientific youths with their scientific instruments, which looked more like gardening tools; and also, for some reason or other, discus throwers, both large and small, sporting plaster underpants for the sake of decency. With time the ideals crumbled, and the same thing happened to this pantheon of the parks: only occasionally, in some remote corner overgrown with weeds, could you come across a mutilated bogeyman with a face like a boot print and, instead of arms, dusty reinforcement wires on which an occasional wrist and hand had been preserved, dangling like a glove. Then these cripples were gradually cleared away too. By the time Maxim T. Yermakov reached the final class in school, from this once-numerous family of statues only ten were left – and only because they stood on the edge of the roof of the most prestigious Stalinist apartment block, erected for the top management of the factory. Withered and wind-worn, they were indefinite silhouettes against the languid heavens and although they had initially all been different, now they seemed identical, resembling shadows or columns of smoke. As the years passed, these final demigods had clearly altered their poses, hunched over and now, instead of gazing forward, they looked down to where the municipal authorities had recently created a pedestrian zone and laid beautiful beige paving slabs. The statues who had outlived their time must have found the seven-storey abyss attractive, they wanted at long last to reach the ground and shatter into crude chunks among recoiling passers-by, thereby recovering their lost materiality, in the way that people redeem their souls after death. Maxim T. Yermakov spotted all this and figured out how to make spectacular use of it.

To start with, after first donning his motorbike helmet to condense his rarefied head, he climbed up to reconnoitre. Discovering among the reinforced entrances one in which the iron door was clucking helplessly with the tongue of its broken lock, he made his way through a trapdoor that wasn't locked into an attic crunchy underfoot with clay pellets and aswirl with the ghosts of pigeons; from there, after breaking the decrepit planks out of a skylight, he climbed onto the roof, promptly receiving a bracing sluicing-down from the strong, imperious wind of freedom. Here every step resounded like thunder; on the rust-red sheet-iron roofing, installed at the precise angle to make it almost impossible to keep his footing, even with half-bent knees; flakes of rust and paint and some other dry, hard garbage bobbed up and down; the dried-up puddles around the rim of the roof looked like rags. Here the statues seemed huge, like grey elephants rearing up on their hind legs. Spreading his feet wide and making his way with small, firmly placed steps along a balustrade that was still whole in places and had crumbled down to the steel reinforcing rods in others, Maxim T. Yermakov crept round all the graven images. Even close up, even by touching their traumatised arms and the rough folds of their garments, whitewashed with bird droppings, he couldn't tell what material they were made from. In the flexed elbow of one, apparently a woman, he discovered a rock-hard carton from a kind of fruit ice cream that hadn't been produced and sold for ten years or more; in profile many of the statues looked like noseless skulls. For his spectacle, Maxim T. Yermakov chose one of the more imposing examples – a male idol of a now indeterminate profession, who was gazing in exactly the right direction: down at an embryonic square right at the centre of the facade, a far more comfortable space than cobblestoned Factory Square – it was even adorned with a little round fountain which, seen from above, seemed to blow twinkling kisses into the air.

The next morning the district riff-raff arrived at the small square, rattling and weaving heavily between the flowerbeds on their bikes – three IZhaks and two Urals. Dangling over his shoulder Maxim T. Yermakov had an old "swear-box" style megaphone which, thanks to the technical expertise of one of the young jackals, now worked on modern batteries. Fortunately, no one had got around to repairing the previously reconnoitred entrance. In the attic Maxim T. Yermakov got tangled up in washing lines tarred black by time and scrunched clay pellets, raising a cloud of dust that set the entire attic space, transfixed by slanting beams of light, shifting in spectral fashion. On the roof the harsh sunlight transformed the metal covering into a slanting, abstract ruler; with the crown of his head Maxim T. Yermakov could feel a ticklish spot of sunlight blazing on the red motorcycle helmet.

Just as he had expected, he could already hear a hubbub down below. When he got close to his graven image – moving far more confidently than the day before, but still at a skewed slant – Maxim T. Yermakov saw people flocking towards the rudimentary little square. From up above the people, consisting of heads and feet that were alternately thrust out and gathered in, looked like snails creeping along, only rather quickly.

"He's going to kill himself! The man on the roof! Look, he's going to jump any moment!" the young jackals shouted, warming up the crowd.

When Maxim T. Yermakov appeared, the crowd started making even more noise. People backed away, craned their necks, dropped handbags at their feet; the upturned faces looked like plates of boiled vegetables. The young jackals piled on the heat, revving up their idling bikes.

"Hey you, ladybird!" yelled a man in the crowd who had a

moustache and a waistline that quivered like a lifebelt in its tight-fitting yellow shirt. "What do you think you're up to, eh? Come down, or we'll hand you over to the police!"

"Ladybird, ladybird, fly away home!" some small kids in back-to-front baseball caps chanted in chorus and scattered in all directions, croaking happily like frogs.

Maxim T. Yermakov drew himself as erect as the abyss clutching at his legs would allow. He looked at his stooping idol, as if asking: "Ready?" The idol remained silent. Its heavy head, with a covering of cylindrical curls that seemed to have been wound on gigantic rollers, was drifting into a cloud stretched to the point of tearing, with insanity shining through it. There was a damp streak on the giant's battered temple, as if the statue could weep tar; between the chiselled fingers of an extended hand, where the winds had blown in a little soil, a stiff, wiry little stalk, bearing a clumped-up, blind little flower, bobbled about like a toy.

"Attention," Maxim T. Yermakov said into the swear-box, but he forgot to raise the visor of his helmet, so the word only echoed in his head. "Attention, citizens!" This time the megaphonic summons rumbled out right across Factory Square and, like a wind-up toy with little toy figures, the square turned another third of the way through its tight revolution and stopped dead.

"Go on, Maxo, tell 'em," the young jackals yelled up to him, waving the bandanas they had taken off.

"Go on, Fatso!" yelled some young hussies with paste-diamond hair slides blazing in unbearably bright flames on the tops of their heads.

"Citizens, I'm not the suicide! I'm the negotiator!" Maxim T. Yermakov was bursting with inspiration that literally raised him up slightly above the surface of the roof, so that the soles of his scuffed Grinders scraped freely over the reddish-brown iron. "Look here! Look at this man!" Maxim T. Yermakov took hold of the statue by its mutilated elbow. "He's been standing here, so handsome, for so many years. And watching you ugly freaks! He's fed up with it! You've finally pissed him off, get it? He wants to jump and smash himself to pieces. But let's ask him to stand like this for another ten years! Admire the view a bit longer! Enjoy watching what assholes you all are! Let him put up with it! How can he get away from you?"

The sound that rose up from below in reply was like a muffled blow on a tambourine, accompanied by a murmuring of little bells. The crowd around the fountain was swelling rapidly, pressing up against the young jackals on their metal ants. A mechanical wailing came from the direction of Lenin Prospect on the right and two militia cars flashing beams of radiance drifted through the human waves like fragile rafts.

"Don't jump, friend! Don't do it! Life is beautiful" Maxim T. Yermakov exclaimed, dropping the megaphone behind his back and putting his arms round the statue.

The first thing he felt was the abiding, integral chill coming from inside the statue, piercing through his jacket and his ribs. Then Maxim T. Yermakov's head seemed to start spinning slightly as the insane cloud turned dark, like a photographic negative, and the sky gave a sudden lurch. In reality it was the statue that had listed over on its crack-riddled pedestal with a heartrending, rasping groan. The next moment the statue hoisted up the flimsy down jacket that overlay Maxim T. Yermakov's body with a snap and scraped across his stomach like ghastly sandpaper as it tore reinforcing rods and lumps of concrete out of its pedestal, like roots with lumps of earth on them, and launched into space with an impassive face, floating down towards the crowd. The statue's motion was devastating. As shocked as if a rocket had just blasted off out of his arms, for a while Maxim T. Yermakov couldn't understand what he was and where he was, he only saw the stone idol slowly turn over in the air and literally explode on impact with the beige paving slabs; through the fractured lumps and grey dust a primitive iron skeleton became visible and the giant's head bounced off and plopped into the fountain, goggling out of it with one eye wide open in amazement. At this point Maxim T. Yermakov suddenly felt that he had very little anchorage: one foot, with air in a boot that had come untied, was dangling over the abyss as the knee of his other leg slithered down the slope of the roof, and the dilapidated section of balustrade that could barely hold back the weight of his horror-numbed body was slowly buckling, preparing to let the negotiator fall. Everything down below was like a dream, the square with the remnants of the idol was inclined at a strange angle, someone who looked like a cockroach was being helped to his feet and a bunch of bluish-grey militiamen were squeezing into the entrance of the building.

With an incredible effort, pawing desperately at the roofing, Maxim T. Yermakov pulled himself back a metre from disaster and got up on all fours, feeling a sticky spot on his stomach turning cold. After that, instinct dragged him along on its lead. He rumbled across the booming iron, broke the fragile planks out of the very furthest skylight, tumbled into the attic, which was still deserted, and then, by good luck, found himself in an unfamiliar hallway and an old woman who was taking out a little bag of modest garbage let him out too. This distant entrance opened into a side street occupied completely by a twin-peaked garbage tip, onto which the old woman tossed her fluttering contribution with a certain degree of elegance: behind the overflowing rubbish containers a grinning young jackal, who by some miracle had figured out the situation, was waiting on Maxim T. Yermakov's impatiently roaring IZhak.

"Maxo, the helmet! Ditch the blankety-blank helmet!" the young jackal screeched as soon as Maxim T. Yermakov flopped, hissing, onto the saddle.

The helmet, decorated with starry dents, went flying onto the garbage tip like some simple saucepan. The bike roared and set off slowly and heavily, picking up speed. Maxim T. Yermakov's head was left unprotected and the air swept straight through it, full of prickly, stinging particles. The clever young jackal, who knew all the holes in all the town's fences, tore through the factory site; the grey buildings were like gigantic beehives, and out of them grey, stinging bees flew into Maxim T. Yermakov's brain. They jolted over the sleepers of a narrow-gauge railway line, skipped under a trembling boom that was being lowered and came out onto a soft country road. Forest plantations flickered past, bright with sunlight, hazy agricultural expanses stretched out and away; the bike seemed not to be moving, merely buzzing and spluttering like a fly against a windowpane. But they got away after all.

At the feast of victors on that rip-roaring evening, Maxim T. Yermakov's head, stuffed with crunchy garbage collected during the pursuit, demonstrated for the first time its ability to project alcohol into space. Maxim T. Yermakov sincerely believed that the clever young jackal who had whisked him away from under the very noses of the pigs was now his friend for evermore. However, that same evening his saviour, baring his rusty little teeth in a grin, declared that Maxo owed him money. So Maxim T. Yermakov gave him money: he sold the red-hot IZhak and greased the young jackal's palms generously, knowing already that he wouldn't be riding the bike round the little old town again. The little old town ceased to exist. Maxim T. Yermakov didn't even bother to enquire if anyone had been hurt when the statue fell, he only saw that the other idols had also been removed; short-lived ghosts lingered briefly in their places, twinkling fragilely, like gigantic mineral water cylinders – and then they disappeared too.

There was only May and June left until school graduation. The little old town was transformed into a blank space, a white spot on the map – as if, despite the warm weather, it was blanketed with perpetual snow. How many white spots like that there are on the map of Russia, how much snow there is in the country! Moscow, only Moscow – how eagerly Maxim T. Yermakov had striven to be there, how hard he had tried to fit into those cheap, cruddy digs, where the baths were dirtier than the toilet bowls at the railway station shithouses, until they gave him a bed in a student hostel; how hard he had worked to pay for college, in a shameful dump of a shop beside a metro station, flogging the citizens shaggy children's toys in poisonous colours – until he had wriggled and twisted his way into his present transnational trading niche, where he decided for the first time that he had made it! And now here he was, sitting in his rented flat as if he was perched on the edge of a precipice, raging furiously as he devoured the sticky mess left over from the cake, snacking on a dried-up heel of lightly smoked salami at the same time. All his achievements were there with him. The bucket of dirty water glowed red in the centre of the room, grains of ice clattered against the window panes, the concealed video cameras peered out of their cracks, wiggling their antenna-whiskers, the social forecasters dozed peacefully on the windowsill in the stairway.

This was three o'clock in the morning. And that was a ring on the doorbell.

There she was. The poor little kitty. Her open fur coat was covered in wet clumps, as if it had been licked by a tongue, the way a cat cleans itself. The yellow dress was crumpled and covered in watermarks from dried-out spilled drinks. The nails were torn, the long, sharp-toed boots were fastened up crookedly, but every last one of the fingers on her trembling hands was unharmed.

"Well, holiday greetings to you! Happy yesterday, my dear!" Maxim T. Yermakov said with an ironic bow.

His face was instantly stung by an oblique slap. Maxim T. Yermakov had never felt any slaps like that before. His left cheek, which caught the cracker, was immediately a whole kilogram heavier than the right one. Apparently his head was by no means as weightless as he had previously imagined. Ah, you little bitch! Three million dollars for your pin money? Here, take that!

Marinka flew back against the door jamb, clutching her face. Maxim T. Yermakov's palm burned and itched as if he had parried a heavy pass in volleyball. The door to the stairwell was still open and a social forecaster, roused from his sleep, climbed up to the landing on light feet, cautiously thrusting out a long, semi-transparent nose and a blinking eye set beside it.

"None of your lousy business, shove off!" Maxim T. Yermakov yelled at him and slammed the door furiously, imagining in passing, at terrible speed, how instead he could have made friends with the officers, found out the timetable of their shifts, invited them in for a glass of tea, enquired after their domestic circumstances, sympathised and felt for them, made his own complaints about women and bosses. Everything heartfelt and human. When it came down to it, what made him any worse than the hospitable old woman Kalyazina from flat four hundred and six? The social forecasters could have used his toilet, with Just Natasha's precious toilet bowl. Instead of which, Maxim T. Yermakov felt like opening the door of the flat and slamming it again, this time making sure to catch the semitransparent nose that looked like a slippery piece of ice.

"Yowa bashtad, Max-ie... Wotta bashtad yowa!" Marinka lisped, somehow managing to straighten up on her heels.

She was clearly well hung-over. Her left cheek was blazing, her long mouth was bloodied and flattened against her teeth, barely able to unglue itself from them. And yet the eyes in yesterday's peacock makeup glowed with such genuine, bright despair that Maxim T. Yermakov felt slightly frightened. What if they really had done something to her? Clinging to the walls of the hallway, Marinka pulled her boots off and hobbled through into the room with the angled-heel gait that women have after wearing high stilettos.

"What kind of show was that you put on? Who was that moron who called me? Are you going to answer?" asked Maxim T. Yermakov, following Marinka and just managing to grab the splashing bucket out from under her feet in time.

"How cyud you, Maxie, how cyud you..." Marinka swayed to and fro, hugging her own lopsided shoulders. "Aren't I even a khuman being? You couldn't care less if I die, is that it? Aren't I entitled to anything g-good at all in my life? Let them cut my fingers off, let them chop my legs off? Like some d-dumb animal? No one will even turn a hair..."

"But you set it all up!" Maxim T. Yermakov yelled with his hands on his hips. "Do you think I didn't hear you answering that halfwit from the bathroom? The receiver was just lying there! There was no kidnapping! No one was going to cut off any fingers. You all had a good time, slept wherever you fancied with whoever was there, and then in the morning decided to improve your financial situation. Where would I get you three million greenbacks from?"

"What's more valuable, a khuman being or three million?" Marinka snarled back, her eyes flashing under louring brows.

"But where could I have got them from? Tell me how you see it happening. Come on, lay out the sequence of events," Maxim T. Yermakov demanded.

He wanted to make Marinka let something slip, something like: You write a will and then you shoot yourself. Then, having said that out loud, she would realise the seriousness of the whole business. Instead of that Marinka threw her head back, scattering her tousled mane across her clenched shoulder-blades like black soot, and howled at the ceiling. She howled from the heart, straining her white throat – and her wailing glissandos were filled with such wild, vulpine despair that Maxim T. Yermakov understood. Only a few days before he himself had sunk into despair – into an entirely unfamiliar, murky medium, more like a liquid than a gas, that had squeezed at his heart the way a current of water squeezes rubber boots against your legs. Marinka's moment of the Great Wipeout had arrived, and she poured out her heartrending complaint about the mismatch between her and her life. About not having been born in a rich, high-ranking Moscow family and not having everything that ought to be hers automatically, just because she lived in the world; about how she could probably have grown up a good girl, with a neat parting on the warm top of her head and eyes filled with sweetness and light – but she had to play the trollop, get down low and dirty, and even then, even then happiness wasn't granted to her, and she could never settle for a life without that simple Moscow happiness, not ever, no way. So tell me, is a human being worth more than three million dollars? Look at me, I'm a human being, where's my money? Why don't you answer, you scumbags? A-ooooh! A-ooooh!

Marinka's absolute intransigence – that was what Maxim T. Yermakov hadn't noticed before. Marinka would beat her head against the wall that divided rich Moscow from the influx of provincials and others – she would beat herself to death against that wall, leave her caked blood on it. There was a kind of grandeur and heroism in that too.

"Okay, go and wash up, I'll make some tea," Maxim T. Yermakov muttered in a conciliatory tone. "You need some sleep, I won't give you coffee."

"Sleep! Wizh you? Are you totally off your trolley, Yermakov?" Marinka smiled a caked red smile, revealing her split gums. "You betrayed me. You hit me. You're capable of hitting a woman, you brute! I've got a wobbly tooth now. You bashtard... " At this point she screwed up her face, making herself ten years older, and the peacock-blue makeup flooded down her cheeks, flushed away by the copious flow of moisture from those two springs that glowed so unbearably bright. "I was going to marry you, Max! Maybe I loved you and I was testing you. Now it's over, understand, it's over! Give me my bag right now!"

With a shrug of his shoulders Maxim T. Yermakov handed Marinka the bucket bag with a dirty fringe that she had dropped on the floor beside her collapsed boots.

"Not that one, you cretin! A big one, or some kind of suitcase! To pack my things!"

Maxim T. Yermakov obediently dragged out of the wardrobe a dismal, hollow-cheeked suitcase with wheels that stuck. He had come to Moscow with it ten years before and lugged it round the city from one lodging to another. A pair of jeans and a t-shirt from the little old town were lying in the suitcase, fused into a bundle that still smelled, through the time and the dust, of some immemorial laundering, plus a short black jacket of polyester fibre that used to whistle as he walked along, but had now clotted into a prune – and everything was such a small size, almost like a child's, although Maxim T. Yermakov was by no means a child when he came to the capital. Before he could even grab his long-lying relics out of the suitcase, Marinka's bright-coloured glad rags started flying into it, instantly withering into a heap in the past tense preserved by the suitcase. Marinka ran round the flat, stomping with her heavy heels, barbarously stripping the hangers in the wardrobe, grabbing a scarf, panties, a crumpled silk gown from here and there. Bottles of nail varnish, swept from the windowsill into a plastic bag, clattered as they landed on top of the glad rags and were buried under angular, dried-out underwear brought from the bathroom, looking like tattered dustjackets from romantic novels for women that had been read long ago; they were followed in by a mug, a spoon and a fork – there was something of the convict about that, as if Marinka was going to jail.

Finally she cast a maniacal glance round the messy, chaotic room, closed the suitcase and pulled the ossified zip shut with furious jerks. The suitcase looked even more dismal now, with one side bulging as if there was an elbow poking out from inside.

"Give me some money," Marinka demanded, struggling to squeeze her feet back into her boots.

It couldn't be helped. Maxim T. Yermakov took out his wallet and opened it, pondering the meagre wad of five-hundred-rouble notes. How many should he give her? If things went on like this, soon he'd have to dip into his special stash, simply to live. Before he could even glance over his shoulder, Marinka had plucked out all the money, leaving the wallet gaping in wide-mouthed amazement, with just small change in its crevices. "Treat the girlies well in bed, never let them give you head," – Maxim T. Yermakov suddenly remembered his Grandad Valera's jingle, for which granny used to threaten to hit him with a French book, even while she giggled. "I can't recall how long it is since I realised that life is shit," he added on his own account.

"Maybe I could give you a lift to wherever you're going?" he suggested reluctantly, following Marinka and his departing suitcase into the yellow lighting of the hallway.

"I can manage. Azh it happens, there's a car waiting for me downshtairs," Marinka blurted out spitefully, floundering in the sleeves of her slicked-down fur jacket. "I hate you now, Yermakov, so there. Oo-ooh, how I hate you. All these years I've wasted on you. Coddled you. Never mind. You'll pay for efery tear I'fe cried. You'll pay with a bullet, that's how. Do you think I'm not a human being? That I've got no dignity? Just wait, we'll meet again!"

With these incoherent threats Marinka finally made her way out into the stairwell, shoving the limping, lopsided suitcase along. The lift, which had probably not gone anywhere since it brought Marinka up to that floor, opened immediately, obligingly rolling its rumbling glassware out at Marinka's feet, and she kicked it furiously. The lift doors closed together and the dark stairwell clattered like the breech of a shotgun.

Shuddering slightly, Maxim T. Yermakov rubbed his chilly shoulders and walked back into the flat. There was a grey track mark from a suitcase wheel on the toes of his high-class Cesare Paciotti shoes; the briefcase, which now lived in the hallway, like a dog with fleas, was slumped against the wall in the stooped pose of a drunk. In the room Maxim T. Yermakov suddenly felt as if he had been robbed. That was the way everything around him looked – as if the place had been looted. Although, in fact, Marinka had taken only her own things, taking absolutely no notice of the other objects, relegating them to the status of junk. But wait: the cubistic inkwell and the other cubistic doodad with two black nostrils for pens were now standing separately on the honoured teacher's desk, but the base of the writing set was missing. He wondered what Marinka could have wanted with that unsightly piece of marble. Just Natasha would freak out. "And all the years that *I* wasted on *you*," thought Maxim T. Yermakov, slumping onto his plundered bed with no woman's body in it.

She's gone – so great! We won't be asking her back.

March, and even April, in Moscow is still not spring. It's the void between winter and spring, when time doesn't move forward, but staggers to and fro, and hot days are jumbled together with icy ones, shuffled up like cards in a pack. The meagre snow that had functioned during the winter months as an accumulator of grime and trash had melted, leaving its withered and faded chattels laid out on display – washed-out scraps of paper, brittle, ash-grey scraps of polythene, flattened cigarette butts. Before the industrious Tajik yard keepers could even rake the lawns, wet flakes started streaming down, reducing visibility and speed on the roads to the approximate level of a foaming car wash, the only difference being that bathing in this slurry didn't make the cars any cleaner; tents collapsed under the weight of snow in the camp ground of protesters against Maxim T. Yermakov. For a week the temperature danced so closely around zero that all water was left in a transitional state resembling glue. Then it turned warm again and dust with the taste of burnt paper was replaced by dust with the taste of ground pepper. As soon as the trees warmed up and buds formed on them, transforming smooth branches into serrated ones, the white flies started flying again and overnight everything swelled up, the ground becoming like a thick sheepskin, tinted reddish-brown by last year's grass. These abrupt changes in the weather gave Maxim T. Yermakov a filthy headache – and the tablets that helped ordinary people had no more effect on him than alcohol.

However, the changeable weather was not the worst of his worries. The local minimarket, which only recently had welcomed him so amiably, flatly refused to serve him. The same thing happened in all the other shops nearby: the security guards put on faces of tin, blocked Maxim T. Yermakov's way and tore the trembling basket out of his hands, responding to his rancorous prods at their solar plexuses with dark smiles. Maxim T. Yermakov remembered that no matter what, he mustn't end up with the militia. Although he couldn't give a damn for Foetus and his state tadpole-heads, he caught himself feeling fainthearted in the face of shop-door security men, who looked like lanky, overgrown schoolboys in their short, jerked-up uniform jackets. This timidity was a bad symptom, very bad; but even so Maxim T. Yermakov started avoiding retail outlets at which food was sold.

He would probably have slid gradually into starvation if not for the accommodating alcoholic Shutov. In his holy simplicity this native Muscovite, indelibly impregnated with a bitter, fleshy scent, reminiscent of the smell of tomato seedlings, who rode jauntily in the militia's imported automobiles to his second home in the monkey cage at the station, clearly did not understand what was going on all around him. When he got back from the office, Maxim T. Yermakov rang the bell at the low dive's leatherette-covered door; the turbid peephole went dark and blinked, after which he had to wait another fifteen minutes, listening to strange sounds, as if they were moving furniture about in the dive. After that the door opened ten centimetres and Shutov squeezed deftly through the gap, like a rat, always leaving one of his tattered, flaking house slippers inside. Sometimes, instead of Shutov, a crumpled hussy, sloppily wrapped in a dressing gown, came out onto the landing, and sometimes a naked woman's arm with gnawed, varnished nails and wet fluff under the armpit was simply thrust out. Maxim T. Yermakov handed over his shopping list, with the money wrapped in it, and went on upstairs. Only a short while later Shutov or one of the hussies showed up with the food and a detailed financial report. Just as they didn't allow him into their flat, they wouldn't enter anyone else's, and hung about on the landing in full view of the duty detail of social forecasters, who cast irritated glances at the unauthorised activities of this antisocial element. At first Maxim T. Yermakov was afraid that the tarts, driven by professional instinct, would attempt to squirm past him like fish, swim into the flat and into his bed. But the hussies behaved quite untypically: they stood to attention, with their crooked legs set close together, leaving yawning gaps like the ones in half-log fences. They were all quite strangely unattractive: crude moles, long mouths, the gristly noses of school swots – and, in all honesty, with legs like that they shouldn't wear short skirts with slits almost all the way to the none-of-that-funny-business. Of course, the alcoholic Shutov's dingy flat wasn't the kind of place where you would expect to encounter Claudia Schiffer out of the blue. The girls were all very diligent – diligence was probably the only positive aspect of their dubious professional competence; there were often explanations on a piece of paper attached to the receipts, written in neat, girlish handwriting that looked like narrow, fine lacework. "He gets them from an orphanage, that must be it," Maxim T. Yermakov thought, meaning the alcoholic Shutov and his workforce. In their financial accounting the inhabitants of the low dive were honest right down to the last kopeck; their fee was always two bottles of vodka, the very cheapest, capable, one might think, of fatally poisoning the girls' anaemic bodies. Maxim T. Yermakov had suggested several times that the alcoholic Shutov should take good vodka. But Shutov, clearly incapable of understanding why anyone would pay more for the same strength and volume, only shook his dishevelled locks with their greasy highlighting of leaden-grey hairs.

"Vodka's not for your health anyway," he explained to his naive neighbour. "Just the opposite."

True enough.

Maxim T. Yermakov kept waiting to see what the social forecasters' next move would be. In spring the tadpole-heads were faced with new problems: immense forest fires started up everywhere and smoke came billowing in from the deep corrugations of the taiga as if the earth had split open there. The news showed blurred, flaming ulcers, the size of entire electric-bright cities, filmed from helicopters, the sparks and flakes of ash raised up into the sky by the heat, the expanses of pine trees blanketed in smoke, with a sheet of phantom snow spread across the ground below it. Siberian townships blazed, homeless victims howled and hugged their children, the vague forms of sooty automobile carcasses stood along the edges of roads, the human casualties were counted in the thousands. New characters appeared in the online game "Light Head" – the fire fighters without whom no serious mission was now possible. The virtual fat man acquired the ability to breathe out mighty jets of flame that instantly transformed special agents, strategists and marksmen into blazing torches. The fire-breathing monster literally blew centuries-old villages and rural streets familiar from TV reports off the face of the earth; the only thing that could stop the fat man was a fire engine that jangled like an alarm clock with a nimble crew.

Basically, it was another graphical explanation for the people of who was to blame for everything. New, more intensive measures had to be taken to neutralise Maxim T. Yermakov. And then one day, as he ran into the office past the picketers, who were daubed dramatically with soot on account of the fires, Maxim T. Yermakov saw something that literally sent his heart sinking into his boots.

Was it him or not? Maxim T. Yermakov thought about it the whole day long, staring at the dusty desktop covered with finger doodles. That man standing there with a blank look on his face, holding the pole of a banner the way that people cling to a handrail in the metro. Too small for Vovan Kolesnikov, too narrow in the shoulders. But nonetheless it was him, Big Vovan: his grey stubble looked as if it was mouldy, his mattress-stripe down jacket looked as if it been sewn from the same collective farm jacket out of which Maxim T. Yermakov had once filched a dirty envelope stuffed with dollars. Maxim T. Yermakov didn't actually recognise Vovan with his eyes, but with his solar plexus, which started jigging in terror. Somehow Skewbald and Kazakh became associated with Big Vovan to form a three-in-one terror: Maxim T. Yermakov was haunted by the phantom of a mirror-bright flick knife, grinning at the spring sunshine pouring in through the window, tickling his skin, trimming his hair that was standing up on end.

What could he do? From the porch to the Toyota, prudently left in a secluded side street, was a fifteen-minute run. And it wasn't that easy to run in the crisp plastic raincoat that protected Maxim T. Yermakov against the rotten vegetables now that spring had arrived – it created a steamy, hothouse atmosphere inside itself. Vovan would probably come again tomorrow. Those ratfink tadpole-heads knew their job all right: they had dug up the one man who could really poison Maxim T. Yermakov's life, brought him here and stood him in a conspicuous spot.

The working day came to an end and people perked up as they poured out of the offices to greet the good weather. In his opaque raincoat Maxim T. Yermakov looked like an advert for some packaged meat product as he trudged along at the back, one of the last. Vovan was standing in the same place, smoking a cigarette, clutching it between his irregular teeth that looked like small stones; the other end of his banner was being held aloft by an old woman with a hooked nose and grey hair, who looked in profile like an old white crow, but it had slumped noticeably at Vovan's end. Heaving a deep sigh, Maxim T. Yermakov prepared to make a run for it – and was amazed to find his legs, suddenly light and uncontrollable, carrying him directly towards Vovan. This was terrible, this was impossible;

about ten metres away from his enemy Maxim T. Yermakov caught a single molecule of that familiar people's cologne, as shaggy as a wasp, and with every step the swarm grew thicker, flowing into his distended brain, as if the wasp's nest was in there.

The disconcerted picketers, mostly elderly women in black gauze scarves, pulled back; the banner gave a crack as it pulled taut, revealing what was written on it: "Yermakov, our children died because of you!" Vovan spat out his *papyrosa* and the glare of his swollen eyes – blood-red and salty blue – focused at a spot somewhere near the bridge of Maxim T. Yermakov's nose.

"Well then, Vova. Hello, now that you're here," said Maxim T. Yermakov, almost unable to hear his own voice through the buzzing of the wasps. The fear made his hand, freed from under the raincoat and held out to his enemy, feel as if it was wearing a prickly wool glove.

Vovan blinked and squinted in surprise at his own dark claw of a hand. Holding the pole of the banner under his arm, he held the claw out, as if he wasn't entirely convinced that it existed. The handshake turned out crooked and painful; Vovan's claw was nowhere near as huge as Maxim T. Yermakov remembered it, with short fingers as yellow as fag ends, but it still possessed an immense, crude power that fused Maxim T. Yermakov's bones together.

"How's life, Vova?" Maxim T. Yermakov asked cheerfully, squeezing out a smile.

In response to that Vovan's mouldy face twitched into a grimace of haunted spite, immediately making it clear that Big Vovan's life was far from sweet.

"I owe you some money, remember?" Maxim T. Yermakov said with a smile so broad that he could feel the springy resistance of his own ears.

"Right," Vovan confirmed cautiously and his voice, rough and hoarse, was still the same voice that used to bring Maxim T. Yermakov out in a cold sweat ten years earlier.

"Let's go to my place, I'll pay you back," Maxim T. Yermakov said with the definite sensation of watching himself in some strange kind of dream.

Big Vovan's eyes, as bloody as fish entrails, started tumbling about in their sockets.

"What makes me so lucky all of a sudden?" he wheezed, cringing.

"I just happen to have the money," Maxim T. Yermakov replied honestly, recalling that he had dollars at home – the "grey" part of his salary, paid in an envelope.

Now it was Vovan's turn to start to waver, trying to step left, right, forwards and back in his battered trainers.

"Let's go," Maxim T. Yermakov said decisively and set off along the half-demolished line of picketers in the direction of the parked Toyota.

After hesitating a little longer, Vovan set out after Maxim T. Yermakov, as if he had been magnetised by the promise of money, and the hook-nosed white crow was forced to amble after them with a cry of protest, until Vovan caught on and simply dropped his pole of the banner on the ground. As he passed the state security van, this time decorated with an advertisement for a tourist agency, including two notional palm trees that looked like green table lamps, Maxim T. Yermakov noted with malicious glee the long faces of the social forecasters on duty. Thoughts flickered through their blinking eyes like the symbols on the revolving drums of fruit machines, until they halted on the same one: if they could have killed him, they would have. "But you can't!" Maxim T. Yermakov exulted inwardly, dispatching a sumptuously indecent gesture in the social forecasters' direction.

It was clear from the start that he would have nothing but trouble with Vovan, who moved uncertainly, swaying to and fro, each foot trying to take a half-step sideways with every step forward. At first Maxim T. Yermakov thought that for some reason Vovan didn't want to go to get his money, but then he guessed that it was just the way he walked: the way people shift a heavy wardrobe, swinging it from one corner onto another. On the comfortable seat in the Toyota, Vovan became small and withered again; it was obvious he had never ridden in such classy automobiles before. After knocking a pack of cigarettes off the dashboard onto the floor, Vovan tried to fish the fallen item back up, squirming himself blue in the face in an uneven struggle with the safety belt restricting him, his massive clumsy legs sticking up like a tank trap. Maxim T. Yermakov drove the Toyota mechanically, thinking: "Why am I doing all this?" The car was buzzing, filled with a swarm of almost imperceptible dots; Maxim T. Yermakov felt as if he was driving a ticking bomb on the passenger seat – only the bomb, extracted from the crowd of picketers and effectively stolen from under the very noses of the social forecasters, now belonged to him for a while.

In the stairwell the duty officers, evidently already informed by colleagues of their Object's behaviour, tried to incinerate Maxim T. Yermakov with their withering glances, but the Object briskly shoved the hijacked Vovan into his stuffy flat. Gazing around, Vovan removed his battered footwear; his socks were slightly different shades of cheap grey cotton and a fat callous peeped out through a hole in one like a red eyeball. In the kitchen Vovan immediately cowered in the corner and pulled his head down into his shoulders as far as the ears, which now looked like vegetables taken out of hot borscht.

"Coffee?" Maxim T. Yermakov suggested sociably, taking hold of the kettle.

"Money."

"Whatever you say."

In the room Maxim T. Yermakov took the pack of dollars out from under a heap of laundry (just recently they'd been giving him the frayed bills that were disliked so much in Moscow's bureaux de change) and counted out twenty-five ragged Benjamin Franklins. Then, as if someone had nudged his arm, he added another five.

"Here, take it. With some interest too," he announced proudly as he came back into the kitchen.

Vovan grasped his unexpected windfall with both hands, which were trembling noticeably. It took him a long time to calm down, he rubbed every bill between his fingers as if he was hoping the friction would separate a hundred bill into two. Finally he packed the dollars away in the inside pocket of his down jacket and fastened them in there with an evasive little button.

"Right, now I can take a drink, if you'll pour me one, of course," he said in a mellower, hideous voice, sticking his huge smelly feet under Just Natasha's snow-white table. "Keep the coffee, what I'd fancy…" At this point Vovan raised his eyes to the ceiling, as if anticipating that a bottle of vodka would come drifting down to him, suspended on silken threads.

Maxim T. Yermakov went over to the bar, scratching the back of his head. He spent a minute trying to choose between whisky, vodka and cognac. Then, prompted by intuition, he raked all the jangling bottles together into his arm, like sticks of firewood. Why save the stuff, when all these elite tipples were damp squibs for Maxim T. Yermakov himself? He basically kept his supply for girls, but girls weren't the most important thing right now. At the sight of such expensive booze Vovan's face seemed to light up with sunshine. Maxim T. Yermakov, having decided to go the whole hog, sliced a heap of salami and opened packs of sliced meat and fish, decimating the reserves delivered the day before by one of the diligent whores.

Vovan consumed alcohol like a pro, with due respect for the shot glass. He filled it right up to the edge, with a rounded hump, hunched over it as he raised it to his half-opened mouth and dashed its contents abruptly into his throat; the movement had a special kind of smooth fluidity to it, reminiscent of the snatch of oars in an impetuous swirl of water. Out of politeness Vovan paid almost no attention to Maxim T. Yermakov's parallel glass, which made fewer moves and never emptied itself, he merely reached out with the bottle occasionally to "freshen it up a bit". Yes, life had turned out shit. He'd done a two-year stretch, every single day of it. No one who hadn't trodden the ground of the "zone" could know what that meant. His mother had died while he was inside. She walked around with appendicitis for a week, afraid they would ask for too much money in the hospital. She was afraid to pay for anything anywhere, thought they would charge her a million for macaroni in the shop. A fool, even if she was his mother. Then, when they took her off in the ambulance, she

discovered they cut out appendices for free. And he'd done his entire
stretch with no food parcels, on nothing but skilly. Well, once he
was back on the outside, he'd worked here and there. Couldn't go
to college after the camp, could he? He'd just done evening classes.
This kind and that. He went wherever the courses had good grants.
He'd been sacked from his last job for being truthful. No one likes
to look the truth in the face. He, Vovan Kolesnikov, had told the
foreman straight: Valerii Pavlich, he'd said, you're an asshole. Of
course he was an asshole, everyone knew it. Well, they gave him the
push on the spot, supposedly for a breach of safety regulations, they
didn't give him three months' pay, said the station didn't have any
money. You can take some written-off equipment if you like, they
told him, start your own business. But what kind of equipment was
that? Pure suicidal it was, forget about any safety regulations. Take
it, they said, you're welcome! Uhu, what kind of idiot did they take
him for…

Ask about someone's life, and you have to listen. Once he was
relaxed, Vovan spoke at length, with the commonsensical obtuseness
of a proletarian who has seen all sorts of things. Every now and then
he squinted down at his own chest, at where the money was hidden,
as if he had just been awarded a shiny new medal. Overcoming his
horror – a feeling like a sticking plaster being repeatedly ripped off
his heart every minute – Maxim T. Yermakov observed his visitor
from the past, rather than listening to him. At the very beginning
of the spring warmth Vovan was covered with a coarse, dark tan
– it was clearly years old, stained in; his neck, streaked with white
wrinkles, looked like fried bacon. The rustic tattoos that once made
Vovan's fists especially terrifying had blurred, like ink on blotting
paper: on his right ring finger a wedding ring that had grown into the
flesh gleamed a dull yellow.

Had Vovan been married? Well yes, he was still kind of married
now. Nadya worked as a machinist at a factory, or maybe she didn't
work there any more. He'd come home once a bit drunk, Nadya
had fallen over herself to throw him out and he, Vovan, had upped
and left. He, Vovan, was always on the side of truth, including in

family relations. That was the way Vovan was, don't monkey with him. But Nadya was a good woman: when that asshole of a foreman gave Vovan the push at the station, she came to take him home. She washed all his things and rustled up some rissoles. And then Maxim's people showed up, the grey men in the vans. They offered him work in Moscow, all he had to do was stand in a picket line, five hundred roubles a day. Nadya started shouting: Don't go, I'm afraid. But there's no point listening to women. Who else would offer him a job like that? And taking a ride into Moscow was interesting too, to remember his young days. And now look how well things had turned out: he'd met an old buddy and the buddy had paid back his debt. Maybe Vovan really should set up his own business. Buy a little house by the sea, cater to the tourists – diving for all comers, ten minutes at three metres down. Always free for old buddies!

"Stop, stop!" Maxim T. Yermakov interrupted, waking from his trance. "What job did you do for that asshole of a foreman?"

"Are you deaf, or what?" Vovan asked in surprise. "I told you in plain Russian: a diver at the diving station in Samara!"

So that was it! That was what all this was about. Maxim T. Yermakov's plan for "shooting himself" and still staying alive had suddenly moved from the sphere of mirages to reality. What was required for a high-quality simulation? For the body to disappear immediately after the shot. Where to? Under the water. A shot to the head on a bridge at night, a somnambulistic flight with the pistol in the slack hand separating from his body like a shuttle from a space station, a brief impact against black ripples, blurred surroundings, enveloping murk, faintness, a hired professional giving Maxim T. Yermakov a hose to breathe from, dragging him as far away as possible, to a deserted riverbank. And then the social forecasters could go whistle, they'd never find him. Let them trawl the bottom, looking for a drowned man. That still left a heap of problems, of course – an honest heir, false documents. But everything could be done for money. He could even have plastic surgery on his face, so that his own mother wouldn't recognise him. But his mother had absolutely nothing to do with this. Afterwards he could send his parents two hundred thousand greenbacks for a life on easy street. Although they'd still live a pauper's life even with a million, or two, there was no cure for that.

The conversation after that was conducted with heads close together, to the jaunty yackety-yack and blaring music of the Autoradio channel, cranked up to full volume for the overworked ears of the social forecasters. When Vovan deciphered a proposal to add another ten grand to the three thousand dollars he had already acquired, he got really excited and turned as proud as a peacock. The reddish-brown folds under his chin started flapping about furiously. Vovan seemed to regard any money that he earned as an award, not recompense for his labours, but a decoration or, at the very least, a medal. Maxim T. Yermakov's proposal transformed Vovan into a potential Hero of Russia. Accordingly, the retired diver, breathing garlic fumes, began describing the difficulties of the enterprise. Equipment was the first. A dry diving suit, a buoyancy control device, special thermal underwear, a mask, this and that, two sets of everything, each costing two hundred thousand roubles. The Moscow River was the second. The flow rate was regulated, a system of locks, like valves in a water main – the current was weak, dead slow, there was about three metres of silt on the bottom, plus sunken water craft, cars and refrigerators. There were even corpses! And the third thing was Maxim T. Yermakov's total lack of training.

"How were you planning to jump? Belly-flop onto the water? Have you seen a stuntman? You'll hurt yourself so bad, I won't be able to pick you up underwater, you won't be able to breathe any air at all." Vovan drilled the lesson into Maxim T. Yermakov, leaning his chest into the plate of salami. "And how's your health? My health was good enough and it still is, but how about yours? Do you know what barotrauma is? Your blood vessels will get ruptured to fuck and you'll end up lying in a hospital bed like some handsome marble Apollo, covered all over in fine veins. And you have to know how to work with the equipment, but you'd be like a fart in a trance, you couldn't even switch on a lamp under the water. How am I going to drag you along? And what if I pick you up underwater alive and pull you out a dead man?"

All this was entirely just. In reality the undertaking looked frightening and extremely uncomfortable. He really would have to jump from a height into murky river water, flounder about in that insanitary environment, clamber out soaking wet onto a boggy riverbank, lie low somewhere for six months, waiting for the money, then make his way out of the country, and obviously not through Sheremetievo airport either. Not to mention the fact that Big Vovan, who set Maxim T. Yermakov's skin creeping, would be hanging around for a long time. But there was absolutely no way to avoid it all. The very thought of always having to live in a flat with built-in TV cameras and drive around with the social forecasters' painted-up vans on his tail was enough to make Maxim T. Yermakov really want to shoot himself for a second. Right, right, that was what they were counting on. He had to make sure Vovan was seriously interested, especially since he could come in useful after the jump. Use him to rent a little flat in some quiet spot outside Moscow, run errands, do this and that. Or get the alcoholic Shutov involved.

"By the way, afterwards you can keep the equipment, both sets," Maxim T. Yermakov suggested in a loud whisper, at the same time insuring himself against buying any old junk that had been glued back together.

"That's great! Now that's what I like to hear," Vovan said with a grin, showing his grey, cracked teeth and bluish gums close up. "Okay, let's go for it. The things you do for a buddy. You give me the money for the equipment, I'll get it in and work with you a bit, find some stretch of water, even if it's a village pond with carp in it. You'll have your own personal training programme. And we'll have you jumping before you know it!"

Vovan received the money the very next evening, the entire sum in brand-new flame-bright five-thousand-rouble notes: he plodded along the familiar route to the parked Toyota, still heated from his activity in the picket line, where, incidentally, he had hit Maxim T. Yermakov on the shoulder with a rotten egg. As he counted the money and tucked it away, he thriftily held his stock of missiles on his knees in a paper bag.

"Do they hand those out to you or do you get them yourself?" asked Maxim T. Yermakov, nodding at the filthy bag with its bottom covered in snot.

"They're mine, they went off, so why keep them?" Big Vovan replied matter-of-factly, fondling the five-thousand notes. "But they bring stuff in every morning, entire crates of tomatoes. And sometimes there are pears, and kiwi fruit, and bananas, I haven't seen it, that's what people say. Sometimes there are only two or three rotten tomatoes in an entire crate. People grab them quick, take them home in their bags. Well, of course, some don't take anything, they've got someone who's died… well, that's their business. It keeps the women happy anyway. They can them, do this and that with them. I'll call my Nadya in, she can stock up with a few cans too."

Vovan didn't seem at all interested in what was happening around him and why he had to throw rotten vegetables at Maxim T. Yermakov. He had a few amorphous ideas tumbling about in his head – about the run-up to the election campaign, about a movie being made. It was none of his business. Once he had the four hundred thousand, he set about buying the equipment. Together with the money, Maxim T. Yermakov handed Vovan his old, greasy mobile phone with a new SIM card and instructed him only to call on business, in order not to flash the number about unnecessarily. But Vovan called him almost every day: he asked for advice, boasted, sent crooked photos of something or other that looked like huge dead tropical fish. At first, after looking round the sites, Maxim T. Yermakov decided that Vovan was jacking up the cost of the equipment, but then he realised that, strangely enough, the retired diver loved his underwater occupation and was avidly making the most of things.

"What bridge were you going to jump off?" Vovan asked about two weeks later, sitting in the rumble and roar of Maxim T. Yermakov's kitchen, where he had made the cosy spot in the corner all his own. "Give or take, there are at least twenty of them here."

Light-Headed

Maxim T. Yermakov wanted to jump off the Krymsky Bridge. Under that bridge, no doubt because it was a suspension structure, the water had a special kind of expression: calm and inviting. The river under the Krymsky Bridge looked as if it was stretched taut, like the safety blanket that firemen, for instance held up so that people could jump out of windows without hurting themselves. No doubt this provocative feature explained why the Krymsky was Moscow's leading bridge when it came to suicides. The Large Stone Bridge wasn't too bad either, with its postcard views of the Kremlin and the samovar shape of the Cathedral of Christ the Saviour; its imperial cast-iron railings with banners and stars were also very convenient for climbing up in shoes.

"You're supposed to be smart, but you're a real fool," Big Vovan responded furiously to this choice. "Are we going to climb out onto the bank right under the feet of people who are out on the town? Or do you think I can crawl twenty kilometres along the bottom with a handy hulk like you? And we have to look at what the bottom's like. Or else you'll jump straight onto a spike, like a butterfly in a collection. I don't want anything like that. I'll have to work on it myself, reconnoitre, see what's what."

Vovan started doing just that, as soon as he'd spent all the money he was given for equipment. He got into the habit of showing up at Maxim T. Yermakov's place at midnight to regale his investing partner with reports from underwater and help himself generously to the contents of the fridge and the bar. He arrived, massive and damp, leaving a trail of footprints on the floor in the hallway, his lumpy toes creaked in his crooked socks and his stomach rumbled on the way to the kitchen, as though there was an aquarium inside him, with a powerful aerator at work in it. He guzzled and drank absolutely everything there, with the exception of coffee, which he despised. The tiny kitchen, filled to overflowing with radio broadcasts alternating with crackling interference, seemed as isolated as a river under the ice to Maxim T. Yermakov's blocked-off hearing; the upstairs neighbours pounding on the ceiling were like fishermen trying to break through a hole in the ice to lower in their bait. It was hard to talk without raising his voice to a shout; he had to slip along under the strata of noise, let his voice nestle against the table top, from which a fork or a knife fell to the floor absolutely soundlessly. Big Vovan managed it better – no doubt that was down to his prison skills, rather than his underwater ones.

According to what Big Vovan said, which Maxim T. Yermakov made out partly by reading his lips, the bottom of the Moscow River and the Yauza were like jelly. Maximum visibility was about one and a half metres. Murky haze, drifting flakes, sunken logs. The broken-off stern of a boat, white and battered, like a whitewash bucket. He'd almost got snagged on it. Nobody cleared anything up, and this was the capital's main waterway, blankety-f...ing-blank! From the bottom the sun was just barely visible, trembling faintly on the waves, like a little fish in a net. And the depth was only four metres, what a joke!

"It's impossible to dive in the centre of Moscow," said Vovan, staring straight into Maxim T. Yermakov's eyes in his agitation, as if inviting him to glance through his dull, glassy, blue peepers and straight into his soul. "The patrols they have there! Sharks! You forget about the Krymsky Bridge."

According to Big Vovan, several times he had seen side tunnels blocked off by metal bars, with bunches of military divers hovering beside them. The tunnels probably led to somewhere in the Kremlin, or to a secret government bunker. The bars were overgrown with waterweed and wriggled as if they were alive, like worms in a jar, and the darkness behind them was absolutely terrifying. Better not go sticking your nose in there! Vovan had almost been arrested underwater on his own, but if he was dragging someone else along, what would happen then? These two divers suddenly appeared out of nowhere and the slippery characters – so help him, they had heads like the civilian boss who came to hire Vovan for the picket line: like long balloons, not inflated very tight – had already grabbed Vovan under the arms. It was lucky Vovan had managed to wriggle free. He was slippery as an eel, Vovan was. And he was lucky too!

As proof of his good luck, Vovan showed Maxim T. Yermakov

some money. He had found a purse and three wallets on the bottom. The woman's purse, half-digested by the river, had only small change in it, he couldn't make out what time it was from, it was all scabby. But the three men's wallets were pretty fresh and very well stuffed as well. Big Vovan carefully dried the money out on the radiator. Probably he could change it for new notes in a bank? A bank was obliged to accept any notes. Vovan's haul was leathery, warped and faded: the only evidence that this washed-out paper had once been money was its distinctive format, not really recognisable by sight, but from a reflex response of rejoicing in the subcortex. Only here and there was it possible to make out Lenin's frowning profile, or the slim mouth of the Queen of England. That meant they were pounds! Big Vovan wasn't giving up hope. He already had a whole rucksack full of dried money like this from his hauls in the Volga. If he was going to set up his own business, it would come in handy. Vovan had also found in the Moscow River a rusty knife without a handle that looked like a fried fish and a heavy's broken gold chain that flowed into the hand and sat there in a hefty heap.

Vovan, by the way, didn't want at all to give up his meagre income from the picket line. He conscientiously stood through his shift (twelve hours every other day), dined with relish on the hot slop from the vats that that were ferried in, struck up acquaintances with certain dubious characters, became one of the best throwers of rotten vegetables, inferior only to the Tatars, who were still unmatched in the power and relish with which they smote the target and the picturesque quality of their blotches. After smacking a tomato onto the streaming plastic raincoat, he waved his soiled hand at Maxim T. Yermakov as if to say: Hi, nothing personal. Sometimes there was a pleasant little nightstand of a woman hovering beside him with her eyes screwed up comically against the sun. She was probably the Nadya he had mentioned and, to judge from the bulky bags standing at her feet, the tomato-canning was coming along well.

Something bad was happening to Maxim T. Yermakov. He could feel some vitally important resource within him gradually being exhausted. Everything inside a human has its own operational limits:

the heart's is longer, the liver's is shorter. How can we define the substance, the depletion of which Maxim T. Yermakov experienced as a decrease in his essential internal pressure, rendering the pressure of the external environment all the more palpable, all the more menacing? What was it – courage, stamina? More likely his screw-it-all attitude. The attrition of this attitude was creating a void in his soul. Maxim T. Yermakov wanted to be alone, without any social forecaster duty-officers with spring-pale faces, without any cameras infesting his flat, without any cartoon double in the online game "Light Head", whose friskiness sucked out his strength in some incomprehensible vampiric fashion, and whose fire-belching gave him heartburn. He yearned to be alone in a wide open space – but this desire sharpened the awareness of his true loneliness, which Maxim T. Yermakov had never thought about before. Not a single genuine friend, even Marinka had disappeared without trace, she never showed up or called. Even Just Natasha, when she came for the rent, didn't sit around any longer, she didn't rub her forefinger across the furniture, just pulled her little head down into her shoulders and cleared out, back into the stairwell, as soon as possible. She didn't seem to have noticed the disappearance of the valuable lump of marble and there wasn't a word about evicting him – they'd clearly had a little talk with her, explained what was what. This was what Maxim T. Yermakov had been reduced to: he would even have talked to Just Natasha now. He would have taken a drink with the alcoholic Shutov. He could feel that being observed night and day, within the walls of his own home, was making him prissy, giving him certain prudish, womanish mannerisms; if a woman suddenly appeared in his bed, the observation cameras would render him impotent. If only it was someone else in Vovan's place! Maxim T. Yermakov felt the retired diver's wet breath on his face all the time; Vovan's face thrust forward confidentially was like a pillow, with which they were trying to smother Maxim T. Yermakov. He had been wrong to think that the social forecasters had no time. Maxim T. Yermakov was the one who had no time.

No time, but just try killing it. As the increase in the period of daylight created several superfluous hours, the day became too long for Maxim T. Yermakov, he rattled about loosely inside the day, like a pea in a glass jar. He went on walks every day after work. Previously he had thought of the Moscow River as simply a strip of unsightly grey water that occasionally glinted on the right or the left as his car drove along, briefly interrupting the angular stride of urban development. Now he looked at the river with new eyes. The Moscow River smelled like an old woman; the sound produced by its waves beating against the embankments, as if they were demanding embraces from the sheer stone wall, was always mawkish. At the same time its waters seemed strangely heavy – which could be explained simply by pollution and all the years that had passed since the bottom was last dredged clean. Only a quarter of the Moscow River was natural environmental water – the rest of its contents found their way into it via the countless arteries of the city, on the way absorbing the biochemical composition of the capital and its fifteen million inhabitants. Essentially, it was the lymph of the megalopolis that flowed through those curving banks; this yellowish organic matter was saturated with information – and the river, unable to bear away on its back the reflection of the Kremlin, as rusty as a half-submerged cruiser, hauled its illegible files off to the Oka, the Volga and onward further into the dead end of the Caspian. Regardless of the weather, reflections in the Moscow River possessed a remarkable durability: demolished by wind and wave, they immediately reestablished themselves, their horizontal elements reassembling, as if they were magnetised, on some firm, well-shaped base that was concealed from the eyes by the glittering of the water.

In some ways the Moscow River was similar in nature to Moscow's mysterious catacombs, which writhed within the hills of the city like living creatures, moved and shifted shape, snarled themselves into tangles and died, leaving behind the mouldy shells of their own forms, which caused famous buildings to settle suddenly and old bell towers to lean over like the Tower of Pisa. The Moscow Metro came from the same breed. A system of strangely voluptuous palaces without any facades or roofs – essentially without external appearance or true substance. The Moscow Metro, circulating seven or eight million passengers a day, stubbornly resisted comprehension by the human senses: there had to be a reason why people stuck their noses into books and snuggled against each other's backs as the train howled, flying along through the slick, oily, black tunnel, suddenly skipping through a station that was like a fossilised skeleton: ribbed vaults, columns overgrown with incrustations, spectral cables supporting sparse iodide lamps flashed by and disappeared. What was that? No way of knowing.

In the metro Maxim T. Yermakov's brain, confined by the impenetrable strata of rock and earth above it, was like a balloon under a ceiling: it bobbled about, shrivelling up. In addition to the currents of air pumped by the ventilation system, his brain also detected certain gentle draughts creeping along the walls. The metro was a glove, constantly being pulled onto an incorporeal hand with multitudinous fingers. In the underground Maxim T. Yermakov felt this movement, not only with his floating head, but with his spine too. In many of the stations he could observe the murky lamps, suspended from the vault above the empty rails, swaying cumbrously and randomly without any visible reason – like buckets of water from the Moscow River being carried on shoulder-yokes. Maxim T. Yermakov perceived that same heave and sway, that same ponderous, competitive dance rhythm in the surge of the river: the rhythm was quite unmistakable, unlike anything else. Now Maxim T. Yermakov found the attraction of this new, visceral Moscow perhaps just as powerful as the pull that had lured him from the little old town to flame-bright, rich, absolutely unique, one-of-a-kind Moscow, which had accepted Maxim T. Yermakov as its own and was drawing him into its deep maw, having first made clear that there was no peace down there in its earth and never would be.

Maxim T. Yermakov resisted. But even so his walks led him ineluctably to the Moscow River. He pensively contemplated the riverboats that looked like various-sized trainers, so battered that he could easily distinguish the left foot from the right. He even went on a boat trip once: the stern shuddered as if it was made of tin, little flakes of white paint danced, the engine seethed and simmered, leaving watery green blisters in its wake. To the right and the left of Maxim T. Yermakov, no more than a couple of metres away, social forecasters lounged against the hand-rail – one of them, with a long nose and narrow, bright-pink nostrils, kept trying to spit onto the water, but the wind carried the glittering, glutinous thread against the side and the social forecaster worked up a new gobbet with the movement of a bird feeding a fledgling from its crop. Further along the edge of the boat someone laughed, a luminous mass of woman's hair flounced about above a suntanned shoulder, empty plastic bottles winked as they floated by in the water, the heavy clumps of lilac on the banks had already withered slightly from plum to prune-colour. The wind and other people's laughter brought a whiff of freedom, seagulls scudded about, banking so steeply that they almost pulled their sharp wings out by the roots – and when they sailed under bridges, their damp, dark iron thrummed faintly. Maxim T. Yermakov could probably even have relaxed in the sunshine, if only the social forecasters on his left and his right weren't so tense. With a twitch of a cheek, the two officers squinted sideways by turns at the briefcase that Maxim T. Yermakov kept clasped in his embrace like his favourite teddy bear. The flat, angular dead-weight of the infamous pistol could be divined within it; just recently the Makarov PMM even seemed to have gained additional weight. No doubt in their secret reports the social forecasters had been noting the Object's interest in the river – and that was a good thing. When the night of the blank round and the leap arrived, the tadpole-heads would say to each other that this had been the most likely outcome all along, because the object had been gazing into the water for ages and that had driven him slightly gaga.

"That's it, I've found the right spot for you!" big Vovan eventually announced, delighted, when he turned up one rainy evening, soaked through, with a wet blur of hair on his head and no umbrella on principle; he probably felt that these streaks of damp in the air were not real water to a professional like him.

"Well?" Maxim T. Yermakov was basically prepared, but his heart gave a sudden, loud beat, interrupting the singer bawling from the radio in mid-word.

"The Nagatino Metro Bridge! It's not too high and the water under it's plenty deep. Apparently it's not the natural riverbed, they dug a kind of channel, so it's still pretty level there even now. And not far off – just swim five hundred metres, and there you are, wild bushes. Ragged and shitty – just what we need. We can climb out, get changed and slip away on the quiet. We just have to hide a bag in advance, with the clothes and all the other stuff you need."

Big Vovan needn't have mentioned the bag: as if Maxim T. Yermakov intended to schlep it through Moscow in an aqualung and flippers. He knew the Nagatino Metro Bridge, he'd been to see it, along with the others. He hadn't thought the choice would fall on this nondescript spot, though. Not exactly an industrial area, an indifferent kind of embankment, in the style of some second-rate regional centre; lots of very bright and very badly tattered greenery – the branches of the trees looked naked despite their leaves, which were like swathes of cloth hung out randomly to dry. The bridge itself was reminiscent of a typewriter: every now and then metro trains slid across it with a carriage-return clatter, while cars and pedestrians flickered along below them, like text being endlessly composed. Any object that ended up here – human being or automobile – seemed to lose all individuality; from the bridge even historical Kolomenskoe Park looked like slovenly scrub, totally bereft of its pleasant, rounded parkland forms. Of course, he would have preferred a better stage set for his suicide. But, on the other hand, the important thing was to do the deed, and the landscapes could wait.

"And I've found something else too!" Big Vovan carried on in a boastful whisper. "I've found a pond where we can practice. It's a remote spot, near Chekhov, seemingly pretty close to Moscow, but there's no one around. It's near enough the middle of June already, I reckon it's time to start."

"But it's cold, only ten degrees, and it's raining," Maxim T. Yermakov protested feebly.

"I'm not inviting you for a little dip. What do you think divers are, full-time tourists? It's no holiday, I can tell you. A diver couldn't give a hoot for the beach season. The water's always cold down deep. But it never rains, I can promise you that! So stop farting about. We've got dry suits, waterproof, that is. And warm underclothes. I got the very best! Look, I've brought you your set, you try it on, flex your arms and legs a bit, and I'll adjust a few bits and pieces on you here and there," – and so saying, Vovan reached in briskly under the table, where his tightly stuffed black rucksack was standing.

"No!" said Maxim T. Yermakov, grabbing Vovan by the elbow. "Not here. Later. When we go to the pond. On the bank."

"What's up with you, afraid of a diving suit?" Big Vovan asked in amazement as he straightened up. "Well, you always were a bit of a coward, no offence intended, and you still are. I'm going to have real problems with you!"

Maxim T. Yermakov gave a crooked smile. Wouldn't he look bright if he started trying on diving equipment in front of the concealed cameras? As it was, there was still the big question of whether the social forecasters were filtering out his conspiratorial conversations with Vovan from the din of the radio. Maybe all these table games of theirs with drinks and snacks had been recorded ages ago, but on the other hand, what could they do? Where else could they have a chat? Doing the rounds of the bars? There was no certainty they wouldn't be recorded there with some kind of high-tech garbage. And there was no certainty that Maxim T. Yermakov would even be allowed into the bars. There were security guards everywhere – in those school uniforms with metal buttons. Shameful though it was, Maxim T. Yermakov felt more intimidated by restaurant doors now than he did when he had just arrived in the capital and didn't have a kopeck to his name. The entire enterprise was a precarious house of cards. Maxim T. Yermakov understood that very clearly. When it all eventually happened, the social forecasters would have great doubts about whether they ought to part with the money. How did their relations of cause and effect develop if nobody had been found? He could only hope the tadpole-heads would believe what they wanted to believe. They were people too, in the final analysis, they were pissed off working for the man, and the chances were that at least some things human were not alien to them.

"Okay, you think what you like," Maxim T. Yermakov said in a conciliatory tone, pouring Vovan a glass of cognac as thick as honey. "But you'd do better to think about the money. You don't find ten thousand dollars lying around on the bottom of a river. And tell me, have you spotted anyone tailing you? Are there any stupid, serious-looking guys plodding around after you?"

"Well, you're a real… chicken, aren't you?! Vovan exclaimed in jolly amazement. "You've got delusions, that's what it's called. You're afraid of life and you imagine spies everywhere. And you an actor, too. How do you play in films with your brains addled like that?

"An actor?" exclaimed Maxim T. Yermakov, amazed in his turn. "Where did you get that idea?"

"Nadka's cousin won a competition on the internet," Big Vovan explained willingly. "They sent him a t-shirt with your picture on it and something else as well, I don't remember what, something like shampoo. On the front of the t-shirt there's your portrait, and on the back of it there's your skull, kind of unusual, looks like Africa. Nadka recognised you straight off, she said it says on the internet that you're a well-known actor, you play in some kind of real show or something."

"Reality show," Maxim T. Yermakov corrected him mechanically. So how about that. Apparently popularity came to an Alpha Object even against the will of the tadpole-heads. Before he knew it, Maxim T. Yermakov might find himself a newsmaker, regardless of what kind of actor he was. But by that time it would be better to be somewhere far away with the money.

"There's one thing I can't understand: you're so cowardly, how can you play parts?" Big Vovan drawled thoughtfully, rubbing his prickly, hollow cheek with his index finger. "I'm not afraid of anything much, but when a whole lot of people look at me at once, then I get frightened."

"What's frightening about it?"

"That's what I can't understand." The intellectual effort had raised the sparse hairs above Vovan's clenched forehead up on end, like a bird's crest. "It's not like I give a shit for what they think of me. Yelling something wild, or cutting up rough, that's not for me, that's for smart-asses who are afraid. I just say my piece and that's all. Anyone who doesn't like it can fuck off. It's just them looking at me… Lots of them, and only one of me."

"There's only one of everyone in the world," Maxim T. Yermakov summed up.

Thanks for phoning on Women's Day, mum. Without that call, Maxim T. Yermakov wouldn't have remembered about the motorcycle helmet. That feeling of security, of being cut off from the informational soup seething all around him, of having all the nebulous channels and branches of his imponderable brain under a solid shell – all of that allowed him the precarious hope that, once enclosed in a helmet, an Alpha Object's head didn't register on the social forecasters' special equipment. It seemed a simple enough little task: to get to a secluded pond without the duty van sitting on his tail all the way. But in the Toyota, closely guarded by an entire team of tadpole-heads, that would be impossible. So it was a helmet and a motorcycle.

His choice would have to be a sports bike. And that was after the old heavy-assed, squat IZhak which had trudged along the soft country roads and could only get up to eighty kilometres an hour on the straight. Of course, he could try a classic or a good chopper, there would be some chance with them too. But to tear away from a standing start and slice through the traffic jams in some unpredictable direction, it had to be a sports bike, a ferocious beast with slanting crystal eyes that got up to a hundred kph in five seconds. They said a sports bike was the most expensive way to commit suicide. That wasn't true, it could be arranged more expensively. What did Maxim T. Yermakov really have to lose? But even so, the mere thought of a sports bike and the kind of speed it had made him feel as if the chair had been yanked out from under his haunches.

Without having really made his mind up yet, one fine Saturday Maxim T. Yermakov set out to go round the bike showrooms accompanied, naturally, by the obligatory secret service Lada 9, tumbling about in his rear-view mirror like a ripe apple in a golden dish. Maxim T. Yermakov didn't even bother to brake when he had an excellent view through an expanse of sheer glass of the bright-lacquer-coated, two-wheeled steeds and the customers drooling over them. He only stopped when an unfinished multi-storey car park, temporarily transformed into a sales outlet, showed up just where it was supposed to be. Inside there was a strange earthy, floury chill and simple yellow electric light, and the bikes looked less glamorous, but more real. The first thing Maxim T. Yermakov did was make a beeline for where they were selling crash helmets. Progress had had its due effect: the stand of brightly patterned integrals looked like an exhibition of parrots. Once his shouts into the depths of surrounding concrete space had attracted the attention of a stoop-shouldered manager with unhinged arms that waggled about strangely as he walked, as if they'd grown out of the spot from which the ends of other people's scarves dangled, Maxim T. Yermakov tried on every helmet they had in stock. Naturally, the one that fitted his visually small head was the very largest integral, the only one of that size on sale, decorated with bright red swirls. A close, cosy fit, not a ripple or a flicker. As solitary as if he had stuck his head up through the sky.

"Okay, now let's go and look at the sport models," Maxim T. Yermakov said in a trembling voice, smoothing down his hair with both hands because it was standing up on end after the fitting session.

"The sport models? Are you sure?" the manager asked, gazing at Maxim T. Yermakov with poorly concealed scepticism.

"Yes, what's the problem?"

"Well... Pardon me, but you're obviously not one of us," declared the insolent manager, who himself looked less like a biker than an office paper-clip. "Sports bikes require skill, plenty of fast-driving experience. And then your figure, how can I put it, suggests an upright posture in a motorbike saddle. Believe me, you'll find that much more comfortable. I can show you a wonderful touring bike."

"What? What are you drivelling about?" roared Maxim T. Yermakov, not even realising that he had grabbed the skinny salesman by the collar of his blue uniform shirt, dragging it out of his sagging trousers like a crumpled rag. "Did I ask for your advice? I came here to buy a donkey!"

"All right, all right, sorry boss!" said the frightened manager, fluttering his arms about, and Maxim T. Yermakov felt the salesman's ridged Adam's apple twitching against the knuckles of his fist. "There's one hard-core model, a real beast, not a bike!"

Breathing heavily, Maxim T. Yermakov let go of the manager, who dashed off into the depths of the shop on an uncertain, zigzag trajectory, stuffing his shirt into his trousers as if they were an empty sack. Maxim T. Yermakov hurried after him, tramping heavily and almost crying. Out of the corner of his eyes he spotted another two blue-uniformed figures, evidently attracted by the incident, approaching from opposite sides of the concrete barn – and one of them, with broad shoulders, was creeping along carefully, holding something in his hand. "Right, now I'll get a good ass-kicking," Maxim T. Yermakov thought drearily, and for a second he even felt annoyed that the social forecasters had slacked off on their routine and no longer tagged along behind their object to check the contents of his shopping basket.

"Hello, excuse me," said the broad-shouldered one, springing up in front of Maxim T. Yermakov with a smile stretching right out to his pink ears. "Could I ask you for an autograph?"

The thing in the beefy guy's hand turned out to be a fan-club poster with a cartoon-style portrait of Maxim T. Yermakov against a background of clouds of flame that looked as if they had been well boiled. "I wonder why there's no sign of these fans outside the office or in the yard?" Maxim T. Yermakov thought sourly as he scratched his pointy signature across himself.

"Wow!" said the one like a paper-clip, shifting his suddenly bright eyes from the portrait to the original. "And I didn't recognise you at first. Well, that makes everything clear!"

Babbling as they went, the salesmen led the celebrity to his future purchase. The Yamaha bike, all yellow and silver, was supremely handsome: even standing still, it already looked if it was rushing along at more than 30 kph. But it really did look too small for Maxim T. Yermakov after all: it was less like a ferocious beast than a blue-tit with a pointed tail, set on wide, virginally black balloon-tyres. Maxim T. Yermakov climbed apprehensively into the saddle; he immediately felt how cramped and painful the racing "prawn pose" was for the folds of his stomach.

"Maybe you should use a double? Some stuntman," the broad-shouldered salesman with a perfectly circular ruddy bloom on his cheeks said sympathetically.

"Got to do it myself," Maxim T. Yermakov said in a muffled voice, adjusting his shoulders and elbows to fit the low handlebars.

Nodding respectfully, the managers started chattering about guarantees and tuning, and saying the suspension had to be slackened off to avoid getting battered black and blue on the patched asphalt. They all decided that Maxim T. Yermakov needed the very best protection and dragged a black and red leather suit out of the stockroom to match the integral helmet he had already bought, and also a pair of incredibly heavy boots and thick-fingered gloves. Having squeezed the sweating client into all this, they stood him in front of a spotty mirror screwed to a concrete column. The reflection reminded him of a poster from the school biology lab, with an impassive man showing off his red musculature – except that the anatomy of the being in the jumpsuit was not human, but Martian. The knees equipped with sliders were dislocated unnaturally, the swirls painted on the helmet looked like projections of non-human thoughts floating in an alien head. Nothing in the appearance of the being suggested that Maxim T. Yermakov was inside it.

"I'll take it all," Maxim T. Yermakov mumbled from inside the helmet. "And some kind of backpack too."

There was a brief moment of acute horror when Maxim T. Yermakov suddenly thought that while he was frittering his time away in the showroom, the tadpole-heads could have blocked his bank account. But the payment went through smoothly, and as he took back his card, Maxim T. Yermakov promised himself to withdraw the remainder in cash. After dropping the client's jacket and briefcase into the boot of his Toyota, the broad-shouldered, sugary-faced manager happily agreed to drive it round to Usov Lane – and the one like a paper clip clearly envied him.

"Right then, I'll take a spin," Maxim T. Yermakov muttered and set off, creaky, clumsy and heavy-footed, towards the bike that seemed to have its cautious, slanting eyes fixed on the little key clutched in the blunt fingers of one glove.

Maxim T. Yermakov rode down the inclined ramp, dangling his feet so that the biker boots scraped along, feeling like a little kid on a wooden horse. The social forecaster's blue rust heap was relaxing calmly in the lazy, leafy shade and, to judge from the rotatory movements of their jaws, the two men inside it were consuming their lunch. They took no notice of the departure of the leather scarecrow with an ornamental head, who glanced directly at them with a flash of his dark visor. "Well, *bon appétit*, scumbags," thought Maxim T. Yermakov and revved up the engine.

The bike roared and leapt. For a split second Maxim T. Yermakov didn't really know where he was. Then he discovered himself on the same street, hurtling along the lane, straight towards a grinning, shuddering jeep that was furiously sounding its horn. He had no idea how he managed to dodge it. The brief encounter consisted of molten patches of blinding brightness, a long howl that went streaking past him and a honking of horns: his own lane – when he finally managed to get onto it – consisted of rear bumpers set out like pieces on a chess board and mirrors sticking out everywhere. The bike, which reacted with delight to the throttle, reacted much less willingly to the brake, and Maxim T. Yermakov jumped three out of four traffic lights on red, feeling like a lucky fly who has just escaped a pair of clapping hands alive and unharmed. Like a horse that hasn't been broken in, every now and then the bike tried to rear up, and Maxim T. Yermakov had to lie forward with all his weight to force the front wheel down onto the asphalt. Maxim T. Yermakov worked his entire weary body, waltzing with the bike, swapping kilograms of live weight and metal weight in order to avoid the crazy obstacles, which became more and more like a mirage of trembling mirrors, reflecting an ever-expanding motorcyclist about to smash himself to pieces. Even so, he decided not to pile on the turns yet, and allowed the sun-spattered Moscow Saturday to lead him along a relatively straight line, as if he was riding through a pipe. Maxim T. Yermakov could barely recognise Moscow – that is, familiar combinations of architectural forms did occasionally appear in long-shot, but in close-up everything was a distorted flickering, every passer-by was like a flick of a fingernail.

Suddenly the pipe brought Maxim T. Yermakov out onto a highway – he thought it was the Novorizhskoe Chaussee, or perhaps it wasn't. The central dividing lane flowed towards him like a silk ribbon. Somehow it happened, quite independently of Maxim T. Yermakov's will, that one new biker's boot stepped up the gear and a glove turned up the gas. And at this point something happened to his sense of balance and space, which had never been reliable anyway: now everything seemed as if the bike and its rider were not flying along horizontally, but scrambling upwards. Extended by speed, saturated with it, Maxim T. Yermakov was sitting up vertically on his coccyx, facing a coarse wall of asphalt with various different vehicles attached to it, like large letterboxes. At first these boxes remained motionless, then they started toppling down onto Maxim T. Yermakov almost too fast for him to avoid them. Someone seemed to have smeared lines of thick green paint to his left and his right with a house-painter's brush; villas of pale and red brick pivoted past like wind-up toys.

Eventually the jumpsuit's promised ventilation system kicked in: Maxim T. Yermakov's sweat dried up, coating his body in sticky cobwebs. Out here on the highway he couldn't avoid turns; submitting to the demands of the bike, which was reluctant to part with its speed, Maxim T. Yermakov hung into a bend like a saddlebag on a horse – and the stripy asphalt flickered past close by, looking from this angle like a battered vinyl record. Maxim T. Yermakov

196

didn't think about anything, he didn't want anything. He was just surprised that there were hardly any motorcyclists on the highway. Only once he saw a group of five bikers up ahead, also travelling at a fair speed, although the bikes they were on were clearly not sports models. The quintet maintained an amazingly steady wedge formation: it seemed as if some precisely regulated magnetism was at work between the riders. Unlike all the other objects of this vertical world, the bikers didn't come tumbling down, but stayed ahead for quite a long time, trembling and swelling up as if they were preparing to explode at any moment; Maxim T. Yermakov even had time to examine their rounded leather backs, decorated in the style of warning notices about high-voltages and children playing with matches. He had to overtake the fivesome on a bend, there was nothing else for it: hanging almost alongside the Yamaha, striking showers of sparks out of the asphalt with his knee, he couldn't give a rotten damn for anything. The bikers trembled again, slid back one by one and exploded there behind him, like confetti party poppers. Still alive by some miracle, Maxim T. Yermakov tore on and on, with confetti – sometimes white, sometimes coloured – glimmering in his eyes; hills sprang up and dived back down with the movements of dolphins and their shadows lying across the road hurtled past, which made time on the highway seem to move exactly the way it does in a speeded-up film, when the shadows of clouds rush by in ragged patches.

Suddenly the sound of the motor dropped; it roared one last time and then died. Gently, raising dust and scrunching quartz chips, the bike and he rode off onto the verge. So much for this over-hyped technology. Extending the kickstand with a clumsy blow of his boot, Maxim T. Yermakov started clambering off the motorbike cautiously, like a woman. His legs wouldn't hold him up at all. His numbed back and backside felt like immense, frozen lumps of earth. Remembering that he still had a rucksack on his back, Maxim T. Yermakov reached into it and groped for his cigarettes, didn't find anything, pulled off his gloves, took out the cigarettes and stuck the filter of one of them against his visor.

Olga Slavnikova

When he pulled off the helmet, it felt as if someone had opened the lid of a boiling kettle. Compared with the blank isolation inside the integral, the silence that surrounded Maxim T. Yermakov was vast and empty. Down at the bottom there was a dry sound, like someone sharpening the glittering stalks of grass with a sharp instrument; up above, the clouds rustled. On the left was a green slope, scattered with rich little mounds of earth – probably the work of moles; along the crest of the slope poplars stood in a dark line against the sun and their shadows, already elongated, seemed drawn in by a child's hand. To the right, literally only ten metres from the highway, space shifted into a long shot; entirely beyond reach, some kind of long building stood in a meadow, with one wall bright in the pre-sunset light; after that everything was a mass of waves and stripes that paled as they stretched out to the horizon; there was a bluish strip of forest with a neat notch in it, as if a front tooth had fallen out – that must be another highway or a firebreak. Maxim T. Yermakov didn't have a clue where he had ended up. But it was quite possible that the social forecasters had already pinpointed the gravitational phenomenon with their fancy, hyped-up equipment.

Although it seemed not. Not since the state security freaks first showed up at Maxim T. Yermakov's office had he felt himself surrounded by such serene emptiness. He felt like sitting down on the grass, and then lying down. This was it, freedom. He felt as if he could remain suspended at this blissful point in space forever, if not for the need to eat and drink. And also, of course, the desire for money. Ah no, Maxim T. Yermakov wouldn't take his claws out of the tadpole-heads until they paid up. It was a two-way bear-hug, that was the problem, but Maxim T. Yermakov had had the audacity to lead the special state committee in the dance, like the lady. In his excitement Maxim T. Yermakov even stamped one foot that was baked into a biker's boot like a pie. Why else would he ever have let Vovan into his kitchen and knackered himself on a sports bike, if not for the ten million dollars? The tadpole-heads owed Maxim T. Yermakov money – for that, as well as all the rest.

As he tried to light up, Maxim T. Yermakov saw that the gloves had turned his hands black, like black widow spiders – just the thing for frightening children. His hands, the lighter and the cigarette were all shaking, they just wouldn't come together. Eventually the tobacco smoke filled his transparent brain, rounding it out blissfully, and the ground under his feet became a bit firmer. Straightening up the tight small of his back with an effort, Maxim T. Yermakov saw the bikers he had passed on the highway. The wedge approached smoothly, with an increasingly loud roar; he could already make out the face of the leader, looking like a sea-urchin, and the wind was blowing up the beard of the second rider on the left, so that he looked like a bikers' Father Christmas in tight black leather. The bikes themselves had the typical long, branching handlebars: set far out in front, the front wheels gave the motorbikes the look of some kind of agricultural equipment – mechanical hoes or mowing machines.

"Hey, dude! You turkey! Full marks!" the bikers yelled above the growling of their engines, and with a salute of their claws they rushed past in a descending roar, as if the page had been turned after them.

Shit! He had to figure out after all what had happened to the bike. Maxim T. Yermakov limped round the still red-hot Yamaha, splattered at the front with burnt-on tomato-and-mustard insect blotches. It was very simple: he'd run out of petrol. Accustomed to his Toyota, a modest and not particularly voracious old lady, Maxim T. Yermakov had simply miscalculated the appetite of his brand-new yellow-and-silver blue tit. He thought he'd passed a petrol station not that long ago: that could be fifty kilometres away. A pity he hadn't waved back to the bikers – they had just appeared on a distant rise in the highway, looking like cartoon ants. Maxim T. Yermakov had heard that bikers were supposed always to help their own; meanwhile, the Saturday highway's infrequent cars, which took so agonizingly long to grow from a spot in the mirror to life size, only increased their speed when he waved his grimy hand at them. He could call a tow truck on his mobile, but he knew what kind of rescuers would come: with square, double-headed-eagle ID cards in their pockets. Oh no, Maxim T. Yermakov had laid out enough money in order not to meet them today at least. So what other option did he have?

Afterwards Maxim T. Yermakov himself couldn't believe that he had made that forced march. The low handlebars made pushing the Yamaha along the shoulder uncomfortable at first, and then agonising. "You stupid jerk," Maxim T. Yermakov muttered through clenched teeth, plodding along dully in his biker boots with a coating of grey dust that made them look like felt. The five-hundred-dollar helmet hanging on the handlebars clattered like a bucket and kept trying to slip off. Without even knowing why, Maxim T. Yermakov didn't set off back towards Moscow, where there definitely was a petrol station, but dragged himself onwards towards the spot where the highway disappeared over the horizon, as if it had taken a run up and done a hunchbacked somersault. With every step he took the uncertainty grew. The very air seemed strange, stratified. In the sky above his head it was still day, but night was already rising from the ground and the sunset-bright grass, standing right up on end, was lined by an under-fur of darkness below.

The Yamaha wobbled about, attempting to lie down on its side or run its back tyre onto his foot; the sweat ran down his back under the jumpsuit, as if someone was drawing on him with their finger. Maxim T. Yermakov plodded on and on, no longer paying any attention to the traffic driving past from in front or behind, sluicing him with eddies of heat and immediately disappearing. All signs of civilisation were remote from the highway: for a while a small town stretched out in a mouldering haze beyond the fields, with tiny copper- bright windows flaring up in the sunset. The highway skirted round a slimy little marsh with dead tree trunks jutting up out of it haphazardly, looking like candles blown out on a cake; invisible frogs thrummed and quavered on various notes in the style of a folksong ensemble from Chukotka. Then the highway crept into a forest enveloped in silence, taking Maxim T. Yermakov with it. In the gap between the crowns of the trees the sky was like a pale river that was reflected in the grey strip of asphalt climbing uphill, higher and higher – but in between the tree trunks it was as dark as in a stove, with only the white glimmering of occasional slim, spectral birch trees, like

200

threads of smoke or undead nocturnal plant life in the depths of the gloom.

Maxim T. Yermakov muttered obscenities under his breath, then yelled them out loud, then muttered them again. He recalled his Grandad Valera, who could move creaking furniture and ignite matches with his special swearwords. The guttural expressions that Grandad Valera used to spew out, with his white hair blazing magnesium-bright and his stick jiggling in his hand, used to send grandma into fits of tremulous laughter. But the stools duly tumbled over, the cupboards swayed, shaking trinkets off onto the floor, and damp matches burst into hissing flame, sometimes an entire box at once. "*Scélérat! Gibier de potence!*" Grandad Valera bawled, dousing his dry salted biscuit of a protruding chin in spittle. "*Gibier de potence, gibier de potence*," Maxim T. Yermakov mumbled as he dragged the stubbornly resisting Yamaha up the steep incline. And his grandad's incantation worked: as soon as they reached the top of the low hill, the bright neon lights of a petrol station lit up down below, with the warm glow of an all-night diner snuggling up close beside it.

Naturally, the social forecasters very quickly figured out what the Object in their charge was riding now – especially since Maxim T. Yermakov didn't try to hide it, he registered his new means of transport with the State Traffic Safety Inspectorate and was given number plates. But the trick of shooting off like a bullet at traffic lights proved remarkably effective. At the starting line the state security vans and Lada 9s, with their wildly boosted engines, appeared like roaring, trembling, ethereal mirages – but as soon as the light turned green, the technological marvel instantly found itself boxed in and reduced to meek, substantial materiality, with the driver's stiff face looking like a flower pot in a peaceful civilian window. The social forecasters were finally stymied; Maxim T. Yermakov was no longer their constant companion in the traffic jams. Flaunting the remnants of his screw-it-all attitude, with the bike and his backside wagging, he shot straight up to 100 kph and away through narrow clefts, corridors and cracks in an unpredictable direction: numerous attempts to box the Object in, with state security vehicles emerging simultaneously from all the side streets, only resulted in incredible blockages that made any further pursuit impossible.

The social forecasters probably had helicopters at their disposal, but no doubt not even the authority of the special committee extended as far as messing up the Moscow streets, overhung with wires and advertising banners. Once outside the Moscow Orbital Highway however, Maxim T. Yermakov sensed, rather than heard, the dull vibration of rotor blades, and out of the corner of his eyes he would glimpse an unusual aircraft, like a black guitar, showering wind down onto the flowing birch forest below. But the vision with two rainbow-glitter halos flashed by and disappeared – perhaps the reason it was hanging there had nothing to do with him anyway. The open space sluicing around the drunken projectile that Maxim T. Yermakov became outside the MOH was a place of solitude and freedom; it was as if there were no radio or TV broadcasts in the ether, as if the mobile phone networks had disappeared completely and all the military and civilian satellites had quietly burned up in orbit. Probably this was the effect of the crash helmet, which had become the Alpha Object's cap of invisibility. When Maxim T. Yermakov returned, like a prodigal son, to his courtyard and his stairway entrance after a burn up, he took great pleasure in observing the features of the officers on duty, which displayed very, very mixed feelings. He could have sworn that one of the principal emotions was a sincere, almost kindred joy; the officers seemed to be finding the sight of the long-awaited Object ever more agreeable – which was not at all what Maxim T. Yermakov wanted.

After a long silence Sergei Yevgenievich Kravtsov, tadpole-head No. 1, suddenly phoned. His angry voice was greatly diminished: perhaps Foetus was somewhere abroad – or perhaps away on Mars?

"Maxim Terentievich, we are extremely concerned," Kravtsov said in a dry voice that scraped at Maxim T. Yermakov's ear as if Foetus was sticking his icy finger into it. "You are very stupidly risking your life, which is essential to our work."

"Go screw yourself," Maxim T. Yermakov retorted malevolently. "You piss me off and I'll drown myself."

After that the social forecasters' vans started behaving far more carefully: they made token attempts at pursuit, rather than actually going for it all-out, and they didn't put on any more performances with several vehicles all emerging onto the main drag at the same time, provoking bitter weeping and wailing at the smashing of perfectly innocent imported automobiles. Maxim T. Yermakov was pleased with himself. No miracle happened, of course, he didn't become a super-sharp sports-bike pilot in the space of a week, in fact he was more like a circus bear who'd been sat on a motorcycle. But nonetheless, he did learn something. It turned out that any wind, even if it wasn't very strong, swept the sports bike off the highway like an empty cardboard box. It also turned out that a wet road surface swerved unpredictably under his tyres and the fine drizzle exuded by the swollen clouds in the evenings was transformed at speed into intensive automatic weapons fire. On the positive side, a connection was established between the Yamaha and Maxim T. Yermakov's body, like the connection between communicating vessels; Maxim T. Yermakov no longer sensed the road via his safety belt, like when he was driving his Toyota, but with his entire spinal column, from his coccyx to his occiput.

He also finally saw the pond that Vovan had taken such a liking to. The stretch of water was shaped like a crooked oval, with a broad rim of dense sedge grass, like a three-day stubble, so that the shifting expressions of the water, especially when the wind blew, were like those of a human face. The water looked as thick as soup. Blank, floury patches heaved on the sun-flecked surface, glistening waterweed swayed to and fro like nets, a fallen tree trunk with malachite-green streaks protruded from the water, and from time to time slippery frogs leapt off it like long gobs of spit. Maxim T. Yermakov was extremely reluctant to climb into a bath like that. But Vovan, with his professional lack of squeamishness concerning water of any kind, was in seventh heaven. He had set up a faded tent that was once yellow on the bank and, apparently, moved into it, pocketing the money allocated by the state special committee to rent a bed in a hostel. Nadya, the bedside-locker woman, was contentedly running the household here too, stirring some concoction with potatoes in a cauldron over an acrid little campfire, churning laundry that champed energetically in a basin, occasionally tossing the fine, soaking-wet strands of hair back off her forehead and freezing for a moment, holding her soapy hand up by her temple, with a broad, vulgar wedding band glinting in the drooping foam. From the lazy but persistent way in which Vovan followed her movements, it was clear that family life was working out just fine.

Maxim T. Yermakov had never seen anything attractive in women of this type: pale, with plump necks and clumpy elephant-legs – but he caught himself envying Vovan: Nadya would never put him under pressure and pump him for money. Using God only knows what kind of tackle, Vovan had caught small, fat carp, the size of a wallet, in the pond. Nadya cleaned them as they feebly flapped their tails, lowered the grey fishy slurry and the scales into the pond and then, not far from the spreading, oily, leaden patches, entered the water herself to bathe. Below the tussocky slope running down to the water there was a strip of grey sand which, at a pinch, could have been called a beach. Before dipping into the water the woman splashed it on herself with her cupped hands, moistening her moles and goose bumps and the wisps of poplar fluff that had settled on her skin; she made one awkward, poignant gesture, when she adjusted the water at her knees, like the hem of a dress. Previously Maxim T. Yermakov had only met discontented women, consumed by the desire to mean more and have more. Nadya was content with her uncomfortable, grotesque existence, with her Vovan – and that made her a prodigious miracle, despite the ordinariness of everything that constituted her plain, unprepossessing person.

Her bathing was sometimes interrupted by an abrupt gust of wind that swirled poplar fluff up into the air like cotton-wool snow; and then the wispy blizzard was immediately cut through by rain and Nadya, white and wet, with brownish water draining onto her stomach out of the cups of her swimsuit, ran to save Vovan's trousers, clumped together on the washing line. But Vovan himself didn't care where there was water: down below, up above or everywhere. Strangely short-legged in a diving suit as heavy as a bearskin, Big Vovan nonetheless looked nimble and graceful, as if he had been born in this rubberised apparel, in the mask and the boots, with the cylinder behind his back. Only the beaked mask seemed funny, making Vovan look like a cross between a bear and a pterodactyl. Robing yourself in all this expensive gear proved to be a complex skill in its own right. First Maxim T. Yermakov had to pull on the special grey underwear, which was a tight fit for him, then the padded undergarment, and then the real torment began: Maxim T. Yermakov fought the diving suit as if it was an octopus, and when his feet and legs were finally in the boots and trousers and his arms were in the sleeves, he found that closing the hermetic zip fastener, which for some reason was set into the back, across the shoulders, was about as easy as hoisting himself up into the air by the scruff of his neck, in the style of Baron Munchhausen.

"That's it, that's it, learn to do it yourself," Vovan kept repeating, standing to one side and scratching the thinning fleece on his breastbone. "Who's going to help you when you go to shoot yourself and drown? No one's going to help you."

The diving had a strange effect on Maxim T. Yermakov, making him feel the way he remembered himself as a toddler of perhaps a year and a half, with bandy legs and a tight feeling in his crotch. And when Big Vovan fastened the belt with the lead bars round his expansive waist and fitted the waistcoat with the air cylinder over it, he really felt like slumping down plop onto his little botty. Eventually Maxim T. Yermakov saw the underwater world. At first the sensation was exactly as if he was being drowned in the toilet; all around him there was nothing but a brownish blur with rumbling yellow bubbles. Later, when Maxim T. Yermakov stopped floundering about desperately, the visibility improved slightly. A crooked array of brownish stratified stones reflected the rippling sunlight; stalks of waterweed, some thicker, some thinner, swayed to and fro; some kind of small animal life flailed wildly, burying itself in the sand; occasionally a small fish flickered by like a wan patch of sunlight. The air fed from the cylinder to the mouthpiece tasted oily. He had big problems with breathing: after a few minutes a blockage appeared in the hose and his head, and Maxim T. Yermakov roared up to the surface, spitting out the mouthpiece.

"Breathe through your gob!" Vovan roared, surfacing beside him.

While Maxim T. Yermakov got better and better at riding the sports bike (thanks to the old IZhak, by this time certainly deceased), he was definitely not destined to be a diver. For some reason, although Maxim T. Yermakov tried very hard to do everything right, under water he ended up turning over onto his back all the time. Emerging out of the gloom, Vovan twisted some kind of valve on Maxim T. Yermakov's sleeve with a ribbed claw; immediately the water's embrace of Maxim T. Yermakov's body tightened, as if it was squeezing him in its fist. That helped a bit to maintain his stability between the cellophane surface and the darkling bottom; the flippers, however, refused to obey him, tangling together and sticking in the clay like planks, and his ears were filled with a taut, painfully inflamed rattling. The much-vaunted "dry suit" turned out not to be so very watertight after all: when he tugged it off, after Vovan had taken the weight of the wet cylinder on his chest, Maxim T. Yermakov always turned out to be damp and somehow waterlogged. Immersion in the brownish puddle left him terribly exhausted; trembling with weakness, Maxim T. Yermakov slurped and chomped indiscriminately everything offered to him by the considerate Nadya, including the pieces of stale grey bread and bony, sweetish-tasting carp.

"Yeah, you're not doing too well with this," said Vovan, stretching out beside the little campfire that had turned grey and was scattering grey flakes. "I can't understand what's wrong with you. Why do you keep slumping over all the time? As if your centre of gravity keeps wandering all through your body. Maybe we should put another stabilizer jacket on your backside."

After ten days of practising almost every evening, a bright idea suddenly surfaced in Vovan's straggly head.

"But you can't just go jumping off the bridge in a suit and flippers, with a cylinder, right?" he asked himself, with absolute amazement written across his dry-smoked features. "That'd give the whole artistic concept away straight off."

"I told you that at the very beginning, you fucker!" Maxim T. Yermakov erupted indignantly.

"Don't you go yelling at me, I'll do the yelling!" Vovan retorted viciously, instantly furious. "Did you warn me that you swim like a sack of shit? You didn't. There's no way I can get a mask on you underwater. Did you think about that, you fucker? The great thinker! Let's suppose we can breathe from the same cylinder, I'll stick my octopus second stage in your mouth, that's standard practice. So at least you'll live. But you'll see fuck all!"

"What about the suit?" Maxim T. Yermakov muttered.

"The suit's a problem too," Vovan said with a solemn frown. "A dry suit's no good. You'll be getting dressed at home, you'll have to put a raincoat on top, slip on a pair of trousers and this and that. But you won't get any raincoat buttoned over a dry suit: you're fat enough anyway, but that's even worse. And a dry suit's heavy, when you climb over the barrier, they'll see it. But that's still not the main fuckup. A dry suit's got air in it, it floats. When you jump in the river, you won't go under straight away. You'll have to bleed off the air, that's three or four minutes. Any fool will spot you floating there, still alive after you shot yourself."

"So what do we do?" asked Maxim T. Yermakov, restraining his fury.

"What do we do? I'm supposed to know? What does your director get paid for?" Vovan's eyes roamed about as he broke up small branches and tossed them into the campfire. "Okay, let's say there is a way out. We'll buy you another suit, for spearfishing, in seven-millimetre neoprene. It's summer, you won't freeze. I'm the one who'll be lying under the bridge and waiting for you God knows how long. Then we'll need different ballast. I'll get you a frying pan weight, that's for spearfishing too, on straps, you could wear it under a jacket. But then there's another interesting point too. It turns out I have to take you in tow underwater. So that makes me your tugboat, on top of all the other hassle. That's hard work!"

"So what? That's what we agreed, isn't it?"

"I don't remember that!" Vovan snapped. "And if I don't remember it, it didn't happen. So anyway, it's eight hundred bucks from you for the ballast and the suit, plus an extra grand for me in person. Up front. If you don't like it, that's your business. You can jump like a frog in all the gear, only make sure you don't catch your flipper on the barrier."

Maxim T. Yermakov heaved a deep sigh. He'd withdrawn his money from the account, and once he subtracted all the outlays on the preparations for his plan, there wasn't all that much left for six months of lying-low. He was pretty much down to the wire. Vovan waited, working his jaw muscles and blowing *papyrosa* smoke out through his pinched nostrils. His faithful Nadya waited behind his back, with a heap of dishes in a basin: walking past, she had stopped when she heard the conversation and frozen motionless, with her grey eyes wide open in an expression of timid hope.

"Okay, you've persuaded me," Maxim T. Yermakov growled.

Nadya beamed, got terribly flustered and trotted off to the water, on the way swatting a scarlet mosquito against her creamy-white neck. Vovan relaxed and took a swig of super-concentrated tea from his smoke-blackened metal mug.

"You've got to understand, I don't just have to drag you along, I'll be doing extra training with you too," he added in a benevolent voice, shattering a flame into sparks with a stick. "So now you and me'll be doing different diving."

The "different diving" began. The new diving suit was a tight fit: when Maxim T. Yermakov squeezed into it he felt like a tightly stuffed cushion. Now he flopped into the pond with his head uncovered, and the water immediately swallowed it alive, grabbing and squeezing its soft, unstable prey and trying to force it in some indeterminate direction. The taste of the pond was putrescent, slightly fishy and slightly cabbagey. He carried it all the time now in his rheumy, inflamed nasopharyngeal cavity. Maxim T. Yermakov squeezed his eyes tight shut in the water, but nonetheless he opened them when his groping hands came across something solid; for the most part this something solid was Vovan, murky-dark, seething like a kettle, a monster with a one-litre face who tumbled Maxim T. Yermakov over like a limp puppet, pulled his stiff, unbending arms off somewhere and then, after giving him a good shaking, stuck a repulsively hard, squeaking mouthpiece in through his half-crushed lips; and then, at last, together with a massive swallow of agitated slurry, oxygen started entering the half-drowned man's body. Learning not to cough and choke under the water was almost impossible, the proper management of smooth breathing seemed to depend on the behaviour of a certain cowardly diaphragm below the ribs, which Maxim T. Yermakov was unable to control. He could only hope that at the critical moment everything would go right. Maxim T. Yermakov was impregnated with the pond, he carried it around inside him – he glugged as he walked, with silt in his legs and a cold little carp quivering in his stomach; it seemed to him that if a human being consisted of 80 per cent water, in his personal case this water came from the pond where Vovan ceaselessly tried to drown him in his wild passion.

"Tough training, easy war," Big Vovan kept repeating as he dragged Maxim T. Yermakov, slithering and puking, into the tangles of sedge grass that were standing in for the shitty river bank under the Nagatino Metro Bridge. "Never mind, another week or two of diving and then we'll do it for the movies."

Before it could be done "for the movies" there were still a few vital questions to decide. Question number one: who could he make out his will to? There was only one answer: Little Lucy. She was the only person who Maxim T. Yermakov knew for certain wouldn't filch the legacy, but hand it over right down to the last kopeck and even be embarrassed to take a commission.

Maxim T. Yermakov went to a notary's office and drew up the document. Should he tell Little Lucy now or call her afterwards, from the next world? No, now wasn't a good idea: Lucy was a simple soul, she could let the information slip somehow when the elated skunks at the office were all chipping in for their dear departed's funeral wreath. Let her cry a bit first, and then rejoice at the news. She'd get some kind of money from the operation anyway, twenty thousand say. Or maybe not, ten would do. Money, even huge money, had a way of melting away in your hands. Well just look, soon there'd be nothing left from the savings he'd scraped together in dribs and drabs for a flat, no more than a damp stain – after that he could just wipe his hands on his pants and give up. He could ask Little Lucy to visit the sham corpse at his secret hideout, bring food, run errands, even cook and clean the place at the weekends. He could trust her more, she wasn't a hussy after all, not a whore like the ones who made such an effort for a couple of bottles of fake vodka – that was probably their professional going rate. Little Lucy would help even without any money, simply out of compassion, out of pity for Maxim T. Yermakov – he could have died after all, and then he would have really suffered!

And incidentally, he didn't know what was happening with her kid. At the office Little Lucy was the same every hour of every day, it was impossible to tell anything from looking at her. Always the same little grey linen dress, crumpled at the front and the back; always the same hairclip, dangling loosely on a few ratty strands of hair, like a snail on blades of grass. Little Lucy wore massive sunglasses on her tiny face now; when she leaned down to the papers on her desk, the glasses fell onto them with a distinctive thud. That dull, plastic thud was heard every time Maxim T. Yermakov walked past the outer office. After once glancing in to see what those scratched lenses were concealing, he never wanted to see it again. The dark circles under Little Lucy's eyes, which shimmered with quiet insanity, could have been left by tea glasses. Maxim T. Yermakov wondered uneasily whether his appointed heiress would come completely unhinged when her kid died.

At the same time strange things started happening to Maxim T. Yermakov. His imagination was running out of control. He imagined the cheap, dim little flat where he would have to spend six months or more without even going outside. He saw a sagging couch with a damp yellow cushion, damp wallpaper with a pattern of ludicrous little flowers, a dusty television that didn't work, but which he still watched anyway, not even noticing other objects in the room. Little Lucy, appearing in this lair on, let's say, Saturdays, would be the only female creature in the whole world for Maxim T. Yermakov. It would even be something like love. She would cook and tidy up and, maybe, who could tell, even do something else for poor Maxie.

Thinking in this way Maxim T. Yermakov, who had grown famished since Marinka took off with her things, involuntarily started looking at Little Lucy with a male's undressing eye. He was amazed at how intensely he could focus on the shallow cleavage in her neckline, with its delicate thickening of shadow. Once he peeped when Little Lucy groggily lifted up her hem and squeezed out a drop of glue onto a ladder in her tights; the vision of that silky ladder and the intimate darkness that he could divine above it, seared right through his dreams. Things reached the stage when that thud of falling glasses gave Maxim T. Yermakov an instant hard-on. It was strange that the alcoholic Shutov's hussies, who were also bony and really ground their bones as they walked, didn't arouse even a hint of any similar reaction. He could probably have come to an arrangement there all right. But as for Little Lucy – it was quite impossible to touch her right now, even a dyed-in-the-wool cynic like Maxim T. Yermakov understood that. There was something criminal in the very lust that was aroused in him by this exhausted creature who, even including her little sparrow's head, weighed only half as much as Maxim T. Yermakov did. But what could be done if Maxim T. Yermakov was fixated on Little Lucy and no one else? What was he actually guilty of? Ah, what a screwing he would have given her right there on that desk of hers, eclipsing all her idiotic work, her wretchedly unhappy life! Just as long as she didn't take her dark glasses off.

With Little Lucy in his loins and a whole heap of problems in his head, which had expanded like an atomic mushroom, Maxim T. Yermakov steered into the yard of his building on a warm, overcast

Friday evening. He had sent Vovan a text message, saying not to expect him today. He wanted to take a rest and maybe, at long last, chew the fat with his good neighbour Shutov, after pouring some alcohol fit for humans into the swollen little monkey. He could assume that in Shutov's line of business he had a wide network of murky connections. Surprisingly enough, his hussies were well sought after, customers flowed to them like ants to an anthill, and all sorts too – from a youth with protruding ears that looked as if they would chirp like fifes if he was smashed over the head to a corpulent old man with a yellow goatee beard and a trembling cane in a hand that looked like a vacuum-packed chicken. Judging from their chastely lowered eyes and obvious skill in merging into the wall, many of the lovers of Shutov's coarse and green forbidden fruit were involved in business that wasn't entirely legal – very probably including the forging of documents. There were a lot of them and the number kept increasing – as if all the feculent strata of Moscow's male population sent their representatives to the den of vice. Maxim T. Yermakov could just imagine them waiting for the girls, sitting in line on battered chairs in the corridor, as if they were in a medical centre or a social security office.

Once he had parked, Maxim T. Yermakov got out unhurriedly into the damp sultry air, onto the asphalt dappled with fine rain. The clouds were like warm ash. On his way to the entrance he cast a habitual sideways glance at the courtyard demonstrators standing there under the sparse, fine-spun drops, some with umbrellas and some without. He glanced, looked and froze on the spot. Blazing brightly among the bunch of nondescript hired hands was the tall figure of a woman in a scarlet evening dress; the wind, creeping up from below as it does before a storm, tossed the supple silk hemline this way and that, wrapping it round the long legs trembling on immensely high heels. The face, like the make-up on it, had blurred slightly, the cheekbones resembled bruised pears, the false gemstones were like tears on her neck. But even so she was splendid – in the way that a woman is splendid when she is about to fire a pistol at someone. For this was Marinka, for she was already raising her outstretched hand holding

212

a heavy black thing that was searching for Maxim T. Yermakov with its baleful, birdlike pupil.

"Hey, hey…" Maxim T. Yermakov backed away, suddenly feeling the slant of the earth's surface under the soles of his shoes.

"You'll pay for all my tears, you rat!" Marinka squealed and immediately the heavy black thing jerked her hand hard, right up to the shoulder and a red-hot drill bit went flying past Maxim T. Yermakov, seeming to shave off the fine hairs standing erect on his temple.

"Drop! Get down!" wild men's voices shouted from somewhere in the distance and Marinka, shifting on her high heels and wiggling her hips like a stripper, took aim again.

As a man used to falling into a clean bed and lying there, Maxim T. Yermakov still couldn't bring himself to sink down into the greasy, swirling dust, and he carried on hovering there with his arms splayed out, like a fat penguin. Another two bullets zapped into the coarse bushes, Maxim T. Yermakov took a cold raindrop that landed on the top of his head for a bullet and a wave of heat flooded right down to his knees. And at that instant a heavy male carcass stinking of sweat and cheap ironed fabric landed on him. Falling onto the asphalt with his leg twisted awkwardly was painful, his knee crunched and burst into flames. Maxim T. Yermakov started floundering about, gasping for breath, with a metal pen protruding from the pocket of the other man's shirt rattling against his teeth. The social forecaster who had tumbled him over was also floundering like a man in a fit, scrabbling wildly with his legs, as if he was trying to crawl over the asphalt, dragging Maxim T. Yermakov, scraped and tattered, along with him. Suddenly he froze, seemingly readying himself to jump up vertically from all fours, and he really did disappear for a moment, but then he rematerialised and went limp. A drop of thick, salty sauce flowed into the corner of Maxim T. Yermakov's distended mouth and he unwittingly licked it off.

With an inarticulate squawk, Maxim T. Yermakov heaved the limp man off himself, so that the man's soft arm seemed to make a sweeping gesture of invitation. The first thing he saw when he sat up in the rain was the scarlet dress, wilted by water. Two social forecasters were holding Marinka with her arms twisted behind her back: the necklace of false stones dangled, swaying senselessly, and the cleavage of her dangling breasts could be seen in the drooping neckline, which gave Marinka a strange resemblance to a slashed and gutted fish. The courtyard demonstrators had clustered tightly together and seemed set to stand to the death under their interlocked umbrellas. Here and there on the glassed-in and barred-off balconies bleary observers appeared, looking like the inhabitants of hanging zoological gardens.

Maxim T. Yermakov struggled to his feet, hissing at his injured knee – and only then got a proper look at the social forecaster stretched out on the ground. A state security man like any other: a narrow forehead with one deep wrinkle, a shaved head the colour of iron, a small scar on a chin as firm as a calloused heel. The only distinctive feature was that he was dead. The social forecaster's wide-open eyes looked polished and didn't blink at the raindrops. A thick, red sauce flooded out from under the head that had caught the bullet, instantly disintegrating in the rain and flowing in a diluted, tinted trickle into the noisily gasping grating of the drain. "What do I care, look how many of them are still alive," Maxim T. Yermakov whispered soundlessly, but it wasn't true. Maxim T. Yermakov had the salty, soy-sauce taste of this man's blood in his mouth, Maxim T. Yermakov's rib cage was a battery that held the electric charge of his agony, Maxim T. Yermakov's diaphragm retained the feeling of weightlessness that must come when the soul leaves the body. When the state security man died, he and Maxim T. Yermakov were a single whole, they were one. They did it together. Closer than a priest, closer than a blood relative – Maxim T. Yermakov had become a printout of this man, who had departed with a bullet in his head intended for the Alpha Object, as if he had received a message that explained everything about Maxim T. Yermakov.

The sharp shock of the rain was still trying to revive the heavy body, wrapped in its cheap, soaking clothes that looked like oil cloth. Eventually one of the dead man's colleagues, an individual with sinuous features that seemed to have water perpetually draining off them, ran up, squatted down beside the body and felt under the slumped-open jaw. He got up slowly and shook his fingers.

"You ba-astards! Let me go, you a-assholes! Let me go-o!" Marinka squealed, looking like a red pepper pod in her totally soaked dress. A whole gang of social forecasters, with the support of some cops who had arrived, was trying to shove her, struggling and twisting her backside powerfully, into a militia car.

Suddenly, as if on command, everyone turned their heads to the right – and from that side, from the direction of Usov Lane, a thoroughly battered black Volga came drifting across a broad puddle, like a black swan with its watery wings slightly raised. "Holiday greetings, asshole, thought Maxim T. Yermakov, wiping his wet face with his wet palm. Naturally, he had guessed immediately who it was that sped through the capital in this glorious Soviet museum piece. And he was not mistaken. The very tallest social forecaster, bending over double in respect, trotted towards the spectral Volga with his umbrella glinting in the rain, just like in some old-time movie – and a crooked man's foot in a black shoe as simple as a galosh was thrust out under the protective dome. The man who climbed out of the Volga with cautious movements, as if he was pulling on his trousers at the same time, was Sergei Yevgenievich Kravtsov in person. As soon as the principal state tadpole-head straightened up, the rain disappeared from the air as if by magic. The early evening sun came tumbling out like an egg yolk out of its shell, the wet foliage sparkled with sizzling rainbow colours, the courtyard demonstrators closed up their flimsy umbrellas and stood there just as they were: frightened, taken by surprise, as pale as poisonous toadstools. Limping and swearing, Maxim T. Yermakov dragged himself over to a green yard bench that looked freshly painted beneath its plump moisture. He plonked himself down, realising that there was no point in feeling sorry for his trousers any more.

Sergei Yevgenievich Kravtsov was annoyed. His remarkable semitransparent head had come out in crimson blotches, as if it had been smothered in passionate kisses. His bloodless mouth was twitching in the way that a lizard's might. The state freak had shown up at the scene of the incident in the same tracksuit that Maxim T. Yermakov remembered, with the stripes on its trousers half-torn off. The top was open over his hairless chest, revealing to the general gaze a gold Orthodox cross, the size of a honey cake – but on Sergei Yevgenievich Kravtsov, on his non-human skin, the gold glinted like steel. After standing for a minute over the dead social forecaster, who was grinning at the clear sunshine with his regular teeth, the principal tadpole-head set off towards Maxim T. Yermakov with long, loose-jointed strides.

"Maxim Terentievich, please be so good as to inform me where your personal firearm is at the moment," he enunciated with cold fury, gazing at the bridge of Maxim T. Yermakov's nose.

"I've got it, where else would it be?" Maxim T. Yermakov muttered. He wondered what picture they had in their minds: was he supposed to have fired back at Marinka, then?

Under the unblinking, dangerous glitter of the state security freak's gaze, Maxim T. Yermakov reached out for his briefcase, which was as inseparable from him as a sick liver. The lock hadn't been opened for many weeks and it stuck. Maxim T. Yermakov finally mastered the crooked little mechanism and the briefcase breathed out a musty, leathery smell and the penicillin odour of a hamburger forgotten inside it. Thrusting his hand in for the item that constituted the briefcase's impressive weight, to his great astonishment, Maxim T. Yermakov pulled out the marble base of a writing set, wrapped in a clumped and tangled lady's shower cap.

"Your pistol was taken by Ms Yegorova, who has just fired at you," Foetus declared in a steady voice.

"I'd already guessed that," snarled Maxim T. Yermakov, shaking screwed-up scraps of paper, tattered strips of yellowed, bone-hard painkillers and tobacco crumbs out of the briefcase.

"Take it," said Foetus, holding out the half-forgotten, sour-smelling modernised Makarov handle-first. "You have displayed criminal negligence and for your own sake I hope that such a flagrant incident will not be repeated henceforth."

"Oh, I'm frightened! Oh, how terrifying! But permit me to remind you, Mr. Kravtsov, that I don't work in your special department. And I didn't ask you for a personal firearm, you can keep it if you like," said Maxim T. Yermakov with an insolent smile plastered right across his face as it dried out in the sun. But he took the pistol.

Yes, wouldn't he look fine clambering up onto the barrier of the bridge, gazing into the river and aiming his index finger at his temple? But how about that Marinka! She'd really gone and shot at him, earned herself a stretch inside, it was the camps for her. She wasn't even concerned about her designer glad rags that would go out of style while she was sewing work mittens in a prison workshop.

"And how do you intend to deal with Ms Yegorova?" Maxim T. Yermakov asked disinterestedly, focusing on the bridge of the special-committee man's nose, which seemed to have a Roman numeral stamped into it.

"According to the full severity of the law," the state security freak replied impassively.

"Well, that's bloody great! These are your fucking games, what's Marinka got to do with anything? You provoked the stupid fool, totally fucked up her brains. And not only hers, by the way! Somebody shot at me earlier, did you know that? They clipped a bit off my ear. And those disaster victims with their toy pistols? What guarantee is there that the father of some deceased family won't take a pop at me for real? Will you put him away too?

"We will," Foetus confirmed in a cold voice. "It's all a matter of the relations of cause and effect, in which you represent a malignant node. One of the most important mechanisms of cause and effect is the law. And we shall uphold the law during this delicate period, whether we like it or not."

"Okay," said Maxim T. Yermakov, involuntarily tightening his grip on the wet handle of the pistol. "Don't expect any complaint from me. And I won't provide any testimony either."

"Your complaint will not be required," the principal tadpole-head declared arrogantly. "Let me remind you, in case you hadn't noticed, the victim of the crime is not you, but another man. Apart from that,

I would like to hope that you won't be able to testify for objective reasons. Because, to coin a phrase, you will no longer be among the living."

"Oh, really, is that what you hope?" asked Maxim T. Yermakov, starting to shake so hard with nervous laughter that he could feel the substantial weight of his own fat on his ribs. "Maybe I should shoot myself right now? Have you reloaded the pistol for me? Because I don't know how, chief!"

At that the state-security freak gathered together deep brown folds of something that looked like the pulp in pear compote around the sides of his eyes and smiled a wistful smile that gave Maxim T. Yermakov a chilly sensation in the region of his heart. Both of them looked at the dead social forecaster, who seemed to have aged several years in twenty minutes. A lanky character was performing a crane dance over him with a camera, clicking it in the dead man's face as if trying to talk to him in bird language. Meanwhile, an ambulance drove into the yard through the long, silvery puddles, beaming and lamenting with its heavenly-blue flashing light. The medics, all with weary, crumpled faces, dragged a stretcher out of the back. The photographer, having completed his final series of click-squawks, beckoned invitingly to the medics. But this cultured gesture was brusquely cancelled by a wave of the state tadpole-head's icy hand: the whole scene froze and shrivelled up, the medics backed away to their ambulance and one woman with braids of grey, lifeless hair dangling from under her medical cap sat down in exhaustion on the kerb.

"Please take a close look at this," Foetus said to Maxim T. Yermakov, pointing to the dead man. "Be so kind as to state what the difference is between you and this man."

"He's dead, I'm alive," Maxim T. Yermakov replied quickly and when he attempted to gather air into his lungs with a convulsive gulp, he felt that spectral electric embrace with all his ribs.

The state security freak said nothing for a while. Two digits were immediately added to the Roman numeral V on the bridge of his nose: in combination with his fastidious politeness, this was probably a sign of the extreme fury that only a coldblooded, high-ranking FSB officer could afford to indulge.

Eventually he spoke, forcing out the words:

"His name is Sasha Novoseltsev, he was not yet thirty and he…"

"Leaves behind a wife and two little kiddies," Maxim T. Yermakov put in with a derisive smile.

"Leaves behind a wife and a little son," the state security freak confirmed balefully. "But the difference between you is this. Today Lieutenant Novoseltsev simply and matter-of-factly did what we have been trying to get you to do for many months. We think up scenarios, dance complicated dances around you, spend countless amounts of state funds – I'm so sorry they don't go into your pocket. Lieutenant Novoseltsev wasn't promised millions of dollars or posthumous glory by anyone. No one singled him out or told him that he was special. He protected you from the bullet with his own body, thereby preserving the possibility of halting the surge of negative energy. He just did it. But you – why can't you do it? What makes your life more valuable than his?"

"The fact that it's mine, how many times do I have to tell you?" Maxim T. Yermakov said patiently. "This Novoseltsev of yours was probably a good guy. If he'd asked my advice before going to work for your committee, maybe I could have changed his mind. But no, he was determined to choose you. And then he got married as well and had a child. So who has he got to blame, that's what I ask. I have no idea why he jumped in front of the bullet today. To be honest, I can't even imagine why. I wasn't acquainted with Novoseltsev, not even for a day, but when I try to picture my acquaintances, you know, sacrificing themselves – can you imagine that it doesn't work with even one of them? I just come up with a load of nonsense, a drunken office party with ritual jumping through the fire. And as it happens, I know hundreds of people in Moscow. Clever, creative people who know how to make money. So are they all abnormal, then? Wrong? If appealing to the people is important to you – that's what the people are like. The same as me."

The principal tadpole-head winced and licked his blotchy lips quickly with a little tongue as hard and white as chalk.

"You haven't told me anything new," he declared contemptuously. "I don't harbour any illusions. In the last fifteen years people like you have become the majority: The human individual is the highest value, and I am that individual. A proud *homo sapiens* in conditions that automatically supply the comforts of life. Even a young lout who lives in some dump in the back of beyond, in shit and poverty, ideally sees himself like you – a manager in a Toyota. Someone who, if he doesn't owe money, doesn't owe anybody anything. But permit me to assure you, Maxim Terentievich, that normality is not a statistic. Even if there are only five per cent of us left, or one per cent – it won't make any difference: we are normal, not you."

"Duty, patriotism, love of the Motherland," Maxim T. Yermakov commented ironically. "I can't understand how it's possible to experience all that inside yourself. It's not private territory. Of course the state would like me to experience it all, but what the fuck do I need it for?"

"Yes. Staggering changes!" the principal tadpole-head exclaimed, clenching his fingers into a fist and holding it out as if he didn't know what to do now with that bundle of bones wrapped in skin. "Ten years ago the subject of discussion was at least comprehensible. Now it has disappeared, evaporated. Sasha Novoseltsev hasn't proved anything to you today. I can't prove anything either, I can only testify. Love for the Motherland is a profoundly personal experience, it's impossible to rid oneself of it by rational means. It is a special kind of enthusiasm, which sleeps little and works hard. It is a furious faith that runs contrary to the present-day situation. If you wish to know, I loathe matryoshka dolls, balalaikas and all those painted wooden trinkets, I hate drunken snivelling and when I hear the words 'mysterious Russian soul' I reach for my gun. But I love everything that constitutes the strength of the country. I love industry and armaments. I love honest improvements. I rejoice when I ride in a good railway carriage from the Tver factory, when I buy good-quality shoes produced in Moscow. I love our secret laboratories, where we are streets ahead of the foreign research engineers. I want to be a part of strength, not weakness, and therefore I love strength in myself and my compatriots. But you, Maxim Terentievich, and those like you, are not representatives of *homo sapiens*, but a waste of space. Pardon the platitude, but you have nothing that isn't sold for money."

"I don't have a lot of what is sold for money, and that bothers me far more," Maxim T. Yermakov countered. "And don't go pushing your morality at me. I like Italian shoes, and anyone who sews Moscow creepers can wear them himself. Why, just because I happen to have been born here, can't I want the very best for myself? Why do they hang the Russian car industry round my neck, when it hasn't produced anything decent for a hundred years? By all means, I'm willing to pay for quality, for slick technology and advanced manufacturing skills. But you, and people like you, make me pay for lack of skill, cack-handedness, brainlessness, sloppy fucking work – and all at world prices, in the name of patriotism. That's the essential truth of our life here. And you're surprised because I'm not willing to sacrifice my life? I'm not prepared to sacrifice anything at all – not an hour of my own personal time, not a single rouble."

"What about the quality of the chocolate you are pleased to advertise?" the state security freak asked with an acid smile, baring a complex stomatological structure of either iron or gold.

"I don't produce chocolate," Maxim T. Yermakov replied in disgust. "I produce advertising. It's a different product. My creative work may not be one of the world's great masterpieces, but it's well up to European standards. I know what to say and what to show to make people enjoy consuming that garbage. But I'm not responsible for the whole shebang, whatever you might think about it. And don't go trying to dump global responsibility on me. Just look at what you've taken on yourselves, bloody patriots. But the private individual is nothing to you, a rotten flea. You destroyed Marinka's life and didn't turn a hair. But you've started going to church, consolidated your moral rights. I reckon your sensors don't even register people one at a time. How large does an aggregation of people have to be before your sense of duty starts stirring? From a hundred upwards? A thousand? Why, you've expended thousands and thousands of little people, as the glorious history of your department demonstrates. And don't dangle that righteous cross of yours under my nose, why don't you fasten up your plunging neckline, close your jacket; that would look more decent."

Slowly, with a sickly grimace, the principal tadpole-head pulled up the plastic zipper and closed the woven collar right up to his bevelled chin, which looked like a peeled potato with a rotten section sliced off with a knife.

"So today's incident hasn't taught you anything?" the tadpole-head summed up in a harsh tone.

"What do I need to learn?" Maxim T. Yermakov asked with a laugh. "Draw your own conclusions about your shitty scenarios. You stirred up the people's wrath, now deal with it, be vigilant, protect me."

The state security freak clenched his frosty fist together again and turned it this way and that, as if he wanted to bite it, but didn't know from which side. Instead of that he waved irritably to the medics, who were tired of standing around for so long, and they came back, waddling along like weary ducks with the stretcher for the social forecaster sprawling on the asphalt. When they lifted the dead man up, his head dangled unnaturally and Maxim T. Yermakov saw the bullet hole caked with black blood, looking like the mark from a burning *papyrosa* that had been screwed violently into the temple to stub it out. The lieutenant's gliding disappearance into the bowels of the ambulance in the form of a tidy, elongated package was accompanied by furious yelping: it was the time of day when the courtyard's dog-owners walked their elderly, red-eyed mutts, and now the entire pack were straining at their leashes, including old Kalyazina's dachshund, dragging its fat little body along like a seal, and as Kalyazina was pulled forward, she grabbed at her terrible yellow straw hat and squatted down on her flabby legs, crisscrossed with a pattern of black veins like dry grapevines.

Maxim T. Yermakov carried on sitting there, slumped like a sack on the rain-spattered bench, feeling sudden exhaustion instead of the triumph of victory; a shimmering insect buzzed in his face, making him jerk, and the pistol dangling in his numb hand almost slipped out into the bright, shaggy grass. The witnesses to the criminal incident gradually wandered off to their televisions, where they were shown more or less the same thing again. The social forecasters pulled up stakes, as always leaving two symmetrical pairs of sentries with thermos flasks and sandwiches.

"Mr. Kravtsov, may I ask a question?" Maxim T. Yermakov shouted at the principal tadpole-head's back as he strode towards the Volga.

"Well?" he said, looking back over his crooked black shoulder.

"I suddenly felt curious: who do I take after as an anomalous Object? My mum or my dad? They seem like perfectly normal, respectable philistines. Or does heredity not have anything to do with it?"

"We've studied that question," the principal tadpole-head replied drily. "The preconditions were present in your grandfather, Valerii Dmitrievich Yermakov. He was objectively a very harmful individual."

And so saying, tadpole-head No. 1 clambered into the Volga one part at a time, like a folding deckchair, and the battered legacy of some District Party Committee departed, pretending at the last moment to have difficulty taking the cramped turn out of the courtyard. "*Scélérat, scélérat,*" Maxim T. Yermakov muttered after him, and for a moment he saw his grandfather's angular shadow in the murky, honeyed air, leaning heavily on a ghostly stick.

An hour went by, or perhaps more. Perhaps a lot more. Maxim T. Yermakov sat on that sticky bench, incapable of doing anything but smoke cigarette after cigarette, which made his mouth feel thick and insipid, like the inside of an old woolly mitten. The sunset clouds looked like scraps of burnt paper – blackened and smouldering, with fire round the edges and none of their daytime whiteness remaining. The courtyard demonstrators disappeared one or two at a time; they dissolved into the dense twilight, into the dark seething of the mass of foliage, until only one, the most steadfast, remained – and on a closer glance, he turned out to be a round-shouldered bush. The yard lamps blinked and lit up – and the air proved to be literally teeming with insects. Large, sparrow-coloured owl moths, little grey moths – and the whole mass of them rustling, as if flour was being shaken out of the lamps. The pistol was still exuding the same unbearably acrid smell; Maxim T. Yermakov, who had never held a gun that had just fired before, didn't know how to deal with these burnt-chemical fumes that had gummed up his nostrils and his lungs. He was overwhelmed, prostrated; even the invigorating thought of ten million dollars seemed to have lost its magic. Maxim T. Yermakov could still feel the imprint of the dead social forecaster on himself – as if he was a lump of rock with a fossilised trilobite in it. He could forgive himself for feeling numb and weak after being shot at and then pressurised. But how could he start moving and keep on going? Or should he say screw it all, just stay sitting here with his ass glued to this bench until he died?

To his left, on the pathway leading to the entrance, he heard a rapid, dull clatter of high heels, as if someone was writing an equation on a school blackboard with chalk. It was one of the alcoholic Shutov's hussies. Maxim T. Yermakov recognised her: she had quite often brought his groceries and always seemed as if she had a cold or had just been crying. The hussy's grotesque skirt, covered with lilac scales, flashed brightly as it jolted about, her bony knees stuck out from under it like two flatirons.

"What's wrong, are you unwell?" she asked in a surprisingly human voice, halting in front of the bench.

Maxim T. Yermakov raised his swollen eyes. The movement of the eyeballs produced a painful effect, as if the contents of his condensed brain had been scooped out with two table spoons.

"What's happened? You look terrible. Can you get up?"

The hussy peered at Maxim T. Yermakov with short-sighted seriousness. Her hairstyle consisted of beetroot-coloured swirls, her narrow face was plastered with make-up, giving it the consistency of eggshell. But the whore's eyes were surprisingly clear and Maxim T.

Yermakov suddenly felt embarrassed.

"I can get up, only what for?" he muttered, stealthily slipping the gun into the limp briefcase.

The hussy thought for a moment longer, toying exactly as a child might with the clasp of her large silver-oilskin handbag that looked like a deflated balloon, the kind they sell at municipal public festivals, along with the inflatable beetles and zebras. The empty bag rustled in the wind and the hussy's beetroot locks tumbled onto her forehead, clearly because of the mental effort she was making.

"You know, it's not good for you to sit there like that," she said eventually. "Come back to our place with me. I don't think Vasilii Kirillovich will mind."

As she spoke the hussy reached out an untanned arm with a scattering of goose bumps to Maxim T. Yermakov and pulled him up off the bench with a jerk that made his overflowing heart glug. Well, after all, why not? Someone had to yank Maxim T. Yermakov out of this deep ditch today. And it wouldn't do him any harm to unstress a bit. He plodded along after the hussy on limp, heavy legs, watching her flat backside in the tight skirt flashing its little lights, like New Year tree decorations. To be honest, he didn't fancy it at all. What if he disgraced himself in comparison with the general male population of the capital? Even if he imagined Little Lucy in their communal bed instead of the whore, the hussy's smell would ruin everything: a hospital kind of smell, bleach and cotton fabric. With such a superfluity of make-up, why didn't she use perfume? And why leave her rounded back exposed like that, when that back looked like an office abacus?

The lift stopped on the fifth floor, directly opposite the door of the den of iniquity, with its padding slashed crisscross and slantwise, and Maxim T. Yermakov could barely resist pressing the button for his own floor. Biting her lower lip, the hussy started squeezing in the bell push: a long ring, three short ones, a pause, then a complicated rhythmical trill that momentarily reminded Maxim T. Yermakov of his mother, her piano and her pupils. From inside the door Maxim T. Yermakov heard the footsteps of a man at home and he foolishly drew himself erect.

"Sashenka, at last, thank God," a very familiar, gentle bass voice said somewhere, and the alcoholic Shutov appeared in the doorway, looking absolutely unlike himself.

First of all, he was entirely sober – and he had been sober for at least a week. The grotesque wrinkles and little blue-grey bags under the eyes had disappeared: the firm features of a middle-aged man had emerged, with angular cheekbones and a nose shaped like a penny whistle. The gingerish beard was still crooked, but it looked respectable. Shutov was dressed in a decent pair of trousers and a clean shirt as white as paper, and his feet were modestly adorned with new velvet house slippers – the old, flaking ones were standing in the nearest corner, like an essential and respected household item.

"Hello," Shutov said to Maxim T. Yermakov, bowing slightly as if he was addressing a complete stranger. "Sasha? Pardon me," he said, again addressing his unexpected visitor, as he took the hussy by her skinny forearm and drew her deeper into the dark hallway.

"Well well, so she's called Sasha, like that lieutenant," Maxim T. Yermakov thought in surprise, looking around curiously at the antechamber to the den of vice. Dangling from the ceiling, as was appropriate in such places, was a naked lamp bulb on a depressing black cord that prompted thoughts of the gallows; on the left a door, once white, that must lead into the lavatory, had turned as yellow as bone with age and hung crookedly in its frame. However, the tidy coat rack on the wall held quite a lot of decent clothes on hangers, and there were five or six pairs of shoes standing in a neat row on the freshly washed floor, like boats in a harbour. Shutov and the hussy whispered with their heads close together, and the host's indecipherable words had an interrogatory, reproachful ring to them, while the hussy answered him in a forceful, clear voice, tugging at the little glass beads dangling on her collarbones. "Do they require a special recommendation for someone to employ their services, like joining a private club in London?" thought Maxim T. Yermakov, starting to feel annoyed at being abandoned by the door on the little rubber mat with "Welcome" on it.

"Well then, you're right, Sashenka, you're right," Shutov finally said in relief, addressing Maxim T. Yermakov as well and seeming only now to acknowledge, with a restrained, gap-toothed smile, that he knew his visitor.

The hussy smiled too, quickly, over her shoulder, and tugged the beetroot swirls off her head. Beneath the haystack that had proved to be a wig was a head of plain, flat hair, damp at the temples and clearly unacquainted with any hairdresser's dye; here and there the dull, rusty tone was streaked with strands of grey, like fishing twine.

"I'll get changed then, Vasilii Kirillovich," the hussy said and slipped away, crumpling the wig in her fist.

"Well, Maxim, don't just stand there, come on in," Maxim T. Yermakov's host said hospitably, setting out in front of him a pair of velvet slippers exactly like the ones he was wearing, and which had clearly never been worn.

"You know, this is the first time I've seen you without any drink in you," Maxim T. Yermakov blurted out, genuinely amazed.

The unrecognisable Shutov smiled again, wiggling his beard and moustache – it was like a little flame snaking through a heap of kindling.

"You'll be very surprised, Maxim, but I don't drink at all."

Well that really was something to be surprised at, no arguments there. Gazing around in a daze, Maxim T. Yermakov followed Shutov into a large room the colour of cardboard and the first thing he saw there was a gleaming, gold icon screen, which for some reason reminded him very vividly of a puppet theatre. The conventional figures with smooth, seal-like outlines were of various sizes, a Blessed Virgin with high, arched brows held an entirely adult, miniature Christ on her knees like a smart toy. Swarthy candles with a colour resembling toffee were burning in front of the icon screen; every little flame had a waxen tear. The glow of the little flames played on the gold of the haloes and simply realising the very possibility of such an expansion of human heads made Maxim T. Yermakov feel the root of every single hair on his own.

"Now, friends, let me introduce my neighbour, his name's Maxim," Shutov announced to the people who filled the room quietly. "He seems to have been through a nasty experience. Sasha brought him."

"All of us here have been through nasty experiences, so welcome," the corpulent old man who was sitting closest of all said in an agreeably husky voice, rising slightly off his chair on behalf of everyone present. The old man had a yellow goatee beard and a birthmark the colour of boiled peas on one fleshy wing of his nose. "He's the one with the stick," thought Maxim T. Yermakov, bowing awkwardly.

He half-knew many of the people in the room. He saw the youth with the fife-like ears, completely immersed in himself right up to the top of his head, with its pale, gleaming forelock; he saw the bogeyman whom he had occasionally encountered in the lift, only now the bogeyman had become an ordinary-looking intellectual type with a receding hairline, square glasses and a burn mark on his right cheek that looked like a ham omelette. The hussies were here too – Maxim T. Yermakov would never have recognised them if he hadn't received a plastic bag of groceries from them every three days.

Bereft of any trace of makeup, their little faces were also bereft of even the slightest inkling of beauty – but had become filled with a strange, spectral tenderness, akin to that of the pale patches on photographic negatives or X-rays. The hussies were dressed in even more fancy-dress style than when they promenaded in their professional uniforms: baggy, shapeless blouses and long skirts, all in dull, dark tones or with patterns of little flowers like dried camomile from the pharmacy or grains of pearl barley. A closer look made it clear that these clothes had not been specially made, but bought in the same cheap trading kiosks as all the shiny skirts and short jackets of clumpy fur: here and there a pitiful little frill with lurex thread or an unpicked pocket betrayed the origins of this consumer crap, which was quite definitely not intended for any kind of praying.

"What do you do here, fancy-dress sex?" Maxim T. Yermakov asked warily, addressing the corpulent old man in the first instance.

The response was general laughter, neither offensive nor offended, only the hussies smiled awkwardly and one, with dark man's eyebrows, came out in red blotches the size of poppies.

"You'll be even more surprised, Maxim," Shutov intervened, displaying his only front tooth again in a smile, "but all our girls are virtuous and many of them are virgins."

That made Maxim T. Yermakov feel more embarrassed than he had felt since he was ten years old, probably since that terrible moment when the neighbours' little jackal had handed him a pornographic magazine to look at, rolled up tight into a flute, but Maxim T. Yermakov had got flustered and dropped it, splashing the pages open in full view of everyone. Nowadays, when sex had finally become a normal need that was satisfied in various ways, Maxim T. Yermakov fancied that there was something indecent about virginity. He suddenly felt as hot as if he had walked into the steam room at the baths, wearing a heavy wool coat.

"Listen, aren't you that Yermakov from the computer game?" a man sitting opposite him enquired eagerly: the man had narrow shoulders and a suspiciously large head, topped by a distinctively shaped yellow forehead that looked like a boiler imbedded in clay.

"Well, I suppose I am," Maxim T. Yermakov muttered, trying to guess if the man worked for the special committee.

"Right, so that's it," the man intoned in an agitated tenor. "You see, I've got two sons, one in the seventh class at school and one in the ninth, and they play it, it's impossible to tear them away. Their schoolwork's down the drain, the older one's given up boxing, can you believe it? They've invented a real plague! Half the school's like that. And there's nothing that can be done about it!"

"Write a letter to the president," Maxim T. Yermakov advised him acidly. "Let the president shut up the whole shop. I'll be all in favour."

The man looked up at him with helpless, watery eyes, blurred with the whitish haze of a grief suffered only very recently, with which he was obviously not coping very well. This narrow-shouldered family man seemed to be one of those people who take any harsh words to heart and only come up with answers after the fact, almost falling under a tram in the process, and sometimes appeal helplessly for justice, even to their own children, deranged by puberty. A perfectly obvious type, except that this particular specimen must have been upgraded somehow, because the small facial features that looked as if they had been flattened by the massive boulder of reason above them, suddenly smoothed out into a smile.

"What am I saying?" he said guiltily. "You suffer far worse from that 'Light Head'. Allow me to introduce myself: Ivan Antonovich Lukin. An individual of no great consequence: I teach geography in the Humanities Grammar School No. 2. But I am at your service if I can be of any help."

Having said his piece, the man stood up and offered Maxim T. Yermakov a gnarled hand covered on the back with coarse little black hairs. Maxim T. Yermakov cautiously grasped this dead-and-alive object, imagining as he did so an entire classroom of pubescent scumbags for whom a geography teacher like this was an inexhaustible source of amusement and object of ceaseless ragging. Then all the others started following Lukin's example, getting up and introducing themselves. Gleb Nikolaevich, Vitya, Irina, Sveta, Igor Petrovich, Volodya, Ilya – for a minute Maxim T. Yermakov felt as if the faces were spinning like a carousel in one direction and the names were spinning in the other. Never mind, it would all come together somehow. The new guest was offered two chairs from different sides at the same time, one dry and fragile, the other massive and crudely knocked together, with a check jacket splayed out on its back in the manner of a Caucasian felt cloak. Maxim T. Yermakov chose the one without any clothing, thinking that obviously no one here lost any sleep worrying about the furnishings.

The main item of furniture was a large oval table, around which the strange company was gathered. The table was covered with a white tablecloth that was far from fresh and crumpled like the sheets on a bed. Flaunting its charms on the tablecloth was a highly artistic still life: seven opened and well-pawed bottles of vodka, lacklustre vodka glasses, a bulky plastic container of beer that occasionally glugged from its innards. Heaped right beside all this, on yellowed plates or directly on the tablecloth, were the drinkers' snacks: potato chips, rusty pieces of herring, some expensive kind of fish with soft, white flesh, crudely hacked boiled sausage and two grilled chickens, obviously bought at the metro station. The still life gave off a palpable stink. Taking a sniff, Maxim T. Yermakov was able to determine the source: the slices of sausage were inflamed and the noble white fish had swollen up so that it looked like white bread.

"Your sausage has gone off, by the way," he announced, afraid that these people would all start regaling him with this stinking food that had hardly been touched.

Shutov, who had taken the place at the head of the table, raised his open hands reassuringly, but before he could say anything the door swung open and in walked Sasha in her changed outfit. She had the simplest possible cotton-print village headscarf tied tightly round her head and the savage's glass beads had been replaced by a dark little tin cross that looked like a fly hanging between her collarbones. Without make-up Sasha's face proved to be a remarkably tender pink colour, covered in small freckles that seemed to have sifted down from her forehead to her cheeks, like the sand in an hourglass. In her hands she was holding a large, paunchy china teapot with a design of blue flowers.

"Vasilii Kirillovich, sorry I was so long, I brewed some tea," she said, stepping carefully with her hot burden.

The other girls immediately jumped in to help, shifting the display of alcohol to the centre of the table, and cups of various shapes and sizes appeared in front of the guests at this strange feast, from classic Kuznetsov teacups with chipped gilding to pale-blue children's cups with white polka dots. The girls set out muslin-thin slices of grey bread and dried apricots on separate plates. The tea that poured out of the fat spout was barely even yellow; some of those there took a little bit of sugar on the tip of a spoon and mixed it into the drink, others refrained. Before setting about their meal they all crossed themselves with sweeping gestures. Maxim T. Yermakov's eyes popped out of his head as he watched.

"Ah yes, Maxim, you're not fasting, are you?" Shutov remembered and turned to Sasha. "Is there anything for our guest?"

"There's fresh cheese, I brought it to take home," she replied smartly. "I'll go and get it."

"Sasha will bring it in a moment," Shutov said to Maxim T. Yermakov. "But don't touch anything on the table, that's just stage dressing. In case the local militiaman drops round to inspect us or some other outsider shows up."

"But what on earth have you got going on here?" asked Maxim T. Yermakov, unable to hold back any longer. Who are you? A forbidden sect? Or maybe another special state committee? An FSB big shot showed up out there today with a cross on a gold chain. Or are you the CIA instead?"

"Oh, Maxim, of course we're not FSB or CIA. We're just people. Although, of course, that's the hardest thing of all to understand. I'll tell you the story."

Vasilii Kirillovich Shutov had been ejected from his scientific research institute by *perestroika* without a kopeck to his name but with a serious market inferiority complex – pronounced guilty for all those years he had spent working on grades of steel that were uncompetitive (which later proved to be untrue). Vasilii Kirillovich's wife, a beautiful, slightly overweight blonde who thought that she resembled Marilyn Monroe, quickly divorced him and married a German, a prosperous dealer in footwear. When she moved to take up permanent residence in the Federal Republic of Germany, she took their son Alyosha with her. Having rapidly absorbed civilised ideas about the correct order of things from her rubbery, rosy-pink federal Fritz, she pedantically extorted alimony from Shutov, even when she had to deduct nothing from nothing. Through all the layers of prosperity in which she was now arrayed, she failed to sense the fugitive metaphysical nature of her manipulations with zeroes, while Shutov, who really did drink a great deal in those years, saw that the world was eaten through with little black holes, each as deep as a universe.

Shutov's unfortunate story was perfectly ordinary, but extra-ordinary things started happening to him. He suddenly started seeing people. That is, he had looked at them all the time before: sometimes in the metro a Muscovite can't rest his gaze anywhere without encountering a stooped back or women's knees pressed together and piled up with handbags. Previously, however, these had been parts without a whole. The crowds of people appeared and disappeared like steam, requiring no intellectual effort from him and possessing no continuation in the future. Now the number of people had greatly increased and the population of Moscow seemed to have doubled. Having been disgorged from their research institutes, colleges and chilly factory workshops, these men and women – dressed in various ways, but all with washed-out faces and wearing terrible shoes that looked burnt – were in no hurry to disappear. Muscovites no longer ran everywhere, the masses of humanity thickened and started simmering so that a busy man couldn't get through them. In the old, long underground passages between metro stations a special, strident wheezing sound appeared, the kind that a wind instrument produces when saliva gets into it. Despite his attempts to suppress his operational intellect with poisonous vodka, Shutov suddenly realised very keenly that nobody needed all these people who had been thrown out in the street. Each one of them was on his or her own, a case apart, an eyesore that refused to be forgotten.

Overflowing with the people of Moscow and barely aware of his own self, Shutov turned to various occupations: he screwed and unscrewed nuts in a semi-criminal service station, where foreign cars of uncertain ownership with various stifling human odours inside them were brought at night and by morning had been dismantled, leaving behind only the seats, dumped in a heap; he gave private lessons, hammering school maths into the small heads of girls with dyed hair, despite their stubborn resistance. But for the most part he found employment as a salesman, trading in videocassettes and women's fur coats that looked like stacks of ginger or grey hay, or mouldy medicinal herbal dust packed in opaque plastic. Once a narrow-chested young priest with a barking cough approached his kiosk and asked for herbs to treat a cold. It was from him that Shutov learned, several days later, exactly Who needed every last one of these little people.

Faith and a life spent in striving towards God seemed such a natural condition to Shutov that he could barely even understand how he had lived before. Many things in the world that had previously been hidden behind a hazy veil were suddenly made glaringly clear. Shutov saw that people who consider themselves unwanted by anyone easily believe slander against their own lives: they regard anyone who has acquired even one kopeck more than they have as being in the right and set them above themselves. Guilty of poverty, of the inability to educate their children or feed their old folks, people became shabby and squalid: they didn't wash the windows, didn't clean their clothes, suffered illnesses for years without going to the doctor. They took even less care of their own mental hygiene. People cast aside contemptuously what they had once accepted as a reflection of the reflection of the Gospel commandments – paradoxically regarding "Thou shalt not kill" and "Thou shall not steal" as hangovers from Soviet times. The new reality demonstrated to them that kill and steal was exactly what they should do – and if someone couldn't, then he could beat himself over the head. A former colleague of Shutov's from the laboratory ("That's him," Shutov told Maxim T. Yermakov, pointing to an unhealthy-looking, chubby man with the inky-blue lips of a cardiac case who was smiling into his cup at the other end of the table) lived by carrying out minor repairs on Soviet televisions with innards impregnated with dust, but he felt genuinely ashamed of not riding around in a Mercedes. Being a human being had become very expensive: hundreds of thousands, millions of dollars. The population "of this country" had been presented with new heroes: successful businessmen, self-confident gentlemen with faceted, glinting eyes, wearing wondrous, expensive ties, who had supposedly achieved everything simply through talent and effort. It was enough to drive you crazy to think that you ought to be like them, but in the darkness that had enveloped life you missed your opportunities, lost your way and backed up, searching for the right fork in the path, but your fumbling hands encountered only a wall. "And you mustn't be weak," the new heroes taught the luckless Soviet types, and the ingenuous people believed them, although most had only enough strength to clench their empty hands into ugly fists. It became the height of impropriety to cite your own honesty to justify your failure: teenagers from the new generation of early developers, as pale as potato shoots, were ready to kill their parents for that, at least in their thoughts. The Ten Commandments had been repressed as never before, with the result that human flesh itself began changing before people's eyes: something happened to men's backbones, which almost never remained vertical, women grew moustaches.

Then the transformed Shutov started searching everywhere for others like him, because the Lord lends strength to all, but a weak person requires earthly company. He met some in churches and some surfaced, tattered and wrinkled, from out of his former life; he managed to get talking with others after catching their lost, bewildered glances in a metro station.

"You must understand, Maxim, we're not a sect," Shutov impressed on Maxim T. Yermakov as he topped up his cup with murky brown tea. "Sectarians always claim a monopoly of the truth and announce the end of the world for the day after tomorrow. We're ordinary Orthodox believers, we simply meet and talk to each other about spiritual and worldly matters."

"But if you hide anyway, why don't you join a monastery?" asked Maxim T. Yermakov, still puzzled. "It's all legal there and the local militiaman probably doesn't come bursting in in his dirty boots."

"It's not all that simple, they won't take everyone into a monastery. For instance, they don't take anyone with under-age children. And then the people here are secular people, not blessed for the monastic life. Except perhaps for our Sasha here..." Shutov said with an affectionate glance at his assistant, who blushed furiously, which Maxim T. Yermakov thought made her little freckled face look like a fly agaric mushroom.

Shutov smiled and held his beard in his hand for a moment, then carried on with his story. He still saw people the same way and now also experienced a burning need to talk to them. He realised that the mountains of false guilt heaped up on little people – for their lack of success, for living in murky Soviet society, for Stalin's repressions and the occupation of the Baltic states – prevented their thoughts from even reaching as far as their own real sins. Stooping under their burden, people stopped looking after themselves, accepting that they were waste material, insignificant trash. However, what Shutov intended to make them see was so simple that it couldn't be captured in words. It was like the air, which you can't see and can't grasp in handfuls. But Shutov became obstinate. Using an old typewriter that flung out crooked letters, he sullied and besmirched mountains of paper. He looked for formulations and he found them. Often taken for a bothersome pedlar in trash, he struck up conversations with morose strangers, asking for trouble, was cursed roundly and squarely, and once, in a discussion with two shaven-headed young heroes with breath tainted by hot internal feculence, he lost four teeth and acquired a broken rib.

"But what's it all good for?" Maxim T. Yermakov interrupted indignantly. "Let the priests preach, that's their direct responsibility. The church should do that, not you!"

"You see, Maxim, it's not easy to understand straightaway, but the Church serves God, not people," Shutov objected calmly, screwing up his eyes and staring into space. "The Church's main task is to preserve the essence and the form of faith from century to century. The yearly cycle of the church service is the representation and lived experience of the New Testament, so that everything happens here and now. Of course, the Church does channel help to the poor and the sick, and gives various benevolent donations. But in this case the temple is merely a place where people meet and decide worldly problems on a charitable basis. The Western Christian confessions are more involved in social reality than Orthodoxy. It's like the difference between applied and fundamental science. Orthodoxy is oriented towards God fundamentally, in an absolute sense. But I'm motivated by worldly concerns. Do you think I pester people? No, they're the ones who enter into me. How can I explain to you? I walk along, looking, and see someone. I take another glance and we're hooked. It's like love at first sight, but fraternal love, Christian love. Only don't imagine I get beaten up every day. I'm almost never mistaken about people."

However, Shutov had made mistakes. He acquired a hyperactive associate by the name of Kuzovlev, a smooth-tongued and smoothly-coiffed young man who, above and beyond the natural blackness of his hair, seemed to have poured a whole bottle of drafting ink over his head. This Kuzovlev, a cinema critic by profession, seduced the inexperienced Shutov into reaching out to people not through individual street enamourment, but on a wide scale and from a distance. Shutov's rough drafts, which were already turning yellow and hard, were given a thorough shaking that dislodged enough dried-out lines of type for four newspaper articles which, to Shutov's amazement, were published – one even in a print run of almost two hundred thousand. Emotional reader's responses followed, Shutov suddenly became popular and he was invited onto TV.

"Well, how do you like that!" Maxim T. Yermakov exclaimed in amazement. "Just look at what's happening in front of our office, demonstrators from all over the country and not a single TV camera, even once. This journalist I know explained to me that I'm no newsmaker, nobody's paid the dues yet. And I understand that anyway. I'm not a little kid."

"Don't forget, Maxim, this was the nineties," Shutov reminded him, raising his brown index finger in the air. "Everything was seething and bubbling, the illusions of the intelligentsia had a direct influence even on the new heroes in silk gloves. Back then some fresh, live material still made it into print without being paid for. But, you know, media exposure ended badly for me."

There were five guests in the television studio that was lit as hotly as a summer beach, on a glassy podium that reflected walking feet in an off-putting kind of way. Shutov's companion on a canvas-covered divan was a fat gentleman with the face of a finicky urchin, with damp ringlets and large, wonderfully well-shaved cheeks that had a bluish, mother-of-pearl shimmer. When the microphone came to Shutov, he spoke passionately and vividly, but was so dazed by the muzzles of the TV cameras that he hardly heard the others at all. Meanwhile the fat gentleman – apparently a representative of a major bank – kept glancing at Shutov with a rapidly-kindling appetite. When the recording was over and the studio went dark, he took his neighbour by the elbow, like a lady.

"I'm the one you need," he declared significantly, fingering Shutov affectionately through the sleeve of his jacket.

"In what sense?" Shutov asked in surprise. That is, he was always disposed to talk to people, but this cute-looking banker failed to arouse in Shutov even a vague shadow of the excited recognition that would attract him towards even the most unlovely and unsafe of individuals.

In reply the banker merely winked a jolly eye, which had not lost its cellophane glitter in the gloom, and dragged the puzzled Shutov into an equipment cubbyhole with dusty cables snaking across the floor and a soup plate that had turned as yellow as a skull, with two dry cigarette butts in it. Here the banker set Shutov in front of himself and examined him from the sleeked-down crown of his head to his new boots of Chinese imitation leather, through which Shutov could be seen screwing up his toes. The banker seemed to be thinking about whether he should acquire Shutov in order to stand on the floor of his hallway, like a large vase.

"Well now, really good, really good," this strange man concluded, clearly satisfied with his inspection. "Very convincing indeed, in fact. Our people like that sort of thing. All you need now is a sound, competent manager."

"What on earth for?" Shutov exclaimed, already sensing something ominous hanging over him.

"Well, what a dimwit you are," the banker said with a condescending smile. "It's not salvation or purity that you want. You want *something else*. Otherwise, why go on television? You write in newspapers too, sermonising. You can save your soul without PR, even better in fact, am I right?"

"Yes, that is, you're wrong, I was invited to the broadcast, so I came," Shutov replied quickly, feeling the powder on his face burning like flour on a frying pan.

The banker wrinkled up his face tearfully, as if he had just that moment spotted an annoying defect in his new acquisition. Shutov even got the feeling that the other man wanted to scratch at the annoying spot with his finger to see if it would scrape off.

"Why act so prim, like a five-kopeck honey cake?" the banker asked resentfully, taking one dancing step back from Shutov. "Anyone else in your place would be singing in happiness, grabbing me by the hand. Manufacturing a product is one thing, but selling it – well, just you try. Hang on, though," said the banker, suddenly brightening up and gazing at Shutov with keen new interest, "you've probably already got an arrangement with Belokorkin, right? Answer me: yes or no?"

Shutov, who didn't have a clue who Belokorkin was, just shook his head and went dashing off, on his way running into some irascible television girls, scribbling something on tattered pieces of paper as they walked along, and entire plump caravans of coat stands on wheels with costumes in covers hanging on them. Losing his bearings completely among these rustling covers, he imagined in horror that television presenters in suits were hatching out of the matt cocoons, each one wearing glittering glasses and clutching a sheaf of news. Shutov was delayed by all this and the banker overtook him at the exit turnstiles: scalding Shutov with a blast of healthy male heat from his open coat as he walked along, he thrust some piece of paper into Shutov's hand, managing as he did so to squeeze Shutov's fingers tenderly and hold on to his bony fist for a moment, like the knob of a lever. Stupefied, Shutov thought it was money. It turned out to be a business card, generously embossed in gold, with a convex bank logo that felt sticky to the touch.

As Shutov made his way home in heavy rain, his umbrella caught on others, his new shoes were transformed into saturated oilcloth and he kept thinking all the time that now he simply had to go to confession. That evening the excited Kuzovlev came running round, asked him about the TV, took a great interest in the banker and asked for his crumpled business card, which he kept. After that events developed in a direction that Shutov could not have predicted. Having secured the support of the good banker and bought himself a vast, shoulder-padded black coat almost the same as his, Kuzovlev jollied and expostulated Shutov into registering a not-for-profit organisation. All of a sudden, out of nowhere, money appeared in the organisation's account. Considerably heartened, Kuzovlev set about doing *something else*. He rented a dark little office, where the old plastered walls gave out an ineradicable smell of cooking and installed in it a drowsy secretary as buxom as a pigeon. Partners that Shutov knew nothing about started visiting this gloomy space, frequently accompanied by muscle in the form of black-leather barrels on short track-suit legs; once a young man with a strenuously smiling and prematurely wrinkled face showed up and offered to discuss with "the healer" the idea of his own personal TV programme. Shutov begged Kuzovlev and the secretary Galya, who spent most of her time playing adroit games of patience on the computer, not to let businessmen in; but the strangers kept showing up.

For some unknown reason, a grey cloud of hostility, still fuzzy as yet, condensed above the organisation. The office was visited twice by militiamen in baggy uniforms, who cast dark, sidelong glances from under the low peaks of their caps at the little paper icons glimmering in the corner; racketeers called in on fact-finding visits, looking exactly like Kuzovlev's business partners, but speaking in deliberately loud, adenoidal voices. Dealers in all sorts of shady goods fought their way in to see the office inmate population of the small detached building that was as rotten as a mushroom and cracked across the corner, and one day Shutov was astounded by a plump woman with a tearstained face, carrying her heavy bags with the same detached, flowing movement as women carry buckets of well-water on a yoke.

"It's not anything godly you want," she said, almost exactly repeating the sinister banker's words as she packed the gold and red jumpers that no one had bought back into her bags. "You want money, foreign cars and politics. What would you want with faith, big wheeler-dealers like you? There's no way to find out the truth about you, the only thing that's obvious is that you're getting rich on human naivety. Go on, get richer and richer…"

And so saying, she floated away, like a planet with her two asteroid-satellites stuffed full of goods, which in her hands seemed to be suspended in a state of weightlessness. Shutov couldn't come up with a response to her grievously unjust comments, and she never appeared there again. Shutov felt uncomfortable and nebulous in the office. He felt completely at a loose end there – and so he was. Kuzovlev, his official deputy, did all the hustling himself and always kept the organisation's official seal, the grubby pawn that became a queen when Kuzovlev breathed on it from the depths of his soul and squeezed out a pockmarked impression onto an accounting document in tremulous reverence.

Shutov received some kind of subsistence wage and was even grateful to Kuzovlev when his deputy took him out to the provinces to work – to address people in four towns in the Urals. In the Urals Shutov saw snowy haze between the crowns of the pines, way up under the clouds, and cliff walls with incredibly complicated masonry-work that was a fantastic black colour among the snowy whiteness, as if pig-iron had been mixed into the stone – but also gigantic, poisonous factory chimneys, urban snowdrifts sprinkled with pungent industrial spices, statues of steelworkers corroded by smallpox, dirty flags hanging above administrative buildings, so heavy that the wind couldn't stir them. Kuzovlev put Shutov up in cheap hotels that were a legacy from the Soviet period and abandoned him for the night. Shutov had to keep the hot-water tap open for a long time before the chilly trickle from the pipe started to warm up. Shutov spoke two or three times a day – always in blank, boxy little halls where seats in the audience rows clattered before he began and the maroon plush curtains were raised, like women's skirts, by the curious. Perhaps because they were dressed so thickly and darkly, *en masse* the people in the Urals looked shorter than he was used to, but separately they were tall with broad shoulders and high cheekbones, like the blacksmith's tongs that Shutov had seen in a museum, and extremely meticulous in getting right down to the essence of things. It was only here that Shutov realised he was not offering any original system of philosophy or recipe for life – but there's nothing harder than trying to tell people what they already know. They listened to Shutov with vulpine eyes blazing from the rows of seats, sent up lots of questions scribbled on scraps of paper and enquired with great interest whether they could buy Shutov's book here or in Moscow. Several times when he was walking into a technical college or House of Culture where he was due to speak, Shutov spotted a glossy portrait of the good banker beside a cinema poster: his smiling face, which was a fine flesh colour, was set against a background of fine-weather blue and seemed to be offering itself, like a fancy round loaf of bread, to all the good people climbing the icy steps in the light of a bilious lamp. Kuzovlev, who had bought himself a mink hat in the Urals on which a sprinkling of snowflakes sat beautifully, blazing all colours of the rainbow on the needles of expensive fur, explained animatedly that the banker was going to speak in the same halls immediately after Shutov, only on economic matters. And it was only after Shutov got back to Moscow that he discovered, by chance, that he had travelled to campaign for the banker, who was putting himself forward as a candidate in a by-election to the Duma. That was the first time since he had been baptised that he thumped his fist on the table.

"Hang on, hang on," Maxim T. Yermakov interrupted the pseudo-alcoholic's story, "if this Kuzovlev was such a murky character right from the start, then why did you keep him around? And you handed over the seal to him too. In case you didn't know, he could have got you in big trouble with the law!"

"God was merciful," said Shutov, crossing himself. "As for Zhenya Kuzovlev – this is the way I describe him now, in retrospect. He was an excitable, goodhearted lad, very fond of dogs, he picked up one with a broken leg, cared for it and tried to pull it through, and he was really grief-struck when it died. He was seduced by many things, but he wasn't greedy: he would buy all sorts of fashionable clothes – then give them all away."

"Well, all right," Maxim T. Yermakov persisted, "but what about that holy father who had a cold right at the beginning? He was your mentor, he advised you. After all's said and done, that was his responsibility, if you went to his church. Why didn't he talk you out of that pratfall with the not-for-profit organisation? Where was he anyway, that priest?"

"Father Nikolai," Shutov clarified in a respectful voice. "If you noticed, I never mentioned my relationship with the holy father. Faith views everything that's important to us in the world from a different, non-Euclidian angle. Remember I mentioned fundamental science? It would be foolish of me now to start explaining all this to you in elementary terms. It has to be taken gradually, from the simple to the complicated. Your practical mind would resist many things. You would be hindered by the tools of logic and everything that you have constructed with their help. For now, simply be advised that faith changes a man, but not the conditions of his temporal life."

Maxim T. Yermakov, who had always regarded the Church as a kind of free theatre for old women, sniffed sceptically at that. But he was interested to hear what happened next. And what happened next was something that Maxim T. Yermakov could easily have predicted, while Shutov had apparently still not recovered from his amazement. For him it was like a dream – a meeting at which he was excluded from the charter members of the organisation. It was like a dream in the sense that people Shutov knew well, who were familiar to him in waking life, were present in a strange situation, behaved strangely and spoke in unnatural voices. The secretary Galya, for instance, couldn't possibly have been a charter member of the organisation, but nonetheless she was and she voted, and her buxom chest was adorned with a large necklace of lumpy turquoise, which Shutov had never seen on her before, but he had seen it – or one very like it – in the window of a little jewellery shop as narrow as a lift cabin, which he ran past every day on the way from the office to the metro. The other dreamlike distortion was that Kuzovlev showed up at the meeting as Shutov knew him before they became closely acquainted:

very young, hoarse-voiced, not recognising Shutov with his quick grey eyes, which seemed to skip about when he was counting the hands raised as rigidly as stakes. After the dumbfounded Shutov had been put out of the office door with his personal mug and the paper icons collected together into a file, he couldn't rid himself of the idea that at *dream* meetings like that, as a rule, there were dead people sitting among the living. A couple of months later he was told that when Galya the secretary was on her way home in a minibus taxi, she was involved in a bloody accident and died on the spot – and, moreover, it was quite impossible to find out if it had actually happened before the meeting or after it.

Nonetheless, the dream had an impact on reality: once again Shutov was left without any financial resources, with a few saddened likeminded companions, who carried on coming round in the evenings, bringing a tin of fish or a packet of buckwheat. His ex-wife's voice on the phone – entirely separate from her blurred image, in which the blonde hair that had stuck in his memory more clearly than anything seemed like a wig – suddenly became harsh and intransigent on the subject of Shutov's life. In the precipitately yellowing pages of the newspaper that had previously published Shutov, an article appeared accusing him of engaging in wholesale trade in alcohol and taking large sums of money from "disciples" who had sold their flats and other valuable property. And then the militia came to Shutov's home and carried out a search, tipping all his languid possessions out onto the floor and slashing open the teddy bear with the threadbare seams that had belonged to his son.

Properly speaking, the persecutors of Shutov and his flagging group fell into two categories. The first – those who constituted the demotic majority – were subconsciously convinced that any movement from lesser knowledge to greater, that is, towards the discovery of the truth, is a movement from good to bad, from light into darkness. They regarded Shutov as a swindler who had used the Bible to camouflage the inflation of his wallet. But there were others who realised that Shutov was precisely what he made himself out to be. And these people decided that Shutov was dangerous. For six months he was summoned to interviews by a calm man with thick hair the colour of boiled meat, who was a picture of radiant health in his civilian clothes – he wore pink shirts under a brown jacket with wheat-coloured flecks. The calm man politely questioned Shutov about his concept of Christian chastity, enquired what kind of people visited his home seminars, who they were, what air they breathed, what their needs were. Despite the man's apparent simplicity, his transparent, X-ray eyes saw right through Shutov to his cringing heart – and every time Shutov left the office with his marked pass, he felt as if he was being irradiated one more time, exposed to an incredibly large dose, and that was why he felt weak, his breath was laboured and his head was buzzing. The idea that the man was trying to implant was actually very simple: Shutov had to co-operate and accept help from the special agencies, and if he didn't, he'd better give up his independent amateur activities, because they wouldn't lead to anything good.

Shutov thought for a long time and realised what the problem was: the state, having recovered from its upheavals, had set about developing a single positive image for everyone – red, white and blue with gold trimmings – and any groups of citizens putting forward a positive image of any other colour or shade had become offenders against a state monopoly on supremely important symbolic capital. After realising that he had become a lump in the porridge, Shutov tried for a while to make plans – perhaps he should sell the flat in Moscow, perhaps their ten or twelve families should go somewhere far away? Buy some solid houses, silvery with old age, in an abandoned village in the Urals, settle down among that natural whimsy of stone and rustle of pine needles, acquire some cows, scythe grass, pray to God? However, the Urals idyll was soon deleted by the realisation that there was no way the settlers would be left in peace, because this would be more than mere independent activity, it would be a seizure of territory. The state would definitely feel the little hole in its own massive hide, the painful prick of dispossession. Shutov could just see militiamen riding in from all sides on motorcycles with sidecars, militiamen in resin-slick motorboats; he could see the cordon of raucous journalists around the village and the Assault Group troops with black knitted heads on camouflage-pattern shoulders, quiet as yet but very seriously armed. It seemed like a dead end.

Shutov's solution was suggested to him by a little drunk dressed in an unseasonably light raincoat that was no better than paper against the cold, and with gaping holes in shoes still caked in autumn mud that had turned grey and set as hard as concrete. The little man's face, of which nothing was left apart from wrinkles and raw bones, testified to a long and extensive career as an alcoholic; he was scurrying about at an exit from the metro, grabbing the empty bottles left on the shoulder of the wall and the steps by the young guys drinking beer and stuffing them into a fabric bag in which the glass grated as he stumbled and shoved people. No one looked at the little man: people surrounded by clouds of damp steam flowed out of the wet January underground, ran through the caustic puddles saturated with chemicals, and even those who ran into the foul-smelling scarecrow hastily averted their eyes. Everything about that alcoholic, from the bloated shoes to the exposed bald patch that looked like an egg in a dishevelled nest, invoked powerful feelings – from pity to disdain for human nature; but even so, he was an invisible man, the only one out of all the people there.

That evening Shutov told his people about his idea. Most of them wouldn't agree immediately to become bawdy recluses: they were embarrassed and perplexed. However Sasha, who was already Shutov's senior deputy and the radiant soul of this entire despondent community, said: "This is to humble us, we should do as Vasilii says and not show pride before the sinners we will impersonate". And then they started developing the cover story of the brothel. In second-hand clothes shops they bought lots of glittering glad rags and rubbishy wigs for a few kopecks and someone brought some battered boxes of old theatrical makeup, all mixed up together in coloured dust. At first the new recluses were afraid of exposure and disaster, but the entire world around them found it amazingly easy to believe in the downfall of Shutov and his devout associates. The neighbours on the stairwell merely shook their heads, the women glowered at the sight of the scantily clad "prostitutes" and tried to bring Shutov to his senses, appealing to the memory of his deceased mother and father and wrinkling up their noses under their steel-rimmed glasses at his alcoholic fumes. The vodka with which he had to rinse his mouth in order to make his breath convincing was a thick, raging ball of fire that seared through his gums right down to the roots of his teeth – and the girls' poor legs turned red from the cold in their fishnet stockings. But Sasha didn't lose heart and she wouldn't let the others lose heart either, she called her colleagues in the brothel "polar explorers". Once when Shutov was dressed for his part, that is, exactly like his alcoholic model, in a paper-thin raincoat, with black circles drawn in under his eyes, he ran into the man from the special organs right there in the street. The man had a firm grip on the hand of a roly-poly four-year-old, a smaller version of Signor Pomidor, who kept trying to smash right through every puddle with his rubber boot – but even when the man was out walking he maintained his professional vigilance, and the child looked as if he had been arrested. Shutov had never been so close to disaster. He thought the state security professional (whose penetrating radiation, accumulated in Shutov's organism, still prevented him from getting out of bed in the morning without feeling dizzy) would immediately see through the fancy dress. However, the man in civilian dress – this time in a big shaggy coat that looked as if horse hair had been added to the cloth – merely smiled contentedly on seeing the former preacher reduced to this lowly, prosaic condition. It was clear that it didn't raise any questions at all in his mind. And neither did anyone else around have any doubt that the ugliness they observed was the truth.

"But even so, I reckon that's a bit too extreme," said Maxim T. Yermakov, wrinkling up his forehead and running his finger round the puffy rings left on the table by indeterminate items of tableware.

While Shutov was telling the story of his trials and tribulations in exhaustive detail, the gathering in the room with icons shrank in size. People quietly got up from the table, crossed themselves facing the weeping candles, squeezed Shutov's sloping shoulder and cast significant glances at Maxim T. Yermakov from the doorway – but Maxim T. Yermakov still couldn't understand exactly what they were trying to express or convey. The girls clattered wet crockery in the kitchen, talking together in brittle voices. The only people left at the table, apart from Shutov and Maxim T. Yermakov, were the old man with a yellow beard, the intellectual type with the burn mark, gazing meekly through his murky glasses with eyes the colour of triple-strength eau-de-cologne, and Sasha, sitting with her elbows propped on the table and her pointy chin resting on her clasped fingers.

"It may be extreme and strange, but it works," Shutov said with conviction. "You know, Maxim, I was astounded when the event that I was afraid of in the Urals happened point for point in Penza! You remember, the Penza anchorites, it was in all the papers. Never mind if they were a sect, the people had withdrawn into an underground shelter to pray to God – and they set the journalists and the militia on them. They dug them out, like animals out of their burrows, even though they didn't want any kind of fuss, on the contrary, they wanted to leave the world behind. But the world came and surrounded them, it wouldn't stand for it."

"But supposedly there were children there, they could have got ill," Maxim T. Yermakov protested, vaguely recalling some TV programme about these hermits, the spooky-looking hole of a cave in a clayey cliff face, freezing-cold strips of polythene, naked roots that looked like melting icicles because of the water flowing over them.

"Come on, Maxim," Shutov exclaimed with a wave of his hand. "Was it really because of the children? How many buildings unfit for habitation are there in the country – no light, no water, wet lumps of plaster falling off the ceilings onto tables, into beds. Who's worried about what happens to the children living there? And people who have been burned out of their homes? I personally know of one situation – a family living a miserable life in a barn, with only a planking partition to separate them from the cow; in winter the inside of the logs is covered with hoarfrost as thick as a sheepskin, only unfortunately, it's cold. And what happens? They were given financial assistance from the state: ten thousand roubles. No, the children have nothing to do with it, it's all a matter of the message, as they say nowadays. Those people didn't simply withdraw to live under the ground, they did it for faith. And straightaway they're surrounded by antibodies, like some dangerous virus. The same thing would have happened to us, believe me, Maxim. When people try to live in their own community according to faith, in purity and chastity – they're not understood. But drunks and alcoholics – everyone understands that. And they take no notice of what they can understand, which is just what we want."

"Well, you know best," Maxim T. Yermakov said with a shrug. "Maybe now I can give you some money for delivering the groceries? Since none of you drink."

"Ah no," Shutov laughed, again displaying that single protruding incisor that Maxim T. Yermakov simply couldn't get used to. "What about the mouth rinse and the stage set? You supply our requirements exactly. So let's leave everything just as it is, and thanks for the vodka."

"Vasilii Kirillovich, may I say something?" Sasha put in, raising her hand like a schoolgirl at her desk. "Of course we had to tell Maxim about ourselves. But why did I bring him here? I was walking along and I saw him sitting on a bench, as white as chalk and sniffing at a pistol. A genuine pistol! And I'd heard earlier, in the shop, that a man had been shot here in the yard. Supposedly a woman shot him, some well known singer."

"She's no singer," Maxim T. Yermakov interrupted abruptly, feeling a sudden, profound pang at the thought of Marinka and how now she must be freezing in the holding cells in her idiotic dress, among the iron grilles and bars.

"I blurted out some silly nonsense, Maxim, forgive me for Christ's sake," Sasha said dejectedly.

"It's okay, I'll survive," growled Maxim T. Yermakov: under the table he pressed his thigh against the sprawling briefcase, making the pistol shift in it, like the leg of a startled neighbour. "I was going to come to see you today, even before there was any shooting. To be quite honest, I've really got my back up against the wall… I thought there was murky water here, and I needed to dive in and lie low until things passed over. Now I don't even know what to say…"

"Just tell it the way it is," Shutov advised him seriously. "We're not blind, we can see you're in a tight spot. We have a general idea of how things are from the computer game and the comrades in civvies on duty in the stairwell. You tell us as much as you like, and we'll see how we can help."

Maxim T. Yermakov glanced uncertainly at the open bottle of vodka and wondered if he ought to drink some of the garbage to keep his courage up, but he sighed and refrained. He had intended to fit the entire story into ten minutes at the most – but the state freak Kravtsov, with his head like the stomach of some ruminant and magnesium flashing in his appalling eye sockets, came to life, along with Blur, who was always somewhere in the corner, as inconspicuous and ineradicable as a spider. The multitude of rank and file social forecasters rose up, with their white button-faces and the symbols on them that hadn't become any more comprehensible in six months. Big Vovan crept out, clutching the wallets he had recovered from the river-bottom, looking like crude black shells. Maxim T. Yermakov tried not to show Little Lucy, to hide her away, but even so, she made her quiet entrance, bringing with her an indistinct child, who could be either alive or dead. At this point in the story Sasha's eyes filled with tears and blazed in her face like powerful convex magnifying glasses; the girls who were clearing the crockery away came out of the kitchen and crowded in the doorway – the one with dark eyebrows looking exactly like a stupid matryoshka doll and the other one, with the long nose, whom he remembered wearing a short, clumpy silver-fox jacket, wiped her eyes with the corner of her headscarf, just like a simple village woman.

The intellectual type listened to the story, blinking frequently, which made his large, lack-lustre eyes look like TV screens showing interference: the old man with the yellow beard grunted every now and then and occasionally looked at Shutov quizzically, as if enquiring whether he should believe this or not: Shutov answered by closing his eyes in confirmation. The only thing that Maxim T. Yermakov managed not to blurt out was about the ten million dollars. In his version of the story Little Lucy was going to inherit his savings, because gutting his bank account just before the "suicide" would look suspicious.

When you talk and other people listen, the time passes quickly. Glancing by chance out of the window, Maxim T. Yermakov saw the incredibly limpid pre-dawn light that happens at five in the morning in summer, when every object is clear and distinct and seems to have been reduced to half its size: the maple tree on which Maxim T. Yermakov's desecrated wardrobe had once dangled reminded him of a black glove turned inside out, the children's swings and roundabouts in the far corner of the deep courtyard looked like a cage for small rodents that had been dismantled. His listeners were already yawning desperately: Shutov's nostrils were trembling and his eyes were watering, the intellectual type seemed to be choking on hot porridge as he tried to swallow it. But the story could not be broken off before it was completed: every character in the tale was given a vigorous oral double and Maxim T. Yermakov had a hazy vision of these doubles uniting with their originals in the present moment, and then everything he had not understood before would be revealed to him.

Eventually he came to that evening – strictly speaking, yesterday evening: he saw lieutenant Novosiltsev again, sprawling on the wet asphalt that was gold in the sunlight, and he could feel that Novosiltsev's compressed electric copy, punched into Maxim T. Yermakov's chest by the discharge of his death agony, was still there, sparking and pricking at his heart.

"I honestly can't imagine why he covered me with his body," Maxim T. Yermakov said slowly, staring at the chipped table. "I feel pain for him, but pain doesn't get me anywhere. For me to blast my head off and, let's suppose, save thousands of people sounds stupid enough. I have to want to do it myself, but I don't have the slightest inner urge to do that. Sometimes I might think something

251

like maybe I ought to, my duty as a human being and all that, but then immediately, it just seems disgusting and absurd, as if I've put on someone else's trousers. Kravtsov, the top man in the special committee, talked about a special kind of enthusiasm today, well, I've already told you his speech pretty much word-for-word. To be honest, I don't understand what he's talking about."

"But I do," the intellectual type suddenly said in a flat voice, pulling off the glasses that clutched at his large, crinkly ears like cart shafts, and starting to rub at the lenses with the end of his shirt, as if he wanted to wear holes in them.

"I basically understand too," the bulky old man said after a moment's thought. "I'm familiar with that feeling."

"So am I," Sasha responded in an unexpectedly harsh, agitated voice.

"Some fucking nun she is!" thought Maxim T. Yermakov, squinting apprehensively at Sasha, with her huge moist eyes glittering militantly, but out loud he said:

"So, in short, you condemn me. But I'm telling you the truth about myself and I won't tell you anything else. A pity really that I was given the chance, I didn't ask for it."

"Maxim, Maxim!" Shutov exclaimed, raising both hands in protest. "In God's name, no one is even thinking of condemning you. You see, acting nobly is not the same thing as acting freely. You are a decent, sincere person. You choose freedom, and that is your right. If we happen to share one of Mr. Kravtsov's feelings, that doesn't at all mean that we sympathise with the special committee. They want to deprive you not only of your life, but your freedom and, moreover, in the act that is most important to any man: the final, decisive act. They oppress you and pursue you. In the final analysis they deprive you of the chance to achieve that exalted spiritual condition without which self-sacrifice is impossible. After all, what is the fatal flaw of all the special committees? They oblige citizens to perform acts that are apparently sublime, but in fact hollow and spurious, and so mock the very values in the name of which they were originally created. But you are upholding, with admirable courage, the higher value which, by virtue of your spiritual weakness, is the one that you currently possess. So believe me, Maxim, everyone here is on your side."

Against his own will Maxim T. Yermakov broke into a broad, stupid smile. Nobody had praised him for such a long time, he couldn't even remember how long it was. In the old days Ika sometimes used to twitch the corner of her withered mouth and force out sour praise; Crap, scratching under his tie knot with his mother-of-pearl nails, used to mutter "Not bad"; Marinka beamed and gushed compliments if she needed money urgently. But none of that really counted. Maxim T. Yermakov suddenly felt warm, even hot, in that cardboard-coloured room lit by the yellow ceiling lamp with dark lunar patches of accumulated dust. He reminded himself that these religious recluses who had given him refuge didn't know about the ten million dollars – but even to him the money suddenly seemed so unimportant that his conscience instantly purged itself of any stain. What seemed important was something else, and Maxim T. Yermakov was finally able to formulate the question:

"When I fight for myself – am I fighting only for myself?"

"It's good that you asked, Maxim," Shutov responded thoughtfully. "I don't know, I can't answer straightaway. You really do belong to a new human type that never existed in Russia before. I would probably call you a foreigner, if people like you had not become the majority in your generation. Formerly, in traditional society, fighting for others meant fighting for a whole that was cemented together by something supra-personal, even if it was barbaric. But now it is only the salvation of free individuals, all individually – which is possible for the Lord, but certainly not for man. You, Maxim, are fighting for others like yourself against a monster armed to the teeth, including moral weapons. And your struggle is far more hopeless than, say, the heroic feat of the three hundred Spartans, and not because of the monster, but because the objective is dispersed, there is no single address. My wish for you is to live long enough to realise that in these matters the Lord is better than the internet."

"Well, that's not very likely, I'll tell you honestly," said Maxim T. Yermakov, frowning. "I don't want to make myself out to be better than I am to you. I really am a common individual who gets grief from other people, from some about God, from some about disasters, from some about relations of cause and effect. But there's only one thing I want: to lie low somewhere for six months and leave the country. I don't have any enthusiasm or patriotism in me. I don't see why this country is any better for me than any others. I reckon it's a lot worse. Bumpy roads, bribes, filth everywhere – why, the traffic cops alone are a marvel, with their magic striped sticks bringing in ten thousand roubles on the side in every shift. Oh no, first I'll look for a place that's deeper, and then one that's better. You see what a swine I am: I came to ask for help, but I don't play along with you, I insult your fine feelings. You've been had too, they forced you to act out a brothel, and you're probably patriots."

"It's all more complicated than that, Maxim," Shutov said softly, shaking his head. "Our Homeland is the Orthodox faith. For faith, just like the internet, it doesn't matter where a person's physical body is, as long as he's connected to the network. Remember what they used to say: 'For the Faith, the Tsar and the Fatherland.' The faith comes first, it is the foundation, the identity as they say nowadays. But that's all fundamental science again, you're not ready for that yet, you don't want it."

"Yes, really, Vasilii Kirillovich, let's talk more about today," Sasha intervened briskly and in the window behind her back a low beam of dawn light sought blindly for a gap between two angular roofs, like a thread trying to enter into the eye of a needle. "Or we'll spend all our time on general subjects and not understand what we should do for Maxim."

At this point the intellectual type, who all this time had been fiddling with his glasses, with his brows knitted, looked up with short-sighted eyes the colour of stale eau-de-cologne and gave a resounding cough that attracted everyone's attention.

"There's no question about what to do," he said casually, reinstalling the ugly glasses on his face – they were no cleaner for all his efforts, only perhaps a bit rounder. "The young man needs a place to live for six months and documents in a new name. Sashenka, my dear, give me a piece of paper and something to write with."

Sasha jumped up, twisted round and set down in front of the intellectual type two clean sheets of writing paper and an old souvenir pen in the form of a yellow plastic goose-quill. Inclining his head towards one shoulder, the intellectual elegantly traced out a single line on one sheet and pushed it towards Maxim T. Yermakov.

"There, memorise that number, and destroy the paper," he said imperiously, and somehow it was immediately obvious that he wasn't an intellectual type after all, but probably a retired officer; sinewy, suntanned, with slightly withered muscles that still retained some strength and a heart tied in a knot. "In a few days' time Sasha will bring you a mobile phone, as clean as a whistle, never used. That phone is for just one single call. When you climb out onto the bank and get changed, use it to call the number in front of you. You'll be given further instructions. You don't need to know anything more as yet, that's a basic principle of conspiracy, as you no doubt understand. And don't give me such a frightened look, young man," the pseudo-intellectual said with a fleeting smile. "I'll be delighted to sow some confusion among the comrades from the special committees. If only for all the good things they did in Afghanistan."

"It's not a frightened look. Thank you," muttered Maxim T. Yermakov. He was a strange character, of course, this man in glasses. He changed every time you looked at him. Maybe he was a former spy, maybe he was from the special services too. So Maxim T. Yermakov would be totally and completely in his hands. But what choice did he have? None at all.

"Well then, friends, the debauchery is over for today," the owner of the brothel announced with an embarrassed smile. The guests, pale-faced and with their bodies looking somehow swollen after the sleepless night, started awkwardly clambering out of the narrow space around the table, leaving the shameless still life as it was, with the two fat-thighed chickens and white fish looking like naked women who had been screwed to death.

"Maxim, when are you going to jump?" Sasha asked in a quiet voice as she saw Maxim T. Yermakov out into the corridor.

"In a couple of weeks, probably," he replied indifferently, clutching in his arms the shapeless briefcase with the hard filling. Suddenly it hit him that these were not just words, that everything was really going to happen, and very soon; his heart suddenly scooped up something cold, like a bucket that has fallen into the well.

"Don't worry," said Sasha, repeating the usual nonsense for such cases. "Everything will be all right, you'll definitely get away."

Two weeks later, in the middle of a fiercely cold August, at half past eleven at night, as agreed, Maxim T. Yermakov drove up to the Nagatino Metro Bridge in the trusty old Toyota that he was now abandoning forever. The August night was black, saturated in raw electricity. He thought it was raining: under some streetlamps the rain looked like a haphazard scattering of steel sewing needles, under others there was nothing. Maxim T. Yermakov rustled and perspired in his stiff diving suit, closed right up his throat with the soft grip of its broad zipper. The "frying pan" – a slab of lead under which a hot, pungent pie seemed to be baking – weighed down painfully on his sacrum. Over the top Maxim T. Yermakov had pulled on an old windbreaker from his Krasnogorie reserves and a pair of tattered jeans, with a fly that wouldn't button up because of the bulky neoprene. Since he had had to get dressed in complete darkness, in the narrow space of Just Natasha's gurgling toilet, extracting the diving suit from a toilet bowl that was icy to the touch, everything that Maxim T. Yermakov was wearing sat crookedly, the way things used to back at nursery-school age, when his humiliatingly warm clothes were pulled on by the attentive hands of strangers.

In all honesty, Maxim T. Yermakov was feeling as chicken as a snot-nosed kid. Beside him, on the passenger seat, lay the pistol, its black adder's scales glittering on the curves, and Maxim T. Yermakov squinted sideways at it every now and then. The day before he had ridden the Yamaha to a wild spot and there, in a remote little ravine, among the ferns and the fallen tree trunks overgrown with grey fungi, he had painstakingly cleared out the clip, tipping the bullets down behind a sprawling root and, just to make sure, clicking the trigger at a huge, black-headed mushroom a couple of times without causing the handsome fellow the slightest damage. But even so, he couldn't get rid of the feeling that in some incomprehensible way a single bullet had still been left in the pistol and the Makarov had hidden it inside its ribbed cheek, like a caramel sweet.

To distract himself from the shuddering and the sick feeling, Maxim T. Yermakov went through his final actions, step by step, in his mind. Immediately after the visit to the ravine he had dashed back to Moscow, to Andropov Street, with a rucksack on his shoulders, and in the rucksack was a small bag containing all his posthumous property. Apart from a tracksuit rolled up into a tight bolster and a couple of compact bricks of money, the bag held a cheap mobile phone, painstakingly swaddled in many layers of polythene and rags. Sasha had bought him this old-age-pensioner's model stuck at the bottom of his bag of groceries and looked at Maxim T. Yermakov with her makeup-plastered eyes as if she had fallen in love. It was better not to remember that moment right now. Maxim T. Yermakov had hidden the bag a little distance away from the site of his anticipated emergence from the water, in a heap of caked leaf mould that had accumulated over the years in a rubbish-strewn little thicket. No matter how hard he tried to disguise his precious treasure, no matter how he heaped it over with old, perspiring plastic bottles and damp pieces of paper – many of them bearing the blackened imprints of seals from human backsides – the traces of his work were still visible. A dozen times that evening Maxim T. Yermakov suppressed the urge to go dashing back to those unreliable bushes and make sure the bag was there, and hold it in his hands. Only the presence of the duty officers in the stairwell – on this occasion they were somehow especially focused, which made them look as alike as twin brothers – held Maxim T. Yermakov back from this rash act.

It was a strange feeling, saying goodbye to his old life. Just Natasha's dull flat suddenly became as dear as if Maxim T. Yermakov had grown up in the narrow space between these walls. The tenant's personal belongings had never merged into their rented interior but always stood out, three-dimensional against the flatness, so that if he wanted he could have collected them all up in ten minutes – but now they had merged with it, put down roots. Many, very many things had to be abandoned. His computer, for instance, that precious, lived-in, cluttered laptop, with the keyboard worn down by Maxim T. Yermakov's fingers so that only blackened little shells remained of the letters. For instance, his multi-brand collection of silk ties that had hardly been worn since the moment when Just Natasha threw his clothes out – he wondered who would get those. The uterine murmurings of the water pipes were like rumblings in Maxim T. Yermakov's own stomach. Somehow the way that things called to him from all sides, wherever he looked, made the fanciful idea that he was really going to die even stronger. By comparison with the faint materiality of this flat, the immediate future was absolutely empty, it gaped open before Maxim T. Yermakov like a huge bank of grey fog. He couldn't believe that this emptiness could be filled with a new life: the bed, walls and view from a window that were waiting up ahead were unimaginable. There was absolutely nothing to get a grip on, his imagination had gone blind. Maxim T. Yermakov had to get a good night's rest on this last night at home, and he made an honest effort to sink into the hot, goose-pimply sleep that cast green shadows under his eyelids – but after about half an hour he would wake up with the feeling that he was travelling in a train. And finally, at the deepest point of a damp and heavy August night, the moment of mental numbness arrived in which Maxim T. Yermakov suddenly lost his faith that things could be bought for money.

He hadn't got enough sleep after all. His hands on the steering wheel of the Toyota were cold, no matter how much he blew on them, and sometimes they lost contact with his head, which had drifted up above the clouds. The Toyota toiled along slowly and the social forecasters' van, as small as a stool, plodded along behind; in the damp air its modestly downcast headlamps expanded into blurred, trembling yellow blotches. But all the same, there it was, the Nagatino metro bridge. And here was the middle of the bridge. They had arrived. In violation of every possible rule of the road – they were no longer important – Maxim T. Yermakov parked. "Am I going to do this for real?" he asked himself with detached amazement, clambering out of the warmth of the car into the fine drizzle that instantly pasted his hands and cheeks with its dank substance. The car alarm squawked. The Toyota went dark. The social forecasters also stopped a short distance away, forgetting to extinguish their tearful headlamps that looked like the enflamed eyes of a sick dog; behind the windscreen, beaded with perspiration, Maxim T. Yermakov fancied that he saw the movements of two coordinated shadows, one of which was wearing a shadowy, double-peaked hat. "I forgot the pistol," thought Maxim T. Yermakov. However, the Makarov turned up in his right hand, angular and awkward, not knowing which way to look.

Maxim T. Yermakov bent over the low barrier. The water was as thick and black as tar: it was impossible to tell which way it was flowing. Serried ranks of residential high-rises burned like firebrands on the opposite bank and their reflections in the water were unfinished, with blurred, shattered lights. He couldn't believe that somewhere down below him, under a layer of tar, Big Vovan was waiting for a bulky body to fall, preparing to provide that body with oxygen. "Come on, bugger it, stop wasting time," Maxim T. Yermakov commanded himself, spotting out of the corner of his eye that the social forecasters were climbing out of their little square van. As if they could stop him. But even so they were coming closer, the cunts, walking on tiptoe. The one in the hat was in front and the other, a husky individual, was hanging back, mincing along, holding an umbrella with its catch released, looking like a dove of peace struggling to soar up and away: there, at last he opened it over his resolute boss's hat with a quiet pop, and immediately the umbrella strained tautly, as if understanding the importance of the mission entrusted to it. All right, you patriots, now you get what's coming to you, prepare to be led astray by the evidence of your own eyes. Maxim T. Yermakov's diving suit was snuffling with his sweat, it wouldn't let him raise his bent leg onto the low barrier. Then Maxim T. Yermakov simply lay down on the barrier on his stomach and hastily tumbled over it, feeling the displacement of his fat supper in his stomach.

Immediately the river water moved closer, came alive and started smacking its lips, its fleshy, female scent came alive and the liquid lights blurred like oil on a black frying pan. Now Maxim T. Yermakov was barely holding on to the icy railing with one hand behind his back and could clearly feel that he was not wearing real shoes on his feet, but rubber boots, through which he could sense every little roughness of the inclined ledge. "Now I'll fall off without firing, and they'll jump in to save me, the bastards," he thought quickly, and his right arm, which had suddenly become much longer than his left one, traced out a strange arc through the air. A firm ring of metal touched his forehead, the eyebrow beneath it trembled and fluttered, and for a moment Maxim T. Yermakov could sense the entire jointed, malevolent little killing machine just waiting for the index finger on the trigger to jerk. "Easy, easy, easy," Maxim T. Yermakov whispered through his clenched lips and then his wrinkled forehead seemed to be kicked by a horse.

For a second he was nowhere, with his stomach in his chest, the biting air was tearing him ragged, the black water was hurtling up towards him from below, and it had suddenly started flowing faster – and then he was deafened by an explosion far more powerful than the shot. He exploded in the river like a May Day fireworks display, in an entire cloud of lead-grey and yellow bubbles – and up above the two social forecasters hastily occupied the same spot where the fat suicide had only just tumbled over the barrier. There was even something human about that, because people always dash to be right at the site of a tragedy, as if they can prevent something retrospectively or at least understand – from the fresh trail left in the air. However, the social forecasters exchanged smiles at the sight of the murky blotch that swelled up in the water – looking very much like the murky blotch of the moon, far higher up, among the grey clouds – and those smiles were sceptical.

Maxim T. Yermakov, incorporeal, with his arms upraised and the windbreaker up round his throat, sank into the thickening murk. From out of the murk a long shadow rose up, seething quietly, a ribbed, rubbery hand was set on Maxim T. Yermakov's shoulder and a mouthpiece was thrust into the drowning man's bluish-grey grin. After pausing a moment, the shadow thumped the target's rounded back with a smooth gesture and that gelatinous tremor roused Maxim T. Yermakov from his stupor, so that he drew in a little of the dead artificial air. His head, a shapeless bubble, broadcast uneven rings of pain into the enveloping mass of water. The head half-opened its heavy eyes in the water: darkness swayed around it in irregular gouts, and one of the darknesses was a man rapidly moving his flat glass face close to Maxim T. Yermakov. In the gloom Maxim T. Yermakov could vaguely make out swollen features behind the glass, looking like fish in an opened can, and he didn't recognise Vovan in this thick, pale nose and hairless brow ridge that glimmered an oily white.

But there could be no doubt it was Vovan. Winding himself round Maxim T. Yermakov like a black ribbon, he grabbed him under the armpits and, continuing to feed him the tasteless air from his tank, pulled him forward, against the taut and strangely lumpy flow of the river. Through his pain and sickness Maxim T. Yermakov felt the river water rinsing his camouflage clothes, gradually permeating, here and there, the thick neoprene of the diving suit: it reminded him very clearly of something – a childhood winter sensation, when you slide down a little slope with an icy crust on your trousers and the cold thaws in through the wool and the flannel nap.

While it was raining up above, underwater a fine grey snow seemed to be sifting down; in the narrow, barely yellow beam of the lamp glowing on Vovan's forehead, some kind of warped iron structure drifted by slowly, covered in coarse hoar frost. Maxim T. Yermakov felt as if he was delirious and dreaming. His body, dangling limply in Vovan's claws, maintained its equilibrium poorly above the darkling bottom – but every attempt to row with an arm or a leg was cut short by a firm punch from above, which momentarily reduced Maxim T. Yermakov's heart to a formless blot. Maxim T. Yermakov allowed himself to be dragged along almost blindly, but sometimes he opened his eyes to allow in the stinging murk, and then on one side he caught the movement of another flexible black ribbon with flippers, the spectral light of a lamp, a grey stream of bubbles. Of course, this doubling up (or trebling, because there seemed to be yet another electric trumpet shape behind, looking like a dull plastic cup) was an illusion, an emanation of his own indeterminate head. Maxim T. Yermakov felt sick, his stomach was cramping convulsively, there were hard, rough nuts in his ears. That oily abyss below him, and the whitish flakes, and the fine, sharp little stars right in front of the circle of the lamp, and the sticky membrane of the water surface above his head, with garbage drifting by, swaying and bobbing – it all reminded him of something, but what? The despair he had once experienced. That night when Marinka left. The same underwater sensation of deep cold and a tight-clenched heart. And the absolute disappearance of time – here, in the darkness. How long had they been swimming already? One hour, two, an eternity?

Eventually the bottom slanted upwards and crude stones emerged, covered with scabs as if they had had fallen from the moon. Sleepy little fish, hanging like clothes pegs on some kind of slimy stems, immediately darted away – and Maxim T. Yermakov, tugged under his armpits, burst with a sudden gasp out of that dense element, became heavy, drew up his legs, spat out the mouthpiece and breathed in damp, living air that smelled of campfire smoke.

They dragged him crudely backwards onto the low bank with tattered, wetly gleaming bushes sticking up on the left and the right. There really was a campfire burning red, like a lump of raw meat being steamed, and Maxim T. Yermakov thought Vovan had lost his mind. And then he saw Vovan himself: he was sitting huddled up in a wretched little black coat, stretching out his hands, scarlet on the underside, towards the heat of the glowing coals; he looked as if there was red pepper sprinkled thickly under his eyes, and those eyes – drops of dark oil in scarlet wrinkles – carefully avoided Maxim T. Yermakov.

Astounded, Maxim T. Yermakov turned to the man who had pulled him out. The stranger, with biceps each the size of a grown man's buttock, had already rid himself of his flippers and air cylinder and now he was pulling off his half-unfastened helmet, working loose his short whitish hair that looked like wet chicken feathers. Meanwhile another frogman was climbing out of the river, with his huge glossy flippers in his raised hand and his mask on his forehead, and a short distance away another one, the third, heaved up out of the water – all in all, six gleaming, black creatures, with masks like red floodlights. And they all tramped out, seething with agitated silt, onto the low, boggy bank, removing parts of their alien anatomy on the way and shouting unintelligibly to each other in damp, trumpeting voices. Then suddenly Maxim T. Yermakov was doubled over, squeezed up into a painful concertina, and his bitter supper splashed out of his bowels into the shaggy grass.

When he came to after a brief spell of non-being that had constricted his brain, he saw before him a pair of black shoes as simple as rubber galoshes, with dappled, rotten leaves clinging to them. Shuddering violently from cold in the wet neoprene, which was discharging the water squeezed out of it onto his body, Maxim T. Yermakov started scrambling and tumbled over ponderously. Sergei Yevgenievich Kravtsov was squatting down in front of him, dangling his grey hands between his small, boxy knees and watching very attentively out of the depths of his shapeless eye sockets.

"Well hello, Maxim Terentievich," he said, swaying comfortably as if he was on springs. "So you did it after all, congratulations. It was beautiful, but pointless."

"So you knew from the very beginning?" Maxim T. Yermakov croaked, goggling with watery eyes at the principal tadpole-head of the country.

"Naturally," the principal tadpole-head confirmed condescendingly. "Actually we were expecting you to try something of the kind. And then this man comes running to us…" Kravtsov nodded briefly in the direction of Vovan, who had half-risen, with his backside jutting out. "He comes running to us and tells us this and that, and your mark's going to jump into the water for a film, he asked me to be his trainer. He came running, by the way, on the very same evening when you took him to your place and gave him money and drink. He perfumed our modest office with your fragrant French cognac. How about that?"

At these words Vovan, still half-doubled over and unable to decide whether to straighten up or sit down, broke into an embarrassed smile and started blinking very rapidly, as if he had been praised to the roof and then even higher.

"Ah, you bas-tard!" Going up on one elbow on a branch that promptly snapped and stuck into him, Maxim T. Yermakov loosed a string of obscenity too filthy to have been heard in his little old town, except perhaps from the most tobacco-soaked and alcoholic-drenched of its inhabitants, and which he could never have expected from himself.

The principal state freak looked at Maxim T. Yermakov with respectful interest, inclining his semi-transparent head to one side with raindrops running down it, feeling their way cautiously. The frogmen moved closer, one or two at a time, dragging the equipment they hadn't finished taking off over the black grass; the slightly opened mouths in their water-pale faces were like holes made with an index finger. The smile on Vovan's face twitched like a lizard squelched under a stone and finally froze in an unnatural curve, and the unshaven Judas' eyes were suddenly misted by an absolutely genuine, hot, trembling veil of tears.

"What's he trying to pull, eh? What's this rubbish he's spouting?" Vovan appealed plaintively to everyone there, clenching and un-clenching his potato-brown fists, drowned in the sleeves of his orphan's coat. "I taught him, I carried him, he couldn't do anything, He's just a bubble of shit! He would have croaked today if I hadn't slaved over him! Some actor he is! Where's the camera? There isn't any camera. It's all a heap of shit, phooey!" And with a shrug of his shoulders Big Vovan hoisted his hunchbacked coat right up to his flabby, mouse-furry ears.

"Well, all right," said Sergei Yevgenievich Kravtsov, slapping himself on the knees and rising lightly to his full height. "Let's just say we can now put this stage behind us, Maxim Terentievich. The damage, fortunately, is minimal: one Makarov pistol irretrievably lost in the river. Here, take another one, and make sure you don't lose it."

So saying, with a sickening crunch, the state freak pulled an object out of the pocket of his shapeless trousers, as if it was his own pelvis – a pitch-black pistol, even more repulsive than the other one. One of the social forecasters, arriving at just the right moment, placed the weapon in Maxim T. Yermakov's filthy hand, as feeble as a jellyfish. This Makarov was much newer than the one that had drowned and Maxim T. Yermakov thought it felt a little bit heavier. It was packed chockfull with death, like a purse of coins. One of the pistol's cheeks was warm – that was unpleasant, some kind of chemical warmth from an abortive male body concealed under coarse folds of fabric, under a raincoat that glistened like cast-iron. The touch of this warmth, well retained in the metal, made Maxim T. Yermakov shudder.

"Don't be squeamish, now. Maxim Terentievich," the principal tadpole-head declared sarcastically, spotting the Object's reaction. "My pistol is now your best friend. Your comfort in the very final and, believe me, most important moments of your life depends on its serviceability."

"Screw you," croaked Maxim T. Yermakov, feeling a blob of nausea spinning slowly in his head.

At that moment the bushes jolted and a large social forecaster with steamed-up oval glasses on a round face like an alarm clock scrambled out onto the riverbank, cleaning something off his fat sleeve. He was clutching the twisted strap of Maxim T. Yermakov's bag, which had one side horribly dented in. The round-faced man was followed out by another two like him, who thrust their army spades debonairly into the ground and started stamping their feet diligently to shake the wet sponge of garbage, clay and grass off their shoes.

"There, Sergei Evgenievich, we had a lot of trouble finding it," the round-faced one announced, displaying his unsavoury find to the principal tadpole-head.

"Well then," the principal tadpole-head summed up, "we're done here for today. Take Maxim Terentievich home, get him a doctor and don't forget to drive his car back to his building's courtyard. What?" he asked in a different, harsh tone of voice, turning to Vovan, who was hovering agitatedly, stretching his gulping, plucked neck out of his grimy collar.

"Begging your pardon, the money's there, in the bag," Vovan explained obsequiously, glancing sideways at the round-faced man, who tightened his grip on the strap.

"Naturally the money's in there," the state freak agreed icily. "Kostya, give Maxim Terentievich what is rightfully his."

The round-faced man, who answered to the name of Kostya, waddled over and set the bag close against Maxim T. Yermakov, who didn't even have the strength to embrace his returned property.

"Begging your pardon once again," Vovan piped up, very much afraid, but starting to get angry. "He owes me money for the training. I could just count it off quickly now, with you here, ten thousand, like him and me agreed. He promised to give me it today, and he won't give me it later! It took him ten years to pay back a piffling two grand!"

Sergei Yevgenievich Kravtsov raised the skin on his browless superciliary arches and fixed his magnetic peepers on Vovan. A pause hung in the air. The two diggers stopped tramping and froze. The round-faced man tried to wipe his little glasses with his chilly fingers, which gave them a crooked, lathered look, and then he took a well-used handkerchief out of his pocket and started industriously scrubbing the squeaking lenses, worming out the microdeposits of dirt right in the very corners.

"What? Well, what? I only want what's due, what I've earned…" Vovan muttered, gazing round and seeing detached faces all round him, literally looking like white stones.

"Mr. Kolesnikov, listen to me very carefully," the principal tadpole-head said in an ominously affectionate voice. "What you have done to Mr. Yermakov is called treason. You betrayed him yourself, entirely voluntarily, no one forced you to do it. Did you think we would accept you as one of our own? You naive man. No one likes traitors, and neither do we. And you will not take any money from Mr. Yermakov. Don't you dare!" he yelled terrifyingly at Vovan, who had made a dash for the bag with a weeping face.

Vovan froze on the spot, looking for all the world like a vegetable-patch scarecrow in his pitiful coat. He tried to say something, but his jaw just flapped about, which made his face look like a round black loaf with a thick wedge being sliced off the bottom by a crude knife. It was evident that the sight of the unapproachable bag was causing him physical suffering.

"All right then," he wheezed, speaking to Maxim T. Yermakov. "So, two old friends met up. You owed me two thousand greenbacks. Now you owe me ten. We'll settle up sometime. I'll pile on the interest so thick, you'll end up running round Moscow with your ass hanging out of your trousers. I'll drown you yet, since you didn't drown yourself, you bastard fucker…"

And then Big Vovan's horrible face moved closer and blurred, there was strong whiff of his harsh, sickening eau-de-cologne and Maxim T. Yermakov, swept off the riverbank by a black wave, lost contact with reality.

Being ill was disgusting. The high-voltage buzzing in every cell of his unwieldy body, the aching in his bones, the painful roundness of his heavy eyeballs, the sweaty sheet. Maxim T. Yermakov puked frequently, he was simply turned inside out – and every time, there by the head of the bed, was an unfamiliar orange basin with a rose of psychedelic proportions – the size of a head of cabbage – daubed on it. That alien basin made the setting of Just Natasha's flat, which Maxim T. Yermakov had left forever in a previous life, seem like an artificial creation, faked for the purpose of some complex deception. In the dingy lodgings where he was lying, the ceilings were too high, the patterns on the wallpaper were too lively, and every now and then they started growing and branching, like those relations of cause and effect, or became even more gorged with red, as if they were Maxim T. Yermakov's own capillaries. The same thing happened with the text of some ponderous tome that Maxim T. Yermakov sometimes tumbled open at random, but only saw blocks of red Cyrillic letters on mirror-glossy paper; the book slid off and fell with a dull thud on the scuffed-up bedside rug, and Maxim T. Yermakov stepped on it when he tried to make his way out to answer nature's call. Mysterious benefactors in the form of blurred carcasses with thick breath grabbed Maxim T. Yermakov under his splayed elbows and dragged him into the toilet, where the patient simply couldn't hit the deep crater of Just Natasha's unwashed toilet bowl with his wobbling streamlet.

Also present in the flat, or whatever it might be, were other hazy people of some kind. They scraped their feet, moved objects around and muttered in indecipherable, thick voices. A hairy male hand in an iron watch carefully raised a tablespoon of trembling, syrupy mixture to Maxim T. Yermakov's lips, while another hand – perhaps belonging to the same specimen of state security man, or perhaps not – held the back of his head, pulsating as softly as a little baby's. At night a duty shadow sat in the armchair, looking like a heap of abandoned coats. Sometimes this shadow was more reminiscent of a man, sometimes of a woman – quite a young one, with a fat-cheeked squirrel's face, leafing through a brightly coloured magazine. One visitor, evidently the doctor, was more distinctively defined than the others: he had a grey moustache protruding from under a long nose, and together they produced the impression of an elephant's trunk lifting a bundle of hay to its mouth. This presumptive medic pulled up Maxim T. Yermakov's damp pyjama jacket and tapped on his strata of thawing fat, extracting some compact, deep-water sounds; then he rolled an unbearably cold, prickly little sphere over Maxim T. Yermakov's body, holding it with his palm and simultaneously watching a monitor in which the picture of Maxim T. Yermakov's insides resembled some geographical region with a volcanic eruption taking place at night.

Apart from the people, there was also some kind of small animal present in the lodgings, most likely a heavy little tomcat. It had the feline habit of installing itself at Maxim T. Yermakov's feet, weighing down the blanket, and sometimes it tried to install itself on the pillow, which was as uncomfortable as a sack of potatoes.

Maxim T. Yermakov pushed the creature off, not wishing to share the caves and pits of his bitter bed with it – then some human shadow would approach gently, take the creature in its hands and set it back in the bed more gently and intimately, right by the sick man's side so that, if he wished, the patient could stroke the sweet, furry universal favourite. This was an entirely superfluous favour; Maxim T. Yermakov couldn't bear felines, especially black ones – and this one was definitely black, as black as the devil, in addition to being strangely weighty and angular. But Maxim T. Yermakov had no time to voice any protest: the presumptive doctor took him by his feeble wrist, squeezed the bright-pink contents of a little syringe into a swollen vein and then there was silence, darkness, velvety sleep.

Only one of the visitors to this flat – or, perhaps, a fevered hallucination – was familiar and even dear to the patient. A bony old man in a brown, slightly decomposed suit, with a forward-jutting chin like a salted biscuit, appeared from somewhere behind the wall and tapped his flaking stick on the night sentry's trouser legs, driving him out of the armchair. The displaced social forecaster gaped at the old fellow, mumbled into his fist, which was clutching his walkie-talkie, and disappeared from view. The old man gazed attentively at Maxim T. Yermakov with murky eyes that looked like boiled onions, while his clasped hands, reminiscent of lumps of wax from a burnt-out candle, rested comfortably on the stick planted between his knees.

"Grandad, you?" asked Maxim T. Yermakov, raising himself up on one elbow and struggling to get a better look at the thick tangle of wrinkles.

Then, under the keen gaze of the sick man, who knew, even in his delirium, that Grandad Valera was supposed to have died, the wrinkles on the visitor's face dissolved and the stick melted into the air, leaving a spectral line lingering for just a few seconds – and there sitting in the chair, leaning forwards slightly, was a muscular fellow about thirty years old, with a forelock shaped like a helicopter rotor blade hanging down onto his forehead and a thin, sarcastic mouth, stretched out more to the left than the right. The suit was transformed too: now it was pair of cheap striped trousers and a jacket with the same stripe. It looked as if a cobblestone had been tied into the knot of the indecently speckled tie.

"Grandad, they told me you're a very malign person. What should I do with them, how can I handle this? Give me a clue," Maxim T. Yermakov asked the rejuvenated phantom, who became more detailed and more real the longer Maxim T. Yermakov looked at him.

"Screw your Short Course, I'm not going to study it," the phantom suddenly said quite distinctly in Maxim T. Yermakov's own voice.

The armchair was gone, and so was Just Natasha's flat. Thirty-year-old Grandad Valera was sitting on a flimsy chair in a room that looked like an office, half of which was taken up by a desk as huge as a cart, heavily loaded with cardboard folders and mounds and piles of papers. A stocky man was sitting slouched over the desk with his fingers woven into a basket; a Soviet decoration glowing dully on his quasi-military field-jacket looked like a part of some industrial lathe. The man's face – like Grandad Valera's – differed subtly from those of Maxim T. Yermakov's contemporaries: it seemed to have a wooden block inside it, unlike the modern silicone and plastic faces.

"Comrade Yermakov, don't treat this sort of thing so flippantly," the decorated man pleaded, cringing. "You may be a Stakhanovite hero of labour, but the Party might not take that into account. You're being honoured with an invitation to join because a worker with your kind of fame can't go around without Party membership. You must understand, it's just not right! It's the same as if you walked around naked!"

Growing excited, the man jumped up from the table, reached into the pocket of his black breeches, took out a crude cigarette case with a rudimentary emblem of the USSR stamped into its lid, looking like a bird's nest with one bulbous egg, and held the case open in front of the imperturbable Grandad Valera. Without hurrying, Grandad Valera thriftily took all four *papyroses* that were lying under the rubber band, put three in his jacket pocket and lit up the fourth, spluttering the match powerfully along the edge of the large box. Then he fluidly breathed out smoke in a ring that grinned in the air and, without the slightest sign of being interested, started looking out of the overcast window, through which he could see a narrow street like the passage between two goods trains, and on it a dejected, worn-out horse with a lack-lustre mane that looked synthetic, feeling at a blade of grass with its soft lips.

The decorated man went back to his official seat and took a sip of brown tea out of a thick glass tumbler in a battered tea-glass holder. Maxim T. Yermakov observed all this while seemingly remaining in his bed, which now had the appearance of some nebulous kind of cradle, and he was amazed at how clearly he understood everything, at the fact that he was far healthier among these delirious ravings than in waking reality.

"You, Comrade Yermakov, are an alien element. There's kulak leaven in you, it seems to me," the decorated man said helplessly – he was obviously the local top manager. "I see I made a mistake when I chose you for the Stakhanovite record. I gave you everything you needed: pit props, trolleys. I assigned four timbermen to you. Alexei Stakhanov only had two for his record. With conditions like that any cutter would have produced your two hundred tons in a shift!"

"Not just any cutter, don't talk nonsense," Grandad Valera responded lazily, screwing up his light-coloured eyes with an unpleasant yellow tinge. "Those cutters of yours – stand them up and they stand, lay them down and they just lie there. And don't you reproach me, Comrade Aristov. It was you who needed the Stakhanovite record, not me. The mine had been underperforming for three years, the state apparatus wanted to put you in jail as a saboteur. You were good at waving your sabre about in the Civil War, but they might not have taken the fact that you were a hero into account either. They'd have exposed you soon enough as a spy for a hostile intelligence service. You used me to save your skin, and that opulent backside of yours too. Can't deny that, can you?"

The top-manager at the desk choked on the remains of his tea and wiped his wet mouth with his sleeve.

"You're the one who's got opulent, Comrade Yermakov," he said in a tense voice, "You earn more than two thousand roubles a month, before the accelerated rate of pay. You were given a free voucher for a sanatorium. You go to the bathhouse for free, to the barber's for free. They allocated you a flat! A separate one! Two rooms for one person! Why do you need a free bathhouse, when you've got a bathroom of your own?"

"So they did give grandad a flat after all!" Maxim T. Yermakov thought, delighted. To all appearances, grandad was delighted with all his bonuses too. He nodded approvingly in response to the outraged listing of the benefits that had fallen to the lot of a "kulak element".

"They still owe me a warrant for shoes and clothing," he reminded Aristov briskly when the other man ran out of breath.

"Go and buy them in a commercial shop! With the amount you earn!" Turning crimson, the top manager took a small, dirty piece of sugar that looked like a chip of granite out of his pocket and stuck it in his badly shaved cheek.

"He wants to smoke," Maxim T. Yermakov realised.

"The commercial shop's pricey," Grandad Valera informed his exhausted manager judiciously. "It's my due, so give me it."

Comrade Aristov stared at young Grandad Valera with eyes that seemed completely sick, as if he couldn't understand why the coal cutter Yermakov was only one man, if he had two rooms.

"Now listen, Comrade Yermakov, why have you dug your heels in, like a bullock at the slaughterhouse?" he said in a conciliatory tone. "Come on, learn this little book. You're literate, four classes of school, after all. No one's going to examine you on it. The whole population studies Stalin's short course on the history of our great Party. You read it too, it's not written in French, when all's said and done!"

Grandad Valera unhurriedly screwed his *papyrosa* into a flowerpot, from which a velvety violet looking like Mickey Mouse was gazing out at him, and transferred his bored glance to the wall above the frustrated top manager's head. Hanging there in an ascetic frame of painted wooden laths was a portrait of a pock-faced man whose remarkable eyebrows, nose and moustache, taken all together, looked like one of those carnival masks that are hung over a normal face with a rubber band. "Comrade Stalin!" Maxim T. Yermakov thought with wicked joy, recognising the pockmarked face. Vaguely, through waves of crackling and marches broadcast on the radio, he caught Grandad Valera's thought that it would be good if portraits like this were sold with a target drawn over them, like the rabbits in the shooting range in the municipal Park of Culture.

"I'd rather learn French than the Short Course," Grandad Valera declared, more to the portrait than to Comrade Aristov.

At that Comrade Aristov slapped himself on the knees and burst into laughter. He seemed all set to squat down and launch into a dance. But at the same time his eyes still looked sick and hunted, with an ominous bloody sheen.

"French? You? With your four classes of school?" he said eventually, after almost choking himself trying to laugh as loudly as possible. "I studied it for seven years in grammar school! I hardly remember a thing! You're from the country, your head's full of mud! How can you *parler francais*?"

"If I learn it in a year, will you stop pestering a distinguished Stakhanovite with your short course?" Grandad Valera asked smarmily and immediately reminded Aristov: "Tuition at home is free for Stakhanovites!"

"Well, in that case! Then of course!" Comrade Aristov said with a grin. "There's Comrade Rumiantseva, she teaches at the workers' faculty. She'll be the one to teach you. French, that is. She won't lie, she never lies to favour anyone. She'll tell us about your progress, just the way it is. Only you haven't got a year, only six months. You have to attend the district convention of Stakhanovites as a Party member!"

"It's a deal!"

Grandad Valera pulled his miner's hand, as coarse as an iron statue's, out of the pocket of his stripy trousers as if it was a great treasure and held it out to Comrade Aristov, who eagerly thrust his own whitish-yellow hand, looking like the little boiled carcass of a bird, into the trap – and Maxim T. Yermakov guessed that in the sequence of relations of cause and effect this unequal handshake had facilitated his own appearance in the world.

Meanwhile the social forecaster on duty had contacted the person he needed on his walkie-talkie and three, or perhaps four figures burst into the room – Maxim T. Yermakov couldn't make objects out very well, he only saw the outlines, filled with some murky substance, like the water in which water-paint brushes are washed.

"Citizen, how did you get in here?" the largest and murkiest of the new arrivals asked Grandad Valera. "Who are you: a neighbour, a relative? Why were you allowed in to the patient?"

Grandad Valera smiled, stretching out concentric wrinkles to his ears, and carried on quietly sitting in the armchair. The men who had come in exchanged glances. As if they were jam jars, brushes soaked in watercolour pigment were lowered into them again and Maxim T. Yermakov could see the darkness being shaken into their heads and permeating their entire corporeal substance.

"Major Seleznev, Special Section," the large man introduced himself officially – he had not just a brush, but an entire mop swirling around in his head. He held out a square ID with a double-headed fledgeling glinting on it to Grandad Valera. "Your documents, please."

"*Vaurien*," Grandad Valera declared smugly, savouring the sounds. "*Misérable*! *Rebut de la société!*"

"What?" Major Seleznev asked in amazement, eddying like a thunder cloud now. Are you a foreigner? Do you speak Russian? Dooyoo speek Inglish?"

"*Infame crapule!*" Grandad Valera suddenly roared straight into the blot that the major had instead of a face. In response the furniture in the room shuddered and the intravenous drip stand, which looked like a gibbet, shook, clinked and started moving across the floor on its own.

"*Monsieur*, or whoever you are, you shouldn't be in here," said one of the social forecasters, presumably the doctor with the moustache, who also seemed to be full of dark watercolour. He leaned down to Grandad Valera and added: "The patient must not be tired. And apart from that, this is a special duty post…"

"Take the blackguard by the scruff of the neck and throw him out!" Major Seleznev interrupted brusquely. "I've remembered what a *misérable* is! Look here, Grandad, if you show up here again, I'll have you put in the cooler, it doesn't bother me if you are French. You can complain to your embassy about us later!"

The murky social forecasters grabbed Grandad Valera by his half-rotted brown jacket and dragged him out into the corridor. The malign old man squatted down, slithering across the floor with his cardboard corpse's shoes and rattling his bones as if he was dropping an armful of frozen firewood beside a stove. The social forecasters, in turn, were dogged in their determination to expel this foreigner who had infiltrated the flat illegally. However, even before the noise in the corridor had died away and the door of the flat had slammed behind the trespasser, Grandad Valera calmly emerged from the wall with a mundane kind of movement, like someone pulling clothes on over their head. For a while the pattern of the wallpaper remained torn at the spot where he had entered, but soon, literally before Maxim T. Yermakov's eyes, the lines of stylised vegetation started growing under the pressure of the human blood that filled them and the wall firmed up again, so that only an attentive eye could now have spotted something like traces of darning at the point of access.

In the meantime Grandad Valera had taken up his habitual position and was staring invitingly at his grandson, as if expecting further questions.

"Grandad, Comrade Rumiantseva – that's granny, did I guess right?"

No sooner did he say that than a hazy woman appeared beside his grandad. At first only her eyes were visible: long and overcast-grey, the colour of low clouds just before rain. Then the woman's image became clearer and Maxim T. Yermakov agreed that the white monkey he remembered as his grandmother could have looked exactly like this, even though she was no longer really young, probably a few years older than Grandad Valera. Her large porcelain face was covered with fine wrinkles, as if the porcelain had been broken and skilfully glued back together again: her short, bobbed hair was hidden under a mushroom-shaped beret that had clearly had dealings with moths. The woman's clothes were rather strange in general. On looking closer, Maxim T. Yermakov could guess that the light-coloured skirt sitting tightly on the low hips was a remnant of a once magnificent tablecloth and the coat had been made out of velvet curtains, complete with substantially worn gold tassels – and, moreover, it was clear that all this interior-decor clothing had been re-sewn several times and shrunk in the process, like a magical shagreen, until it had been reduced to the meagre wardrobe of the workers' faculty teacher. Miss Rumiantseva resembled most of all a female brownie – the faded spirit of a vanished St. Petersburg apartment, who had decked herself out in patterns, rags, prints and scraps of memories of former times.

"Don't get distracted, Comrade Yermakov," she said severely to dandified Grandad Valera, who was gazing with piercing intensity at Miss Rumiantseva's white neck.

Granny and grandad were sitting in a bright room speckled with shifting patches of sunlight and drifting through leafy shadow; messy exercise books with corrected exercises were laid out on the table in front of them and the venerable textbook stood there, leaning against a glass jar with a bouquet of wild flowers that looked like a cloud of small white midges. The sun was stinging the nickel-plated balls of a wide, emphatically empty bed, where a mound of pillows lay neatly arranged in muslin, like a fat bride. Miss Rumiantseva was dictating throatily in French, clasping her long fingers tightly together. Suddenly Grandad Valera, scraping his elbow across an exercise book, took hold of Miss Rumiantseva's square shoulders and pulled her towards him, knocking over his own chair and hers. Miss Rumiantseva shook her bobbed head and started slapping her hands against the eminent Stakhanovite's swollen muscles. Then she suddenly froze, looked very intently at Grandad Valera's terribly embarrassed grin, put her hand on the back of his head, squeezed a handful of coarse curls tight so that there was no way he could break free, and pressed her mouth firmly against his.

"So that's what they were like, the young lady and the hooligan," thought Maxim T. Yermakov, taken aback and at the same time delighted.

"So that's it," he said out loud – although in the indeterminate space that emphatically dramatised the action, rounding off the corners of rooms and objects, the concept "out loud" was highly relative.

"Yes, that's it," Grandad Valera answered "out loud" without opening his long mouth. "She was the *vaurien*. The hooligan, that is. Your granny, Polina. She knew so many French swearwords – the French themselves don't have that many on the tips of their tongues. They were underlined in her books. She taught me them. I used those bad expressions in the test in front of my Party comrades. Polina was sitting beside me, all strict and severe. She translated something quite different into Russian for them. Then Comrade Stalin's portrait fell, during that test. It quivered first, then slid down the wall and fell on the floor. After that the comrades lost interest in me. Ideological saboteurs – that was what they were, with the Leader falling like that…

After that Maxim T. Yermakov saw all sorts of things – either in a dream, or in delirium, or in fits of clairvoyance that were accompanied by an excellent sense of well-being and additional light, as if he had a miner's lamp glowing on his forehead. He saw a mine shaft, an irregular tunnel curving up and to the left, with rails as narrow as a step ladder; he saw a coalface lit up by flickering electricity, looking as if it was made out of coarse lumps of silver. He saw low trolleys, looking like iron baths, loaded up with this finely fragmented silver, and above the trolleys – a half-decayed, fragile sheet of iron with the words "Mind the cable". Unfamiliar expressions drifted into his mind: "bring to grass", "block lava", "coal bed cleavage". Stocky, grimy men in boilersuits that seemed to be made out of dented tin

Olga Slavnikova

were trimming fresh logs with axes and propping up the vault of the
ceiling so vigorously, it seemed that up above the birches must be
quivering. Grandad Valera, up ahead of them all, naked to the waist,
but wearing a dashingly cocked cap and with his muscles rippling
like mercury, was working with a jackhammer: he didn't go charging
in head on, but drilled with neat precision at weak points that he
judged by eye – and, like a theatre curtain descending, like a sea
wave crashing onto the shore, the next ton fell off the coal face.
Somehow Maxim T. Yermakov understood his grandad's delight in
his working skill, in struggling face to face with the mighty mass of
coal, which really did consist of a balance of weak points, a stack
of prehistoric timber. This delight had nothing to do with the Party
committee, or the director of the mine, Comrade Aristov, or the
Stakhanovite movement – it didn't even relate to his pay and his new
flat, it was Grandad Valera's own, personal, pleasurable pastime. It's
a terrible thing to say, but if grandfather Valera had been a bourgeois,
like the ones they drew on posters as bubbles with skinny little legs
and top hats, with big bags of money that looked like pigs – he would
have used this money to buy himself a good mine and hewed coal in
it without any pay at all.

The Party committee and the mine director Aristov only spoiled
Grandad Valera's enjoyment by dragging him round conventions,
meetings and amateur performances. Although Grandad Valera
wasn't a Party member, the papers wrote about him, including
Pravda. A little photo-correspondent in a worn commissar's leather
coat made him hold his jackhammer in a way that no one had ever
held one. When the eminent Stakhanovite Valerii Yermakov walked
up, stoop-shouldered, from the hall to the presidium, people in the
back rows stood up to get a better look at him. The hero of labour
himself, once he was at the table on the stage, with his shoes and
knees in full view of everyone, fell like a circus artist who has been
sawn in half, so that her legs and the top part of her body are separate
from each other.

It was exhausting and embarrassing to sit in the front row at a
concert, watching the Komsomol girl gymnasts making a pyramid

and seeing the naked white legs of the fat athletes at the bottom trembling like live fishes with the strain, and the girl at the top, the lightest, crookedly waving a little Soviet flag. The eminent Stakhanovite accumulated a dozen young pioneer ties, tied onto him at triumphant assemblies by sickly young lads who seemed to have been trimmed with a plane. Labour collectives sent the hero presents – all sorts of different things, including a ruddy Ukrainian *bandura* painted in bright colours: Comrade Rumiantseva sceptically plucked the strings of the weepy instrument and hid it as far away as possible, after wrapping it in woollen shawls, so that it wouldn't make a sound. Comrade Rumiantseva also forbade him to switch on the magnificent radio in a dark, polished-wood box that had been given to the eminent Stakhanovite by the Voronezh Radio Plant: she couldn't stand marches and Soviet poetry with resounding rhythms in marching time.

"I can't stand marches either," Maxim T. Yermakov told his attentive Grandad Valera, who was blinking his waxy, warm eyes in the armchair. "They actually make me throw up, especially when someone is marching as well."

"But do you like this kind of music?" Grandad Valera asked impishly, imperceptibly becoming his grandson's age once again.

Maxim T. Yermakov listened. Something famous was being played, something recognisable even to his ignorant ear. But in the elemental surge of sounds the moments and fragments of recognition disappeared like wooden chips in a stormy sea, and he couldn't believe that all this was being produced manually by a woman with a round head and bobbed hair operating a grand piano the size of a Mercedes. Comrade Rumiantseva's fingers took in the entire width of the keyboard and were reflected in the polished lid in spectral rapids and breaking waves: the performer's half-closed eyes reproduced the soft, dreamy expression of a cloud when the sun is just about to peep out through a gap that is brightening and thawing.

Maxim T. Yermakov looked closer. The grand piano didn't fit completely into the little room, which was obviously the smaller of the two in the separate flat allocated to the eminent Stakhanovite: the complex anatomy of the instrument simply didn't seem to be suited to the right-angled construction of the building. In any case, the door into the little room didn't close, and Comrade Rumiantseva was practically sitting in the corridor, leaving not a single cubic metre of silence in the Stakhanovite's residence.

"To be quite honest, I don't like any music," Maxim T. Yermakov admitted. "Granny's playing is hardcore, for sure. But I'd rather stop my ears."

"I always used to stop mine with cotton wool," Grandad Valera chuckled. "Seal yourself off, and it's like thunder growling in the distance, and that's okay."

"Didn't granny take offence because you weren't, let's say, an admirer of her talent?" Maxim T. Yermakov enquired, feeling sorry for Grandad Valera facing that elemental musical surge.

"She didn't take offence, she swore at me," Grandad Valera told him with obvious satisfaction, as if he was saying how deliciously he was fed at breakfast, lunch and supper. "She could give me a clip round the ear too, enough to set my teeth rattling. Of course, she was a great mistress of her instrument, but still not the most progressive. Once I took her to a concert where a Stakhanovite musician was playing."

"A Stakhanovite musician?" Maxim T. Yermakov exclaimed in amazement. "But a musician's not a worker to go setting labour records!"

"We were all Stakhanovites back then," Grandad Valera explained readily. "Tractor drivers and engine drivers and cotton pickers. A Stakhanovite movement even sprang up in the special services for the arrest of enemies of the people. There were the Vinogradov women, weavers, who serviced more than two hundred looms, and this musician serviced two pianos in concert. Nothing to it really."

"Really?" Maxim T. Yermakov asked with his eyes gaping wide in amazement. "You mean two, actually simultaneously?"

"You don't believe me?" asked Grandad Valera, tugging the earthy cuffs of his funeral shirt out of his mouldy sleeves in a foppish bourgeois gesture. "Your granny was very doubtful about it too at first…"

He had to believe it. Maxim T. Yermakov saw (we could say "with his own eyes", if physical vision functioned in that strangely refracted, incredibly clear space where he was) a large planking stage, probably in a workers' club. The backdrop was covered by a huge portrait of the leader, with waves running across it from some adjacent structures being dragged about backstage. In the foreground stood two grand pianos, with their open keyboards facing each other: one was snow-white and the size of a large jacuzzi, the other was scuffed and black, with crooked candle sticks covered in wax: standing between the two instruments, looking like a chess pawn, was a black concert stool. The audience husked its sunflower seeds as it waited for the maestro's entrance – and then the maestro came skipping out, small and snub-nosed, with shaggy hair and a starched shirt-front that protruded absurdly from his tailcoat. Flashing a wild glance at the audience, the virtuoso gave a sweeping bow, flung back his tails and plonked down onto the stool.

He started with the black piano, falling on the instrument like a vampire attacking its victim. He tormented and pounded it, setting the concert grand's entrails booming. Under his incredibly rapid fingers the keyboard swayed and heaved about like the caterpillar track of a working tractor. This, however did not continue for long: with a toss of his head and a push of a foot clad in a wrinkled lacquered shoe, the maestro swung round on the stool to face the white instrument. There, before the uterine roaring had faded away in the belly of the black instrument, the musician hammered several selected keys, eliciting a flat wooden sound that sounded false even to Maxim T. Yermakov's ear.

And so on and on, swinging this way and that on the stool, pushing off hard with his foot like a kid on a skateboard: all joking aside, the Stakhanovite maestro honestly serviced two instruments for the entire concert. At least, there was always some kind of sound coming from the stage. Maxim T. Yermakov wouldn't have taken it upon himself to judge whether this sound was music. Judging from the martyred expression on Comrade Rumiantseva's face as she sat shoulder to shoulder with her heroic husband in the front row, it was a crime. The maestro himself, however, seemed pleased with it. He kneaded, tickled and hammered both howling instruments recklessly: every now and then, overcome by a performer's passion, between changes of keyboards he performed several additional turns on the spinning stool, setting his coattails fluttering like flags. Eventually the latest spin of the stool made the musician dizzy and the maestro went tumbling down onto the stage together with his stool, flashing the pink soles of his concert shoes through the air.

The audience broke into wild applause and people cried, "Bravo!" from the boxes. The maestro jumped up as if nothing at all had happened, dusted himself off and held out his open arms to accept the bouquets being carried up onstage by blushing Young Pioneer girls.

"He's not a pianist or a Stakhanovite, just some kind of clown," Maxim T. Yermakov commented, glad that the pianos had finally stopped howling. "What happened to him afterwards, I wonder?"

"The comrade accepted the Stakhanovite commitment to service not two, but four instruments at his concerts," Grandad Valera replied imperturbably. "But during a rehearsal the comrade fell off his stool, as he did just now, and shattered a vertebra in his neck."

"Yes indeed, a truly heroic death," Maxim T. Yermakov said with a crooked smile. "Well, Grandad, shall we have a smoke?"

Grandad Valera gladly pulled a rather dilapidated pack of Kazbek *papyrosas* out of his pocket – the good people who dressed grandad in the morgue had forgotten to take them out of his jacket. The two Yermakovs, senior and junior, often smoked now right there in the room, even though the murky guardians of order, catching the smell of tobacco smoke, would come to throw the "Frenchman" out, tediously arguing among themselves over who had let him in again. Grandad, however, returned before his fragrant *papyrosa*, left glowing on the edge of the ashtray, had even gone out. There were more and more darned holes in the walls of the room, in some places not completely grown over with the pattern of the wallpaper: the lines of vegetation had worn too thin from the effort of knitting back together, and sometimes they seemed to forget their pattern and rhythm, filling the void with a kind of improvisation or childish scrawl. However, this didn't bother Grandad Valera in the slightest. He smoked his vile tobacco that burned with a loose, red flame in the same adroit, man-of-the-world manner that Maxim T. Yermakov remembered from his childhood; the smoke that grandad breathed out from what he had under his rotten jacket was clearly a substance from another world, more like a powder, and the slightest coating of it – visible now here, now there – gave real objects a certain lunar transparency.

Those were probably the best cigarette breaks in Maxim T. Yermakov's life; sometimes the grandson's cigarette collided in the ashtray with the grandfather's crude Kazbek *papyrosa*, and then it was as if they were conjuring together, as if they were reading the future in the ash and dust. On some occasions the thoughtful Comrade Rumiantseva would join them, setting her firm hip in its tight skirt on the armrest of Grandad Valera's armchair: she was holding a long, elegantly poised cigarette-holder and breathing out a strange, glimmering smoke, as if she was passing a super-fine silk scarf through a ring. For the first time in his life Maxim T. Yermakov felt that he was in the bosom of his family – and it wasn't so very important that this agreeable family circle consisted of the dead.

He saw many different things in this clear, distinct delirium. He saw the crooked steps of some institution, with crude little flowers looking like leopards' spots in a flowerbed in front of it and an automobile that had once been white parked there, looking like a washing machine on four bicycle wheels. He saw a rutted winter road that looked like an unwound bandage, with the clayey imprint of wounds, repeated again and again, getting smaller and smaller for as far as the eye could see, and along the sides of the road, the steppe, covered in raw, glassy snow, thickets of dead weeds, encrusted with icy seeds, and a grey horizon that seemed to have been blurred with a finger. He saw the same steppe baking-hot and prickly with hoar-headed, whiskery cereals, he saw an immense hound in the dust beside a wicker fence, with fur like peat, and its pale, trembling tongue lolling out. He went down in a metal-barred cage, probably into a mine, felt the shuddering of the platform under his coarse soles, making him feel as if the earth's nasal cavity was about to sneeze at any moment. He saw a little ginger-haired man with a quilted jacket over his naked body breaking the thick, fibrous disc of a sunflower. These were all grandad's memories – random and shuffled together randomly, and yet, by virtue of some subtle attribute, immortal. Comrade Rumiantseva was constantly present in them. Wearing just a worn cambric shift with embroidery that was reminiscent of scars, she sat in front of an old mirror murky with age, and her red mouth floated in it like an autumn leaf. She read a book, slowly turning the pages as if she was holding the text suspended to check its transparency. She sank her large, strong teeth into an apple and laughed with her mouth full, letting a trickle of juice and spittle run down onto her smeared chin. Already grey-headed, with lead in her hair and dry furrows running down her hollow cheeks, she fed a sluggish infant from a half-empty breast that looked like a pancake.

Yes, that was right, from some family conversations or other Maxim T. Yermakov knew that granny had had his father when she was no longer young, after the war. Grandad Valera wasn't in the army, he was evacuated and hewed coal in the rear (there were glimpses of goods trains, entire cities of snow-covered goods trains, a massive antediluvian station looking terrifying in the gloom, grey cones of light wandering across the sky like gigantic stilts and there under the night clouds – a regular tapestry of German bombers, looking as if it had been sewn in cross-stitch). Gradually Maxim T. Yermakov began to understand why Grandad Valera the Stakhanovite was such an especially malign individual. He had split into two layers. The image of Grandad Valera was a painted phantom, inflated with all the resources of the PR of that time – it didn't correspond to the real Grandad Valera. For instance, while Stakhanov, who had never been called Alexei, changed his name and passport following a mistake in the newspaper *Pravda*, Grandad Valera categorically refused to nourish the parasitic phantom with any of his personal reality. He was a normal peasant, a kulak by nature, with a passion and muscular desire for hewing coal and an idler and slacker in everything else, who had turned his bath into a yellow swamp until Comrade Rumiantseva put an end to the outrage. Like every kulak, Grandad Valera loved gain, especially in the form of money (how magnificently Maxim T. Yermakov understood him there); after his own rural fashion, he was a dandy and a fop, on Sundays he wore yellow and red bourgeois half-boots – a parrot on each foot. But without any feeding, the phantom languished. While Grandad Valera's own life became more interesting and varied (in the background the outlines of two entirely different women appeared: one a fresh, young Komsomol girl, literally with fire in her blood that made her plump body glow like a pink lamp, the other tall and as lean as a pencil, who never wore underclothes because of her progressive principles) – and at this very time the variations on the theme of the phantom became rarer and rarer. Previously the newspapers had printed many photographs of the Stakhanovite Yermakov – at a meeting for the opening of a new House of Culture, in a reading room with his elbows propped on a book, at a May Day celebration with a bundle of balloons filled with murky sunshine and a smile right out to his ears. Gradually only one photo was left in use, at the coalface, supposedly working, in which the eminent Stakhanovite had white fish-eyes on a coal-black face; from one publication to the next the features of this face known to the entire country became more generalised, losing their connection with the original, so that all that was left of grandad in the photo was his best canvas duck suit, donned instead of a boiler suit especially for the photo-correspondent and covered with the filth and grime of the mine.

It wasn't just Grandad Valera – the entire country lived alongside its own phantom, with a gigantic, life-size illusion of the USSR, supporting which consumed not only material resources, but also human lives. This illusion was a kind of contiguous territory, where the sun shone more brightly, where the young had an open road ahead and the old were respected, the grain stood in a solid wall in the fields, coated in gold leaf, and a wrinkled, toothless, old collective-farm worker cautiously screwed a glass vessel – Ilich's light bulb – into a socket and it suddenly blazed up like a firebird in his gnarled hand. In real life, with its sparse, prickly grain, worn and rutted roads and humpbacked little towns, the phantom showed through mostly in the form of red fabric territorial markers and the black plates of radio speakers yelling from poles; the red banners with hammers and sickles were actually the banners of a different state – one that didn't even exist, but was none the less foreign for that. However, the inhabitants of this plain, poor reality supported the existence of the phantom with great willingness, even enthusiasm, feeling that they were its future citizens. Against this background Grandad Valera, who had been assigned one of the key roles in sustaining the illusion, was an absolutely genuine saboteur. He let everyone down, he absolutely refused to become the person he had been appointed to be, he sent everyone to hell.

"You know what, Grandad, I wouldn't have agreed either, they can fuck off," Maxim T. Yermakov declared with relish, delighted with his deceased relative, who had already made himself entirely at home in the room and thoroughly saturated it in his otherworldly tobacco fumes.

"Listen Maximka, will you forgive me?" said Grandad Valera, suddenly embarrassed and squeezing the handle of his stick tight in a bundle of wax and bones. "I shouldn't have flogged you with nettles that time. You understand, a man's not interested in little children, they just get in the way. But I really overdid it that time…"

"Was that when I took your watch to pieces?" Maxim T. Yermakov laughed. "Forget about it, Grandad. I'd give any kid a worse hiding than that if he tried to spoil my things. You forgive me, I still feel sorry for that watch of yours."

At that Grandad Valera winked and, pulling on a half-rotten strap, heaved that selfsame antediluvian "Flight" watch up out of the depths of his tatters: it goggled murkily, like an old man's eye behind a magnifying lens. The hands of the watch had rusted to the dial and left gingerish blurs on it – but on the other side the exposed mechanism glinted, blinked and ticked exactly as it had when Maxim T. Yermakov stuck his tweezers into it. No one can know which memories will be the very best afterwards. While the deceased grandad was still alive, he and his grandson had regarded each other with bewildered affection, realising that there was simply no way they could embrace.

"Grandad, so what should I do now?" Maxim T. Yermakov asked as his thoughts returned to the reality that was lying in wait for him, growing denser now, acquiring form and outline, beyond the membrane of delirium. "I made my dive, tried to get away from them, and look, they grabbed me by the tail. And I still haven't managed to get any money out of them for all their fine tricks. And living under their constant surveillance is hard, it's stifling and repulsive. When I think that this is forever, I really do want to shoot myself."

"You play for time, more time," Grandad Valera said vehemently, shaking his mysteriously working watch under his grandson's nose, and this almost physical proximity made the watch blur and swell up to the size of a light bulb. "You could get married too. A wife holds a man, won't let him go to the next world. Marriage is a great help against death. And if this lot start bothering you, smash their faces in!"

"Did you try that?" asked Maxim T. Yermakov, looking doubtfully at Grandad Valera, whose yellow ribs, protruding from his tatters, made him look a bit like a hussar. "You know, they're past masters at face-smashing themselves."

"Oh, I tried it all right!" exclaimed Grandad Valera, clenching his hand into a clammy knot.

Immediately the fist increased in size, was covered in unwashably graphite-stained miner's skin and went flying with terrible force into the cheekbone of a massive military man, and even though the military man's head was set very firmly on his shoulders at chin level, the blow sent his blue uniform cap flying. The man's white, bumpy shaved head looked like a snowman's and it set Maxim T. Yermakov thinking about the species of kinship between this archaic specimen and the state freaks who were putting pressure on him in the present day.

"Resisting the security service? Why you great blankety-f…ing-blank!" With a tomato swelling under his squinting eye, the military man pulled a massive revolutionary Mauser that looked like an iron goose out of its holster.

"Shoot! Come on, shoot the eminent Stakhanovite!" exclaimed Grandad Valera, theatrically ripping open the sweaty singlet on his chest. "Let's see what Comrade Stalin will have to say about that! What Soviet power will say!"

At the mention of Comrade Stalin the military man's deathly pale features, which seemed underlain by ice, not bone, subsided strangely and the Mauser in his massive hand lowered its barrel. Maxim T. Yermakov looked around. The eminent Stakhanovite's flat had been ransacked. The naked iron bedstead was wreathed in chicken feathers from the slashed pillows. The chest of drawers, with the drawers pulled out and legs and sleeves dangling out of them, looked like a scene from a horror film, with the dead rising from their graves. Another NKVD man, with pointy ears and sharp elbows, was investigating a new pair of absolutely transparent lady's stockings as they performed timid dance steps in the draught. Another two were demolishing, brick by brick, the French library with the patterned spines that Maxim T. Yermakov remembered so well, forcing the books wide open with a crack and shaking the alphabetic mass, no doubt hoping that all those little counter-revolutionary symbols would come tumbling out. Comrade Rumiantseva, with a downy shawl over her sharp shoulders, was flashing her mirror-bright eyes from the corner, like a furious cat. The meek search witnesses, an old couple with identical long wrinkles that made them look like contour maps of the same area, were sitting on chairs close by, with their venous hands held in identical positions on their knees, not daring to raise their eyes to observe the aggressive search. And meanwhile, outside the open window it was a wonderful summer night, the full moon was blazing in a polished sky and moon dust was trembling in the air like fine, pure snow, settling on the slopes of the roofs and the round-shouldered poplar trees as they lazily flapped their over-ripe, silver-black leaves.

The blow to the cheekbone and the shouting halted the picture as if someone holding a remote control had pressed "pause", and only the leaves outside the window carried on moving. The Mauser in the military man's lowered hand froze absolutely still, making it seem that if the man who had been punched in the face opened his fingers, the weapon would stay hanging there, half a metre above the parquet, covered in fingerprints and with the safety catch off.

"We have a warrant, Com... Mr. Yermakov," said the NKVD man who was fiddling with the stockings, breaking the silence. Judging from the harsh expression in those deep-set eyes that looked like two hard metal thumbtacks, this man was the senior member of the group.

"Arrest me! Me! A decorated man, a Soviet deputy!" shouted Grandad Valera, continuing his assault on the NKVD men and clearly enjoying the performance. "The whole country knows me! Who knows you? *Racaille*! *Brigand*! *Ignoble personnage*!"

These foreign incantations set the light in the room blinking, the round bronze chandelier decorated with the crests of the republics of the USSR – obviously a gift from somewhere – started shaking violently and fine, faceted crystals sprinkled down out of it, like water through a sieve. Looking closer, Maxim T. Yermakov saw that the disorder in the room was dual in nature. Some of the devastation, as coarse and banal as if it had been dug with a spade, was the result of the search; among all this, over and above it, certain bright stars stood out: a blue vase, shattered to smithereens and the juicy blots of ripe fruit – the results of grandad's magic. Before the very eyes of the NKVD men and the witnesses a matchbox crushed on the parquet floor started hissing and flame burst out of the greyish little heads with intense pressure, like water out of a broken-off tap. With her habitual dexterity Comrade Rumiantseva flung bright water onto the dancing flames from a metal mug and the room was filled with white bathhouse fumes. Now the space was plunged into trembling, stratified semi-darkness, and the moon blazed in through the window like a powerful floodlight.

"Well then, well?" Grandad Valera exclaimed defiantly, swathed in vapours. "Aren't you afraid that you'll be arrested yourselves for overdoing things? And you too," he said to the old witnesses, who couldn't possibly be as innocent as they appeared to be at first sight.

The NKVD men exchanged glances and the oily whites of their eyes glittered. To judge from the look of cautious concern on their faces, the outcome promised by the eminent Stakhanovite was entirely possible.

"We ought to call Comrade Ozolinsh," one of the two dismantling the library said in a low voice. When the old male witness heard that suggestion, he squared his shoulders and stuck out his little academic beard that looked like a sheep's tail. Apparently this quiet little informer knew exactly who Comrade Ozolinsh was.

The senior NKVD man frowned, straightened out the folds of his tunic under his belt with his thumbs and set off towards the corridor, where a telephone that looked like a confidential little briefcase hung on the wall. Just as he was about to pick up the hefty receiver fitted with some kind of extra mouthpiece, the glittering metal cup on the apparatus burst into a trill that ran along everyone's nerves like an electric charge through wires.

"Usoltsev," the NKVD man introduced himself drily into the receiver, but then immediately pulled himself up to attention and his face became detached, as if he was following the little spot of a plane, one of Stalin's falcons, high up into the sky. "Yes, sir! Yes… No! As you say, sir!" And he hung the receiver up very, very gently, as if it contained Comrade Ozolinsh, or perhaps his deputy, who had just curled up in a ball and instantly fallen sleep.

Shattered, the NKVD man took off his cap by the peak, wiped his forehead with his sleeve, and the shape of his head, covered with thick piebald hair, also looked extremely suspicious to Maxim T. Yermakov. There were several faces hanging in the doorway of the room like a bunch of balloons: Grandad Valera's face was not among them, he was too self-possessed and brazen, but Comrade Rumiantseva's face looked absolutely dead and the flames of the next world were trembling in her wide-open eyes.

"Hmmm… Well now… There's been some kind of misunder-standing, the senior NKVD man stated uncertainly, evidently not knowing how he could wriggle out of the situation now, when the security organs never made any mistakes in principle, but this time they had overshot the target a bit. "An accident," he explained loudly to the little old man, who was thrusting an unsteady finger at the bridge of his nose and the frame of his glasses, which were trembling and glittering, as if water was being poured from one lens to the other.

The otherworldly flames in Comrade Rumiantseva's eyes turned wet and became even more terrible, she opened her dry, caked lips gracelessly, but didn't make a sound.

"Please forgive us, Comrade Yermakov, it was an accident," the NKVD man shouted into the room, from where an answer came in the form of French expletives and a hollow explosion of crystal.

Without waiting for anything more, the officer waved to his fellows and the military men filed out of the devastated flat against a blind draught that felt at things on its way in. The mark under the eye of the man who had been punched in the face had already turned dark and now resembled a tablespoonful of blueberry jam; for some reason he wiped his boots very respectfully on a woman's blouse that happened to be under his feet, as if he was not leaving the flat but entering it. The witnesses plodded after them, supporting each other at the elbow, both the same sex now, greatly frightened, and murky emeralds, each the size of a grape, dangled on the old woman's stretched earlobes. The door slammed shut.

"Well, then, have they cleared off?" Grandad Valera asked, sticking his head out of the room lit with crooked, blinking emergency light and, once he was sure they had, he lazily resumed his seat in his customary armchair. Comrade Rumiantseva turned away sharply and seemed to start pushing hard against the whitewashed wall of the corridor, her little shoulders shaking under the downy shawl that was as grey as dust.

"Stop it, don't go bawling your eyes out!" shouted Grandad Valera, half-turning around. "It's finished, they've gone! They didn't take me! It's all over! Although, of course, not all of it was," he muttered under his breath, taking his inexhaustible pack of Kazbek, brown from the damp, out of his tattered rags.

"But what happened afterwards, Grandad?" asked Maxim T. Yermakov, leaning forward.

"What… We left, we were evacuated, and the building with our flat in it was bombed out!" the deceased old man exclaimed bitterly and sucked the hot, living flame greedily into his *papyrosa*. Our lot or the Fritzes, how can you ever tell? We came back and there was a pit where the house used to be, and green water in the pit, with a mangled bicycle sticking up out of the water. There was only the French library left, we lugged it to Kazakhstan and back again. We couldn't take the piano away with us, no matter how much your granny swore about it. So there you are!"

"Yes, a shame about the flat," sighed Maxim T. Yermakov. "A real shame. And look at me too, I can't get hold of one, can't get a place to settle down in. And what about those guys with the Mausers? Did they come back for you later?"

"Na-ah!" said Grandad Valera and rakishly blew out three transparent rings of smoke that floated in the air like jellyfish. "See how useful it can be to poke a man from the secret police in the eye!"

"Hang on, that wasn't the reason they left you alone," Maxim T. Yermakov laughed. "They got orders over the phone, didn't they? They were scared of their own bosses, not your fist!"

"Time!" said Grandad Valera, gravely raising a parchment index finger with a dead man's sprouted fingernail, as black as tar. "If I hadn't offered resistance to the security services, they would have already taken me away to the slammer. And they wouldn't have let me out of there. Because they would already have broken the Stakhanovite's bones and generally reduced him to a condition in which no one can be sent back home," said Grandad Valera, with a thoughtful glimmer of what he used for looking out of his apparently empty eye sockets, out of the depths of his intracranial space, which definitely had no beginning and no end. "Time, Maximka, a very important thing! Observe it. Sense which way it's flowing, who it's working for. And if it's working for you – make the most of it! Don't be shy! Draw things out, if time's still on your side. And definitely get married. A wife is the best protection against death.

Although you still won't be immortal, even with a wife, that's for sure," Grandad Valera added philosophically, opening the remnants of his jacket to display his yellow hussar's ribs, with a dried-up heart hanging on some kind of hairy cross-braces behind them, looking like the cocoon of some large butterfly and clearly preserving a secret, colourful, bright life.

"Who can I get married to?" thought Maxim T. Yermakov, breathing in the sweetish tobacco smoke with its savour of the next world. "Marinka? She's in prison, and God forbid anyway. Sasha? A good girl, and a fucking convent's not where she ought to be. Only she'll boss me around and complain about me to my neighbour Shutov at the slightest thing. Or Little Lucy?" The mere thought of Little Lucy's weak little breasts set something stirring in Maxim T. Yermakov's trousers. "There's the child, the sick child," he reminded himself. Then immediately the sensible idea surfaced from somewhere that before the time came for him to make a decision the child would probably have died already.

Meanwhile he could hear damp, hoarse sounds from behind Grandad Valera's back. Comrade Rumiantseva was sobbing brokenly, wiping her face obliquely with her hands, and her arms were wet to the elbows with tears. She still seemed to be pushing against the wall, which was covered with imprints of her, greyish-blue on the whitewash: her despair seemed capable of moving the corridor, the Stakhanovite's entire flat, or a mountain like Mont Blanc – but not capable of helping her at all.

"There, see, that's women for you," Grandad Valera said helplessly, hoisting his rickety framework of bones out of the armchair.

Growing more solid with every step (the stick he was leaning on turned into the shadow of a standard lamp on the way), Grandad Valera went back to his time and his flat. With a movement that Maxim T. Yermakov could never have expected of him and would hardly ever be able to repeat himself, the eminent Stakhanovite touched Comrade Rumiantseva's tangled, spiky hair. Pushing away hard from the splotchy wall, the woman grabbed hold of her husband. Seeing them stand there with their arms round each other, so young and yet together looking like the gnarled, whimsical trunk of an old tree, Maxim T. Yermakov suddenly felt that he was a leaf on that tree, bright-green and transparent to the rays of the sun.

"I'll marry Lucy," he decided, gazing emotionally at his grandad and granny fused into one. "Why should I deny myself, after all? I want her, and that's all. I'm not to blame. Her eyes are even a bit like Comrade Rumiantseva's, without the black glasses. Just look at the way they cling to each other, grandad probably doesn't realise I'm watching them."

No sooner did Maxim T. Yermakov think that than Grandad Valera swung round sharply, jerking his unshaven chin up over the top of granny's head, and shouted in a voice that was like the simultaneous squawking of an entire flock of agitated crows:

"Maximka, there's a pistol in your bed!"

Time did not exist in the delirium. Or perhaps it went round in circles, like all the clocks in the world, and afterwards Maxim T. Yermakov could not have said if he had lived through any particular episode once, twice or multiple times. Grandad Valera appeared sometimes as a thirty-year-old with a thick head of curls and a *papyrosa* dangling from his lower lip, sometimes as an old man with a salty beard and riddled with arthritis, with wrinkled joints that had proliferated on his body like some tree fungus; sometimes he appeared as the something that now lay under a gravestone glinting like a dull mirror in the little old town's cemetery, baked to a silvery sheen by the heat. This something wasn't frightening at all, in fact it was touching, it walked unsteadily, like a child only just learning to take its first steps, and tried very hard not to litter the armchair or the floor with parts of itself. It was what Maxim T. Yermakov saw while associating with this third version that convinced him that every human being's skull can accommodate the universe.

But one fine morning Maxim T. Yermakov awoke purged of his illness and with his mind clear, although he was as weak as jelly. He had no idea how long he had been lying there like that: Just Natasha's iron alarm clock, which appeared to display the convex time of ten-fifteen through a magnifying glass, looked like some kind of Martian mechanism to him. The murky-silver sunlight coming from the unwashed window was already completely autumnal. While Maxim T. Yermakov was trying to sit up in bed a couple of pigeons landed on the outside window ledge, scraping their claws on the sheet-metal surface: the birds themselves were almost invisible, but their blue, deep shadows on the glass were perfectly clear, unfurling first one polydactyl wing and then the other.

Maxim T. Yermakov could feel a foreign object in the folds of the blanket. Rummaging warily, he encountered something surprisingly familiar that fitted comfortably into his hand. Still warm from sleep, the brand-new Makarov gazed straight into his face with its stupid little black hole. "Maxim, there's a pistol in your bed," empty space said in Grandad Valera's voice and glancing around, Maxim T. Yermakov immediately spotted a darned patch on the wall with squiggles that hadn't grown back together properly.

So that was what they kept putting back in the patient's bed with such tender care. Looking round and sniffing at the air, Maxim T. Yermakov guessed that there were still plenty of social forecasters in the flat. The air in the room was chilly and inconsistent, half street-air, the way it is when outsiders keep coming in and going out repeatedly – during a funeral, for instance. And in addition, there was a clear smell of smoke and burned food coming from the kitchen, together with the sound of plummy male voices, discussing something animatedly. "I'll fuck them all out of it," Maxim T. Yermakov promised himself, tugging his shabby old plush dressing gown, covered in loose-thread hangnails and bobbles, off a chair. To his amazement the dressing gown not only closed, but actually overlapped. The wall of the corridor in which Maxim T. Yermakov found himself was hung with strangers' clothes and the floor was covered with cheap shoes smelling of plastic. The poorly cleaned mirror, into which Maxim T. Yermakov glanced out of habit, showed him a gaunt face that looked like an empty mitten. Rubbing the woolly stubble on his chin, Maxim T. Yermakov drifted on in the direction of the kitchen. There were the social forecasters, five or six of them, sitting at Just Natasha's messily set table. They were the same ones, full of agitated turbidity, who had thrown Grandad Valera out of the flat; now they looked normal, only perhaps excessively solid; every cubic centimetre of their pumped-up flesh seemed to weigh far more than the norm. One was the doctor – or the one whom Maxim T. Yermakov had taken for a doctor in his delirium. This man with greyish-blond hair was now manifested in tangible detail: his broad face was white and moist, but the wrinkles were red, as if the threads of quilting had been drenched in blood. Maxim T. Yermakov almost decided this was a continuation of his delirious capillary visions. However, the presumptive doctor got up off his stool without changing in any way and demanded angrily:

"You're sick, who said you could get up?"

And now the others sitting at the table turned towards Maxim T. Yermakov. They conformed perfectly to the standards of their serious department: muscular, compact, with polished jaw muscles, dressed very cheaply and plainly in pale, drab sweaters; as an exceptional piece of licence, one of them had hair that was smoothly combed back and had been styled, which made his head look as though it had been painted brown using a housepainter's brush.

"And who, I wonder, gave you permission to sit and guzzle in my kitchen?" Maxim T. Yermakov asked defiantly, supporting himself against the doorframe in his weakness.

After Maxim T. Yermakov said that, the social forecasters lost all interest in him and went back to what they were doing before, which was tearing a dried-up omelette to pieces on a frying pan; the frying pan itself, from being brand new, had become black and burnt, as if a meteorite had hit it while Maxim T. Yermakov was ill.

"Go back and lie down, I'll come and examine you soon," the greyish-blond medic said indifferently and started gathering murky egg-yolk off the frying pan with a piece of French baguette.

"Screw that!" Maxim T. Yermakov exclaimed indignantly. "I told you in clear Russian, clear out. This is still my own private territory. I'll call a doctor myself if I need to."

"There's gratitude for you!" the blond man said, pulling a mean face. "We take care of him as if he was a little child. And all, by the way, in the line of duty. We could have been solving more important problems if you, Mr. Yermakov, had not decided to jump off a bridge and given yourself double bronchial pneumonia in the process."

"Don't try to snow-job me. I am your most important problem," Maxim T. Yermakov chuckled and suddenly felt a strange weariness that made him want to sit down right there, on the unwashed floor, with its blackened splotches of food, fluffy with dirt.

The nearest social forecaster, the one with the head that was painted brown, jumped up off his stool and grabbed Maxim T. Yermakov under the arms, His grip was painful and it pierced right through the sparse flesh to the bones. Through the heated wool of his sweater he gave off a commingled odour of cheap perfume, shower gel and some other male toiletry items; the pimples on his forehead, smeared with some kind of tinting cream, reminded Maxim T. Yermakov of dead flies. He suddenly guessed that the social forecaster was in love and struggling to deal with it the best way he knew how.

"I'm sorry, you know, but we can't go," the brown-headed officer said in a pleasant, honest voice, thereby indirectly confirming Maxim T. Yermakov's guess. "We don't have the right to abandon our watch. Who's going to give you the injections and feed you? And if we've made a bit of a mess of the position, never mind, I'll wash all the dishes straight away. That's easily done."

Maxim T. Yermakov cast a sideways glance at the kitchen sink, full almost right up to the brim with dirty water: the heap of dishes in it resembled a sunken ocean liner.

"Okay, leave the garbage tip, only, for God's sake, clear out of here into the stairwell," he wheezed accommodatingly. "I'll call my neighbours, they'll help me and tidy the place up."

"Which neighbours are they, if I may ask?" the blondish doctor put in briskly. "Would that be Mr. Shutov and his ladies? They've gone, let me tell you that immediately. Far away and for a long time. Don't expect any help from them."

"What do you mean gone, where to?"

To hold himself steady Maxim T. Yermakov grabbed at the

doorpost and the social forecaster who was holding him – and grabbed something thick and chunky that turned out to be a hairy wrist with an iron watch. Maxim T. Yermakov recognised that watch: it was the one that had spoon-fed him sweetened medicine and bland porridge with warm milk.

"Don't be upset for them," the owner of the watch said right into Maxim T. Yermakov's ear. "Everyone had had enough of the old lush, that's all. It was too embarrassing to walk past that flat, you probably know yourself what they got up to. The girls ran up and down the stairs half-naked. The residents on this stairwell put up with it for as long as they could, and then they wrote a collective complaint to the militia. The militia came and picked up the whole lot all at once. What did you expect? That Shutov's got as many violations on his charge sheet as a dog has fleas. I've got a girlfriend, she's a nurse. Comes here to help during my shift. Well, I used to meet her at the metro station so the freaks wouldn't bother her. And she felt really ashamed that I was bringing her here, as if she was the same as those little whores with the red knees…"

"Doesn't she feel ashamed any more?" Maxim T. Yermakov interrupted with an unsavoury grin.

"No, not now," the social forecaster replied with honest confidence.

The first thing I have to do, thought Maxim T. Yermakov, is get the situation clear in my mind. Get the situation clear. Somewhere close by there's a black, yawning abyss and people disappear into it like burnt-out matches: Marinka, Sasha, Shutov and the others. Somewhere very close by. I could accidentally step into it and the edge of reality will crumble away under my old slipper.

"By the way, who's that ratfink Frenchman who comes to visit you?" put in the largest of the men sitting in the kitchen. Maxim T. Yermakov recognised this burly man with the tiny berry-red nose and a jaw like a bucket as Major Seleznev, Special Department.

"My grandfather," Maxim T. Yermakov declared curtly, expecting the special services man to apologise for that "ratfink".

But no apologies followed.

"So you have relatives outside the country, do you?" Major Seleznev asked in amazement. "Our data base doesn't hold any information like that about you."

"Yes, outside the country, on the other side of a very important border," Maxim T. Yermakov said mockingly and suddenly imagined the boundary line between life and death, blurred and pale, like the solid dividing line on the highway at two hundred kph, when all the markings come away from the road surface and turn transparent.

"Does your relative have keys to this flat?" Major Seleznev enquired in passing, wiping his fleshy fingers with a wad of pink paper napkins. "Did you give them to him?"

"Do I have to answer that?" Maxim T. Yermakov replied furiously. "I definitely didn't give you any keys!"

"I suppose not," the major said with a frown. "But I'm much more interested in why that visitor doesn't show up in the recordings from any of our video cameras. Is it some special kind of screening technology? Or exceptional agility? Is he a Ninja, then, your old Frenchman?"

"Work that out for yourself," Maxim T. Yermakov thought malevolently, but out loud he said:

"Okay, I'm not going to answer any questions. I'm sick, take me to bed," and he raised his elbows to make it easier for the social forecasters to take hold of him.

"Shall I help?" asked a social forecaster with the same basic features as all the rest, getting up off his stool.

"No need to bother, you carry on eating!" the brown-headed man responded, carefully putting his arms round Maxim T. Yermakov. "I'll get him there and lay him down and give him his medicine. And I'll wash the dishes, why shouldn't I? It's not that hard, is it?" the social forecaster muttered obligingly in his happiness.

"What's your name?" Maxim T. Yermakov asked in a stifled voice.

"Victor, you can just call me Vitya," the social forecaster replied eagerly. "And my girlfriend's called Katya. That's right, careful not to lose our slippers. And we lay ourselves down carefully, that's it… Now let me have the slippers. We'll adjust the pillow… Comfy? And where's our pistol? Ah, there's the pistol, it fell on the floor. We'll tuck it in right beside you…"

This Vitya really proved to be very diligent. He went to the shop for groceries and brought back plastic bags stuffed absolutely full in both hands, always with milk dripping out of them. He washed the mountains of dishes left over from the other shifts, running water that was almost boiling out of the tap, and after Maxim T. Yermakov complained to him about the battered teflon frying pan, he cleaned it down to the scratched bare metal so that it rang like a tambourine. He put in the effort to cook boiled grain and soups that had an almost imperceptible industrial aftertaste and, despite Maxim T. Yermakov's protests, carried on feeding the patient with a spoon, so that eventually the Alpha Object even became accustomed to the feeding hand in the iron watch that ticked, scraped and knocked like a miniature locksmith's workshop.

"I'm left-handed," the diligent Vitya felt it necessary to explain, every time he hit the patient's cheek with the spoon.

Without the veil of delirium, the girlfriend Katya proved to be an individual with plump cheeks that had a bloom as bright as radishes, fine hair that was almost transparent, gathered together into a ponytail, and bushy eyelashes that looked like tooth brushes loaded with toothpaste. She shouted at her diligent Vitya in a repulsive croaking voice and fiddled capriciously with the food that he cooked, but that only made Vitya even happier. "Well, you're a real shithead," Maxim T. Yermakov thought to himself, watching as the social forecaster laid nicely browned griddle cakes, lacy round the edges, on his girlfriend Katya's plate, and she wrinkled up her face.

After long-repeated demands and a bit of light blackmail, the two of them helped Maxim T. Yermakov go up to Shutov's flat. The memorable door, now barely held in place by its hinges and the crooked tooth of the single lock, was glued to the doorpost with several pieces of paper bearing identical greyish-blue stamps that had corroded through them. That shoddy Soviet-made door, the only one of its kind in the entire armour-plated stairwell, was spattered with something: the tar-black spots could have been oil, they could have been ketchup, they could have been blood, and there was one separate dark streak that looked like a tongue being stuck out. Maxim T. Yermakov prodded at the doorbell, which turned out to be a disconnected decoy. Diligent Vitya breathed damply on the back of his neck, which sent rainbow ripples running through the Alpha Object's head, and meanwhile the girl Katya, with one plump foot in a pointed shoe propped on one of the steps, talked on her pretty rhinestone-spangled mobile phone.

"Yeah, it's a real snazzy jacket, the shortened model… Only half-price. Fifteen. Fifteen what? Thousand roubles, of course. Brought from Italy a month ago. The watch? Of course it's an original. An original copy of a Chanel. Listen, girl, did you read all the words in my ad or not? Can you even read at all? If you can't, there's no point even calling!"

Maxim T. Yermakov imagined how now, if he was in an American movie, he would knock out the door with a roundhouse kick and it would fall flat inside, raising dust. And there inside, for instance, would be Shutov, alive and well, rinsing his mouth out with vodka with a thick, bubbly gurgling sound and wiggling his beard. Or there'd be a note hanging in an obvious place from the pseudo-intellectual type who had promised to help and sent the mobile phone. But Maxim T. Yermakov couldn't even lift his foot to strike the door, and his leg was trembling at the knee, so instead he flopped against the door with his entire weakened body, like a piece of meat falling onto the cutting board. He staggered back and flopped again. At the second blow the dry pieces of paper with the seals burst, a crooked crack appeared between the door and the doorpost and a filthy, horrible smell leaked out of it – some acrid processing chemical in equal parts with floral air freshener.

"What are you doing?" Vitya exclaimed in fright, grabbing hold of Maxim T. Yermakov's bruised shoulder. "You can't go in there! And you mustn't strain yourself! What will I tell my boss?"

"And the boots are too narrow for me," his girl Katya continued, still talking on her mobile while Maxim T. Yermakov choked on the perfumed dust flowing out of the dark crack. "Barberry, have you heard of that firm? A very expensive firm. No, I won't let them go for less than thirty thousand…"

Little by little Maxim T. Yermakov started moving around the room independently. The darned-up sites of Grandad Valera's entrances had an odd convex feel to the touch, as if there really were holes under the wallpaper and they had been stuffed with cotton wool. In the first drawer that he opened in the wardrobe, Maxim T. Yermakov found the small bag that he had hidden in the bushes before the jump into the Moscow River. The two wads of dollars with rubber bands round them were lying entirely untouched on the bottom, under the old clothes. Maxim T. Yermakov hid them away hastily and then shook a plastic bundle out of the screwed-up tracksuit; it looked as if it was glued together with something sweet. Tearing open the wrinkled polythene, he took out the old-age-pensioner's mobile phone, with its battery completely dead; despite the pseudo-intellectual type's instructions, it was wrapped in the sheet of paper with the telephone number. No matter how hard he tried to stick the charger into the back of the phone, or how long he wiggled the feeble plug in the socket, like a loose tooth, in search of electric power, the mobile phone remained as dead as an ancient Egyptian scarab beetle. Then Maxim T. Yermakov cast caution to the winds, dialled the conspiratorial number on his normal mobile and listened, panting, to the cold electronic space, full of dry, shifting snow. "This number is not in service," the space stated in an icy, synthetic voice. And no matter how many more times Maxim T. Yermakov tried, he always got the same result.

One day he switched on his computer and checked his emails. In all the time he had been ill there was only one message – from the office, to inform him that he had been granted unpaid leave. A malicious violation of the Labour Code of the Russian Federation– well, he couldn't give a damn. Maxim T. Yermakov was absolutely unconcerned about where the social forecasters found the money to buy the groceries and who was now paying Just Natasha her legitimate thirty thousand roubles. Unable to resist, he crept down his inbox list until he found the message from Little Lucy with the link to the online game "Light Head". Well, how about that! A blank page. They'd erased an entire virtual culture, and with it the achievements of Lucy's little kid, who might be dead or alive, Maxim T. Yermakov didn't know. Intrigued, he turned to his search engines and looked at the blogs, where there were some surprises in store for him.

"Maxim Yermakov was alive and now he's dead," declared *Humanist*, memorable for his user-pic of a cartoon cat wiggling its backside. "He drowned in the Moscow River. That's why they closed the game down, in mourning."

"It's a shame," commented *Milena*, the sugary blonde. "Are they all idiots, or what? It's the same as burning an actor's films or an artist's paintings when he dies. They might as well burn down the Pushkin Museum. Pushkin died a long time ago."

Raven: (a user-pic of a huge old bird, with a tail like a yard-keeper's broom) "Girl, have you ever even been to the Pushkin Museum?"

Milena: "I've been twice."

Paladin: (a handsome, unshaven individual with piercing blue eyes and a chin indecently reminiscent of a pair of hairy man's balls) "They shouldn't have cancelled the entire project just because of the star. What a project it was, people! A computer game, plus real-life action, a new concept of the actor's interaction with the viewer. Super-topical, provocative, a complete new genre. There's never been anything like it anywhere in the world. Post-post-modern! Puts all the Guggenheims in the shade. And as usual, we Russians will invent it and then just drop it on the floor. The foreigners patent it and exploit it."

Hell-demon: (another old acquaintance) "Exactly! Everything just falls out of our mouths. We invented radio and the steam engine, we invented almost everything, then we end up backward savages, like. They should have just changed the actor, that's all. Richard Harris died too, but no one stopped the Harry Potter project because of that. They just keep on filming. They never back-pedal where money's involved, the fuckers."

Humanist: "I'm gonna unfriend you for swearing in my diary."

Hell-demon: "Go fuck yourself!"

Humanist: "You go fuck yourself."

Paladin: "But how did Yermakov die? Did he simply drown? Does anyone have any intelligence data?"

Milena: "Who knows? Actors are dying like flies. They found Vadim Kurkin dead in his flat from his heart, he'd been lying there for a week. Yevgenii Matveev wrecked his car and killed himself. They were still young. The serials finished them off. Yermakov was the youngest and most talented, IMHO."

Raven: "He got arseholed on booze and went in for a swim. That's the whole secret."

Humanist: "There are rumours going round that he was poisoned by the river. A military chemical leak on that very day. He swallowed some of the water by accident and couldn't even shout. The security guards pulled him out, but he had this red hole instead of a throat and his cheek was corroded, full of holes. What a way to go."

Milena: "A pity all the same that he drowned and didn't shoot himself. Everyone was really hoping he would."

Paladin: "Yeah, the hopes of all the gamers and viewers were disappointed. Professionals don't let down the consumers of a product like that. So it isn't part of the script, Yermakov really did drown in the river. And our big-shot showmen lost their heads and dropped the ball. Peace to the remains of a classy baddy!"

This news from the computer brought Maxim T. Yermakov out in a cold sweat. So he was dead. He'd drowned. In their dreams he had. Maxim T. Yermakov wondered what was out in the yard now. He stole over to the window on tiptoe, conspiratorially moved aside the nylon net curtain that smelled of dust and looked into the world outside for the first time in many weeks. The spot where the lowlife protesting against the very fact of Maxim T. Yermakov's existence always used to loiter with their placards looked strangely empty. Stray dogs were lying on the trampled lawn like furry clothing abandoned by the lowlife. So the social forecasters had changed their tactics. No doubt they had some colossal dirty trick up their sleeve, but the question was what? And he had no one to ask for advice. Maxim T. Yermakov was absolutely alone – and in his former life he had felt as if he had people plastered all over him. If only someone would come to visit the sick man with a bag of mandarins. Maybe the social forecasters weren't letting anyone in. Now that he had recovered some strength Maxim T. Yermakov was ready to fight the freaks on duty for everyone who rang the bell at Just Natasha's long-suffering door.

And a few days later a visitor did show up. The former lover of truth from NNT-TV and now free European, Vanya Golikov, had put on some serious weight. His outstanding nose had acquired a spider's web of purple veins and his large cheeks shook like two full hot water bottles. Vanya's clothes were all inexpensive cotton, badly washed-out, but somehow Maxim T. Yermakov got the feeling that now he had a nicely rounded bank account somewhere. In his delight Maxim T. Yermakov was about to throw his arms open to embrace his old friend, but immediately he sensed in front of him the springy and strangely corrugated personal space that Golikov had grown in Europe.

"How about a drink?" Maxim T. Yermakov suggested urbanely, moving back a step.

"Who have you got in there?" Golikov asked warily as he walked through into the room. The question was about what was going on in the kitchen. There was hissing and crackling and a cloud of bluish smoke billowing out of the door: diligent Vitya was frying meat rissoles, tossing them onto the frying pan as if they were grenades.

"Oh, there's a whole story to that! That's an FSB man in there. Just the kind of story you need!" Maxim T. Yermakov exclaimed enthusiastically, seating his dear guest on the divan bed.

Golikov, however, reacted sluggishly to the story, with a certain degree of polite interest and a certain degree of sympathetic sarcasm. He sipped the thick cognac, leaving cloudy marks on the edge of the glass, and at the dramatic moments in the narrative he jerked up his famous bushy eyebrow, the size of a haystack. He hadn't thought to remove his dirty trainers when he entered the flat, and as he swayed his leg he shook waffles of dirt off them beside the divan.

"Okay, Max, I get the whole picture," he interrupted lazily as soon as he decided that his reserves of politeness were exhausted. "To be honest, no matter who I meet in this Moscow of yours, they all come out with some heartbreaking story about themselves. I even feel embarrassed for them. Mother Moscow's really worn me out in a week."

"Are you saying that everyone's got a story like mine?" Maxim T. Yermakov asked, offended. "Are they all under pressure from special committees trying to force them to commit suicide?"

"Well no, of course not, yours is the most convoluted case," the new fat Golikov admitted reluctantly, with the divan squeaking under him like a snowdrift. "But every person is on his own, everyone's sore spot is the most painful one for him. And in Russia everyone has a story to tell, so basically everyone's in the same boat. And you've really pissed the civilised world off with all your suffering, to be quite frank. No one's interested in hearing about you any more."

"*About you*? And who are you then?" Maxim T. Yermakov asked in amazement and immediately felt Golikov's personal space stiffen and inflate slightly, increasing the size of the veins and loose pores on his outstanding nose like a magnifying glass

"Max, my friend, I'm not the same person I used to be, I haven't been for ages," Golikov laughed and stroked the top of his head, where a small bald spot peeped through the thick thatch like a maturing root vegetable peeping out of a vegetable patch. "Ten years ago I would have grabbed your story and sunk my teeth into it. But that old bastard, journalism, is ancient history now. There's no way to do anything for this country, even if you beat your brains out against a wall, do you understand that? The civilised countries see Russia as a new blank spot on the world map, they don't know about it and they don't want to know. And they're right not to. Who do you think I can sell your story to? And anyway, I'm in an entirely different field now. I'm not one of those talentless losers who can't break away from the Russian tit and go prowling round Moscow in search of grants for their cross-cultural projects. My project's all-western, there isn't a cent of Russian money in it. My business is penguins now."

"Making films about them, are you?" Maxim T. Yermakov enquired acidly.

"Our project is saving endangered species from environmental pollution," Golikov replied spiritedly. "Have you ever heard of Humboldt penguins? They live in South America, there are only ten thousand pairs left. According to the forecasts, the Antarctic emperor penguin is going to end up in the Red Book too soon. Research has demonstrated that the penguins' feathers are glued together by pollution. Now volunteers all around the world are sewing special jumpsuits for penguins out of environmentally clean materials, the patterns and list of materials are on our site. My job is to take delivery of this clothing, certify it and send shipments to the Antarctic and the Puñihuil Islands."

"And how do they put these jumpsuits on the penguins?" Maxim T. Yermakov asked in amazement. "And anyway, do they like living in your clothes? At one office party we put a paper cup with spangles on a cat's head, taped it to his ears so he couldn't pull it off straight away. Well that cat tumbled about and hammered that cup against the floor until he tore it off, together with the fur. He depilated his own ears. Maybe the penguins writhe about like that in your clothes, or even worse than that, they die of terror? Haven't you enquired about that?"

"That's not my cup of tea, there are specialists for that," Golikov said with a shrug. "This is a very inspirational project for me, because it brings together thousands of people in voluntary work. We get mail from the States, from all the countries of Europe, from Japan, even from Singapore. And we have the very highest standards, by the way. We reject garments for any deviation from the patterns. It's a really big job and now I've got stuck here." At this point Golikov slumped over to one side and tugged some crumpled printouts out of the back pocket of his coarse, spacious trousers. "I have here our mutual credit history. I've added it up and you owe me eighteen thousand roubles. But you check it all, in case there's something I've forgotten. And I'll just take a quick look at my emails, if you don't mind."

Without waiting for an answer Golikov plonked himself down on the computer chair, which shifted under him, and signed on to the internet, setting the monitor blinking like the window of a high-speed train. Maxim T. Yermakov puzzled over the sheets of paper creased into the form of Golikov's massive boulder of a backside. Eight mohitos, cognac – who drank that and when? Five hundred bucks for a broken mirror at the Pea Club. Yes, there was something like that, a mirror did get broken, Maxim T. Yermakov remembered the shower of slivers sparkling in the beams of the spotlights, like some massive electrical short-circuit – but at the time he was sitting at the bar and passing alcohol through himself, with a head like a fire-cracker. Two chicks at two fifty a time – possible. Okay, but what was this here? The Dungeon restaurant – he'd never been there in his life. But anyway, Maxim T. Yermakov couldn't remember much about the other column either, the one that listed his expenditure and therefore, Golikov's debts. Life as a dream.

Meanwhile Golikov was enthusiastically running the mouse around the desk like a kid with a toy car and muttering to himself in German. Maxim T. Yermakov could give him the money now and then all contact would be broken off with this man on whom he had secretly been counting all this time.

"Will you take it in dollars?" he asked in a dispirited voice, realising that a mutual credit history, like any dream, was not amenable to checking.

"*Gut*! Even better!"

Sighing and shielding himself from Golikov with his back, Maxim T. Yermakov reached into his hiding place. In the wads of money that had been left untouched by the social forecasters, the dried-in moisture had withered the edges of the dollars slightly, like autumn leaves. He couldn't take them to a Moscow-street bureau de change any more. But the European Golikov accepted six hundred-dollar bills without any objections and stuck them in his bulging breast pocket. He had as many pockets on him as there are mail-boxes on the wall of the entrance to a block of flats.

"*Gut*," he repeated contentedly, slapping himself on his rounded knees and getting up. He already had the resolute face of a traveller who just needs to call in somewhere for his baggage and set off to the airport.

"Will you have lunch?"

Maxim T. Yermakov started in surprise. Diligent Vitya, in an apron with a bright, cheerful pattern, was smiling out of the smoke-filled kitchen: his brown, gel-soaked hair had melted slightly in the kitchen heat, as if it was chocolate. Golikov gave a cautious half-smile and backed away half a step just to be on the safe side.

"That man, is he really from the FSB?" he asked in a voice that was suddenly falsetto.

"Sure he is!" Maxim T. Yermakov exclaimed with a sweeping gesture towards the blushing social forecaster. "Vitya, what's your rank in your special committee?"

"Senior lieutenant!" Vitya replied smartly. "I just wanted to say that lunch is ready. Meat rissoles with potatoes and a salted cucumber. "Although it did get a bit burnt today, look…" and he sheepishly displayed a plate of something greasy and black, looking like slices of hot asphalt.

"Thanks, I'm not hungry," Golikov said in a strangled voice, turning pale. "I think I'll be going."

"No wait!" Maxim T. Yermakov blocked Golikov's way and saw the European's personal space stiffen again, and once again he seemed to see Golikov through a magnifying glass, turning fluid and moist. "You tell me you're not interested? But you're afraid of my special committee men. Your knees went rubbery and your hands started shaking. Am I right?"

"I just don't want any problems," Golikov replied in his falsetto voice, shifting from one foot to the other in an attempt to get out into the corridor.

"But I've got plenty of problems!" said Maxim T. Yermakov, even stamping his foot in its shuffling slipper. "I'm a bundle of problems. But I'm not afraid of any FSB. Look how well trained I've got them! They're tame! Have you ever seen anything like it? They go to buy my groceries! And they nurse me, and cook for me, and serve me lunch. Well, Senior Lieutenant, will you serve me your burnt rissoles in bed?"

"Why, you creep!" diligent Vitya said disappointedly.

He looked round the kitchen with bewildered, watery eyes, pulled the rubbish bin closer with his foot and dumped the whole heap of hot, congealed rissoles into it. When he looked at Maxim T. Yermakov again, his eyes weren't bewildered or watery any longer. He was someone entirely unfamiliar, red with rage, with his eyes narrowed viciously; now the pimples smeared with tinting cream looked more like a coarse crust of oxides on red-hot pig-iron.

"Vi-itya! Vityok! What's going on in there?" the girl Katya's voice called through the kitchen smoke – apparently she had been sitting in there all the time.

"Shut up," the unrecognisable Vitya barked over his shoulder, with the air of a man committing suicide.

Everything went quiet in the kitchen, so quiet that the cooling frying pan could be heard hissing under a stream of water. Katya was keeping her head down. Suddenly the hand in the iron watch, the one that had spoon-fed Maxim T. Yermakov, grabbed the collar of the dressing gown at his throat and Maxim T. Yermakov felt himself tied in a knot. He started gasping and lost his slippers. The unrecognisable Vitya examined him swinging to and fro, like a pendulum, with keen eyes that seemed to see him for the first time. The murky smells of Vitya's gel and perfume, mingling with the hot, carnal smell of his male fury, produced the alcoholic breath of fermenting home-brew.

"What sort of man are you, you creep?" the social forecaster said, breathing intensely. "What makes you feel so sorry for yourself? What are you saving yourself for? Sasha Novosiltsev died because of you. He took a bullet for you. Well, you'll carry on living, but so what? Will you buy a new flat? A new car? Well flats and cars exist without you. You didn't make them, you didn't build them. What do you amount to anyway? What kind of great treasure are you? We nurse you and serve you lunch, just like you said. We're counting on you, hoping your conscience is going to wake up, believing that it has to. Something human in you has to wake up. Do you think soldiers like us are just pawns? Without any human feeling in a soldier, none of the commanders' orders will work. It's all built on human feeling. But is there nothing there inside you? Well, tell me, nothing at all?"

And then the unrecognisable Vitya shook Maxim T. Yermakov so hard that his entire spine felt like a well-chain when the bucket falls off it. He heard a bustling sound on his left: it was the dumbfounded Golikov, who couldn't manage to slip past this conflict that wasn't his on his way to freedom, and he was scrabbling about in his own personal space like a mouse in a one-litre glass jar.

"You'll have to cook some more rissoles," Maxim T. Yermakov forced out hoarsely, smiling into the special committee man's face with frothy spittle on his lips. "Go on, thump him in the face," he heard Grandad Valera's cracked voice say right in his ear, and he caught a sudden, close smell of earthy, cold dampness and the sweet odour of black roots. "You just can't lie quiet, can you, Grandad," Maxim T. Yermakov replied in his thoughts, and the next second his cheek was spread across the bone, closing his left eye, and his teeth were swimming in something salty that was swelling up rapidly.

"That's not from the special committee, that's from me in person," the unrecognisable Vitya said with dignity, wiping his fist on his cheerful apron, which was slightly incomplete and less cheerful along one blurred edge, like a waning moon, because Maxim T. Yermakov's left eye wouldn't open, on the contrary, it was being overgrown by a hot, dense cushion and the initial pain from the blow was already dispersing, but the entire structure of his head, its entire skewed architecture, refused to settle back into place.

"Well, I think I'll be off," Golikov's voice said somewhere far away, as if he was already back home in Europe.

"He's cleared off," the social forecaster commented. "Okay, don't faint, don't make out it's all that painful. I'm left-handed," diligent Vitya felt compelled to add before he started rippling, folded up elegantly into the air and disappeared.

So now it was time to go to work. Like going to a different planet. His trousers hung on him like a sack and if not for the old suspenders, they would have dropped to the floor. A barrel could have fitted into Maxim T. Yermakov's jacket with him. A strange sensation of his own boniness, a rickety skeleton inside him, protruding here and there in hard, slippery bumps. The bruise so generously planted by diligent Vitya had still not dispersed and in its glimmering, lilac-and-rainbow wrinkles his bruised eye looked like a butterfly's wing. He was a fine sight, no denying it.

The end of September, the trees are transparent, the wind drags their fallen leaves about below them, scraping at the asphalt with dry claws. Limpid, spectral light, and such emptiness all around, as if something has been taken away, but you can't tell what. A traffic jam with no end to it in sight, the glitter of powdered silver. In the rear-view mirror the scowling, battered bumper of a Zhiguli-7, and in the Zhiguli two duty officers, both clutching some kind of food in their fists and tearing at it with their teeth. Not a single protester outside the office, nothing left of the protesters' bivouac except heaps of packing crates with poisonous blotches from rotten vegetables and square patches of felt on the grass where the tents used to stand. Maxim T. Yermakov strode towards the office, light now, in clothes that flapped in the wind, catching the low, sidelong glances cast at him, and his smile, beaming into nowhere, was as blind as a spot of sunlight.

Maxim T. Yermakov's work-station was so overgrown with dust that it looked as if it was completely encased in a dirty canvas slip-cover. Some joker had placed two orchids as curly as a sheep's coat on the desk. There had been changes in the office. Ika had suddenly got herself a promotion and now her place was occupied by a man who had always worked for their competitors, a skinny, bilious intriguer with a large number of wrinkles running across his bald forehead and a long, sticky mouth that became twice as long when he imitated a smile. At the first conference with his new boss, Maxim T. Yermakov wasn't allowed to say a word. His chocolate business had already been handled for a long time by a team of strangers who had arrived with the boss. Maxim T. Yermakov caught a glimpse of Little Lucy in her secretarial front office – or rather, of the very smooth, tightly combed back of her head and her bloodless little hands, looking as if they had been covered in cigarette paper. He was surprised himself at how much this fleeting encounter moved him. For some reason he couldn't bring himself to ask the office workers he knew, how things were with Lucy's kid and if there had been a funeral.

The ones he knew – well, they had now been seriously diluted by new arrivals, cocksure and loud-mouthed, who mostly walked around in fluffy beards of the most varied shades, no doubt in compensation for the hairlessness of the new boss, whose densest growth protruded from his long, crumpled ears. The new boss apparently had no idea what to do with this unfamiliar colleague returned from cold storage. After an unpleasant, empty pause that made the pit of his stomach feel equally empty, Maxim T. Yermakov was handed a scraggy little project to promote a line of Russian-made creams, in which a Western partner, greedy for new market segments, had decided to invest his money. The creams were greenish and brownish substances that gave off a harsh pharmacy smell; when they were squeezed out of the tubes, they muttered and blew murky bubbles, like mushy peas. The promotional budget, the allocation of which was actually still in question, was barely even enough to develop a half-decent corporate style and not a single kopeck was envisaged for any other promotional activity – in short, the project was certain death for whoever took it on, and Maxim T. Yermakov understood that perfectly well.

"Well then, we wish you success and have no doubt you'll achieve it," a member of the new team told him sneeringly in farewell – a stocky, laid-back young guy who had two little cheeks and a snub nose that were like ruddy crab-apples, with everything else covered by a thick coating of hair the colour of black earth.

"Try giving that beard a wash, man," Maxim T. Yermakov advised him, and from the expression of what remained free of the hairy thickets he realised he had won himself an enemy.

The social forecasters carried on shadowing him. They had cleared out of the flat, but taken up their former position in the stairwell, and they accompanied him round town in their slovenly vans with coatings of suede-leather mud and mendacious inscriptions like "Divans moved". Without the support of people with big placards and toy pistols, the special committee men looked lost and lonely. Diligent Vitya rang the doorbell one evening and handed Maxim T. Yermakov a document that had been reduced to the condition of a tattered rag in his pocket; complete with a signature that looked like a cardiogram of a heart attack and a scoffing FSB stamp, the document informed him that a Yamaha motorcycle belonging to Maxim T. Yermakov had been removed for safekeeping and was located at the special garage at such-and-such an address, from where the owner could retrieve it on presentation of a long list of documents, including a certificate from a psycho-neurological clinic. "…or the heirs of this individual" – that phrase stood out in bold print, although it remained unclear whether the heirs also had to provide documentary proof that they weren't psychos.

Grandad Valera didn't appear through the wall any more, only in dreams a couple of times: he was sitting on his own grave, overgrown with wild grass, and eating a hardboiled egg, dipping it into wet salt poured straight onto the ground. "We live in a time when everything is becoming meaningless: love, wealth, dignity, patriotism," said Maxim T. Yermakov, squatting down beside him. "Ah, Maximka, maybe I didn't thrash you enough, I should have thrashed you harder and more often," the deceased old man replied with a sigh, brushing crumbled egg yolk off his rotten jacket.

Meanwhile the world was not standing still. The world, it seemed, was rapidly going to hell. Certain paradisiacal resort islands, where hundreds of Russians were holidaying, were devastated by a tsunami of unprecedented power; captured on an amateur video, it gave the impression of the disaster of the century. First the ocean changed its colour and swelled up like a bruise; then the horizon heaved up in a glittering crest and literally one second later a whitish mass of water, like grey spring snow being pushed by a bulldozer, came crashing down on the beach with its teeming human figures, the fluttering, protesting palms, the boxy little houses. Unconfirmed figures put the death toll at four thousand. Yet another war was going on in the Caucasus: tanks swayed through a haze of dust and flame, rockets blazed white vapour trails across the azure sky and entered helicopters overloaded with refugees like a thread entering the eye of a needle. In Kamchatka volcanoes came to life, blazing like the industrial giants of the first five-year plans, and buried several villages in rich, hot ash in a single night. Automobile accidents changed their nature everywhere: now two vehicles that collided attracted everything travelling on four or two wheels, the way a lamp attracts midges. In a mere few minutes ten more accidents accumulated on the site of the first and the heap of twisted, battered metal, splattered with human blood like ketchup, only very gradually lost its magnetic force, only very gradually released those who were creeping past in the free lanes and on the shoulders of the road. And finally, one fine day the price of oil collapsed. Nothing seemed to have changed all of a sudden, but a strange, waxy pallor invaded people's faces and other colours faded too, and many people got the feeling that they weren't watching reality, but a film shot in black and white. Goods in shop windows suddenly wilted and frayed: they were no longer engorged with human cupidity, no longer animated by dreams of how all this would be consumed and worn – and it turned out that they were nothing but rags impregnated with dye, nothing but wood, iron, carbon. Terrible to say, even money itself withered, not only roubles, but dollars and Euros too, for those who had them. There were rumours going round the office of impending layoffs and reduced salaries. Everybody was casting dark sideways glances at each other, trying to guess who would be the first to get the push, the women became terribly touchy and resentful and their painted little mouths looked like mosquito bites that had been scratched until they bled. Even the hairy team of newcomers was no longer so unified: opposition to the boss arose, led by the very fiercest of the bearded ones, who in full face looked like a tattered bird's nest with a clutch of large, speckled eggs. Many looked hopefully to Maxim

T. Yermakov, assuming it was clear that this superfluous specialist would be the first to be fired. Aha, in their dreams.

Out of the blue, towards the end of the working day, Sergei Yevgenievich Kravtsov phoned in person.

"How is your precious health?" he enquired jauntily.

"What do you want?" asked Maxim T. Yermakov, cutting straight to the chase.

"Do you watch television or the internet? Do you perceive a trend?" Sergei Yevgenievich Kravtsov was clearly wrought up, perhaps even drunk. "Is your conscience not bothering you at all?"

"Not in the least," Maxim T. Yermakov replied quite sincerely. "This is our old conversation all over again. You shoot yourself if you like, but I'm not going to. Your entire department can camp out in my stairwell, or you can fuck off out of it, if you like. I don't plan to go searching for the meaning of life and I don't intend to prove anything to anyone. I like being alive better than being dead, that's all. For me personally, that's enough. You can collect the little pistol, it's yours. Like you, I don't want what's not mine."

"Oh, I understand your position, I understand," the state freak said irritably down the phone line. "If a man isn't endowed with wealth and power, it's almost impossible for him to believe that so much depends on him. You can't feel it. You can't touch it in the air. Oh, that terrible innocence of the little man! He doesn't owe anybody anything, everybody owes him. Cure his illnesses, educate him, and he's never to blame for anything. It's an abomination! The fundamental abomination of our times!"

At this point Maxim T. Yermakov couldn't believe his ears, because he could hear almost genuine, caustic tears in the voice of the principal tadpole-head. Those tears could probably have been dripped into the keyholes of locks on the most powerful safes in order to break into them.

"Now, let's take a Russian man," the social forecaster said confidentially and Maxim T. Yermakov heard a large glass container sob in his hand. "He lives in Ryazan, Kazan or the middle of nowhere. He has genuinely grafted hard for ten or twelve hours a day all his life. But he doesn't want to any more. He eats, drinks, shifts papers or lumps of metal from one spot to another somewhere or other, rants against the authorities, envies the official who takes bribes. There's no question of any refurbishment in his shitty little Khrushchev-era flat, he can't even be bothered to hang his trousers up in the wardrobe. His woman does wash the dishes, but she's more interested in hearing about the heroes of her soap opera than real live people. She might have been a B-student in school, but since then she's degenerated so far, she wouldn't even recognise herself. But there they are, not to blame for anything, nobody created the right conditions for them! They were tricked during privatisation, you see, when their factory's holiday camp was sold off to businessmen. But just to tidy up after themselves, to sort out the mess they live in, do they need special conditions for that? They don't work, they don't read any books at all, they only watch shit on TV – and they're blameless? Are no demands to be made on them? Well, Maxim Terentievich, yes or no?"

Maxim T. Yermakov didn't answer. And once again at the other end of the line a bottle glugged pathetically and its contents hissed gently as they streamed out into a glass. "Fizzy mineral water!" Maxim T. Yermakov guessed. "Well, Sergei Yevgenievich Kravtsov, you're some performer!" Nevertheless, Maxim T. Yermakov had to admit that, on the whole, the picture painted by the social forecaster was accurate.

"My own people fail me," the social forecaster exclaimed with a little Dostoevskian catch in his voice and drained the invisible glass in tense gulps. "The people are to blame. Only it's impossible to prove that to them. We tried it at the beginning of perestroika, but ran into a brick wall and switched to the concept of the authorities being at fault. And is it any better in the West? The man in the street there is more brainwashed than here in the old Soviet days. He doesn't want to hear anything except confirmations of his own comfortable clichés. Freedom, freedom! There is no freedom without freethinking. Without the ability to think with your own head! There's no freedom anywhere without that! And freedom is actually an uncomfortable sort of thing, it's about time our dear Common Individual grasped that."

"Ho, ho! And what right does your department have to preach about freedom?" Maxim T. Yermakov enquired ironically into the phone, with as much feeling as if he was speaking directly into Sergei Yevgenievich Kravtsov's ear that looked like a wax flower from a wreath on a grave.

"You, Maxim Terentievich, also think in cheap clichés, 1937 and all the rest of it," the social forecaster parried arrogantly. "Freedom is the material with which we work. In the perspective of our research, freedom is a part of the biochemistry of living creatures that goes by the name of relations of cause and effect. The pattern of these relations' growth presents an extremely strange picture to the human eye. The hierarchies of which we are consciously aware are by no means the bearing structures of these multidimensional creepers, they are merely the bars on the murky window through which we observe them. The relations of cause and effect can latch onto an oligarch or a yard keeper, like bindweed. They have already woven a dense tangle around you, because they can't move on, so they wind themselves round the obstacle again and again. Naturally, you don't sense them on yourself. You think that evil men with fancy I.D.s keep telling you lies, and for some weird reason they've planted a pistol on you…"

"Don't you even hope that's the reason I keep telling you to go to hell!" said Maxim T. Yermakov, interrupting the social forecaster in full flow – perhaps he was drunk after all… "Do you think all you have to do is convince me and I'll start cooperating? I know you're not lying. I know that. The idea does come into my head. But you have to understand what I mean by that. It just arrives, that is, it drifts in, of its own…"

"Good, come on, tell me about it," the state tadpole-head, suddenly benign and attentive, told him encouragingly.

Maxim T. Yermakov checked himself. He suddenly realised that he had gone too far. Someone seemed to have scored a direct hit on his head with a grenade launcher; it swelled up like a balloon and carried on expanding. Inside it, in real-time, an airplane falling into the sea snapped into pieces like a chocolate bar in silver foil, a huge red-brick building subsided and collapsed with a grimace of inexpressible disgust; thick, rich lava crept into a grubby little town and children's clothes hanging on a line flared up, fragmenting into blazing scraps. Somehow or other Maxim T. Yermakov knew for certain that if he did not exist, then neither would any of this. The social forecaster in the phone held his breath and became like syrup, waiting to be poured into his brain. Yes, Grandad Valera was right, he needed to get married urgently.

"So what am I waiting for?" Maxim T. Yermakov asked himself.

He simply stuck the phone in his pocket after pressing the off button. The office corridors, rendered soundless by the synthetic floor covering, were empty and stuffy, the main body of employees had already made good their escape into freedom and a few tardy individuals were pining as they waited for the lifts in a dry, dusty beam of sunlight that made the human figures look like murky glass bottles. Maxim T. Yermakov darted down two floors of stairs. He reckoned that if the kid hadn't died yet, Little Lucy must have dashed off to the hospital already, but if it was all over with the kid, she was probably in no hurry to get home.

Little Lucy was there in her secretarial front office: a frail figure with one shoulder higher than the other and shoulder blades jutting out of her back like shards of broken crockery. She was watering some kind of half-rotten plant the colour of boiled cabbage and just kept on and on pouring the quivering trickle out of the glass, taking no notice of the fact that the water had already surged up in the plant pot and was overflowing onto the windowsill. All the other plants in the front office were boiled-cabbage colour too. "Now why am I feeling so nervous?" Maxim T. Yermakov asked himself: the inside of his head was like a cloud. "If it's yes, it's yes; if it's no, it's no."

"Maxie?" Little Lucy turned round, still pouring the wavering trickle, now onto her own skirt.

She was looking astonishingly good. Her make-up was applied neatly and thickly, with her cheekbones rouged so that they looked like little New Year lights. It occurred to Maxim T. Yermakov that this was pretty much the style in which they made up corpses in the morgue. Lucy was dressed in new things too, the satin blouse with a pattern of small maroon flowers, like open sores, was still bruised from its shop storage. There now – no one, not a single normal man, would have even spared a glance for this tragic scarecrow. But Maxim T. Yermakov gazed like a sex maniac at the gap between two faceted buttons, where a tiny little mole was breathing, devouring it with his eyes.

"Hi, Lucy, I was walking by and I saw you were still in your office," he lied, although both of them knew there was no way Maxim T. Yermakov could walk past Lucy's front office on his way out. "We haven't had a proper talk since I came back to work. How are things, Lucy?"

Little Lucy didn't answer. She slowly turned away to the window, beyond which the gigantic, murky crystals of nearby office centres were gradually filling up with electricity and the pure sky of the clear autumnal twilight was sheer ice. For some reason Maxim T. Yermakov sat down at Lucy's work station, where everything was covered in sticky, tarry rings from Lucy's mug, which was standing right there, rusty inside from tea, like a section of water pipe.

"How's Artyom?" Maxim T. Yermakov asked in a strangulated voice, although everything was clear without even asking.

Another silence. Maxim T. Yermakov heaved a deep sigh and bared his teeth. There was something unbearable, impossible in the way Little Lucy was hunched over, running her finger across the windowsill. She was spreading the water running out of the plant pot – the convex pool, with whiskery scraps of soil, glinting like polythene. Outside the window spry automobiles groped with their electric feelers as they scattered from the car park, the twilight in the front office thickened and in the twilight white objects became visible, looking as if they were lathered with soap. Somewhere on one of the upper storeys a sickening drill sank its sting into a wall and set to work, and this crescendo of sound made Maxim T. Yermakov shudder.

320

"You think it turned out like that for Artyom because of me," he said, twisting his hand into a fist with a squeak. "You do, you can't help it. If I'd shot myself then… But it's not necessarily so. Perhaps he and I weren't connected, do you understand me? And I'll tell you straight, I didn't shoot myself and I'm not planning to. But I don't know what to do for you now, Lucy… Take anything you want!" And then Maxim T. Yermakov filled his chest with air right up to his very chin and blurted out: "I'll marry you, if you want!"

Little Lucy started. "Okay, now she'll turn round and I'll look into her eyes," Maxim T. Yermakov commanded himself and looked. Little Lucy's eyes were exactly like Comrade Rumiantseva's: a soft, overcast, grey colour, the colour that clouds are just before rain.

"Yes, I do want to," Little Lucy said simply and smiled, with her entire tiny little face trembling like a reflection in water.

They set off slowly to Lucy's flat. Maxim T. Yermakov seemed to be driving his Toyota in inverted space, in a strange land through the looking glass, where everything moving closer simultaneously moved away; the cars around them trundled along as if children were pulling them on strings and they honked at Maxim T. Yermakov when he switched from one twitching lane to another one just like it. Only intervention from on high could possibly have saved them from having an accident. On the way they lost all the social forecasters following them in two, or maybe three, Soviet automobiles that looked like rickety old furniture: unable to adjust to Maxim T. Yermakov's new driving style, the special committee men got stuck in the traffic jams. But who could have adjusted to it? Only a total screwball could have repeated the movements of the Toyota, skipping about in the flow of traffic like a pawn lunging forwards to become a queen. In the front seat Little Lucy simply couldn't manage her seatbelt, it kept jumping out of its slot, recoiling upwards with an elastic whistle and skewing her flimsy blouse, which made Maxim T. Yermakov's mouth go dry and his tongue feel as if it was made of sand.

Surprisingly enough, their route took them to Malaya Dmitrovka Street. They drove through a deep-arched passage, faintly lit by a light bulb in an iron birdcage, and found themselves in an old courtyard where the branches of trees covered in bark like elephant skin reached right up to the top storeys. The entrance hall astonished Maxim T. Yermakov with its immense, hollow resonance and a strange, empty plinth in a niche, supporting a jar full of ruddy water with cigarette ends – and the double door of the flat, which Little Lucy unlocked with trembling keys, was twice the height of a man. The first thing Maxim T. Yermakov sensed once he was inside the huge, dark corridor hung with paintings was a pungent smell of medicine. The next instant Lucy dropped the keys and her handbag on the floor and nestled against him, so that he could feel her taut little heart beating through her blouse and the silly lace cap of her bra – two beats together, and then another two, and all this noisy beating didn't leave a single second to say anything.

And then, dancing a strange tango, removing their own and each other's clothes, tugging off long, clinging sleeves, they ended up in a dark room where they ran into an unfolded divan bed with a whisked-up sheet on it. They still couldn't kiss properly, their hungry mouths kept dawdling on a cheek or an ear, the upholstery of the divan scraped at their heated skin and Little Lucy's rolled-off panties dangled on her ankle like a funny fabric bracelet. Naked, she resembled a dragonfly with no wings. Inside she was surprisingly strong and muscular, she seemed like a vessel full of that primeval, moist, pulsating substance from which life arose. She had vaccination marks that looked like oat flakes on her shoulder. What Maxim T. Yermakov received from her, what he experienced in her, far exceeded any official norms, any service ration or standard entitlement to earthly blessings. She had entire geological deposits of moles scattered across her pale, super-thin skin. It was so hot in her tousled hair that fingers plunged into those tresses burned with fire.

It was a very long night, as the first nights of lovers always are. Sometimes they both sank into brief slumber, and then the molecules composing their devastated bodies rose up into the air like innumerable white midges. What the social forecasters sitting

322

in their green Moskvich, parked beside green garbage containers to which it seemed to be related, saw in the window of the flat under surveillance was something like a school chemistry experiment: flickering light, fibrous vapours like cotton wool filling some kind of rounded, enclosed volume that resembled a flask. There was a moment when Maxim T. Yermakov, waking up beside sleeping Lucy, who had crumpled up the moist sheet on her little breasts, saw her body looking as if it was sprinkled with a thick coating of powder, and there were particles of the powder hovering in the air. And he also remembered a glass with the remains of tea and a swollen slice of reddish lemon, standing at the head of the bed on a warped sheet of paper; on the chairs and on the floor there were heaps of straggly stuffed toys, so huge that they were really part of the soft furniture cluttering the room; a mirror in semi-darkness, on a door – he thought it was a half-open wardrobe – with a single vertical column of mercury; hazy crockery in a cupboard, looking like sleeping ducks and chickens. Twice, or perhaps as many as four times, the lovers shuffled to the shower. In the long narrow room the enamelled bath, with its metal content that was probably the equivalent of a small armoured car, amplified the sound of the water to the rumbling of a mountain torrent, and the long-since desiccated children's things hanging on the drying stand by the naked black window had become so small there, they would probably only have fitted a two-year-old. Probably everything in the flat, apart from these wrinkled-up clothes that reminded him of little mittens, was exaggeratedly large, one and a half times, or perhaps even twice natural size; when Lucy, trying to find some woman's cream or other, switched on the chandelier in the middle of the night, the rainbow glimmers of its mobile crystals on the immensely high ceiling reminded Maxim T. Yermakov of a planetarium.

It goes without saying that they were late for work in the morning. Lucy, who was afraid of her new boss in the way that any normal woman is afraid of a rat, went dashing to the metro, but Maxim T. Yermakov, in a state of total corporeal bliss, took his time lounging about in the traffic jams, and along the way he bought an immense, indecently expensive bouquet of roses, thirty-five of them, all ballroom-gown snow-white, which he pulled out of a sobbing plastic vase. The first thing he did – insolently, paying no attention to anyone – was lug the roses to the little front office. Along the way frightened colleagues who had grown unused to any kind of blossoming shrank away from him. Lucy, who was intently hammering out the latest piece of crap on the computer for her boss, was the same and not the same as yesterday: her fingers pranced over the keyboard, her ring glinted, her hair was tousled, hovering like sunlit smoke over her inclined head. When she saw Maxim T. Yermakov craning his neck above the roses, Lucy whistled.

"Catch!" said Maxim T. Yermakov, tipping the heavy roses into Little Lucy's outstretched arms: he was as proud as if he had dragged a mammoth into the cave.

"Oh, wow! Where am I going to put them?" Lucy exclaimed in horrified delight, breaking into a blush that was pale, but alive.

She had her arms around an entire thicket of wet stems that were almost arboreal in their botanical vigour, fused layers of dark-green leaves and thorns with drops of water. It was genuinely hard to imagine in this office any vessel capable of accommodating a bouquet like that and what Maxim T. Yermakov was trying to say with it.

"Maxie, you know, you don't have to marry me," Lucy suddenly said in a quiet, serious voice.

"Oh, yes I do," Maxim T. Yermakov replied confidently. "I won't get ahead of myself and start talking about love, I don't know about that yet. But all the signs are that you are for me and I, likewise, am for you. My grandfather pointed you out specifically, and the old skeleton wouldn't give me bad advice."

Just at that moment the new boss emerged from his office, smoothing the remnants of his hair towards the back of his head with both hands. At the sight of the couple with the bouquet his long mouth unglued itself and the cramped concertina of wrinkles on his forehead stirred into motion.

"What?" said Maxim T. Yermakov, turning towards him. "She's

getting married to me. Have you got a problem with that?"

"Well now, that really is your personal business," the boss replied in a hostile voice, gazing only at Lucy with his unblinking, electric-yellow, reptilian eyes. "Please keep your personal business outside working hours. Especially with my secretary."

And then a small miracle happened. Only yesterday Lucy would have crept under her desk in the face of a murderous gaze like that, but today she just tittered quietly into the bouquet.

That evening the two of them went to Just Natasha's newly alien flat to pack his things. The social forecasters standing watch in the stairwell, whiling away the time with some melancholy little mechanical toy that shambled slack-jointedly across the windowsill, cast dark glances at Little Lucy as she walked by. After Just Natasha's devastating assault, there were almost no effects left to pack: the bulkiest item was a dilapidated bag with collapsed sides from IKEA, which was now inhabited by old, wrinkled clothes brought from the little old town, but for some reason these were the very things that Maxim T. Yermakov didn't want to leave behind. The oldness of those almost childish T-shirts, with designs that had been reduced to dry flakes of paint, the oldness of the jeans that now looked like grimy plastercasts removed from broken limbs, aroused a strange feeling in Maxim T. Yermakov, as if he had already been dead for eight years. But even so, the packing went cheerfully, Maxim T. Yermakov and Little Lucy stuffed themselves, clearing out the contents of the saucepans in the wet fridge and tossing the dishes into the sink. Just Natasha no longer even existed. Maxim T. Yermakov felt like hopping about on one leg. His previous farewell to these walls had been painful, as he abandoned their security before his flight into the unknown, but now it was as if he was leaving a loathsome hotel room where he had been stuck on a long business trip. He could just feel the social forecasters' bugs that were stuck all over the flat, overheating until they were ready to burst into flames, like match-heads scraped along the side of the box. As he was already trundling out of Usov Lane, Maxim T. Yermakov realised he had left his top-brand neckties behind on the divan, rolled up into a ball, and decided he couldn't give a damn. And then, when they finally reached the immense corridor of the previous day, all the baggage instantly went tumbling to the floor and they didn't remember about it again until the morning.

Thus began Maxim T. Yermakov's new life in a new place and in a new capacity. Lucy's substantial old flat was exactly the kind that he had dreamed of as he sliced thick chunks off advertising budgets and hassled real estate agents. Four rooms with immensely high ceilings, bearing on their distant surfaces the remains of thickly whitewashed mouldings reminiscent of little snowdrifts; scuffed blue and gold wallpaper; wide, bleary windows that seemed to admit the outside light through a stratum of their own accumulated images, their own memory, concealed in the thickness of the scratched panes. Massive furniture a hundred and more years old, with patches that looked like pumice thanks to the assiduous efforts of woodworm, stood side by side with misshapen creations of the 1970s, including the folding divan bed upholstered in synthetic hessian, on which Maxim T. Yermakov and Little Lucy spent their sleepless nights – reluctant to approach the twilit bed under a slanting, sail-like canopy that had been standing, made up and ready, in the genuine family bedroom for twenty years or so. The walls of the flat, including the corridor, were hung with rows of pictures that left no free space. Some of them were three metres by four, like in museums, and covered with an incredibly delicate network of cracks; they showed distant Umbrian expanses that seemed to have been painted in ice cream and crème-brulée, and academic, long-legged women's bodies that looked like pink dolphins. Others were small, set in deep gilded frames like caskets, and the semi-naked mythological characters were the size of a little finger. The entire private gallery must have been from the nineteenth century, there wasn't a single modern work that would have violated the gloomy magnificence with a square apple or a one-eyed face. Modernity in general had difficulty establishing itself within these venerable walls – in different rooms Maxim T. Yermakov counted five televisions that didn't work, with screens that seemed to be stuffed with slushy, melting snow; there wasn't a single television set that did work. The flat of his dreams was very badly neglected: the battered parquet flooring creaked underfoot; the taps, wrapped in half-decomposed scraps of rag, oozed and spurted as if they weren't plumbing fixtures, but the truncated stumps of chimerical cripples. Euro-standard refurbishment was required, and Maxim T. Yermakov delightedly readied himself to open his wallet and roll up his sleeves. However, he decided it wasn't possible to set about redecorating immediately, because the flat was haunted by a little ghost.

Along with the paintings, there were a lot of framed photographs in the flat, half of them of children. An affiliation with previous generations – and also, very probably, with the next world – could be discerned in the awkwardness of the Sunday-best outfits and the quality of the photographic prints, the oldest of which resembled nebulous specimens of ground coffee. But even so, the faces of the grandfathers and grandsons were almost identical: tender and jug-eared, all looking as if they had a cold, with the upper lip overlapping the lower one in a slender little hood: perhaps that was the reason why, or perhaps it was because all these children were already on the far side of the great dividing line, that it took Maxim T. Yermakov a long time to realise which one of them was Artyom. He couldn't bring himself to ask Lucy, who never spoke about her son, but spent long hours in absolutely silent tidying of the room furthest along the corridor. One evening, after Little Lucy tugged on her hair that had grown out and went dashing off to the hairdresser's, Maxim T. Yermakov stole into the sacred shrine. Gazing out at him from a black frame on the table was a sombre little boy who, to judge from the impression created by the other photos, should now have been about sixty earthly years old. A pointed forelock shaped like a sparrow's little wing, eyes so much brighter than the dull lead below them that they looked like glass or ice. He could have grown up to be a CEO – or a cosmonaut.

"Hi," Maxim T. Yermakov said to the little ghost.

His foot immediately landed on something boxy and angular, and set off as if it was on a roller skate, so that Maxim T. Yermakov almost lost his balance. The little tin toy truck shot out from under his foot and flopped over onto its side with its button-wheels spinning.

Maxim T. Yermakov looked around him. A child's wooden bed, tightly covered with something grey, like a suitcase on a stand; on the table a TV-style monitor choked with dust and a brand-new keyboard – so this was where the boy Artyom had hunted the virtual Maxim T. Yermakov. Perhaps he would have got a kick out of seeing the high-class baddy in the flesh? There was no way of knowing now. On the walls, a few seascapes with dirty-pink sails tinted by the sun of the century before last, plus a child's drawings: little ships decorated with sharp-toothed garlands of pennants, triangular little people, like fir trees, including one creature with a rainbow-bright flower on its hemline and a caption: "MUMMY". Located above Artyom's bed was what must have been an extremely valuable exhibit from the private collection: glassy-yellow mountains of water swirling about and in the distance a ragged sailing ship, looking like a scrap of cobweb, plunging into a misty chasm. And in the foreground, with magnetic reflex spots of light cast from some mysterious source, a boat battling the waves. The inclined picture, which seemed about to spill the raging elements down into the bed, had more than likely given the kid nightmares. Not for anything would Maxim T. Yermakov have allowed something like that to be hung in his child's bedroom, even if it was a genuine Aivazovsky. Women didn't understand that all this culture-schmulture of theirs turned children into psychopaths, not little prodigies. Now there was an interesting thought: when Maxim T. Yermakov's son was born, would he be another repetition of the collective family portrait, or would he turn out different, unique? Maxim T. Yermakov's father in the little old town had jug ears too, although now they looked like socks in the process of being removed from feet. "Come on now, be born," thought Maxim T. Yermakov, addressing his future child. "I'll buy you a super-cool computer and a football, and a skateboard, and then a motorbike. With you tucked under my arm there's no way the state freaks will get me." At that point he seemed to sense a vague response from out of the multi-dimensional fluctuations of mental space, as if a heavy drop had fallen into his brain, sending out concentric ripples.

A week later they put in their application at the registry office. This municipal district institution greeted the bride and groom with a cold, official, reverberating hollowness, in which the clopping of Lucy's heels on the sugary artificial marble filled the entire vestibule. The large female members of staff who strode along the corridors here in gala dress had high busts that looked like shop counters displaying costume jewellery; however, the bride and groom's documents were accepted by a commonplace little man wearing an unironed white shirt under a little jacket as black as carbon paper. His entirely bald head, the colour and shape of a turnip, aroused a strong suspicion in Maxim T. Yermakov's mind that he was another social forecaster. But the man accepted a little envelope of dollars from Maxim T. Yermakov with the alacrity of an automaton designed to do precisely that – which advanced the date for the registration of their marriage from early December to late October.

During the eighteen days remaining until the wedding, things happened. A curious, almost incredible confluence of circumstances, including a young trainee office worker trying to have a secret smoke at an open window, the futile sparking of her cheap lighter and a rush of air that suddenly enveloped the smoker in the window's dusty net-curtain, which a feeble, bluish spark instantly transformed into a blazing cocoon, resulted in a fire on Myasnitskaya Street that was larger than any within Moscow's living memory. Entire rivers of liquid fire streamed out of shattered windows and up towards the pink night sky, in shop windows rows of dummies flared up and melted, closely parked cars, literally standing on top of each other, barked and whooped in various voices, while here and there petrol tanks exploded and schematic little human figures thrashed about in hell. The sight of the blazing buildings was like a fiery X-ray, they were reduced to fragile skeletons as people watched. The squads of fire-fighters who surrounded the disaster were almost powerless, jets of water and foam, directed into the thick of the raging blaze, seemed themselves to be liquid fire. There was coverage of the appalling blaze in all the news bulletins. As Maxim T. Yermakov watched what the reporters had managed to film on a brand-new plasma screen, he could turn towards the window and see a glow in the sky nearby – a bright patch like the ones that drift by under your eyelids if you press on them.

Twelve dead and three hundred missing. Eighteen dead. Twenty-four. Eighty-six.

"Maxie, you mustn't feel responsible, don't take it to heart," Lucy kept repeating plaintively, dashing to and fro across the room in a lopsided dressing-gown. "Just don't leave me…" and she embraced Maxim T. Yermakov and his chair from behind with surprising strength, her thin arms suddenly like twisted steel cables.

"Don't get all het up, Luce, what kind of idiot do you take me for?" Maxim T. Yermakov replied with his face blurring into a complacent smile. In the clenched ring of that little woman's arms with the little blonde hairs on them standing up on end, he felt absolutely safe. *Quod erat demonstrandum.*

While they were preparing for the wedding, signs started appearing that indicated Maxim T. Yermakov was on the right road. Actually it was always the same sign, to wit Grandad Valera, manifesting himself at a distance, although there was no doubt that it was him. Grandad didn't come to the flat on Dmitrovka Street: Maxim T. Yermakov surmised that he was prevented from penetrating the walls there by the paintings, that their layer of paint, containing not only material pigments, but also a toxic admixture of human talent, formed an insuperable barrier for a dead man. Once Maxim T. Yermakov saw his grandad at a petrol station: he was standing beside a trashy food-and-beer kiosk, slowly unwrapping a melting ice-cream on a stick, as if it was a flower, although he could only devour it with his eyes, and not actually consume it. Grandad Valera also hovered about for a while in the bridal salon while Lucy gasped and squealed as she tried on tons of voluptuous, inflexible dresses, all of which without exception were too big for her; grandad waved to Maxim T. Yermakov over the saleswomen's heads with a withered hand that looked as if it was wrapped in a tight, desiccated glove and quietly drifted behind a mannequin.

The wedding was small and clandestine. The real estate agent Gosha-Cherdak and his perky girlfriend with slanting green eyes and a hairstyle like a fox-fur cap were invited as witnesses – no one else could be found. Maxim T. Yermakov hired a limousine, streamlined and white, with lots of porthole windows, that looked like a small airplane without wings; sticking close up behind the limousine, a grubby, rattling van, loaded with God only knew what, crawled all the way to the register office, with a fat-handed social forecaster at the wheel. In a heap of silk and lace and a funny veil with spangles, Lucy was very pretty, bewildered and embarrassed: compared to her the other brides looked like snowmen to Maxim T. Yermakov. Social forecasters dolled up like grooms kept tabs on the perimeter of the vestibule, where black-and-white couples surrounded by relatives awaited their fate. Eventually Mendelssohn's march rang out through the wide-flung lacquered doors for Maxim T. Yermakov and Little Lucy's turn. The lady registrar, tightly encased in a white suit and seemingly placed there as an example of what all brides become after thirty years or so, was vociferously triumphant; the wedding rings from Tiffany trembled on the little plate on which they were proffered, and Lucy's ring finger, as Maxim T. Yermakov encircled and embraced it with a band of gold, was as translucent as a test tube full of blood. The social forecasters loitered in corners, as inconspicuous as floor-standing vases, and the thought flickered through Maxim T. Yermakov's mind that they were actually everywhere, successfully disguised, by virtue of the absence of anything human in them, as furniture and plumbing fixtures. And the crowning highlight was that Grandad Valera also showed up for the wedding. He appeared quietly, bleeding through the band of pale sunlight from the window like moisture through fabric, and furtively took up a position behind the witnesses. This time he was dressed in his life's best stripy suit and holding out in front of him a weedy bouquet of wild harebells – it was a mystery where they had come from on the threshold of winter. Afterwards, in the restaurant, these flowers of grandad's were discovered, limp and damp, fading rapidly in the harsh air of reality, among the armful of bouquets that Lucy had put on the windowsill – but she absolutely could not recall who had given them to her.

No one at the office knew about the modest celebration for a long time. Lucy was too shy to announce it and Maxim T. Yermakov could understand her, because he realised how recently their colleagues had taken up a collection for Artyom's funeral wreath. Lucy wouldn't even drive to the office with her husband in the car, she ran off to the metro in the morning, and to put an end to this Maxim T. Yermakov started going on the underground with her – and then leading her by the hand all the way to her secretarial front office, which was looking much prettier now, after all the houseplants had blossomed together. Maxim T. Yermakov had not been in the Moscow Metro for several months before this, and he didn't like it inside there at all. Everything had become strangely drab. The tons of heavy, damp air that had passed through thousands of lungs seemed to contain dark particles of human souls, and the sensation of an incorporeal hand drawing the underground tightly into its innumerable fingers had grown stronger. Down in the metro traffic jams formed, just as they did up above, but here they were constituted directly of human biomass: absolutely impenetrable crowds accumulated in the connecting passages, overloaded escalators carried them up and down like potatoes in a vegetable warehouse, but to squeeze into the narrow mouth of that channel you had to stand, shuffling your feet, for fifteen minutes. Maxim T. Yermakov realised that these human throngs were more dangerous than the traffic jams up above and he tried to shield Little Lucy with his body, feeling how laborious her breath was, how her ribcage turned as taut as a football when she breathed in.

Grandad Valera materialised in the metro several times. Usually he was standing on the platform as Lucy and Maxim T. Yermakov's carriage set off, with his graveyard rags fluttering in the howling vortex swirled up by the train, and no matter how fast he was swept past the window, Maxim T. Yermakov always had time to see that the grey mask of skin on the dead man's skull wore an expression of alarm and sadness. One day Grandad Valera also skipped into the carriage like a bony grasshopper and started squeezing his way through between the tight-packed passengers, folding himself up like a canvas chair. Clearly trying to attract Maxim T. Yermakov's attention, he pointed with his stick at women's black, bulky handbags with big scratched buckles – but since every second woman in the carriage had one like that, Maxim T. Yermakov couldn't understand exactly what his grandad was trying to communicate.

However, Grandad Valera was quite clearly signalling that the metro was a bad place to be – that is, he was confirming what Maxim T. Yermakov himself sensed. And Maxim T. Yermakov sensed that the tunnels and stations of the metro were part of the overall system of Moscow's catacombs, part of the root system of that immense void crowned with clouds that always loomed up above overpopulated, terrifying Moscow – and that those roots were gradually dying. Hence the stale, fusty air and the dingy light, and the jangling feeling of danger that never left Maxim T. Yermakov until the moment when he finally led Little Lucy, harried half to death, out through the heavy glass doors that swung with a flat, sweeping impact. With a great effort he just barely managed to persuade her not to go down into the underground any more. It was an entirely different matter in the Toyota. Of course, they left an hour earlier, drowsy and heavily primed with caffeine – but it was warm in the car, the radio murmured quietly and the rivulets of autumn rain, lit up on the windows by the electricity of the street, were a symbol of happiness, like tinsel on a New Year's tree.

At weekends, instead of culture-schmulture, they now enjoyed going round the shops. At first Maxim T. Yermakov was afraid of sticking his nose inside them, expecting the salesgirls to squeal and the brawny security guards to throw him out into the street with Lucy looking on. But nothing of the sort happened and Maxim T. Yermakov pushed the rattling trolley with his purchases along in front of him with the proud feeling of a master of life, keenly imagining how in a while he would be pushing along a stroller containing a goggle-eyed, well-nourished infant in exactly the same way. It turned out that Lucy, the owner of a flat worth close to two million dollars, had never tasted mangoes, or avocadoes, or even smoked sturgeon. Through Lucy, through her wonder at all this splendour from perfectly ordinary supermarkets, Maxim T. Yermakov came to love food again. In the evenings they held gluttonising sessions at home, genuine food orgies, frying huge steaks of pork until the fat ran amber-yellow, hacking salamis and dry-cured fish to pieces, grabbing a jumble of sweet, sour and salty foods without any order, licking their splayed fingers and thumbs, each one of the ten with a different flavour. Their kitchen table was like an inspired artist's palette – smeared all over with colourful mud. Despite the appalling number of kilocalories consumed right up until midnight, they didn't put on any weight. Maxim T. Yermakov remained as he had emerged from his illness, half-melted away, his skin hanging on him like streaks of stearine on a hot candle. And he really did feel a constant warmth inside, the kind that a candle probably feels when its own flame makes it flesh-warm and it acquires the translucence that is intrinsic to young human flesh; all the heavy food was probably burned up in this fire without a trace.

Maxim T. Yermakov's altered dimensions obliged him to change his wardrobe completely. He was no longer greatly interested in brand names and even caught himself feeling indifferent to luxurious indulgence – all those delicate textures, golden logos and special looks; Little Lucy, on the other hand, enthusiastically studied the male product range and dug up a sweater or a suit somewhere in the boutiques that was an absolute must-have. They went to get the sweater, they went to get the suit; in the monumental wardrobe that was like a paunchy carriage, the section that Little Lucy had set aside for male apparel was already completely stuffed, they had to force the bulky wall of clothes apart in order to hang the new things. On the whimsical baroque door of the wardrobe an oval mirror glowed quietly, entwined in a carved grapevine and looking in its old age like murky, greenish mica; Maxim T. Yermakov was reflected in it as the hero of a film in black and white, and there was something romantic about his thinness, the dark triangular patches under his eyes and his deep, louring glance. At last Maxim T. Yermakov believed that he really was the main hero of his own life.

Suddenly, despite all the whirlwind shopping, the family had enough money. Maxim T. Yermakov realised that now the advertising budgets, which always came with a fine, fatty, tempting morsel attached, were of no more than theoretical interest to him. He carried on working in slipshod fashion on his wretched line of cosmetics – anything to pass the time until the end of the working day. The cosmetics' manufacturers, two yellow-haired women in damp down jackets, arrived from the Altai region, bringing a heap of samples that they tipped out onto his desk, suggesting that now he could check out the quality of the products for himself – as if the quality had any relevance for the advertising. Maxim T. Yermakov raked the samples into a plastic bag and gave them to Lucy, together with the instructions on twelve pages of blurred, indistinct photocopies. These instructions, which Lucy conscientiously deciphered, despite the almost illegible patches of text that looked like prints from a boot sole, didn't contain a single advertising idea and were meticulously tedious, like technical specifications for some kind of lathe-turning or metalworking job. Maxim T. Yermakov actually felt concerned that Lucy might suffer some harm from the cosmetics, especially when he saw her face plastered with a thick mask that made it look like a crude clay pot. But, contrary to all his expectations, the potions had a magical effect, Lucy became radiant, and the gauzy wrinkles under her eyes that had been depressing her disappeared completely. When he saw the product's potential, Maxim T. Yermakov was surprised by the enthusiasm it kindled in him. Two weeks later he had prepared a presentation that was attended by a whole bunch of bearded faces, sitting round the table like different versions of a sceptical Karl Marx, with the new boss at the head of the meeting, scratching the sparse stubble on his neck and blinking rapidly. The slogan "Only what's good for you, no extravagance" meant the design costs could be kept down to peanuts, and the concept of "playing at poverty" attracted thousands of ordinary women who had never even glanced in the direction of the luxury sector. From the profound resentment in the eyes of the bearded individuals, from the way their hairy fingers drummed on their doodle-covered papers, Maxim T. Yermakov realised that he had won, squirmed free like a cat, and landed squarely on all four feet at the very spot where, according to his colleagues' plan, he should have crashed and spilled his guts out.

The social forecasters were behaving modestly, keeping their heads down. For some reason they had been unable to infiltrate Lucy's dry, spacious stairwell and kept their vigil out in the yard, in cramped Moskviches and Zhigulis streaming with grey precipitation – two at a time, as always, gawking through a windscreen wrung dry by its wipers and looking like two passport photos of the same person. Sometimes Maxim T. Yermakov didn't even notice them for days at a time. Of course, the social forecasters were present everywhere, just as before, they escorted the Toyota along its entire route, trudged into shops after the newly-weds and fingered goods after they did, actually subjecting the new, entirely innocent garments to a full-scale search, with an investigation of every pocket and hypercritical examination of every label. But even so, after this irksome manifestation, in some strange way they disappeared from view. That is, of course, if Maxim T. Yermakov looked more closely, they showed up all right, but without making a special effort he only saw one in a whole week, buying the copper-red corduroy trousers that he himself had tried on but not bought. In short, the social forecasters, being everywhere, seemed to dissolve into space, becoming yet another obscure, harmful pollutant in the air of Moscow, and Maxim T. Yermakov began thinking that now his situation was not so very different from the situation of ordinary citizens living in this immense country contaminated with invisible people and factories. And if that was so, he could put up with the half-dissolved social forecasters for another fifty years if need be – in the same way everybody put up with them and got on with life.

Basically, Maxim T. Yermakov cautiously allowed himself to assume that the insane affair that had sucked him in almost a year earlier could have a happy ending, the way things happen in novels. However, one event required to render the happiness package complete was still lacking. Maxim T. Yermakov hoped, believed and tried very hard every night: he personally bought two cardboard-boxfuls of pregnancy tests, setting everyone in the crowded pharmacy grinning. Every morning he issued Lucy with her regular paper strip and after she locked herself in the bathroom, he started getting absurdly nervous, catching dishes that jumped out of his hands and looking at his watch. Lucy slipped out of the bathroom as quietly as a fish and immediately sneaked off somewhere without saying anything, but everything was clear without any words. Everything was fine, only at the very beginning of the day there was a minor emergency, a tiny breakdown in relations, and something trembled, unsecured, between them, until once again the moment came for Little Lucy to lose her dressing gown somewhere along the way from the shower to the divan bed. Maxim T. Yermakov understood that very little time had gone by, New Year hadn't arrived yet and the late Artyom, the ghost-child with little eyes of ice, was still sitting in his carefully tidied room, not allowing his brother or sister to be born.

Meanwhile the New Year holidays came closer. The slush in the streets lit up with colourful fire, and at key points around Moscow giant fir-trees were erected, looking like Kremlin towers disguised in jester's outfits. Little Lucy brightened up and launched a full-scale clean-up. As he helped her, battling with the antediluvian vacuum cleaner that either didn't suck at all or stuck fast to the old, faded carpet, Maxim T. Yermakov realised that this flat, to which he had come to spend the rest of his life, was full of childhood. His family residence in the little old town belonged to some different type – adult, or even geriatric – and that was why it had the smell of boredom. Apparently raising one child – Maxim T. Yermakov himself – had not been enough for it to become a fully-fledged family home. But here, inside these venerable walls with their multiple layers of repainting, at least four generations of jug-eared, delicate children, mostly boys, had grown, played, been ill and blotted school exercise books. Their childhood was everywhere: in the course of the cleaning he would come across a spill-proof porcelain inkwell, or a half-ruined box containing some table game, or a herbarium with scribbled inscriptions that had turned grey with age and desiccated leaves and petals that looked like fragile dragonfly wings. The New Year tree decorations, extracted from deep cardboard boxes lined with crumpled silver, were also of various ages, with a range of a hundred years or more. There were plenty of mirror-bright little birds with their paint peeled off, attached to iron clips, lots of little cardboard squirrels and fawns with threads tied on in God only knew what year, and the very oldest decorations were made of scratchy painted cotton wool – clowns and gnomes lumpy to the touch, with little glued-on porcelain faces like decorated fingernails. The springy, fresh fir tree resisted, thrusting out its prickly, quivering, clinking branches – but it was decorated nonetheless, against its will and against the grain. And beneath it, in the glimmering mica of the artificial snow, Little Lucy planted her favourite stuffed animal toy.

"Hey, what's inside it?" Maxim T. Yermakov asked curiously as he picked up the huge teddy bear with hind legs the size of a child's felt boots.

"What do you mean? Heroin, of course!" Little Lucy laughed playfully, taking the bear from him and hiding it behind her back.

Light-hearted and full of high spirits, for the festive meal she dragged out loads of mismatched antique tableware with all sorts of moulded extravagances, and to go with her simple little dress she put on a pair of old gold earrings that had turned as dark as autumn thorns, with large, bluntly-faceted, brightly-glinting diamond kernels. Having stuffed themselves greedily well ahead of time they waited, with a bottle of champagne as dangerous as a loaded cannon, for the chiming of the clock on the television. When the serious, pale president with heavy eyes of cast glass had said his piece against the background of Red Square and the tense, dragging toll of the chimes had begun, Maxim T. Yermakov released a champagne cork that shot hard against the wall, a voluptuous jet flooded the tablecloth and Lucy's dress with effervescent patches of foam, and at last they clinked their carelessly filled glasses and kissed.

"Maxie, we have everything now!" said Little Lucy, wrenching herself out of his kiss as if she was surfacing through a hole in the ice on a river.

"Of course we do, Happy New Year," said Maxim T. Yermakov, not understanding at first.

"Ma-axie…" Little Lucy drawled reproachfully, looking down at her champagne-soaked stomach, as flat as a frying pan.

And at that point the New Year pyrotechnics said it all for Maxim T. Yermakov, zapping and blasting and whistling, scattering dense swathes of coloured polka dots across the sky to the feeble, diluted-sounding cries of people who had spilled out into the street. The young couple didn't watch any more television after that. On that New Year's night they moved for the first time from the divan to the large family bed, dismantling the fused layers of bedding with their subtle smell of decay and the cobweb-grey sheets that had been lying there for goodness knows how many years. The bed was as lusty and hunchbacked as a live bear and several times the novices trying to settle into it almost tumbled off onto the floor. The slanting, moulting canopy sprinkled fine, fibrous particles onto their overheated bodies; outside the window thick, creamy snow poured down on overheated Moscow as if it was streaming out of a milk can and that night, in the seclusion of the old flat and the old bed, it felt as if a new, good – and therefore completely unimaginable – life was starting.

January had passed and the future was unfolding as if nothing had happened. No matter how much Maxim T. Yermakov tried to hurry the processes along in his mind, Lucy's stomach hardly expanded at all, merely changing its form slightly, as if a rounded shell had parted its valve slightly under the skin. Work was total bedlam, Maxim T. Yermakov was totally snowed under. After his success with the bog-mud Siberian cosmetics they had heaped a mountain of projects on him and given him back all his chocolate, and now he spent all day every day dashing round production companies, who had moved offices in the meantime, like all the other Moscow businesses that appeared in the buildings of the capital and disappeared from them like little balls under a shell-game artist's cups. Throughout the working day Maxim T. Yermakov was almost in several places at the same time – and so the half-dissolved social forecasters had to attach additional details to the Alpha Object, and they loitered in the hazy blur of wintry Moscow like planks of wood half-submerged in bitterly cold waters. Even Maxim T. Yermakov's tiredness was blissful. Now at the weekends he sprawled in front of the TV, allowing Lucy to wander round the shops on her own, leaving her alone for the time being to face the immense selection of rattles, tilting dolls that glugged, little blocks, little ducklings and little kittens – to face the entire multicoloured, plastic, easily washed reality substitute that grown-ups make that way because none of them remember what they were like as babies. When Lucy went out for a walk, she phoned Maxim T. Yermakov every fifteen minutes and sometimes she spoke as much as a thousand roubles worth of all sorts of tender nonsense in a single weekend.

Meanwhile the world around them was tearing itself to pieces. Whatever else might have happened in all the time that Moscow had existed, there had never been any earthquakes there – but notwithstanding, one night the young couple were woken by a mounting crescendo of rattling tableware, feeling as if they were on the handle of an immense spoon that was slowly stirring the red brew seething in the bowels of the earth. The heaps of plates in the sideboard shuddered from the top down to the bottom and back up from the bottom to the top, the chandeliers swayed like the crowns of trees in a strong wind, the pictures rustled on the walls, the clocks hiccupped and chimed. But before the young couple, already hurriedly dressed, could grab their money and their documents, it ended, and everything stopped dead, slightly crooked and off-balance, as if the world had raised its foot for the next step and frozen like that, listening. And that really was the way things were – standing poised, almost overbalancing, half a step into the future. The earthquake left Maxim T. Yermakov with the feeling that sometimes comes at the very beginning of flu, as if weak currents of electricity were running up through his body from the earth to the sky. But worst of all – Maxim T. Yermakov unexpectedly started sensing people. Through Lucy, he suddenly came to understand that other people also existed. Other people's deaths frightened and alarmed him, as if someone was clapping his hands loudly or yelling in the room where he was sitting and there was no way he could throw the bastard out. Death was a clap, death was a loud yell right in his ear, and sometimes there were absolute downpours, bursts of automatic fire that prevented him from even reading or watching a movie properly.

It was a weekend and there was a sci-fi serial on TV, one stupid enough to let him switch off completely from reality.

"Maxie, you've got so terribly lazy lately, come for a walk with me," said Little Lucy, already dressed in a pink down jacket that made her look more pregnant than usual. She blocked off Maxim T. Yermakov's view of the screen and the star ship creeping across it that looked like a machine lathe lit up with little light bulbs.

Yawning, Maxim T. Yermakov looked out of the window. There was much more genuine reality out there than in the overheated room, and definitely more than in the TV: a repulsive fine snow was sprinkling down like iron filings and the parked cars in the courtyard were already crusted with it; a sparrow, frozen through, was huddled up on an ice-bound branch, like a child's hand clenched into a fist in a mitten.

"Just what you need, going out in this kind of weather," Maxim T. Yermakov said to Little Lucy as he saw her out into the hallway. And he didn't even kiss her goodbye.

She phoned five or six times after that: she was on Hunter's Row, choosing a new shirt for Maxim T. Yermakov from out of a seemingly infinite number of possible options: striped shirts and checked shirts and shirts with some kind of webbed ribs that Maxim T. Yermakov couldn't even imagine.

"You don't wear green, do you?" she asked yet again in a brisk, businesslike little voice. "Maybe I should get you the cream one?

341

But the green one's really good quality, I really like it! Why don't I take both?"

"Luce, you make the decision and buy something," Maxim T. Yermakov replied impatiently – his aliens, with anatomies that looked like Scotsmen with bagpipes, were attacking an Earth space station at that very moment. "And come home, it's lunchtime!"

He followed the space massacre for a while, rejoicing in the knowledge that the shots from the fantastic weapons, which also resembled wind instruments, weren't real, and when an earthling tumbled gracefully to the ground among the smoke-blanketed scenery or an alien subsided into a heap, drawing in its snotty snorkel-flutes, no one died, they all stayed alive, and in reality they were all actors who were probably already shooting a different, even more idiotic, serial now. But even so, an otherworldly chill licked at his heart, which felt like a cool peppermint. Growing impatient, Maxim T. Yermakov reached for the mobile phone to dial Lucy, who was already late – and at that moment the world gave a quiet gasp. Acting like Maxim T. Yermakov's virtual head, the world released a foul odour of fermented intoxication with a pop, and it took several very, very long seconds for him to realise that the sound had reached him from the metro station on Pushkin Square.

Afterwards, when a Moscow Public Prosecutor's Office operational group investigated the explosion, the pieces of the jigsaw fitted together to form a picture that was rather patchy, with poorly matching edges, but basically consistent. Many witnesses had seen a bulky, middle-aged woman at the Teatralnaya Metro Station, wearing a dirty-pink down jacket over a baggy black dress with a glittering Lurex hem that had been trampled into a fibrous mass and a Muslim headscarf right down to her eyes. The woman stood at the station for a long time, obviously waiting for something that wasn't a train. She was holding a floppy black handbag with an imitation gold clasp the size of a tin can, and the protruding corners of something like a long box could be seen through the bag's sides. In fact, the woman herself looked rather boxy, like a stove built of large bricks to fit the down jacket. No one paid any particular attention to her, but they should have. The people of the capital should have looked into this visitor's eyes, as ecstatic and appalling as if they had been raised to molten heat by some internal fire. But the metro passengers went running by, piling into the departing trains in tight bunches, and so remained alive.

At last the visitor's wait was rewarded. Running down the stairs from the Hunter's Row Station, caressing the banister with her hand and the steps with the soles of her shoes, came an ordinary young Moscow woman with nothing remarkable about her except the glimmer of happiness on her narrow little face – the blindness of happiness that made her walk in a strange way, like the zigzags of a pond-skater across the smooth surface of the water. The young Muscovite was wearing a down jacket exactly like the one that the visitor to the capital had, only clean and neatly buttoned. The woman in the Muslim headscarf leaned forward, but instead of greeting the young Muscovite, she let her pass by and fell in behind, looming up over her and crowding her brick-built stomach up against her, so that for a brief moment it seemed as if the Muslim woman was guiding the Moscow woman along the platform like a puppeteer guiding a big puppet, the same size as himself, across a stage. Some old man in dishevelled brown rags – probably one of the beggars who work the trains – tried to squeeze in between the two pink down jackets, but the visitor to the capital pushed the nimble grandad aside so forcefully that he went flying, striking his back hard against a column and literally shattering into pieces that showered down inside his tattered rags and only just managing to grab the round bony bowl of his head in his hands like a basketball.

With a toot of its whistle and a flash of its lights, the doomed train pulled in, on its way to Tverskaya Station. Panting for breath, the visitor to the capital stuffed the daydreaming young Muscovite into a carriage, and was immediately offered a seat by a passenger with a dilapidated book glued to his nose – a pale student who had precisely two minutes left to live. The woman plonked herself down and immediately started rummaging in her monstrous bag,

Olga Slavnikova

jostling the people beside her with her elbows. Meanwhile the old ragamuffin, who had somehow found his way into the carriage after all, put on a genuine blitzkrieg performance, wiggling and wobbling about, and for greater effect releasing something like white smoke directly out of his skull, the way a puffball releases spores when it bursts. The passengers, taking all this for an original trick, started thrusting scraggly ten-rouble notes into the old man's rags, and in the crush they didn't notice that the money tumbled straight through the artist and onto the floor. Almost all the passengers were already walking dead.

Afterwards explosives specialists calculated that if the "bricks", amounting to the equivalent of eight kilograms of TNT, had gone off in the tunnel, all that would have been left of the entire ill-fated train was the twisted skeletons of the carriages and tattered scraps of meat, roasting-hot from the blaze. Even if any of the passengers had survived, the rescuers would not have been able to reach the injured – the recent earthquake had caused only a single crack in the roof, but it was monstrously huge, running right along the vault, inflamed and swollen with disturbed soil, and the tunnel would simply have crumbled in the explosion, like a snapped wafer. However, the old imbecile managed to attract the suicide-bomber's attention after all. She gaped at him with her wide eyes filmy like cold soup, and her hands froze in the belly of her bag without completing their movement. In this way she lost thirty precious seconds and the entire train had time to draw into Tverskaya, where a large crowd of people was waiting for it, flashing past the windows like dummies in shop windows.

With her packages getting jammed along the way, the young Moscow woman in the pink down jacket started pushing through the crush towards the door. At that the suicide bomber snapped out of her trance. All the passengers turned their heads at the sound of her piercing, inhuman scream, like a circular saw on iron. The woman screeched, squeezing her eyes shut, displaying the little gold nuggets of the worn-down molars in her mouth and at the same time her hands, immersed in the bag, jerked as if someone inside there had

344

bitten them – and that was the last thing that dozens of people saw in their lives. The explosion was like an all-encompassing photo-flash, recording them all for eternity before they were dead. The dilapidated book opened its wings like a wise little bird and pressed itself against the student's face so that he wouldn't see one of the carriage's metal rods flying towards him in a blinding flash of lightning – and a second later the student could no longer feel anything at all.

According to the testimony of people who were in Tverskaya Station at the time, when the explosion occurred, the ill-fated carriage reared up in the air and lashed out like a horse. Broken glass spurted out of the windows of the train like water out of high-pressure hoses; a fire immediately flared up inside the shattered carriage and the flames tinted the jets of glass as if they were boiling. The reverberations of the explosion were drowned out by a human scream as powerful as an opera choir. The flickering electric light faded and darkened; acrid, yellowish-grey smoke filled the station and the indicator panels gleamed in the smoke like dull mirrors. For a moment or two people froze, and then the crowd dashed for the exit, thickening to an intense blackness at the escalators that had stopped dead; there was a dull, ribbed sound of tramping feet on metal steps, collective heavy breathing, and children wailing. Those who breathed through their caps and scarves held up better, but many people, befuddled by the products of combustion, had some kind of hallucination. Eyewitnesses claimed they had seen a human figure on the vault of the ceiling, scuttling along on all fours with the agility of a cockroach; the creature was dressed in the noxiously smouldering, ragged, brown remnants of a man's suit, and supposedly it was shouting out French words that made the marble facing of the walls peel off like a snake's skin. In any case, people ran for it, not believing that everything was already over. And the fewer people there were left in the station, the more obvious became the horrifying blotch of gruesome vomit discharged onto the floor: broken glass, lacerated iron, something absolutely white, rapidly becoming saturated with blood, a plump man's hand wearing a wedding ring, a gutted handbag, a mobile phone, buzzing and squirming like a fly with its wings torn off – and rising up among all this, the dark mounds of dozens of human bodies, one of which, in a pink down jacket, with one cheek torn open and trembling like a gill, was still trying to crawl.

Maxim T. Yermakov tried calling Lucy several times, always getting the same answer: "This number is temporarily unavailable". He tried to watch the T.V. serial for a while, but the screen had become absolutely meaningless. Maxim T. Yermakov glanced out of the window: against a background of deliriously tender winter clouds, crude, curly smoke like the wool of a black sheep was drifting from the direction of Pushkin Square. It was pointless trying to deceive himself: the space around him had turned malign, menacing, unfit to live in. Muttering: "All right, bugger it, I'll just take a look," Maxim T. Yermakov grabbed the first jacket he came across in the wardrobe, got tangled up in it, straightened it out somehow and darted outside.

In the yard acrid industrial fumes were already seeping through the insipid smell of snow and the sky was like an ashtray. Clutching the mobile phone in his pocket, Maxim T. Yermakov rushed towards the metro – in the same direction as a stream of hundreds of other people with eyes full of avid, impatient anxiety. The fine snow melted painfully on his panting face, like midges biting, something hard and sticky was jutting into the back of his neck – scowling and baring his teeth, Maxim T. Yermakov found the glossy label, tugged on it and tore it off, together with a scrap of glossy lining. He realised he was dressed too smartly and not warmly enough in this jacket as blue as a toy balloon that Lucy had bought a month ago in the TSUM department store. No one had helped him choose the right clothes to wear, in the way that Maxim T. Yermakov had become accustomed to just lately – and he suddenly felt terribly alone, terribly hurt that he had to go through all this. "Never mind, she can't just disappear, she'll turn up," he muttered, slapping his new winter trainers down in the black, chemical puddles generously nourished by the snow. Hurrying to keep up behind him, the social forecasters bounced their civilian fellow-citizens aside with their broad shoulders.

As he expected, Tverskaya Street was closed off. All the exits from the metro were venting a faint, transparent blackness and the closest one was smoking like a faulty stove. Without standing on ceremony, Maxim T. Yermakov jostled his way right through to the tape barrier and was on the point of stepping over the vibrating strip, tearing it apart or pulling it down when a militiaman's massive grey-uniformed arm was lowered across his path.

"You can't go in there, sir, that's only for the rescue services," the huge cop with a grainy pockmarked face said in a hoarse voice. "If you're a journalist, go over that way." The massive arm waved in the direction of a smaller, separate crowd with wires, cameras and microphones that made it look like an angry squid, ready to devour the official speaking in front of it, who suddenly removed his hat from his lead-grey head with an awkward movement.

"I'm not a damned journalist!" Maxim T. Yermakov howled, frightened more than anything else by that contrite baring of the bureaucrat's grey locks. "My wife was in the metro! Coming to this station! Her phone hasn't been answering for an hour!"

The cop lowered his arm slightly and sighed.

"Clear enough," he said, embarrassed. "You can see what's going on. My own mother was killed in a plane crash. But all the same, you can't go down there, that section could collapse. Sorry, my friend, you'll just have to be patient."

"And my sister and her husband were drowned on a ferry," put in a small-calibre militiaman with an over-large uniform cap that sat on his head as if it was a fist. "Everyone's been hit one way or another."

"Yes, it's like there's a war going on," the huge militiaman growled. "Everyone's been hit, that's for sure. But don't you go frightening yourself ahead of time," he said to Maxim T. Yermakov. "Go over there and take a look beside the ambulances. That's where they're giving first aid to the light cases. And don't you forget that right now no news is good news for you. If you don't find your wife, that's good. She'll show up."

The huge cop's voice sounded insincere – and it didn't chime at all with what was going on all around. Firemen in black-striped overalls, with satchels like telephone booths on their backs, were dragging endless, scraping hoses into the subterranean furnace and loaded stretchers were drifting out in the opposite direction, up the slush-covered steps that were almost invisible in the smoke. Something in a tattered man's suit was carried past, with a bandaged head that looked like a cabbage. An elderly woman was lugged out, with her long-barren stomach blossoming in bloody patches like roses. A young floozy covered in fake diamonds tried to raise herself up on the stretcher, and the little round open mirror in her hand flashed about like a torch in total darkness, although it was bright daylight all around – her plain little face was covered in fine cuts, like clippings of hair after a trim at the hairdresser's. One after another they carried past three, five, eight, glossy sacks shaped like maggots and the size of a human being. Maxim T. Yermakov jerked forward to look, but then one sack that was torn gaped open and the flap fluttered in the wind. Lying inside the sack was something like an Egyptian mummy moulded out of black plasticine, and the marks left by the huge fingers of whoever moulded it were visible. Fitful female weeping echoed over the square, like the sound of musicians tuning their instruments in the orchestra pit, and bronze Pushkin lowered his head towards the spot at his base where the ever-present bouquet of scarlet carnations lay, fading under a sprinkling of snow.

Through the impatient horror of Little Lucy's absence, Maxim T. Yermakov vaguely felt something else: the fear of being recognised. Now, when he was bewildered and weak, in this slick jacket that was like glass in the wind – he could be caught unawares by some of the furious victims. Apparently, however, his appearance had changed so much that he fitted in without being noticed, becoming one of the crowd. You could say he had gone over to the enemy. And no sooner did Maxim T. Yermakov think that than he was engulfed from behind in a dense wave of someone's perfume and the someone slapped him on the shoulder.

"Well, look who it is, long time no see!"

A small nose with a blotch on it, a head of wild, shaggy hair – standing there in front of Maxim T. Yermakov was Dima

Rozhdestvensky in person. The yellow journalists' journalist was clearly well hung-over, but had already remedied his condition with vodka; Rozhdestvensky's left cheekbone was swollen and as yellow as a lemon.

"Why have you soaked yourself in cologne like that?" Maxim T. Yermakov asked irritably.

"Life stinks," Rozhdestvensky replied philosophically. "But what have you come here for? To gloat, as it were, over the life's work of the Classy Baddy? That was what they used to call you until the game was wiped off the internet. Is it true what they say, supposedly you got married?"

"Yes, I did," Maxim T. Yermakov replied rancorously. "My wife's in there." He nodded towards the gaping jaws of disaster, out of which more mute black sacks had been carried.

"Is that right?" Rozhdestvensky said delightedly, brightening up. "That's just great! Classy Baddy loses wife in disaster! That's my story, that's it!"

"Why 'loses', what sort of bilge is that, you creep?" said Maxim T. Yermakov, almost crying as he grabbed Rozhdestvensky's collar and hoisted him up. "You say that again and I'll smash your brains out on the road, you shitty crud."

"You can kill me later, afterwards," said the journalist, twisting himself free sharply and leaving Maxim T. Yermakov with a nettle burn on his hand. "Remember, I told you: pay a big enough price and you'll get in the news. I'm with the Moscow News Channel now," he boasted, then twisted his head round and shouted: "Afanasii!"

In response to the yellow journalist's shout a lanky, bearded individual appeared out of the crowd – his beard was the colour of wood, with one chip that moved separately, together with his lower lip, and he had a TV camera that looked like a little black goat perched on his shoulder.

"Are we shooting him?" he asked, with a rapid glance at Maxim T. Yermakov from under his drooping eyebrows and deftly set the camera on a tripod with a click. "Stand a bit further to the left, please," he said to Maxim T. Yermakov, aiming the optical muzzle at him.

"Right, don't look at the camera, look at me and talk to me," Rozhdestvensky commanded briskly, with a spongy microphone carrying the TV channel's logo already flashing in his hand. "Let's go," he said, turning to Afanasii and pulling a white sheet of paper folded in four out of his pocket.

Afanasii bared his teeth in a grin and glued his face to the viewfinder. Rozhdestvensky unfolded the blank sheet of paper in front of the camera's muzzle – it was as grubby as the yellow journalist's handkerchief would have been if he had one. Maxim T. Yermakov suddenly felt like a blank sheet of paper that was just as grey along the folds, with one ugly corner jutting up in the wind. Without saying a word, he swung round and walked off, and after a few steps he stopped hearing the yellow journalist's plaintive howls punctuated with crude obscenities. Something was spinning and clattering in Maxim T. Yermakov's head, as if it was whipping up his nebulous brain into a frothy cocktail. Raising his head, he saw the source of the sound: hanging over closed-off Tverskaya Street, swaying like a little shoe on a woman's foot, was a small, elegant, red-and-white helicopter. Identically red-and-white ambulances kept shooting out from under the helicopter and hurtling off up the incline of the road with flashing lights wailing and fading, in the direction of Leningrad Prospect.

That was what he had to do.

Maxim T. Yermakov dashed back to his own yard. From all the water they had soaked up out of the puddles, his trainers felt heavy and sticky in the cold, as if he had three kilograms of fish on each foot. The Toyota was asleep, dreaming, with an icy crust on its back. Swearing oaths to God and the devil that he would have the electrics in the car changed, Maxim T. Yermakov started the engine at the third attempt, watching out of the corner of his eye as the social forecasters who had come tearing up manoeuvred beside the sugar-dusted garbage tip in their roaring Moskvich, leaving black marks in the cigarette-paper snow. After circling round the yard, ploughing up a couple of lawns that were as damp as sponges and jolting the Toyota's frame and bodywork violently on a terrible pothole like the gap where a tooth had been pulled out of the asphalt, Maxim T. Yermakov slipped out onto Tverskaya Street through Nastasinsky Lane.

He had never driven round Moscow in winter at such a crazy speed before. No traffic lights or road signs existed – owing to a disaster of federal significance, the crossroads were manned by teams of militiamen who flashed by like grey pillars. Bronze Mayakovsky leapt out like a grasshopper, Belorusskaya Station appeared and disappeared like scenery on a revolving opera stage. Moscow turned out to be a small town at a speed of almost 120 kph: now Leningrad Prospect had opened up and started shooting past, flickering its streetlamps like someone striking matches. Maxim T. Yermakov was only concerned about one thing – to stick close behind the speeding ambulance, with that sideways drifting of wheels scrabbling in snowy mush as it hurtled along. He saw the large figures 03 written in red paint in front of him – he thought he could see them with his eyes closed. In the curtained windows of the back doors, staggering silhouettes with almost no colour sometimes appeared – perhaps it was medics trying to do something for the injured victims on this frantic, slippery ride. Maxim T. Yermakov clung to the thought that Little Lucy was there inside, that it was probably her – that created something like an invisible cable between him and the reanimobile, and the cable dragged the Toyota along when its own motor wasn't powerful enough.

Then the ambulance turned off, shot through three or maybe four sides streets strangely bevelled upwards towards the sky and shot back out onto a main road, and Maxim T. Yermakov stopped understanding where he was and where this high-speed dash was taking him. He simply followed in the ski tracks of the reanimobile. It didn't look like Moscow any more: pine-tree trunks like sticks of salami flickered past on the verge of the road. Then long, flat buildings appeared up ahead; it had to be a hospital campus. The ambulance turned and drove in along a slip road, medics ran up and started unloading an entirely lifeless, long old woman, whose blood looked like tar on the bandages that had come uncoiled. After shaking the wheels out of the stretcher, they trundled the old woman off at a run, with a terrible rattling, towards glass doors with a sign that said "Admissions". Maxim T. Yermakov parked crookedly and dashed after them.

If, during the time that remained to Maxim T. Yermakov, anyone had asked him what hell looked like, he would have replied that hell was faced with white tiles and there was an aspidistra in the corner. He was the first relative to reach the clinic to which they brought the most terrible and bloody blossoms of that day's explosion. No one recognised him here either – or, rather, they didn't even acknowledge the fact of his existence. Maxim T. Yermakov literally threw himself at the medics in their heavily-breathing gauze masks, but their eyes, which all looked like women's eyes on the covered faces, refused point-blank to see him. New victims kept arriving all the time, many covered in burns like red toads; someone was screeching regularly in a thin voice behind a pleated screen; a heap of scorched, sliced-up clothing lay on the floor and in places the caked-together rags retained the shapes of bodies, like pieces of tree bark.

Feeling desperate enough to pass out, Maxim T. Yermakov went outside for a smoke two or three times. It seemed like the dead of night already: the snow was smoke rising from the ragged summits of the pines, the moon in a break in the clouds was solid rock, as crude as a millstone. A hoarse woman's voice behind him made Maxim T. Yermakov shudder. A cigarette was skipping about in the doctor's long fingers as she kneaded it, and she asked him for a light. The lighter lit up pear-shaped cheeks and a gauze mask lowered onto a double chin; the doctor's small head, like a stump on her broad, dumpy body, paradoxically suggested to him that she worked for the special committee. Choking on his poisonous suspicion and the fierce tobacco, Maxim T. Yermakov explained the circumstances that had led to him loitering here.

"Ludmila Viktorovna Yermakova?" the doctor repeated interrogatively. "There is someone by that name."

"Well?" exclaimed Maxim T. Yermakov, grabbing the doctor by her fat elbow so that she stumbled.

"They didn't get her here," the doctor told him apathetically, still sucking greedily at her cigarette after being grabbed.

"What do you mean, they didn't get her here?" asked Maxim T. Yermakov, turning cold. "Where is she now? What's the address?"

The doctor gave a stiff, forced smile and looked in a vaguely downwards direction.

"Ludmila Yermakova expired on the way to the clinic," she stated without any expression at all and adjusted the jacket thrown over her sloping shoulder. "Injuries not compatible with life, what else could you expect?"

At that moment Maxim T. Yermakov felt absolutely nothing, but the crude millstone of the moon suddenly seemed to be toppling over and crashing down, it was about to crumple the immensely tall pines like grass and flop into the snow, throwing up cold, hazy dust. Darkness was advancing, enveloping the sources of light, the white street lamps over the slip road shrank strangely, so that they looked like mushy boiled potatoes.

"Where?" Maxim T. Yermakov asked in a strangled voice.

"Who are you to her, her brother, her husband?" The doctor sucked her cigarette right down to the filter in truly masculine fashion and stamped out the butt. "I can see you're the husband. All right, come on. Only bear in mind that no one's interested in you now. We don't have any time for relatives. More than twenty casualties have come in already, and they keep bringing in more and more of them. If you faint and collapse – you'll just stay lying there on the floor, understand?"

Maxim T. Yermakov nodded energetically several times and carried on nodding after the snuffling doctor had dragged him into the admissions area and entrusted him to the care of either a nurse or an orderly – a fierce, bushy-browed individual, standing firmly on stubby, slightly straddled legs amid the chaos of the catastrophe. Gesturing for him to follow her, the orderly led the insensate Maxim T. Yermakov down a long corridor painted with government-issue blue paint. The corridor contained nothing except a lopsided, badly sagging wheelchair, which Maxim T. Yermakov stumbled into. Directly above the wheelchair, the cover of some kind of electrical distribution board was half-open, and the thick tangle of wires under it made the inside look as if it was stuffed with straw: Maxim T. Yermakov was amazed that he was noticing such stupid details as he walked along.

The corridor ended at a dull iron door: sighing, the orderly pulled a crude key the size of a chicken bone out of her pocket, the lock champed four times and cold reached out through the door as it squeaked open – not the cold of winter streets, but the dead, fusty air of a fridge that hasn't been washed for a long time. Behind the door concrete steps appeared and Maxim T. Yermakov walked down them as if he was sinking into a pit, first with his left foot, then his right foot.

He saw a long row of tables covered with stainless steel, with the black sacks he had seen recently lying on them. Some were squashed up two on a table, and there was a grotesque, heart-rending intimacy in the way they huddled together. As always in such places, there was the hollow sound of water dripping somewhere and every drop struck as hard as a liquid bullet. The orderly gestured for Maxim T. Yermakov to stay where he was. Walking forward a bit, she started counting the sacks as if they were items of luggage, and her carrot-like index finger was clearly no magic wand capable of bringing the dead back to life. The orderly must have intended to open the right sack at once, but she got the wrong one twice; she leaned down and tugged back the zip, first to reveal a bloodless, man's face in a thick, black beard, and then something shapeless, with bony, forward-jutting teeth, that in life had clearly been a blonde-haired woman or man. Maxim T. Yermakov felt a momentary relief, suddenly believing that everything that was happening was a mistake. But just then the orderly found what she was looking for, opened the zip wider, adjusted the sack the way people adjust a hood on a child's head and stepped back, pursing her parched lips disapprovingly.

Maxim T. Yermakov probably ought to have felt something

different at that moment. Something else, not this strange, alienated helplessness at the sight of Lucy in a black plastic hood, with her cheek ripped open and simply lying on her face like a wet rag. If she was alive, they'd have arranged plastic surgery, for any amount of money. He could see straight away that her eyes had been closed by strangers: the eyelids were crumpled up, there seemed to be a small amount of soapy water in the sockets. Their unborn kid must have been really surprised when they cancelled his ticket. Who was he, down there in the limp, clotted womb: a translucent little shrimp, a fingerling fish? Maxim T. Yermakov, the father of a pink tiddler, now and forever. Lucy lay in the sack, her hair dishevelled and her head cocked back unnaturally as if she didn't wish to discuss what had happened. Her fine hair was tousled the way it used to be in the morning, when she got up for work; Maxim T. Yermakov straightened out a tangle and shuddered when he felt the cold frontal bone under his fingers – and there, inside, some kind of vestigial activity, something like minute electrical tremors before the final darkness. And then the black sacks with bodies in them surrounded him from all sides, swelling up, as if the flabby sacks were inflating like balloons, slowly straightening out their broad sides.

"Hey, mister! Don't you fall in here!" Maxim T. Yermakov heard the orderly's frightened voice say.

He didn't fall and even made his own way out of the basement; he retained a dim memory of crawling up the steps on all fours. Several times his nostrils were assaulted by sal ammoniac, which set his head flashing like magnesium, and things around him congealed, like in photographs: two male feet moving away on a trolley, with toes like yellow toadstools, all the rest covered over with a sheet; someone's hand in a rubber glove, glistening like the fat out of a chicken, reaching for a glinting surgical instrument; a bunch of keys spread-eagled on the floor, clearly not hospital keys, but from an apartment, a key-ring pendent in the form of a little crystal, faceted heart, cracked inside. Maxim T. Yermakov was thrown out of various areas, pulled along crudely by his jacket, shoved into the tiled admissions area again and again. The doctor he had met tried to get through to him with soundless words that she moulded out of the lumpy air with her vigorous little mouth, but he just waved her aside and sat down right there on the floor, beside the aspidistra. "Just look," he thought, doubled up with pain under the aspidistra's leaves, as dirty as shoes, "how fast the time flies. There you are, feeling afraid of something, wondering what it will be like, how you'll survive if it happens – and it already has happened."

Maxim T. Yermakov made it back home almost by guesswork, waltzing among the ragged bandages of dry snow swirling across the road, sometimes getting caught in phrenetic explosions of light and honking from oncoming vehicles. At home he collected together all the alcohol he had – two bombs of champagne, an opened bottle of red wine, as thick as sealing wax, a quarter-litre of vodka, something else slapping about in a green bottle, it could even have been vinegar – and he drank it all in tense gulps, every swallow like a knot with a coin tied in it. Maxim T. Yermakov's head was pounding continuously, like an immense canon: a salute in honour of Little Lucy. How could it happen? They'd only just got married.

After that an indeterminate amount of time passed by. Maxim T. Yermakov abandoned the office, his boss, his projects. They called him from the office: they already knew everything there. Maxim T. Yermakov couldn't tell one voice from another and he hung up without listening to what they wanted to say. Apparently they had taken it on themselves to organise the funeral. So okay, let them organise it. Meanwhile Maxim T. Yermakov sat in one corner or another of the flat that had turned so quiet, sometimes finding himself doubled up on the shoe bench in the hallway, under the canopy of Lucy's arctic-fox fur coat, like a little rabbit under a pine tree; once he spent an indefinite period on the toilet with his trousers down, and the seat glued itself to his backside, like a ring to the planet Saturn. Occasionally he went outside for purposes unknown, still in that blue, tender jacket, smeared on the front with something like black glue; again there was no one to give him the right clothes, even when the temperature outside dipped to minus twenty Celsius. It looked really cold, the hoarfrost sparkled and glittered everywhere like sinister sandpaper, the patches of snow on the pavement were like bird droppings. Maxim T. Yermakov sat on the shoulder of the wall of Tverskaya Metro Station, watching the tops of the passengers' heads as they descended into hell; in the crush several people at once walked down one step at a time together, and that was like some kind of devastation, as if the strata of the earth were shifting or a building was subsiding, floor by floor. In the frost Maxim T. Yermakov's feet turned to stones, but he didn't feel a thing and would have stayed there for a long time if not for the tiresome social forecasters hovering in front of him and beating out a tap dance with their stiff, standard-issue uniform shoes. Overwhelmed by dreary boredom, Maxim T. Yermakov trudged wearily back to the flat.

It was strange that only recently, when he went back to Lucy's flat, he used to say he was going home. Now, unprotected by Lucy's presence, he felt like a burglar loitering at the scene of his crime. Yes, he felt exactly like a criminal. It turned out that Lucy had been killed because of that semi-corporeal, fluctuating item that in some miraculous fashion had clung to his shoulders, like a will o' the wisp on a snag in a bog, for thirty years now. On the other hand, all people's heads were semi-corporeal – on what scales could thoughts be weighed? All right then, if he had given in to the social forecasters and shot himself, how could he and Lucy have got married? There you have it gents, a puzzle with a wolf, a goat and a cabbage. The imprint of Lucy's head was still there in the crumpled pillow. Maxim T. Yermakov didn't touch it. He remembered vaguely from some book or movie that a pillow preserved a person's smell longest of all, and if you sniffed it, it would seem as if they were there. But he didn't sniff it, he simply looked at that precious little hollow, which was gradually disappearing like a track in the snow. It was being covered over by the fine drift snow of time, and this rendered visible the substance of which human days consist.

The most grotesque thing of all now was sleep. Maxim T. Yermakov couldn't stretch out any more on the carved family bed or the sagging divan where he and Lucy had begun a new life. The sleeping space in Artyom's room was taken too. Maxim T. Yermakov arranged himself in a perfunctory manner on the dusty couch in the drawing room, with its springs that swayed about wildly under an ancient tapestry. Sleep flatly refused to come, sleep dawdled brazenly. The deafening ticking of clocks filled the entire flat. When oblivion finally did arrive, Maxim T. Yermakov found himself in a completely different place from where he used to go when he fell asleep before. It was an entirely unfamiliar province, a blighted, alien place, where he encountered numerous glossy-black, ripe-looking balloons; they jostled and chafed against each other in colossal bunches, swayed under ceilings with their filthy-white threads dangling down, and in his dream Maxim T. Yermakov realised that each balloon was a person. There was a New Year tree there too, with black decorations and tinsel, looking as if it had been smeared all over with pitch. But even so, in his dream Maxim T. Yermakov didn't know about Lucy's death and he remembered in the moment he awoke – as if he was making up for lost time in a sudden dash. "I wonder," he asked himself, "how many days or months have to go by before the reality and the dream coincide again? When I'm asleep, it's like being in the past, before Lucy died. The news hasn't reached there yet, it meets me as soon as I open my eyes, falls on me and crumples me up, it won't let me breathe, it won't even let me cry." It was strange to recall that only very recently Maxim T. Yermakov had been trying to decide whether he should marry Lucy or someone else. In reality Lucy had already been his wife when she was still peeing in her nappies. It had all been fore-ordained. But now, fuck it, she wasn't in this world any more.

Once, when Maxim T. Yermakov had only just woken from what he now thought of as sleep and was trying to wash himself with cold water that escaped through his fingers, someone rang the doorbell. An insane hope. Why not, all sorts of things happen. Wiping himself down sloppily with a clumped-up towel, Maxim T. Yermakov set off with a skip and a dash into the hallway. But it wasn't Lucy at the door, or someone from the clinic with good news, but Big Lida, Crap's faithful aide. She looked like a home-grown simulacrum of a Hollywood star, complete with dark glasses that were steamed up after the frost.

"Well, Maxie, just look at the face on you," she declared instead of saying hello. "Do you look in the mirror at all? Or have you gone on the sauce big-time?"

"I don't. I haven't." Maxim T. Yermakov replied in a dreary voice. "What do you want?"

"The funeral's tomorrow, I told you that ten times on the phone," Big Lida informed him, tugging off her rather grimy white gloves one finger at a time. "Have you got the things ready for the morgue? No, I can see you haven't. Maybe you could let me come in?"

Maxim T. Yermakov moved aside with a sour grimace and Big Lida proceeded into the flat, lowering her flowing mink off her shoulders on the way. Maxim T. Yermakov reluctantly accepted the scent-laden fur coat and slammed it, hunchbacked, onto a hook on the tall hallstand. Stroking her tightly wrapped denim hips, his uninvited guest strolled round the rooms at a leisurely pace, stopping in front of the very biggest paintings and touching all the shiniest trinkets. Maxim T. Yermakov plodded after her, observing with a bored glance the wavelike movements of her ponderous body, which reminded him of a chubby mermaid.

"Yes, a nice little flat, impressive," Big Lida said eventually in a pensive voice with a clear note of feminine pique. "Have you got anything to drink?"

"No," Maxim T. Yermakov replied quickly. "Get on with it, do what you came for."

He flung open Lucy's section of the carriage-sized wardrobe in front of his guest – something white fluttered gently inside it, a light-cotton summer frock – and stepped back, crossing his unfamiliarly bony arms on his chest. Big Lida snorted resentfully, lifted her dark glasses up onto her forehead and started rattling the loose-jointed hangers to and fro. Every now and then she pulled some item of clothing out into the light, examined it captiously and even felt the material, as if she was intending to buy it. The sunglasses stuck out on her forehead, reflecting the chandelier. Maxim T. Yermakov tried not to look, but he still saw Lucy's little dresses; the new ones, still with labels, had remained shop glad-rags, but the ones that had been worn were suddenly as faded as if they had been hanging there lifeless for a hundred years or more.

"There, I think that will do," said Big Lida, holding up the matted little suit of grey sheep's wool in which Maxim T. Yermakov remembered Lucy being so unhappy and straightening out the sleeves.

"No, not that, no way!" Maxim T. Yermakov protested and at that very moment he heard the monotonous cheeping of the mobile phone somewhere in the depths of the flat.

The mobile phone turned up on the kitchen table, among the unwashed cups in which the old ground-coffee remains were like dark, dried-up gouache. Maxim T. Yermakov thought at first that it was another call from the office, about the funeral. But it was Sergei Yevgenievich Kravtsov, who Maxim T. Yermakov had forgotten about completely.

"I know about your loss," the principal tadpole-head of the country said in a funereal voice. "Maxim Terentievich, please accept my profound and sincere condolences."

"Let's consider them accepted." Failing to find any cigarettes on the table, Maxim T. Yermakov fished a crooked stub out of the overflowing ashtray. "And now fuck off, I'm too busy to talk to you."

"Maxim Terentievich, wait a moment before you tell me where to go," the state freak continued hastily. "I have important news for you. Important even against the backdrop of recent events. Hear me out."

Maxim T. Yermakov was about to repeat, with more precise directions, the address for which the principal tadpole-head should set out immediately, but something in the freak's voice put him on his guard. A new intonation, contrite and conciliatory. It would have been better if he'd done the heavy, piling on the pressure, Maxim T. Yermakov was already used to that.

"Okay then, tell me about it." Maxim T. Yermakov set fire to the cigarette butt and the half-empty paper flared up and burned his tongue. Fuck it! No point getting agitated, the worst thing that could happen in his life already had. Now the tadpole-heads could sing and dance on the ceiling for all he cared.

"Maxim Terentievich, our department has committed a prodigious error," the tadpole-head in the phone said contritely. "Believe me, such things only happen very rarely. A malfunction in an extremely delicate piece of apparatus. I cannot put into words how sorry I am that this had happened."

"Meaning what?" Maxim T. Yermakov jerked like a lunatic and shoved the small teapot off the table: it exploded on the floor like a round china bomb. The strong brew tumbled out in a half-rotted lump, like earth out of a flowerpot. Why did everything age so quickly without Lucy? The curtain on the window over there seemed to be coming to pieces, and the dishes were starting to look like empty egg shells.

"Maxie, what's wrong?"

Big Lida appeared in the door of the kitchen – she had come running at the noise. It was only now that Maxim T. Yermakov noticed she had turned older somehow, she had spongy spider's webs of wrinkles under her eyes and what looked like cotton wool sticking out through the designer holes in the jeans tightly encasing her low hips.

"Get out of here, let me talk!" Maxim T. Yermakov yelled at the uninvited social worker, who staggered back into the corridor, clutching an armful of Lucy's clothes. "I didn't mean you," he told the state freak in the phone, who was sighing patiently.

"I know you didn't," the principal tadpole-head of the country replied meekly. "Well then, Maxim Terentievich, what I'm basically trying to tell you is this. An appalling, deplorable mistake has taken place. Only today we have finally confirmed that you are not an Alpha Object. Yes, you do possess certain psycho-physical deviations from the norm, but they have no connection at all with those relations of cause and effect that are studied by our department. In short, you are a perfectly ordinary, entirely unremarkable individual."

"Well fucking hellfire!" Maxim T. Yermakov exclaimed, jumping up off his tumbling chair and giving vent to such a long string of obscenities that Big Lida emerged out of the semi-darkness of the corridor again, with the surprised look of a fish disturbed in murky waters.

After blurting out all the unprintable expletives that he could get his tongue round, Maxim T. Yermakov found a mug on the table with a murky liquid in it that he thought was probably a crust of tea and sugar soaked under the tap, and downed it all at a gulp.

"And now what?" he asked when he got his breath back. "So you can harass a man like that for a year, then simply say sorry and that's the end of it? What if I really had shot myself? Who's going to answer to me for this so-called mistake of yours?"

"I am prepared to offer you every possible apology imaginable," said Sergei Yevgenievich Kravtsov, reverting to his usual dry tone of voice. "Naturally, not in any financial form, if you are referring to that again. Maxim Terentievich, you are a cynical man, are you not? So let's talk cynically. Let's look at the real results of what you call harassment. Your situation today is incomparably better than it was a year ago. Your deceased spouse wrote a will leaving everything to you, we've checked that through our own channels. You have become the owner of a flat that you yourself could never have bought, no matter how much you stole. The flat contains a collection of paintings that is valued at approximately one million three hundred thousand dollars. Ludmila Viktorovna's grandfather, the late academician Chebotaryov, was a passionate collector. He also collected coins and, in round figures, his numismatic collection is worth another five hundred thousand. Look around the flat and see if you can find this property, the albums containing it are probably in the drawing room, in the bottom of the antique carved sideboard, under the tablecloths. By the way, if it is restored, the sideboard is also worth money, like many other pieces of furniture and other items. You, Maxim Terentievich, are now a wealthy widower. And at work you have become a valuable specialist, they are so keen to keep you that soon they'll let you steal again. Not bad at all, am I right?"

"Thanks," growled Maxim T. Yermakov, suddenly feeling in his soul the kind of furtive warmth that had once warmed it when he managed to carve a good chunk off the budget for himself. But it was only a reflex response: the deceptive whiff of joy was tainted with a frosty chill. "So it's all down to you, is it, that everything's so hunky-dory?" he asked with the wry chuckle of a swindler caught in the act.

"Yes, precisely so," the principal tadpole-head of the country replied confidently. "Let me remind you, Maxim T. Yermakov, that relations of cause and effect are my speciality. And as a specialist I can say that not all these connections can be traced using our common sense. It only seems to us that they are something like arrows between little circles signifying statistical conditions of the real world. In actual fact there are no statistical states, there is only movement, the multidimensional interweaving of the living shoots of causality. In short, if it were not for our department's error, you would now still be stuck in a rented flat, dreaming of saving up enough for two rooms inside the Garden Ring Road. As I recall, you requested ten million dollars from us. You have received less, approximately half as much, but in your heart of hearts you weren't really counting on so much anyway. So life is looking up, Maxim Terentievich! You are literally to be congratulated!"

"What? Go stuff your congratulations up your ass, you bastard!" exclaimed Maxim T. Yermakov, interrupting the state freak's philosophising, and feeling that the tears he had tried in vain to shed for so long had suddenly gone on the offensive. "Do you have any idea what you're saying, you cunt?"

"I understand it," the principal tadpole-head replied suavely. "But do you, Maxim Terentievich, understand exactly what you have just heard?"

Maxim T. Yermakov fell silent, staring fixedly at a picture that looked like a trough of soaking laundry. The rising tears were a raging conflagration. Only one thing was important now – not to blubber down the phone. He had to get rid of everybody and be alone.

"Maxim Terentievich, just half a minute more of your time," the principal tadpole-head said hastily, as if he had sensed that the former Alpha Object's finger was already on the "Off" button. "We have one final piece of business with you. Not for tomorrow, of course, a funeral is a sacred responsibility. But the day after tomorrow I would ask you please to hand in your personal weapon. Please check that it is where it ought to be. Remember the incident in which your pistol turned out to be in a quite different place from where you assumed it was? I trust there will be no repetition of that. Our regulations are very strict where weapons are concerned, you must understand that."

Without bothering to reply, Maxim T. Yermakov switched off. If he didn't let loose his tears right now, immediately, his entire face could get chemical burns as it was literally burst open by the corrosive discharge of his tear glands. Unfortunately for him Big Lida just wouldn't shove off. Here she was again with those dresses, carrying them in both hands, like banners, and the dresses blurred into trembling, hot, rainbow-coloured blotches.

"Maxie, look, maybe this one, with the flower pattern, it's a summer dress, of course, but it's all the same to her in the grave, isn't it, what do you think?" Big Lida lifted one hanger a bit higher and something white fluttered on something brown. "Max, what's wrong? Oh, he's crying! Maxie, you poor thing…"

"Go away," Maxim T. Yermakov forced out with an effort, feeling the overflowing moisture running down his nose against his will.

"Don't be silly," Big Lida drawled languidly. "Maxie, how would you like me to console you?"

Moving very slowly, Big Lida hooked the hangers with the bright rainbows somewhere on the door and drifted towards Maxim T. Yermakov, on the way unfastening little buttons with her large white fingers. The drowsy smile on her face pitched and swayed like a red float. Maxim T. Yermakov was suddenly nose to nose with her beetroot-red satin bra and its overflowing, sourish-milky-white contents.

"I ca-han't," said Maxim T. Yermakov, turning away.

"I get it," Big Lida sighed disappointedly. "What unreliable apparatus you men have. Don't be upset, Maxie. You'll manage all right, if not today, then some time later. Okay, then I'll take this dress here, with the flowers, and the white shoes, I found them in the hallway. We'll do everything in fine style. I'll take care of you tomorrow. Don't worry, I won't leave you on your own!"

So saying, Big Lida stuffed the unfortunate dress into a plastic bag and at long last set off towards the door, glancing into every mirror that wasn't curtained over along the way. It was torment for Maxim T. Yermakov to wait while she pulled on her boots, flung the mink swankily across her shoulders and blew him a sweet kiss, like a pink pie. As soon as the locks clicked shut Maxim T. Yermakov fell against the wall, trembling.

The wall was as wet as if the upstairs neighbours' water pipe had sprung a leak. The couch, to which Maxim T. Yermakov had groped his way blindly, seeing nothing but a blurred kaleidoscope of rainbow colours, had got waterlogged too and started smelling of dogs. Utterly exhausted by all his sobbing, Maxim T. Yermakov suddenly fell asleep.

When he woke up, it was the dead of night. Outside the windows Moscow was murmuring vaguely, like a restless sea. His numb leg, full of ants, was like a bottle of sparkling water that had just been opened, his crumpled face hung on him like a loose, prickly sack. Something had happened before Maxim T. Yermakov crashed out. Sergei Yevgenievich Kravtsov had called and told him something good, something important.

What?

About the will and the rich inheritance? No, that was crap. What good was an inheritance and all those valuable things, if without Lucy everything decayed, not by the day, but by the hour? Take that picture opposite the couch, yesterday it was a portrait of a rickety grandee with woman's hips and a little wig, but now the paint had cracked and the large scales made the grandee look like a carp. Maxim T. Yermakov got up with an effort and walked, limping on his unstable leg, along the line of his inherited canvases. That was right, of course: not pictures, but burnt oven trays, even the gilded frames had flaked until they were black. And there was the carved sideboard, with the ruins of dishes behind its faceted panes of murky glass. Maxim T. Yermakov took hold of the ring of a handle to take a look at the much-vaunted numismatics collection, but the handle came out of the rotten wood like an old man's tooth. So he shouldn't even bother: no doubt at this very moment the coins in the sticky albums were turning into black, scaly scabs. Chances were that while the social forecasters were searching for the real Alpha Object, the flat would be blown high by the endeavours of some fucking spaced-out terrorist. So okay, that didn't bother him.

What else had the principal tadpole-head of the country said? That Maxim T. Yermakov wasn't any kind of Alpha Object, but an ordinary individual. "So they'll get off my back at last, stop dogging my footsteps everywhere and sticking their video cameras all over the place. A great stroke of luck for me, I don't think." The social forecasters didn't deserve any delighted gratitude from Maxim T. Yermakov. And apart from, that, the social forecasters would still be around, they'd just move a bit further away, but Maxim T. Yermakov, with his experience, would still be able to sense them. He'd see the rusty vehicles with the boosted engines on the streets, pick out the stony faces with the high cheekbones in a crowd. "You're not going anywhere," he thought, "this place is contaminated."

So what was it then, that rescue line, that sure-fire way to simply cancel tomorrow's impossible, inconceivable funeral?

The pistol.

He had to find it immediately.

Maxim T. Yermakov dashed round the drawing room with his teeth chattering. Where on earth had Lucy put it? And he couldn't ask her until he found it and did what he had to do. A closed circle, that was funny. For a moment Maxim T. Yermakov thought that he and Lucy had left the pistol behind at Just Natasha's flat, which had been completely erased from his memory, together with everything it contained. No, that couldn't be right, or the social forecasters would have forwarded the Makarov by personal delivery. That meant the weapon was somewhere at home, he had to sit down and think. Suddenly, with piercing clarity, Maxim T. Yermakov saw Lucy, in her baggy home-wear T-shirt, emptying out the blue bags, transferring stacks of faded clothes to one drawer in the chest of drawers, with the flat thread of a little gold chain blazing bright round her neck, hanging across a vertebra as smooth as a pebble. God, how painful, after pain like that there was nothing to be afraid of.

There was the chest of drawers. The same kind of carved monster as the sideboard. The brass fittings had turned green in just a few hours. Maxim T. Yermakov tried to figure out whether he would have to break out the deep drawers with some instrument that was also half-ruined, but at the very first, tentative jolt, the front panels of the geriatric item of furniture simply dropped out and shattered into rotten pieces at Maxim T. Yermakov's feet. Holding his breath, Maxim T. Yermakov thrust his hand into the gaping innards. He felt as if he was scrabbling about among the ash and the coals in a cold stove. God forbid that the Makarov should turn out to be nothing but a rusty lump of iron, no good for anything.

There it was! Maxim T. Yermakov pulled the thing he was looking for out of the dusty remnants. Brand new, robustly solid, smelling of oil and fresh iron. Nothing had happened to it. Hand in the weapon? Sure thing – and here's the hole from a doughnut to go with it. Maxim T. Yermakov laughed triumphantly. Now that everything had been decided and become inevitable, this Makarov was the only thing in the world that belonged to him utterly and completely.

Lucy couldn't have gone too far yet. Her shell – that old, tattered diving suit for living in this world – was lying, frozen, in the morgue, and she was somewhere around here, if not in the flat, then definitely in Moscow. Supposedly the dead lingered for ten days in the places where they used to live, and only five had gone by at the most. Just for a moment Maxim T. Yermakov had the feeling that he could use the pistol to call Lucy, rather like a mobile phone. Never mind, now he'd do everything right and catch up with her, and then they'd move on together. It was a good thing he wasn't a genuine Alpha Object after all, or things would have turned out the way the state freaks had wanted and tried to make happen. Maxim T. Yermakov might not have been able to make himself hand them a present like that on a plate. But now he was free. Wouldn't that be a surprise for the social forecasters! But that was fine, a few firecrackers up the backside would be good for them.

Maxim T. Yermakov had to check how the pistol worked. He walked through into the bedroom and took his pillow off the bed – carefully, so as not to damage the precious imprint on the pillow beside it – the hollow was already barely visible, with just a faint shadow inside it. The pistol jammed and twisted in some kind of mechanical cramp, and that made it twice as heavy. Bloody hell, what was wrong? Aha, the safety catch was still on. Now it was off. Oh, fuck me! His hand jerked back all the way to his shoulder, the pillow puffed out a little fountain of fluff and collapsed onto its side. Excellent, it could kill an elephant. His head felt drunk after the shot, probably like other people's heads felt after they consumed alcohol. It was okay, rather pleasant in fact. If it was the same after the real shot, Maxim T. Yermakov wouldn't mind.

And now – a few preparations.

He had to get changed and shaved. Scraping his palm over his rustling chin, Maxim T. Yermakov glanced into the splotched and spattered mirror in the bathroom. Yes, Big Lida was right: faces didn't come any more hideous than that. It was like a dead hedgehog. Suddenly Maxim T. Yermakov felt an otherworldly tremor from the mirror's oscillating depths, surging and heaving in dense waves. Maybe he ought to follow tradition and cover all the mirrors over with some kind of cloth? Only what for, really? What if Lucy could peep out of there and give him a sign? But what Maxim T. Yermakov took – just for a second – to be a sweet ghost was only a fluffy towel that had dried into a twisted rope hanging on a hook.

Right then, down to business. What if one of the neighbours had heard the shot and called the cops; if they turned up they wouldn't let him prepare for his journey in peace. The disposable razor that he hadn't changed for ages jerked and skipped about like an old harrow – and finally it cut his skin in the most sensitive spot. The pink-tinted foam looked like whipped cream with syrup. Maxim T. Yermakov dabbed hastily at his shaved neck; the cut right under the chin bled richly, oozing out Maxim T. Yermakov's filling, as if Maxim T. Yermakov was a sweet pie that had been bitten. A scarlet trickle ran across the Adam's apple that was working up and down, reached the wet neck of his T-shirt and made a kind of water-colour blot. The sight of his own blood suddenly plunged Maxim T. Yermakov into paroxysms of animal terror. This was all happening for real. In a few minutes he wouldn't be here any more. Maxim T. Yermakov swayed, saw the ceiling above his head, covered in bruises from some ancient leak, and a thick water pipe with midges dancing round it – or in his eyes – like black threads tied into little bows.

Somehow he made it to the couch, smoked five or six tasteless cigarettes one after another and calmed down a bit. It couldn't be helped, he couldn't stay here, after all. It wouldn't be any more frightening than jumping off a bridge at night. Over there on the other side Grandad Valera was probably already bustling about, preparing a reception for him. So he had to hurry. As he sat there, Maxim T. Yermakov's eye happened to fall on his mobile phone. He remembered how, at the New Year, when the whole sky was a glittering explosion of coloured lights and pregnant Lucy was greedily devouring the side of a chocolate cake, he had turned sentimental in his happiness and suddenly wanted to call his parents in the little old town. He hadn't called then, and he couldn't call now. So he never had managed to forgive his father and mother for their bumbling, unhappy life.

"Marinka, wherever you may be now, forgive me and don't think ill of me. Sasha, dear golden-freckled nun, pray for me, maybe you can make it work."

A short while later Maxim T. Yermakov, in a clean white shirt as angular as a sheet of paper, was sitting in the grandest armchair in the flat, which was upholstered in tooled and gilded leather – a chair in which he had never sat before, not even once. The pistol, ponderously heavy and smelling of gunpowder, was also ready. What a strange thing it was to do, really – point a pistol at yourself. It was awkward, with the left hand or the right, it gave you the feeling of riding backwards in some antediluvian old jalopy. Maxim

T. Yermakov glanced curiously into the round, black little hole. "Hi there, what part are we going to fire at? I don't fancy the head, the social forecasters were far too insistent about that." He tried pressing the hard muzzle against his tense, bristling ribs, behind which his heart was bounding – heavy, alive, clumsy. No, probably better not do it like that, what if it wasn't outright? They'd operate on him, bring him back, take the gun, and what could he do then – hang himself with his shoelaces? All right, he needed to think for a moment, catch his breath. Maxim T. Yermakov lit another cigarette and the usual Parliament seemed to be made of wood. "Well, my friend," he thought, addressing the Makarov, "maybe you should light one up too, your hole's just the right size for a cigarette, it would look neat. All right, let's try in the mouth, like in the movies. Fuck it, that iron's really hard – ribbed and rounded and the taste is already like sour blood in advance." He tried pushing the barrel a bit deeper and almost puked. Just like some girl during her first blowjob. No, that way was no good.

Maxim T. Yermakov settled himself more comfortably in the chair, put his elbows on his knees and pressed his wrinkled forehead against the barrel, as if he wanted to prove he could be more obstinate than the pistol.

At the count of three.

There was a crash and a jerk and Maxim T. Yermakov sprang back and away from himself, like a billiard ball rebounding off the cushion after a blow from the cue. Struggling drunkenly to control himself, he floated out clumsily into the centre of the room and saw the body he had left behind, slowly tumbling out of the armchair onto the carpet. The shot-through head, with a tuft of hair sticking out like a chip of wood where the bullet had exited, had turned palpably heavier, filled up with sluggish, dull matter, and at the back a bald patch that Maxim T. Yermakov had never known about during his life showed bright through the hair. Meanwhile, everything around him had become permeable, everything consisted of grains and patches of searing energy; as an experiment Maxim T. Yermakov passed through the sideboard and back, and felt as if he had taken a hot shower. He asked space a question and received the reply that Lucy was busy right now, but would be free soon. But where was Grandad Valera? Speak of the devil, there was the old man moving aside the black pictures and climbing though the wall like a hole in a fence.

"Well, Maximka, that was a really batty thing to do. Those social forecasters of yours put one over on you and no mistake. Okay, it can't be helped now. Come with me, you fool."

Not on Lubyanka Street, but in a completely different part of Moscow, one in no way remarkable to look at, in building number 17, with a flat roof and a bored expression in its windows, there was an office. The furniture in the office was probably originally from the 1970s: the upholstery of the chairs had turned dull and greasy, the surface of the office desk had buckled like a washboard and come away here and there in stained chips. But the complicated leather armchair that looked a bit like a dentist's chair was from a completely different age, with numerous adjustable brackets supporting instruments with obscure purposes and wide armrests reminiscent of tyres, bearing a relief design that was clearly a sensory keyboard. Lying in the chair, enveloped in a black robe, was the creature known to Maxim T. Yermakov as Sergei Yevgenievich Kravtsov, aka the principal tadpole-head of the country. Standing behind his back, just as it stood in every big boss's office, was the Russian flag, draped in dignified folds, although the colours of this tricolour were strangely bright and so luminescent that they left painful, quicksilver zigzags under the eyelids. Above the flag, where the President's portrait hung in every boss's office, here too there was a standard frame of the requisite appearance and size. But there was nothing behind the glass in the frame: only a piece of grey cardboard with a thin, velvety layer of dust and a coarse, blackish-brown patch.

The tadpole-head was roused from his shallow slumber by a strident ringing sound. The entrance door, which looked like a flimsy slab of chipboard, was retracted into the wall with a hydraulic sigh, revealing at least five centimetres of ribbed steel filling, and the individual whom Maxim T. Yermakov called Blur entered the office, smoothing down the dry tuft on his shapeless head. Since the time of his first and last meeting with the Object in Crap's office, Blur had changed greatly: his head was covered with a strange growth, like the remains of paper that had been glued on and torn off again, the tuft on the top of his head had turned completely transparent and a moustache that looked like a small fish's skeleton had sprouted above his upper lip.

"Ah, Victor Nikolaevich, glad to see you, welcome." The principal tadpole-head leaned forward and the chair under him shifted its position with animated-movie flexibility, seeming to re-assemble itself anew out of its coal-black component parts. "Well, how's our business in Novosibirsk going?"

"Almost smoothly," replied Blur, reaching out to his boss with a hand that seemed to have more fingers than a man was supposed to have. In response, the boss freed his own hand, consisting half of ice, from the folds of his black robe. The handshake between these two was like the coupling of insects from a different planet.

"I heard that everything worked out here too, in the end," said Blur, taking a seat on a Soviet chair that thrust its legs stubbornly against the floor with all its might.

"Yes, in the end," said Foetus, massaging his sunken eyes, as red as blisters. "Liquidation was achieved last night. We've never had so much trouble with an Object as with this Yermakov."

"You took a risk, Sergei Yevgenievich," Blur remarked cautiously. "Was it advisable to inform the Object of our alleged error?"

"It was," the principal tadpole-head of the country replied confidently. "It was necessary to remove the block that had formed in the Object's mind against our direct intervention. He had to feel that he was free to take the necessary decision himself. You can take a look at the recordings later, by the way, the files are in your computer."

The social forecasters said nothing for a moment. Outside the snow was falling in thick waves, here and there pale daytime lights trembled, the buildings in the vicinity were like grey shadows on a gigantic white wall. The winter's day was exactly the same as when the two men sitting in the office went to see Maxim T. Yermakov. As if a whole year had never happened and a man had never existed. As the world without Maxim T. Yermakov was obliquely buried under a quiet shroud, the dense sounds of Moscow faded to a barely audible whisper, and somehow it was clear that today nothing was going to happen.

"I'm just not entirely clued-in about the latest explosion in Moscow," said Blur, breaking the silence as if he was coughing hollowly into his fist. "According to our forecasts, there ought not to have been a terrorist attack on the Moscow Metro for another four months. And the object's wife was not to be involved in it."

"Yes, we organised that incident," Kravtsov confirmed irritably. "Induced a premature birth, so to speak. But what other option did we have left, would you care to tell me? If we had delayed for another two weeks, half of Petersburg would have been demolished. We broke the rules, I agree. A one point five per cent deviation of causality along the thirty-eighth vector."

"One point five per cent isn't much," said Blur, taking a handkerchief dried into a lump out of his pocket and blowing his nose with a sound like a page being torn sharply out of a book. "I beg your pardon, Sergei Yevgenievich, I caught cold in Novosibirsk."

"You and I especially should take care of our health," the principal tadpole-head said sententiously, "with our risk factors. And by the way, I know as well as you do that one point five percent will be offset in about ten years' time. But it was the minimal pinpoint breach, without which we couldn't have solved the problem. Do you think I don't feel sorry for the stupid girl? Rushing in to marry that Yermakov, when everyone with even the slightest scrap of intuition had washed their hands of him. Why, he positively reeked of danger! He stank, like a garbage dump. To be quite honest, in a year I got thoroughly fed up of him."

"But you know, I'm going to miss him," Blur confessed pensively, tamping down his unfamiliar moustache with his fingers, like the tobacco in a roll-up cigarette. "Just for my own interest, I ran his data through the new variational programs. Do you know what I got? With certain different values of base-four and base-eight, he would have become a Hero of the Soviet Union."

"As far as I'm concerned, he's a common-or-garden son of a bitch," the principal tadpole-head said with a frown. "Anyway, you and I know that in a war the good people are simply killed straight away, and it's the bastards who do the heroic deeds and win the medals. In any event, we've done our job. Perhaps we fudged it a bit, but it was the only possible way. I can take some leave at last, I haven't had any for four years."

"Where will you go, Sergei Yevgenievich? To a warm sea? To Egypt or Thailand?"

"No, to my folks in Severodvinsk," the principle tadpole-head sighed sadly. "My mother's seriously ill, we might not see each other again."

"Well, Sergei Yevgenievich, a safe journey to you, and I hope your mother gets well." Blur rose clumsily to his feet, stuffing his handkerchief into a deep trouser pocket reaching down almost to his knees. "I'll get some work done, it's been piling up."

"Off you go, and don't forget to call into the medical unit afterwards," the principal tadpole-head of the country advised him by way of farewell. "If anything comes up, I can be contacted day or night. Download the new codes in the technical section."

"Okay."

The person whom no one thought of as Blur any longer shuffled, stoop-shouldered, to the door, and from there he glanced back at the dimly lit office. The principal tadpole-head was dozing again, with his cheek twitching. Meanwhile above him, in the framed emptiness of the portrait, something was trying to condense, and the blackish-brown patch, now endowed with the outlines of curly hair and cheekbones, smiled out vivaciously at its electorate.

Russian Literature from Dedalus

Dedalus features Russian Literature in translation in its programme of contemporary and classic European fiction and in its anthologies:

The Little Angel – Andreyev	£6.99
The Red Laugh – Andreyev	£6.99
The Fiery Angel – Bruisov	£9.99
The Prussian Bride – Buida	£9.99
The Zero Train – Buida	£6.99
The Dedalus Book of Russian Decadence – Lodge	£12.00
Before & During – Sharov	£12.99
Light-Headed – Slavnikova	£12.99

Ebook only:

Eugene Onegin – Pushkin   £8.99

Forthcoming in September 2016:

The Rehearsals – Sharov   £12.99

For further details visit our website www.dedalusbooks.com or email us at info@dedalusbooks.com or write to Dedalus Limited, 24–26, St Judith's Lane, Sawtry, Cambs, PE28 5XE

Made in Yaroslavl – Jeremy Weingard

'This fine comic novel is set in the Soviet Union circa 1983, and follows two shameless fraudsters – very much forerunners of the present day Russian gangsters who are all the rage these days – as they search high and low throughout the Soviet Union in search of the essential ingredients that are needed to make up the renowned Yaroslavl pickled cucumber. Yes, pickled cucumber. And they only have a very short time to convert a factory from making knitted jumpers to producing pickled cucumbers before it is inspected by the Ministry. The novel shows how, under a repressive system of government, it is very hard for the average person to remain honest. It is even harder for our heroes, who must face down the triple threat of jealous rivals, the mysterious Guild Of Master Picklers and the humble pickle worm. Throughout these escapades, they keep up their spirits by inventing new ways to insult the intelligence of each other and of anyone else who will listen. A lovely satire then and a romp to the heart of the Soviet empire.'

GM in *Crack Magazine*

Full of zany, Eastern European humour and fatalism. Essential reading for gherkin lovers everywhere...

£9.99   ISBN 978 1 903517 73 4   210p   B.Format

Before & During – Vladimir Sharov

Oliver Ready's translation won the 2015 Read Russian Prize.

'*Before and During* remains a disorienting read. The novel invokes real historical events and people (Tolstoy, Madame de Stael, Saint John of Kronstadt, Alexander Scriabin and Stalin, among others), swirling them into a phantasmagoric alternative chronology. Stories germinate within other stories, unfolding in astonishing variations. The clarity and directness of Sharov's prose – wonderfully rendered by Oliver Ready – are disconcerting, almost hallucinatory. His writing is at times funny, at times so piercingly moving, so brimful of unassuaged sorrow, that it causes a double-take.'

Rachel Polonsky in *The New York Review of Books*

'If Russian history is indeed a commentary to the Bible, then *Before and During* is an audacious attempt to shine a mystical light on it, an unusual take on the 20th century's apocalypse that leaves the reader to look for their own explications.'

Anna Aslanyan in *The Independent*

'*Before and During* is a Menippean satire in which historical reality, in all its irreversible awfulness, is for a moment scrambled, eroticized... and illuminated by hilarious monologues of the dead... There are wonderful stretches: an exegesis of Tolstoy's failure to achieve the good in his own family... an astonishing olfactory history of the First World War and Revolution through Scriabin's music. How Sharov resolves the rejection of death is especially good.'

Caryl Emerson in *The Times Literary Supplement*

£12.99   ISBN 978 1 907650 71 0   348p   B. Format

The Rehearsals – Vladimir Sharov

New Jerusalem Monastery, seventeenth-century Moscow. Patriarch Nikon has instructed an itinerant French dramatist to stage the New Testament and hasten the Second Coming. But this will be a strange form of theatre. The actors are untrained, illiterate Russian peasants, and nobody is allowed to play Christ. They are persecuted, arrested, displaced and ultimately replaced by their own children. Yet the rehearsals continue... A stunning reflection on art, history, religion and national identity, *The Rehearsals* is the seminal work in the unique oeuvre of Vladimir Sharov, Russian Booker Prize winner in 2014.

'Sharov has assimilated, perhaps more than any of his contemporaries, the artistic and philosophical legacy of both the nineteenth and twentieth centuries of Russian literature. Like Dostoevsky, he is excessive not in order to deny, misrepresent, or flee reality but, rather, to capture it more accurately.'

Thomas Epstein, Boston College

£12.99 9 Sept 2016 ISBN 978 1 910213 14 8 304p B.Format

The Prussian Bride – Yuri Buida

Oliver Ready's translation of *The Prussian Bride* was awarded the inaugural Russian Translation Prize.

'The Kaliningrad region is in an odd geographical and historical situation. Since the collapse of the Soviet Union it has been cut off from the rest of Russia, sandwiched between Poland and Lithuania. The region itself is only recently Russian – it was once East Prussia and its Russian inhabitants replaced the indigenous German population after the Second World War. Yuri Buida's magnificent collection of stories about his home town reflects these anomalies and presents a powerful and hilarious meditation on dislocated identities.' Tom MacFaul in *The Times Literary Supplement*

'Another triumph for Yuri Buida, this is the second of his books to be translated into English, and like his first – *The Zero Train* – it was shortlisted for the Russian equivalent of the Booker Prize. It has also won a prestigious Apollon Grigoriev award. Buida was born in 1954 in the Kaliningrad Region... Buida wrote and invented details about the area, and this is the resulting collection of 31 tales. The book makes for a surreal experience: his characters include widows, whores, resurrected politicians, madmen, orphans and ghosts, and they exist together in a dream-like blend of fantasy and bitter memory. All the extremes of human emotions are exposed: murder, abuse, passion, debts of honour, devotion, compassion are all here. Appalling, haunting and uplifting, this book is unlike anything you have read before, and completely unforgettable.' *Kirkus Reviews*

£9.99   ISBN 978 1 873982 06 2   363p   B.Format

The Zero Train – Yuri Buida

'Set during the Soviet era, this remarkable novel was shortlisted for the Russian Booker Prize. A remote, police-run settlement called the Ninth Siding exists only for the mysterious Zero Train that halts there. Buida uses the idea as the basis for a haunting, Kafkaesque parable of Russian history.'

Recommended by Harry Blue in *Scotland on Sunday*

'It's a brutally powerful book, set in a landscape of railway track and sidings that could have been postulated by Beckett, but shot through with grotesque, surreal lyricism. "All the women he'd ever known had smelt of cabbage. Boiled cabbage. Every single one." Except Fira. He saw her naked once, washing, "...her heart and its bird-like beat, the gauzy foam of her lungs and her smoky liver, the silver bell of her bladder and the fragile bluish bones floating in the pink jelly of her flesh." A sensational novel, moving, unforgettable.'

Brian Case in *Time Out*

'*The Zero Train* is the most remarkable book I've read this year. It has been hugely successful in Russia, and was shortlisted for the Russian Booker prize. This chilling, brilliant and deeply moving novel goes to the heart of what Stalinism did to individual lives.'

Helen Dunmore in *The Observer Books of the Year*

£6.99   ISBN 978 1 903517 52 9   140p   B. Format

The Dedalus Book of Russian Decadence – edited by Kirsten Lodge

'A journey to the dark side in this collection of horrifying dramatic and erotic stories and poetry never before translated into English, delving into the darkest depths of humanity. This read is definitely not for the faint-hearted, with its morbid tales of death, cruelty, sensuality and corruption.'   Kate Griffin in *The Big Issue*

'By the end of the 19th century hope in Russia that literature might have provided either political or spiritual salvation had withered, leaving writers ripe to fall under the spell of JK Huysmans' apocalyptic decadence. The French-born movement, which espoused the notion that "civilisation is in decline, reality as it exists is contemptible, and that the decadent hero, who is neurotic and sexually deviant, must create an alternative world for himself alone", had a direct appeal to writers such as Valery Briusov and Feodor Sologub. However, what overthrew that civilisation ensured that a literature concerned with "perversity, despair and collapse" was hardly known for much of the 20th century. The stories and poems here wallow in lust, madness and death. Briusov's *Now that I'm Awake* is Poe taken to extremes when a husband discovers that a drug-induced fantasy with his innocent wife is real. Sologub's *The Poisoned Garden* is ruled by a *femme fatale* and plays with the fairy-tale genre. Lodge's collection is a welcome introduction to an important strand of Russian literature.'
                                   Isobel Montgomery in *The Guardian*

'*The Dedalus Book of Russian Decadence*, subtitled *Perversity, Despair and Collapse*, is a bravura wallow in emotional filth and would cheer anyone up. An hour or two in the company of these panting self-poisoners will make you feel bloomingly fit.'
                      Duncan Fallowell in Summer Reading in *The New Statesman*

£12.00   ISBN 978 1 903517 60 4   350p   B. Format

The Dedalus Book of Vodka - Geoffrey Elborn

'In Russian literature, the drink that steals away men's brains is vodka. Tolstoy, repenting his youthful follies ("lying, thieving, promiscuity of all kinds, drunkenness, violence, murder"), founded a temperance society called the Union Against Drunkenness, and designed a label – a skull and crossbones, accompanied by the word "Poison" – to go on all vodka bottles. In the event, the health warning wasn't adopted but Tolstoy's views on vodka seep into his fiction, as do Dostoevsky's in *The Devils* ("The Russian God has already given up when it comes to cheap booze. The common people are drunk, the children are drunk, the churches are empty"). Chekhov was more ambivalent. As Geoffrey Elborn shows in his new cultural history, *The Dedalus Book of Vodka*, he was torn between his knowledge as a doctor and his understanding of human nature. Two of his brothers were alcoholic, and he denounced vodka companies as "Satan's blood peddlers". But he sympathised with the Russian peasantry, for whom vodka was nectar. And in his stories and plays, those who drink excessively – like the army doctor Chebutykin in *The Three Sisters* – are portrayed with humour and compassion.'

Blake Morrison in *The Guardian*

'Dedalus tend to favour books which put decadence or licentiousness in a literary, historical context. Elborn's agreeable overview of vodka's 600-year evolution, its eventual global spread, and the cultural and sociological weight behind this – may therefore be their perfect book. Predominantly associated with Russia, this allows for some choice extracts from Chekhov and Dostoevsky novels; Elborn thinks enough of his audience to give these much more attention than James Bond.'
Buzz Magazine

£15.00   ISBN 978 1 907650 04 8   240p   B. Format Hardcover